G. Allen Wilbanks

COVEN WARS

BOOKS BY G. ALLEN WILBANKS

DEAD TOWN SERIES

Dead Town

Assassin's Spell

Coven Wars

ON DANGEROUS GROUNDS SERIES

Testing Grounds

Proving Grounds

Hunting Grounds

NOVELS

A Life of Adventure

When Darkness Comes

Deadly Seven

SHORT STORY COLLECTIONS

Thirteen Rooms

Not for Bedtime Stories

Deep Dark Thoughts Publications LLC

Coven Wars

Visit my website at www.gallenwilbanks.com

This is a work of fiction. All characters and events in this publication, other than those clearly in the public domain, are fictitious, and any resemblance to real persons, living or dead, is purely coincidental.

Paperback: ISBN 978-1-952630-18-7

E-book: ISBN 978-1-952630-19-4

Cover design: MoorBooks Design

G. Allen Wilbanks

COVEN WARS

DEAD TOWN

Book III

Deep Dark Thoughts Publications LLC

For Jen, Allison, and Samantha

PROLOGUE

"Vi? Can you help me with this, please?"

"Yeah. Just a second, Mom."

Violet jumped up from the dining room table and turned toward the kitchen. Her father and two brothers remained seated, talking over one another as they vied for opportunities to take control of the chaotic mealtime conversation. None of them even seemed to notice Violet rising to her feet.

Liam, Violet's boyfriend, rose from his chair to help. She put a hand on his shoulder and gently eased him back into his seat.

"Stay," she told him. "Mom and I have this. You relax and let us take care of everything tonight."

Liam relented, embarrassed at being catered to but reluctantly settling back into his spot at the table.

"If you're sure," he said to Violet's retreating back. "I can help if you need anything. Anything. Just ask."

"Let the ladies handle dinner," Violet's father said to Liam. "Elizabeth doesn't want us in the kitchen getting in the way. Besides, this is a good time for us to chat and let me get to know my daughter's special fella a little bit better. We haven't seen much of you recently."

Violet grimaced at her dad's comment. She could tell from his tone that he was in the mood to see if he could make her boyfriend squirm a little, but she also knew Liam was a big boy, and he could take care of himself if her father started asking too many personal questions.

As she entered the kitchen, she spotted her mother pulling on oven mitts while watching the microwave clock count down its final few minutes on a timer. Her mother absentmindedly hummed a nonsense melody to herself as she waited for the alarm to beep.

"What can I do to help?" Violet asked.

Without looking, her mother gestured with a mitted hand toward one corner of the kitchen's center island. "Grab the salad and take it to the table. You guys can get started on that, and I'll pull the casserole out of the oven when it's done. Oh, and grab the bread, too, if you don't mind."

"You got it."

"Thank you," her mother said, still watching the timer.

Violet picked up the large plastic bowl holding their dinner salad and paused for a moment to watch her mom pull open the oven door and peek inside. Her mother's long blond hair was tucked up into a neat bun, and she wore a flower print dress she typically only pulled from the closet when she and Violet's dad were going out on a date night.

Violet and Liam had been seeing each other for a little over a year and a half, and her mother still went out of her way to look nice whenever Liam came over. It made her feel good that her mother thought so highly of him. Unless of course that devious cougar was only dressing up so she could hit on her daughter's boyfriend.

"Vi? What are you smiling at?" her father asked as she set the salad bowl on the dining room table.

"Private joke," Violet told him, still grinning. "Mind your own business."

Kyle, the oldest of her two younger brothers, snatched the salad bowl the moment it hit the table and slid it towards himself. He began to shovel lettuce onto his plate as if he hadn't seen solid food in weeks.

"Kyle," her father snapped. "Let the guest serve himself first."

"C'mon, Dad," Kyle complained. "It's just Liam. He doesn't care."

"Really, Mr. Rose. It's all right…," Liam started to say.

"It's not all right. It's common courtesy. And what have I told you about that 'Mr. Rose' stuff?"

"Um, right. Grant. Sorry, I'm still getting used to that."

"Dad," Violet said, slapping her father's shoulder reproachfully, though with no real force. "You're making him uncomfortable. Knock it off."

Her father's face stretched into a broad smile. "Ow," he complained theatrically, rubbing at his arm. "You're getting too big to be thumping your old man around like that. Besides, Liam isn't uncomfortable. Are you, Liam?"

Liam shrugged noncommittally. "No, I…,"

"Stop," Violet said, followed with another smack on her father's arm.

"Fine. Fine." Her father threw up his hands in surrender. He laughed, and Violet could not help but chuff softly in amusement back at him.

Grant Rose was a big man. He stood slightly over six and a half feet tall, and his chest and arms were thick with muscle from many years of loading and unloading crates at the local trainyard. Although he had accepted a promotion and a desk job four years ago, he still retained most of that hard-won size and strength.

Many people upon first meeting her dad found him gruff and intimidating. Liam had been terrified of her father during their first meeting, and, if she was being completely honest, for several months thereafter. Violet knew better, however. He was loud and brash at times, but at home, to his family, her father was little more than a blustering kitten; all hiss and puffed-up fur.

Violet had never felt anything but love and affection from him.

He was simply "Dad" to her.

Grant waved his hands at Violet, gesturing her away. The heavy gold ring he wore on the ring finger of his right hand flashed in the overhead lighting of the dining room. The ring had a three and a half carat ruby set into its wide square face that twinkled with a deep scarlet brilliance. It had been a gift from her mom when her father got the promotion at work.

Her dad had been shocked by the present, at the extravagance of such a purchase, and he practically demanded that her mother return it.

When he asked why she would ever spend so much money on him, she had kissed him on the cheek and told him, "Because I knew you would never do it for yourself."

Since that day, Violet had never seen her father go anywhere without that ruby on his finger. It was part of him now.

"Go. Sit down with your guy," her father said. "I'll be good. I promise."

"Shit," Violet said suddenly. "I forgot the bread."

"Vi!" her mother's voice echoed from the kitchen. "Language."

Her youngest brother, Monty, laughed at the expletive as Violet ran back into the kitchen to grab the bread.

Violet scooped up the basket piled full with fresh baked sourdough rolls, and strolled back into the dining room. Her mother followed close behind this time carrying a glass casserole dish that contained a bubbling, steaming concoction of potatoes, cheese, and sausages. Violet placed the bread on the table and slid a metal trivet closer for her mom to set down the hot dish in her hands.

Monty's hand darted into the mound of sourdough, seizing on a roll. The boy froze before removing his prize and peered cautiously toward his father. Grant sighed loudly, then announced, "Go ahead. I guess it's every man for himself tonight."

Violet's mom cleared her throat quietly.

"And woman," Grant amended. "Monty. Toss me one."

Violet's youngest brother grabbed another roll after setting the first one on his own plate. He flipped the bread across the table, past Kyle's head and into his dad's waiting hands.

"Monty!" his mother exclaimed, horrified.

"Sorry, Mom," the boy said, although the wide grin on his face suggested he was not in the least bit sorry.

"And you," Elizabeth turned to face her husband. "Don't encourage that kind of behavior at the table. Especially with guests here. We don't want people thinking we behave like animals in this house."

"Sorry, Mom," said Grant mischievously. He held up the roll in his hands. "Should I throw it back?"

Monty held out his hands expectantly.

"Absolutely not. Put that on your plate and behave."

Violet settled into her chair beside Liam and placed a hand on his leg. She squeezed apologetically.

"Like a circus," she muttered, embarrassed. "Sorry. My family sucks."

Liam only chuckled before holding up one hand towards Monty.

"Can I get one?" he asked, and Monty dutifully hurled another roll.

Violet groaned and glanced toward her mother. "Are all men just children?"

"Every last one of them," her mother confirmed.

Monty held up a third roll from the basket and raised his eyebrows at Violet.

Before she could decide if she should tell him to drop it or accept the fact her brother would probably throw it at her whether she wanted him to or not, a loud crash from the front of the house interrupted their dinner.

The front door burst open, the latch and deadbolt tearing through the wooden doorframe and releasing a shower of splinters into the air. As the door swung in, the hinges bracing it torqued out of true from the force driving it open. A sound like a gunshot echoed through the home when the doorknob struck the entryway wall, burying itself in the plaster and sheetrock.

Before anyone at the table could move, three women rushed through the shattered entryway and into the front foyer. Two of the women were tall, with long blond hair; one heavy, the other thin. Their third companion, a short Black woman, appeared to be leading the charge. The three were an oddly disparate group, varying in ages as well as sizes, with the youngest in her twenties, and the oldest appearing to be somewhere in her fifties or sixties.

The only thing they all appeared to have in common was the uniformly black clothing they wore. That, and the deadly serious expressions on each of their faces as they invaded the Rose family home. These intruders meant business, Violet sensed, but what could they possibly want here?

Each of the women carried a wooden staff in her hands, holding it out in front of themselves like they were aiming a lethal weapon. The image was surreal, and Violet couldn't help thinking it looked like a scene in some kind of fantasy tale, with rogue wizards storming a castle.

Violet's father was the first to react, lurching to his feet and pushing his chair back to give himself room. By this time, the three women were already into the dining room. The short woman in front uttered a few quick words that Violet did not catch, and her father fell back into his seat with a surprised shout. He blurted out a word that Violet knew her mother would not approve of. Under the circumstances, however, it seemed appropriate.

As her father collapsed onto his chair, Violet saw flashes of color moving throughout the room. They appeared to originate from the staves in the hands of the unknown invaders. At the same time, she felt something constrict around her chest, pinning her arms to her sides and anchoring her where she sat. From the startled expressions of her family around her, they were each experiencing similar mysterious confinement.

Violet's father struggled to stand again, but it was clear whatever held the family immobile was strong enough to hold even him helpless. With the realization that he could not break free, he stopped fighting and glared toward the three unwelcome guests in his house.

"What do you want?" Grant growled. "Who are you, and why are you here?"

"We are here for her," said the smallest of the three, further confirming to Violet that this was the leader, or at least the spokesperson of the group. The woman leveled a menacing finger in Violet's direction. "We have instructions to take her with us."

"No" shouted Violet's mother. "No!"

"Elizabeth," Violet's father said calmly. "It's okay. Vi isn't going anywhere."

"Isn't she?" asked another of the women. The tall thin stranger, an unpleasant looking woman with a narrow pinched face, stepped around the table toward Violet. "How do you think you're going to stop us."

Grant wrestled with the invisible bonds again, but they continued to hold without any sign of weakening.

"If I can't stop you, I can still come after you. There isn't anywhere you can go that I won't find you and get her back," he warned. His eyes flashed as bright as the ruby on his finger. "I'll never stop coming after you."

"We figured that would be your response," said the group's leader. "That is why we decided to make sure that can't happen."

The small woman moved her staff in a short arc. Grant grunted and his face went stiff with pain. Violet watched in horror as her father rocked backward, twisting and writhing in wild convulsions. The muscles in his neck grew tight, and a trickle of blood began to run from his left nostril. The trickle increased to a steady flow, then a gush of crimson. Blood poured over his chin and onto his shirt as the big man continued to thrash and make agonized noises.

"Grant," sobbed her mother, but otherwise no one spoke as the gruesome scene continued for several long seconds.

The blood finally slowed, then stopped, as did Grant's grunts and cries of pain. Violet cried helplessly, unable to move and unwilling to look away. Her father's head drooped, his chin striking his chest with a relaxed finality.

He did not move again. Violet prayed he had simply passed out from the pain and blood loss, but a part of her, deep down, knew he was not merely unconscious.

"Grant?" said her mother again, more softly this time. "Grant, are you okay?"

"No, dear," mocked the heavyset woman in the trio, the eldest of the three, speaking for the first time. "He is not okay."

Violet thought she noticed a glint of something green circle around her mother's head. Elizabeth's eyes grew wide in panic as an irresistible force, similar to the one holding them all hostage, forced her chin up to an uncomfortable angle.

The large woman standing over Elizabeth reached a hand into the folds of her black dress and removed something from a concealed pocket. Violet recognized the object as a small dagger. The blade was short, no more than three inches long from tip to handle, but it did not need to be any bigger when its intended target was held helpless and immobile. Elizabeth remained trapped by the unseen bonds, unable to evade or protect herself from the weapon.

Without preamble, the woman stabbed the dagger into Elizabeth's exposed throat.

Violet screamed. Blood sprayed from her mother's neck, painting the table in front of her with gory cardinal streaks. She heard her little brother, Monty, wailing and pleading for his mother to be okay.

"Mommy. Mommy."

"Stop this," Liam called out. "You don't have to do this."

The women ignored him. They circled the table, all three now with daggers in hand. They attacked their restrained victims in a coordinated flurry of violence. Violet listened to the cries and pleas of her family, silenced one by one in front of her. She watched blood flow, and the life and light drain from the bodies and faces of the people she loved most in the world.

Monty was the last to go quiet, his final cries for his mother silenced by one vicious cut under his left ear.

As fast as the carnage began, it was over. The only remaining sounds in the room were Violet's own muffled sobs. She at last closed her eyes, trying to shut out the horrors around her, but even behind closed lids, she continued to see the still bodies in her mind, the dining table awash in red ichor, and the three murderers in her house, gripping their blades in blood-soaked hands.

Even if she could have escaped the visions, the smell alone would have been more than enough to crush her. The sharp acidic odor of freshly spilled blood filled her nostrils. She had never smelled it before, but she knew it for what it was.

It was the smell of death.

Fingers tangled in Violet's hair and pulled her head back sharply. She kept her eyes closed, waiting for the pain of a knifepoint to find the exposed skin of her throat. Death would be a relief, she thought in what she believed to be her final moments. Whatever waited for her could certainly be no worse than the hell she had just been forced to endure.

Instead of a blade in her neck, she felt the bindings that held her in place loosen and slide away.

"Okay, girl. It's time for us to go."

Surprised to still be alive, and perhaps more than a little disappointed, Violet opened her eyes. Around her, everyone at the table lay dead, slumped in place like discarded and forgotten toys. Their bindings must have also been removed, because both Kyle and her father had fallen out of their chairs, collapsed into lifeless heaps of flesh on the floor.

Violet knew, even if she did miraculously make it through this day alive, her existence as she understood it had died with the people in this room. She was no longer the person she had been when she and her mother sat down at this table to eat mere minutes ago. That Violet was gone forever. She was a broken thing now, a damaged item that nothing and no one could ever completely put back together. And it was not just Violet herself that was different. The entire world had changed around her in the blink of an eye; in a single beat of her heart.

What had previously felt safe and protected had become cold and threatening. Where once there had been love and joy, only cruelty and violence now waited for her.

Nothing would ever be the same.

She raised her head to meet the stares of her attackers. Violet wanted to memorize their faces, to burn them into her brain so they could never fade away. She owed these women something that she intended to pay back. Not today, perhaps. No, she was far too weak right now. But a tiny voice in the back of Violet's mind told her that she would not be this weak forever. Someday, somehow, she would make herself stronger. Strong enough to find these women again and repay their evil deeds.

Someday.

In this moment, she only needed to remember what they looked like.

Her gaze shifted from one woman to the next, locking eyes for a moment with all four of the strangers in her house.

Four? Hadn't there only been…?

"Alyssandra?" asked the heavy blond woman, surprise clear in her voice. "What are you…?"

A tall, thin scarecrow of a figure with dark skin and sharp features stood in the room. Violet had not seen her enter. She wore all black like the others. She even held a heavy wooden staff in her hands like the three who had broken into Violet's house. This fourth stranger did not appear to be a friend of theirs, however. As soon as her presence was noticed by the others, the woman did not hesitate. She hefted her staff and uttered a single word.

"Cut."

Violet watched as a spectrum of colored lights flashed from the end of the raised staff. The woman who had been addressed as Alyssandra shaped that light into a flat disk that expanded throughout the room. Although the growing circle passed harmlessly over Violet's head, it struck the three women standing around the table, slicing them neatly in half where the edge of the rainbow arch touched them. The shortest of the three was cut through the neck, and Violet watched in renewed revulsion as the woman's head toppled from her body like a prop in a badly made horror movie.

The sounds the dying women made as they fell to the floor, spilling blood and entrails, turned Violet's own insides upside down. She retched, coughing and choking, though there was nothing in her stomach to eject.

Alyssandra moved behind Violet and laid a hand on her shoulder. Violet shuddered and flinched away, and the thin woman removed her hand, stepping two respectful paces back.

"I'm sorry, child," she said. "I knew these witches intended to take you, but I had no idea that they planned to do…," she gestured at the bloodshed around them, "this. By the time I realized their true intentions, I was far too late to stop them. Please forgive me for my failure."

Violet sat mutely in her seat. She had so many questions, she did not know where to start. She was also still deeply in shock from the attack on her family that she had been forced to witness.

Unsure if she should scream, cry, or leap at this strange woman and try to claw her eyes out, she settled for asking, "Did you say witches?"

Alyssandra nodded. "You do not realize it yet, but you have the potential to become a very powerful witch. Others have noticed you and are watching you closely. I have seen your ability." She pointed at the corpses of the bisected women. "They have seen it and so have many others."

Alyssandra took a step forward and Violet shied away. The woman retreated again.

"I have been trying to figure out a way to approach you and ask if you would allow me to train you. I knew other covens would also seek you out, but I did not realize the manner in which they would contact you. If I had, I would have come to you sooner or offered your family some form of protection. I regret my poor judgement led to us meeting in this manner."

Alyssandra extended a hand. "I cannot fix this. I cannot bring your family back. What I can do is offer you training that will allow you to protect yourself so nothing like this will ever happen again. Will you allow me to do that much for you?"

Violet heard everything Alyssandra said, but she was unable to process it properly. Coherent thought was not something she was fully capable of at the moment. Grief, fear, anger, and a thousand other emotions churned her brain into a soup of confusing ideas and images.

She opened her mouth and took a shaky breath before asking again, "Did you say witches?"

CHAPTER 1

Mitch Loman held Violet's hand as they strolled through the hillside town, traversing the up and down sidewalks of Carmel-By-The-Sea. The late June sun shone warmly in the eastern sky, lighting the day but not yet bringing the temperatures to an uncomfortable level. A dense cover of old growth Monterey Pines, Cypress, and Oak trees provided a layer of shade and comfort for the steady stream of visitors wandering among the folksy downtown shops. In addition to the natural shelter, overhead canopies covered every street corner and gap between establishments, giving a cozy secluded feel to the community.

Mitch mentally noted the assortment of businesses they passed, peering in at a variety of museums, wineries, and family-run restaurants tucked in among the normal touristy stores full of T-shirts, hats, and other overpriced, novelty rubbish. The buildings all appeared to be old-style wooden homes converted into businesses, along with a few newer structures carefully designed to blend in with the existing surroundings. It was obvious to any observer that the city was carefully managed to maintain a small town feel despite having become a popular vacation destination over the past few decades.

Along with the other businesses situated along the sloping streets, Mitch also found a surprising number of storefronts for realtors advertising properties for sale. He supposed it made sense. A lot of people would probably love the opportunity to purchase a home in the densely forested hills only a few minutes' drive from the ocean. And where there was demand, there of course must be someone willing to provide a supply.

Pausing at one of the realty offices, Mitch glanced at a price sheet in the window advertising a local two-bedroom home located on a quarter acre of property.

"Wow," he muttered. "I guess I won't be moving here anytime soon. A Sacramento cop's salary wouldn't cover the property taxes, much less the mortgage."

"What are you looking at?" asked Violet, peering over his shoulder at the listing. "A house? Are you interested in living here?"

"No, not really. I was just curious what it would cost. I figured if it was cheap, this would be a great location for a vacation home. I guess I'm not the only person that thinks that. Ah, well. Maybe I'll win the lottery one of these days. At least we can afford to come visit for a vacation."

"Not a vacation," Violet reminded him. "We have business first. After we deal with this poltergeist, we can relax and play tourist for a little while. We aren't expected back home for a few days, so we have plenty of time to play."

Violet squeezed his hand and gently tugged him along behind her.

Business before pleasure, Mitch lamented as he let Violet lead him to their next destination. He gazed at the long black hair of her wig trailing down her back, the ends of the dark strands almost reaching her waist. The wig was part of her "business attire," as she referred to it, along with the pale, almost white, makeup on her face accented only with dark circles of kohl around her eyes and bright red lipstick to add one shocking splash of color to the goth personae. In deference to the summer heat, she had opted for black shorts and a black T-shirt rather than her preferred ankle-length black dress.

People expected a witch when they hired Violet Rose, and she was more than capable of dressing the part.

Mitch, who owned no work wardrobe other than a collection of black police uniforms, had gone with a light, button-up shirt and cargo shorts. "Dad shorts" Violet had called them, before shaking her head and grudgingly allowing him to leave their hotel room that morning.

Downtown Carmel consisted of fewer than a dozen crisscrossing streets, and it took only a few more minutes of casual walking to reach the business they wanted. Mitch and Violet stopped when they reached the front doors of a boutique-style, independently owned bookshop. The building looked like it might have been a church at one time in its history, with slender, dual doors, and a tall, peaked gable, all painted white with a light gray trim. The front face of the shop was narrow, taking up little space at the street level. They might have easily walked right past it if Violet had not been specifically looking for the address.

Although the façade was unimpressive in its size, the building was deep, stretching far back onto the property behind it, reaffirming Mitch's opinion that the structure had once served a more important purpose for the town. On the tiny front lawn in front of the doors was a wooden A-frame sign that proclaimed, "The Book Nook."

It was past ten o'clock in the morning, and all the other businesses along this street were already open and busily greeting customers, but hanging on the secured doors of The Book Nook was a smaller sign announcing the store was currently closed. This had been at Violet's request. She did not want customers inside the shop, getting in her way or possibly being injured while she worked.

Violet turned to Mitch. "Are you ready?" she asked.

He shrugged and cocked his head in a slight sideways nod. "Sure. I guess so."

Violet's blue eyes darkened, and her brow furrowed. "This isn't a joke, Mitch. This isn't like the echo stuck to an old pocket watch we faced before. This could be a full-blown poltergeist, and I want to know that you are taking it seriously." She touched his chest with a pointed index finger. "Are you ready?"

Mitch straightened his shoulders and stood a little more erect. Violet seemed genuinely worried for him. There was still so much he did not know, and if she was concerned about what they might find inside the bookshop, then he would take this matter seriously as well. He held up his right fist, showing her the gold ring on his middle finger and the large ruby set into its center.

"The ruby is fully charged if I need it. My spirit is pulled back as deep as I can hold it so it will be safe. I'm ready."

"And what will you do when we go inside?" she asked him.

"Nothing, unless you tell me to," he promised her.

Violet nodded and finally let herself relax. "Okay. Good. Let's go see what we're up against.

Together, they traversed the few feet of concrete walkway to the front doors of the bookshop. Violet took the lead and knocked, rapping her knuckles against the wooden door frame in a rapid staccato.

A few seconds passed before they heard the sounds of locks being turned from the other side. One of the paired doors pulled open a crack and two suspicious dark eyes peered out at them.

"Yes?" the man inside responded.

"Mr. Aaron Pavali?" asked Violet. "Are you Mr. Pavali?"

The man's gaze travelled over Violet, taking in the pale makeup, long black hair, and black clothing. He glanced briefly at Mitch, but seemed to dismiss his presence quickly, turning back to give Violet another careful appraisal. Mitch did not blame the shopkeeper one bit. Of the two of them, Violet was definitely the more impressive figure.

"I am. And you are…?"

"Hello, Mr. Pavali. I'm Violet Rose. We spoke on the phone a few days ago about … your unique situation in the bookstore. This is Mitch Loman. He's assisting me today. May we come inside?"

The door pulled open to reveal a young man with unkempt black hair and thick dark eyebrows that seemed to be attempting to hide his muddy brown eyes. His face was long, with a narrow jawline and deep lines around his mouth and nose. A heavy growth of stubble covered his chin, cheeks, and upper lip. The facial hair was so dark that even freshly shaved, Mitch guessed he might still appear to have a visible five o'clock shadow.

The store owner was several inches shorter than Mitch, perhaps no more than five feet, eight inches tall, and he wore brown slacks under a too-large gray sweater with leather patches sewn onto the elbows. The only item missing for a book seller, in Mitch's estimation, was a pair of thick-lensed glasses, perhaps the kind with a heavy beaded chain that hung around his neck. Disappointingly, the man's vision seemed fine without artificial assistance.

The interior of the store looked like a cross between a private den and a reference library. The side walls of the long narrow space were lined with dozens of shelves filled to the point of physically sagging under the weight of hundreds, perhaps thousands, of books of all colors and sizes. Each row of shelves was identified with a large, carved wooden sign mounted on top, indicating the genres and general pricing of the tomes in question. In contrast to the neatly organized books, down the middle of the room, four bulky, mahogany-colored tables had been haphazardly arranged, each surrounded by worn, but comfortable-looking lounge chairs for patrons to sit and peruse their prospective purchases.

Mitch wondered idly if the shop ever sold anything. If customers could sit and read any book they wanted without it costing them a cent, why would they waste their money to take an item home?

"You're here to get rid of our ghost?" asked the shop owner.

"I'm here to ascertain what the problem is," Violet said carefully. "If it is something I can deal with, then I'm prepared to do my best to remove it from your shop. On the phone, you told me you think the spirit is attached to a book you purchased several months ago, is that right?"

"I think so, yes. A gentleman came into our store with a first edition, hardback copy of The Red Badge of Courage. He wanted five thousand dollars for the book. Well, I of course purchased it immediately. I paid him cash. A first edition in the kind of condition this book was in is easily worth three times that price."

"Did the man who sold you the book tell you why he was letting it go so cheap?" asked Mitch. "Deals that sound too good usually come with some kind of catch, don't they?"

The shop owner remained quiet for a moment.

"Mr. Pavali?" prompted Violet. "Did he tell you anything about the book he was selling?"

Aaron Pavali sighed. "I asked him why he wasn't asking for more. I thought the book might be stolen from a family member or something like that. When he said the book was haunted, I thought it was a joke at first, but he really seemed to believe it. I didn't ask any more questions and bought it."

"So, he did warn you," Violet mused.

"I don't believe in ghosts," Pavali said defensively. "I didn't believe, I suppose I should clarify. At the time, I even thought we could advertise that our shop had a haunted book. To the right clientele, that would be a huge draw. It might even increase what we could charge to sell it."

"Okay. You bought the book, put it on your shelves, and then what?"

"The ghost started making appearances in the shop a couple days later. At first it would just appear and occasionally scare off a customer or two. I didn't see it myself until almost a week later. By that time, it was starting to get more aggressive, more violent. It would throw things around the shop and do damage to merchandise."

"So, what did you do next?"

"I called the guy that sold us the book. He absolutely refused to buy it back."

"I'm not surprised," Violet said. "Would you?"

"I suppose not," Pavali admitted.

"Do you know the book's history? Did the seller give you any background on how it came to be haunted?"

"When he sold it to me, he mentioned that he had gotten it at an estate sale. The previous owner had been killed during a burglary. Later, I researched the estate sale online, you know, to make sure the book wasn't stolen, and that it was auctioned off legally. When that all checked out, I did a little more digging. A news article reported the man that had been killed lived alone. He was shot when two people broke into his house looking for valuables. I don't know if the victim is the ghost or not, but that's all the information I could find."

"When did you reach out to Eugene Torgerson?" Violet wanted to know.

"Who?"

"Eugene. He's the ghost chaser that gave me your name. When did you talk to him?"

Pavali's bushy eyebrows rose in recognition. "Ah, Eugene. Right! He came to me, actually. He heard about us from one of the customers the ghost chased out of the store. Spent an entire night locked in the bookstore with a bunch of cameras and equipment. The next morning, he tells me I have a poltergeist, like I hadn't already figured that out, then tells me he knows someone who might be able to help. He asked if I would like him to call his friend, and I told him I would. I assume he was referring to you."

Violet nodded. "He was."

"Why didn't you get rid of the book?" asked Mitch, although he already knew the answer to this question. "You could have sold it to someone else, or tossed it into the trash, or maybe burned it. Why do you still have it?"

Pavali hung his head dejectedly. "I can't find it. It isn't where I put it, and the only explanation I can think of is that the ghost moved it so we couldn't get rid of it. Is that possible?"

"It is," Violet told him. "It's actually probable. Poltergeists are capable of moving physical objects, and the spirit inhabiting your book likely knows you would try to get rid of it."

"So, how do we find it?" asked the shop owner.

There was a sudden bang from the back of the shop, as if something heavy had fallen from one of the shelves onto the floor. A soft muttering could be heard from somewhere among the bookstacks at the rear of the store.

"Is that our poltergeist?" asked Violet. "Or is there anyone else in the store?"

"That's not the ghost. That's Dayo."

"I thought I asked you to keep the store empty of customers."

"He's not a customer. He's my husband. He was putting together some online orders we wanted to ship out later today."

"Does he know about the poltergeist?" asked Mitch.

"Of course," said Pavali. "We're married, and we both own equal shares of the store. I'm not going to hide something like this from him. In fact, he saw the ghost before I did."

"Can you ask him to come out here?" said Violet. "I would like to know where everybody is before I start. I don't want any accidents because I didn't know somebody else was here."

Aaron Pavali walked a few paces toward the rear of the store, then called out, "Dayo. Could you please come here? Our guests would like to meet you."

A bald, dark brown head poked out from between two rows of shelves. The man identified as Dayo stepped out into the open aisleway at the center of the store and waved awkwardly toward the strangers in his shop. He was taller than Pavali, but still not quite as tall as Mitch, with a close-shaved black beard covering most of his face. While Pavali was dressed exactly as Mitch would have pictured a bookshop owner, Dayo was much more comfortably attired in jeans and a tight-fitting T-shirt that showed off his muscular torso.

Pavali gestured for Dayo to join them.

"Ms. Rose, Mister…?" he paused.

"Loman," Mitch supplied.

"Mr. Loman. This is Dayo Akoro, my husband."

"Hello," responded Dayo. "It is a great pleasure to meet you both." He extended a broad, calloused hand and shook both of theirs.

Mitch noticed a heavy inflection in Dayo's speech. He sounded like he might be from South Africa, but Mitch could not be certain as he was not overly familiar with the regional accents.

"Mr. Okoro, it's a pleasure," Violet returned the greeting. "We were just explaining to Mr. Pavali that we would like everyone in the store in one place while we work, so there aren't any distractions or accidents. In fact, if you don't mind, an empty store would be even better. Would you two like to head out for an early lunch while we take care of this … problem?"

"Oh, no," said Pavali immediately. "I'm staying right here. I don't want to leave and come back to a destroyed shop and thousands of dollars' worth of damage."

"If you are concerned about damage, we can simply leave. You are free to find someone else to attempt the exorcism. Or perhaps you might get lucky and find the missing book on your own."

"What? You would come all the way here and then just leave? What kind of shakedown are you attempting?"

"Aaron, please calm down," said Dayo softly, placing a hand on Pavali's shoulder. "We need their help, so there is no point to aggravating yourself and our guests." Turning his attention to Violet, he asked, "What do you need from us? You wish us to leave?"

"No," said Pavali again. "I'm not leaving."

"Ms. Rose," Dayo continued in a more friendly tone than his husband's. "May we stay?"

CHAPTER 2

Dorothy "Dot" Kristiansen sat at her desk, hands poised over her keyboard as she perused both screens of her dual display monitors. The left screen showed a spreadsheet of monthly expenses for Dasan's Terrace Police Department, including several bold red numbers indicating where the department had gone over budget. The chief had asked her to review the costs and determine if there was room for cutbacks or to let him know that it was time to ask the Sheriff for more funding.

The monitor on the right had pricelists and pictures of several fur-lined children's boots she was considering buying as a present for her three-year-old son's upcoming birthday. It was the right screen that currently held her attention.

Dot grabbed the computer mouse next to the keyboard and moved the screen's cursor to hover over the "Buy" button on a particularly cute pair of boots she thought would look absolutely adorable on Bear. She hesitated before clicking, pondering what size to order. It was still early summer, with many more warm days ahead. It might be six months before her son could comfortably wear the shoes, and she was concerned his feet might grow during that time.

"Aaugh," she muttered, removing her hand from the mouse. "What do I do?"

"What do you do about what?"

Chief Simon Jefferson stood in the entryway to the administrative offices lobby, holding a thick manilla envelope tucked under one arm. As on most days, he wore a gray suit, professionally tailored to fit his large frame. The heavy clothing on a warm day, coupled with a brisk walk up a flight of stairs to get to the second floor of the police department building, had left him with a light sheen of sweat on his forehead. He wiped at the moisture with the palm of his free hand.

Dot smiled toward the chief and waved. She was not startled by his appearance as she knew his Tuesday morning meeting had recently ended and he was due back in his office at any moment. In addition, she had heard him coming through the doors, panting slightly from his trek upstairs.

"I'm trying to pick out a gift for Bear," she told him. "He doesn't really need anything. He's going to be four, so it's either going to be clothes or toys, but he has plenty of both at the moment."

Simon approached Dot's desk and slipped behind her to peer at her computer monitors. The chief was not fat, and he was not heavily muscled, but rather somewhere in between. Although barely average in height, he was broad through the chest and shoulders, and his general size dwarfed Dot's tiny frame as he stood behind her chair, peering over the top of her white-blond head. He looked at the boots on display, then glanced at the budget spreadsheet on the second screen.

He grunted, then asked, "Any wiggle room?"

"If there is, I'm not seeing it. I think we need a bigger budget, especially if we stay this active and have to keep paying overtime for the landscaping crews."

"Things will die down eventually, but we're probably not out of the woods yet. I've been waiting for something really bad to leap out at us ever since Chang'e went underground."

"How was your captains' meeting?" Dot asked, changing the conversation to something less stressful than the missing homicidal witch.

Simon straightened and grunted again.

"The usual. I don't know why the sheriff insists I keep attending these things. Ninety percent of what they talk about doesn't impact Dasan's Terrace, and the ten percent that does involves events I can't share with the general staff. I end up sitting silently through every meeting, grinning and nodding like an idiot."

"It's good that you know what everyone else is doing, though," Dot said. "Besides, you need to keep up relationships with the other captains in the department."

"Now you sound like the sheriff," complained Simon.

Dot smiled, amused at Simon's complaint, then pointed back at the shoes. "So, what do you think? Should I get Bear winter boots now, so they don't go out of stock? And if I do, should I get them a size bigger to let him grow into them? Maybe I should wait for Christmas to get them."

Simon paused, staring at the back of Dot's head. His lips curved down into a concerned frown as he observed his administrative assistant.

"What's wrong, Dot?" he asked.

"I don't want to wait too long and then not be able to get the shoes I want for Bear, but I also don't want him to outgrow them before he gets a chance to enjoy them."

"Stop. I'm not talking about shoes. I'm talking about you. You may be the sensitive in this department, but I know you pretty well. You and I have worked together for a few years now, and

I've gotten pretty good at knowing when something is bothering you. Something that has nothing to do with shoes or budgets or anything else we've been discussing. Go on. Tell me I'm wrong."

Dot shook her head, then turned her chair to face Simon. "No. You're not wrong. It isn't really anything I can explain though. Not yet. It's just a … feeling … that something is coming. Something bad."

"A dream?" Simon asked.

"Yeah."

"About Chang'e?"

Dot shrugged. "I don't know. I haven't figured it all out. That's why I wasn't going to tell you."

Simon crooked a finger at Dot. "Come on," he told her. "My office. Let's get comfortable and talk."

Dot rose from her desk and dutifully followed the chief into his office. Simon slipped his suit coat off, mopped his face unceremoniously with the sleeve, then draped it over the back of his desk chair. He sat and pointed at the three cushioned seats on the opposite side of the desk. Dot settled herself into one of the proffered chairs.

"From the beginning," Simon said. "What was your dream, and what do you think it means? Do you think it was a portent?"

Dot glanced around the room, searching for the right words to answer the chief's question.

"I only had the dream once so far. Last night was the first time, so I can't guarantee it was anything more than a dream. But, if I had to guess, I would say that yes, this was a warning. It felt too real, too imminent, to be random."

Simon rocked back in his seat, laying his hands in his lap. "What did you see?"

"I saw the willow tree, the one that stands alone on a green hill. It was nighttime, and a hard wind was blowing through the tree making the branches thrash in all directions."

"You've seen the willow in other dreams. It's the one that represents Dasan's Terrace, right?"

Dot nodded. "Whenever I see this tree, it means something is about to affect the cemetery or the people that work here."

"Okay, so there's a storm coming, and it will happen at night?"

"No, Simon. The dreams are never that literal. You know that. The wind means something is coming that will affect everyone here, but what that something is, I don't have a clue. The fact it was nighttime could mean any number of things, or nothing at all. It might mean that we won't see what's coming until it already happens, or maybe someone here is hiding something from us. Darkness sometimes means secrets or schemes, or yes, sometimes it simply means nighttime. It doesn't matter anyway because that wasn't the most disturbing part of the dream."

Dot paused again and Simon waited patiently for her to continue, content with letting her tell the story at her own pace.

"In the dream, I climbed the hill to approach the tree. When I was close enough, I could see three ravens in the branches. Two of the ravens sat in the middle of the tree, clinging to the moving branches as the wind blew them around. The third raven was at the very top of the tree. This one had glowing red eyes, and it didn't move at all, not like the others. It was completely unaffected by the storm blowing around it."

"Did it cause the storm?" Simon asked.

Dot shrugged. "I don't know. It only sat there, watching the two ravens below it. The two birds further down in the tree began to cry out at the red-eyed raven. It answered them and the winds died out, leaving everything perfectly still. One of the ravens on the lower branches flew away. As soon as it left, the second raven flew off, following the first and leaving the red-eyed one alone. The moment the second raven disappeared into the distance…,"

Dot stopped. Her already pale complexion turned sickly gray as she recalled the details of her dream. When it did not appear that she would continue speaking on her own, Simon gently prodded her.

"The moment it disappeared … what?'

"When the second raven left, the tree caught fire. The flames consumed everything until the entire tree was reduced to ash. The hilltop was left with a black ring of smoking ground. Everything was gone, Simon. Everything was completely wiped out."

"It's okay," Simon reassured her in a soft, soothing tone. "It's okay. We don't know what it means yet. We don't know if something bad is definitely going to happen, or if this is a warning so we can stop it before it gets out of control. Right? You said it yourself; it could be anything."

Dot took several breaths to calm herself.

"You're right. I don't know what it means. But Simon, it feels really bad."

"I know. What you told me sounds awful. Still, instead of panicking over the unknown, let's take a moment and focus on what we can figure out. I know you are still trying to decipher what your dreams mean, but is there anything in this one that makes sense to you?"

"Right," Dot agreed, straightening in her chair and squaring her shoulders with resolve. "What do I know? Okay, first, the ravens are common symbols. I see them a lot in my dreams. They represent figures of power, usually people that control strong magic and have the ability to affect the events around them. That could be practically anyone in Dasan's Terrace. It could be you, or Mitch, or one of the stronger witches."

"Or you?" asked Simon.

"Or me," Dot reluctantly acknowledged.

"The red eyed raven at the top of the tree. Do you know who that might be?"

"No. I have no idea. I only know that they're powerful. They felt malevolent, too. I don't think they have any love for anyone associated with Dasan's Terrace. Could be an outsider, or maybe it's someone who is going to turn on us because of something that hasn't happened yet."

"What about the two others?"

Dot shook her head. "I don't know who they are either. One thing I am almost certain of though, is that the ravens that flew away are important. The act of leaving didn't start the fire, but the fire only started after they left. If we can figure out who the ravens represent, and why they fled from Dasan's Terrace, we have to make sure they don't abandon the cemetery."

"And that will stop the fire, or whatever it represents from happening?"

"I don't know if it will stop the fire. The bad thing might happen regardless of anything we do. But I think if we don't stop these people from leaving, we absolutely will not be able to protect Dead Town from whatever is coming our way."

"Where should we be looking?" asked Mitch, letting his gaze travel along the rows of shelved books for sale. "Does the poltergeist typically come out at a certain time of day?"

Aaron, the less pleasant of the two shop owners in Mitch's estimation, waved a dismissive hand. "It comes out whenever it wants to come out. Usually, to throw a couple books at customers and chase them away."

"Is that a pattern?" Mitch tried to clarify.

"What?"

"The poltergeist comes out when customers are in the shop. What about when it's only the two of you in here?"

"It is typically very quiet in the store when there are no customers," said Dayo, understanding what Mitch was asking. "The ghost does not come out much while it is quiet. When there is noise in the store, it seems to become agitated."

"Are there any locations in particular that it seems to frequent?" Violet added. "Are there particular parts of the store that it seems more protective of?"

"I have not noticed a specific area where it stays," said Dayo. He stroked one side of his bearded face with the fingertips of his right hand, considering the question further. "Although if customers stay near the front of the shop, it does not appear as frequently as when they wander towards the back."

Mitch took a few steps along the middle aisle of the bookshop towards the rear of the store. "If we accept the premise that the poltergeist came from a man killed in his home during a burglary, it would make sense that the ghost only becomes agitated when it feels its territory is being invaded. When the two of you are alone in the store, things are quiet, and the poltergeist isn't disturbed."

"But when customers come in," said Violet, continuing the thread of Mitch's thought, "it reacts like someone who is being attacked in their own home. So, to draw it out, we need to make the poltergeist think it has unwelcome guests."

Violet leaned toward Mitch and patted him on the head affectionately. "Very clever."

Mitch grinned, inordinately pleased by the praise. "Did I earn my Scooby snack?" he asked.

"Maybe two. But it will have to wait until we're done here."

Violet turned to the storeowners. "While we figure this out, you should stay near the front of the store. This could get violent, and I don't want you in the line of fire. I can't focus on removing the poltergeist if I have to protect bystanders as well."

Dayo nodded. When Aaron looked about to object, his husband hooked him by the arm and led him toward the business' front counter.

With the owners safely tucked away, Violet and Mitch wandered toward the rear of the store, warily exploring the bookshelves around them and watching for any signs of movement.

"What should we steal first?" Mitch asked in an overly loud, theatrical voice.

"What?" demanded Aaron from the front of the store. His tone was high, almost shrill with indignation. He started to march toward the back to confront Mitch, but Dayo again took him gently by the arm.

"Hush," said the calmer man. "Remember what they are doing."

"Oh, yes. Um, right," stammered Aaron, embarrassed.

Mitch watched the exchange for a moment, amused that his acting had worked so well, at least on the living inhabitants of the store. He turned back toward Violet and continued. "So, anyway, what looks good to you?"

"All these books look really good. I bet we can sell them for a lot of cash," Violet announced, playing along.

As they made their way deeper into the store, Mitch came across a large cabinet filled with multiple rows of tiny drawers. The broad wooden case was tucked away between two of the omnipresent rows of bookcases, and it only became visible when he reached the exposed space between them. The cabinet was an old style, library card catalog. It was constructed with a darkly stained hardwood Mitch could not identify, and each of the small file drawers had a curved brass handle affixed to its face.

Mitch recognized the item immediately, though he had not seen anything like it since he was a child. And even back then, the card catalogs he had seen were largely decorative, as most libraries had begun transferring their inventory onto computer files before he was born. Although the filing cabinet was obviously old, the drawers and framework were remarkably well preserved.

With genuine admiration, Mitch approached. He slid a few drawers open and closed experimentally, and they glided in and out with ease. They were empty inside, but that did not detract from his appreciation of the craftsmanship.

"Wow. This thing is beautiful," he said. "Violet, you need to see this. It looks brand new."

"How much do you think we could get for it?" Violet asked.

"Hmm?" Distracted by the historic relic in the store, Mitch had momentarily forgotten what they were doing. Violet's question brought him quickly back to work. "Right. Um, I guess to a collector this could be worth quite a bit. I know I'd love to have something like this in my study at home. Assuming I had a home big enough to have a study."

A heavy *thump* startled Mitch. He spun around, searching for the source of the noise. A book lay flat on the floor behind him, motionless and innocuous looking, but he was certain it had not been there when he walked into this aisle. It must have fallen from one of the shelves when he wasn't looking. Strangely, as he scanned the bookcase closest to him, he could not see where the tome had come from.

Violet pointed a finger toward a bookrack further away, indicating the third shelf up from the floor. Mitch saw a gap between two hardbound publications still standing undisturbed in their proper place. The space seemed much too far away for the book at his feet to have simply fallen.

"Coincidence?" Mitch asked, already knowing that it was not.

Violet did not bother to acknowledge the question.

"I think we have its attention. Keep talking. We need to agitate it enough to make an appearance. Unless we bring it out, we may never find the book it attached itself to."

Mitch nodded. "Okay. If you want agitated, I can do agitated."

With both hands, he grasped the edge of a shelf in the case nearest to him and began to shake. The sturdy furniture was bolted to the wall and affixed to the floor, apparently to prevent patrons from attempting this very action, but Mitch kept pushing until he was rewarded by a tiny wobble.

"I'm going to tear this place down," he announced loudly. "I'll set the house on fire if I have to, and I'll shoot anyone that tries to stop me."

Books launched from the shelves to either side of Mitch, this time with much more force than the first publication already on the floor. Two heavy volumes struck him in the ribs simultaneously, one from the left, one from the right. He yelped and darted out of the aisle toward safer and more open spaces, trying to escape any further unexpected barrages.

"Eyes open," Violet told him. "We need to find the poltergeist and trace any tethers back to its origin."

"No, I'm fine. Thanks for asking," Mitch replied, rubbing at a sore spot under his arm where a sharp corner on one of the books had caught him.

Violet winked at him. "Poor baby. Do you want to wait outside where it's safe? I'll come get you when it's all over."

Her jovial expression quickly faded, however. Violet raised her voice and called out toward the ceiling, "We aren't afraid of you. We're coming for you. I promise when we find you, we will take everything you hold dear and then, before we're done, we'll kill you."

The response was immediate. A moan filled the air around them, like a hard wind blowing through the eaves of a decaying house. There were no words, only an inarticulate wail. The cry was wild, animalistic.

Something was angry.

Mitch shivered, but he was unsure if his reaction was due to the incorporeal moaning, or Violet's threat. He knew she was only trying to draw out the poltergeist, but she sounded so serious. He believed every word she said. Fortunately, so did the ghost.

Movement within one of the bookshelves drew Mitch's attention. A formless silver-gray mass flowed from between the spaces in a row of books, appearing like a thick fog rolling through a copse of densely packed trees. The ethereal mass pulled itself together as it appeared, collecting into something roughly human shaped, though no clear details or features were discernable. What might have been the suggestion of a head, torso, arms and legs roiled and churned, expanding and contracting as the figure drifted in the air before them.

This was not a true ghost, Mitch reminded himself. It was not the trapped soul of a human being, forced to remain on the physical plain of existence after death. This was a poltergeist, a residue of extreme emotions left behind by someone during a violet demise. The creature in front of him was not a person, but rather a manifestation of terror, hatred, and pain, seeking to punish anyone and everyone it encountered as repayment for its own anguish.

The apparition was mostly mindless, driven by rage, not conscious thought. It was not to be taken lightly, however. This creature could still be dangerous.

The poltergeist swept an arm across the bookshelf from which it had appeared. Several hardbound novels launched from their wooden perch and flew through the room toward Violet. She barely took notice of the attack, shifting a fraction to her left to avoid the only book that had been propelled with enough accuracy to be even a minor threat. It fluttered harmlessly past her before crashing onto the floor and skidding to a stop near one of the padded reading chairs.

While the poltergeist seemed fixated on Violet, Mitch decided this was his opportunity to end the confrontation quickly. He searched inside himself, finding the deepest recesses within his physical body where he had safely secured his soul before entering the store. He released a tendril of his true self and allowed it to stretch outward. The narrow extension of spirit trailed along his right arm and into his hand. Mitch watched as the glowing projections of his soul sprouted from each of his fingertips. All the practice and training he and Violet had done over the past weeks was paying off, and he could feel the control he now had over his essence. It obeyed his mental commands as if it were an extension of his body.

When Violet used her soul for an exorcism, she manifested a single narrow blade of spirit, a scalpel-like instrument, perfect for delicate, precise cuts. Mitch, however, had none of her finesse. He saw his soul curl from his fingertips like the heavy claws of a hunting predator. Where Violet performed with the skill of a gifted surgeon, Mitch was all about brute force and exerting maximum damage in his attacks.

He took one step toward the distracted ghost.

"Mitch, no. Pull back. Now!"

Mitch heard the urgency and tension in Violet's voice. He did not understand her concern, but he did not have to. He trusted her. Pulling his soul back into the protected depths of his body, he backed away.

Though he had acted quickly to the warning, he was too late to avoid being noticed.

The poltergeist turned from Violet, focusing instead on Mitch's retreating form. He realized it must have sensed his intended attack, somehow recognizing the threat that Mitch represented. The poltergeist reacted from some kind of primitive survival instinct that was triggered when he had gotten too close.

Mitch remembered his first meeting with the ghost of Lieutenant Tim Delaney. He shook hands with Delaney and the lieutenant had recoiled, immediately disliking him. Did all ghosts have this ability? Would they all see him as a threat to their existence?

Now was not the time to be distracted, Mitch warned himself. The poltergeist was the priority. The creature faced him, seeming to assess the situation as it decided what to do next. Two hollow sockets in the head where its eyes should have been focused on him. Another opening in the face formed, creating a much too wide mouth that drifted eerily from one side of its countenance to the other.

The creature wailed angrily and darted forward. Forgoing its previous tactic of throwing inanimate objects, the poltergeist this time opted for a more direct assault. Instinctively, Mitch tried to protect himself from the charge. He pulled at the magic stored in the ruby in his ring and threw up a defensive shield between himself and the attacking spirit. The poltergeist passed through the barrier as if it didn't exist, striking Mitch in the stomach.

Mitch shouted and clapped his hands against his body in shocked surprise. Expecting the contact to hurt, it took Mitch several moments to realize he had not experienced any actual pain when the poltergeist passed through him. He swept his hands up and down his torso, frantically searching for holes or signs of blood.

After exploring his intact chest and stomach in great detail to reassure himself he was fully intact, he relaxed. The ghost was apparently harmless and had done absolutely no damage. The creature might be an angry spirit, but it was still only a spirit after all. It could not touch him.

Mitch released a small chuff of relief, chiding himself at his panicked reaction to the attack.

The poltergeist was similarly realizing its charge had generated an unsatisfactory effect, and it darted at Mitch once again. Unphased this time, Mitch stood his ground and waited for the specter to pass through him as it had before.

The poltergeist hit Mitch in the chest like a cannonball fired at close range.

The breath was crushed from his lungs and he whoofed loudly as the impact lifted him off his feet and hurled him backwards. Fortunately, he fell directly to the ground. The angle of his tumble kept him from ricocheting into a bookshelf or any other furniture that could have caused more serious injury.

"Shit," he wheezed, trying to pull air back into his body. Mitch rolled to his side and searched desperately for the poltergeist, hoping he was not about to be struck again.

"Don't waste your magic on it," Violet told him from where she still stood in the bookstore's main aisle. "It doesn't do much on ghosts. That's why regular witches aren't much use in exorcisms. Also, when poltergeists attack, don't just stand there like a mounted target and let them hit you. At least try to get out of the way."

"Thanks," Mitch gasped. He wanted to say something more scathing in reply, but he was still struggling to breathe normally.

Violet extended a slender blade of spirit from the fingertips of her left hand. Mitch could see the strand of her soul like a shining silver filament. The poltergeist responded immediately, turning its full attention to her. Violet immediately retracted the tendril. She had no intention of attacking, she merely wanted to draw the ghost away from Mitch long enough for him to recover and get back to his feet.

The angry apparition bolted toward her, screeching its frustration. Violet waited until it was almost on top of her, then took one step to the side, turning her body to allow the poltergeist to fly past without so much as brushing against her. She looked like a matador gracefully avoiding a charging bull. The specter, realizing it had missed, dove downward, disappearing through the floor.

Mitch pushed shakily to his feet, clutching at his chest. His ribs had only recently mended from being injured a few months ago. He did not think they were rebroken, but the shot he received from the poltergeist had hurt like hell. He scanned the room rapidly, looking for any signs of the ghost's reappearance. Mitch did not want to take another blow like the last one.

Violet approached and placed a hand over his heart. Mitch felt her magic suffuse his chest as she examined his internal organs.

"Nothing permanently damaged," she announced. "You're going to hurt for a while, and probably have some very colorful bruising, but you'll live."

"That's reassuring," he muttered. "What now?"

Violet shrugged. "The plan hasn't changed. We still need to find the book the poltergeist is attached to. I don't know if we can lure the thing out again. It's probably afraid of us now that it knows we can hurt it."

"Speaking of which, why did you stop me from trying to get rid of it?"

"That would have been a huge mistake. This poltergeist is a lot stronger than most. Did you notice it turned on you the second you exposed your soul?"

"Um. Yeah, I did see that."

"This thing will fight back. It might even succeed in doing quite a bit of damage before you or I can destroy it. That would be really bad. Do you remember what I told you happens to exorcists that don't know what they're doing?"

Mitch nodded. "I do."

Violet had lectured him extensively about exorcists that acted carelessly while eliminating ghosts. Their souls became torn and tattered from repeated injuries. When enough damage occurred, the afflicted exorcists often lost their minds, going completely insane.

"We don't want that, do we?" Violet chided.

"No, ma'am. We definitely do not. So, how do we find the book? I didn't see a tether to follow."

"I didn't either," Violet admitted. She twitched her mouth, and her nose wrinkled prettily as she considered their next move. "I suppose we have to search the entire store. It's most likely somewhere…,"

"Watch out," Mitch shouted. He thrust his hand over Violet's shoulder, pulling at the stored magic in his ring.

He had only a second to shape the magic into a blue disc of power, placing the shield between the back of Violet's head and the massive brass bookend that leapt off the bookcase behind her. The metal projectile sparked as it struck the magical barrier and bounced away.

The cowardly attack from the hiding poltergeist could have caused Violet serious injury if Mitch had not seen it and reacted at the last possible instant.

"I'm empty," Mitch told her. "That was the last of what I had in the ruby."

"Then the sooner we find the book, the better." Violet leaned into Mitch and gave him a quick "thank you" peck on the cheek before turning to assess the store around them and any possible places a hundred-year-old book might be hiding.

"The poltergeist didn't get agitated until we got this far," he said. "I think we should check this area more closely before we start a general search of the store. The owners also said the ghost appeared to customers more often near the back."

"I agree," said Violet. "You go left, and I'll go right. Keep an eye out for the poltergeist or any more ambush attacks."

Mitch returned to the bookshelves where he had first encountered the angry spirit. He figured that it was as good a location to begin his search as any. Maybe the ghost had appeared because he was getting too close to the book it was attempting to keep hidden. He scanned the novels on the shelf in front of him and wondered if he was going to have to check every single one of the thousands of books in the shop.

Then inspiration struck. He called out.

"Mr. Okoro?"

"Yes?" came the answer from the front of the shop.

"What does this book look like? Can you describe it for me?"

"It's a cream or tan-colored hardback book. About eight inches tall and an inch thick. Perhaps a little more. The cover is plain, with black lettering, except for the first letter of each word in the title. The first letters are red."

"Thank you," Mitch responded. Now he did not need to check every book. He only needed to find tan hardback books with red and black lettering. That eliminated better than ninety percent of the shop's inventory, although ten percent still left a lot of books to examine.

He let his eyes trail over the rows of publications, starting with the books at the top of the bookshelf and working his way down. Whenever he noticed a pale hardbound book, he paused long enough to examine the title more closely before moving on with his search. Every now and again, he would stop his hunt to check his surroundings for hostile manifestations or flying objects.

The books on the surrounding shelves proved innocent enough. Mitch even pressed himself flat to the floor to check the narrow gap between the shelving units and the carpeted floor they stood upon, just in case the ghost had managed to slide the book in question underneath. He found nothing but dust bunnies and old cobwebs.

He was about to leave and move on to the next aisle when his eyes strayed back to the card catalogue cabinet he had been admiring earlier. The heavy wooden furniture was situated with its backside against the wall where it could best be seen and appreciated by patrons of the shop as they perused the various stacks of books. The cabinet was also where Mitch had been standing when the poltergeist put in its first appearance.

Mitch lowered himself to the ground again to peer underneath the cabinet. Curved wooden legs held the furniture several inches above the floor, plenty of space for a wayward book to have landed.

The space was clear. He saw nothing but more of the nondescript gray carpet that covered most of the bookshop's floor.

Next, Mitch worked his way to the side of the cabinet, trying to get a look behind it. The card bureau was pushed back almost flush with the wall, and he could not see anything in the limited shadowy space. He tried to wedge his fingers in the narrow crack between the cabinet and the wall but could not gain any purchase. Refusing to concede defeat, he used his left hand to grasp the base of the furniture, leaned his right shoulder against the smooth wooden surface, then heaved the side of the catalog upward. Using the momentum of the lift, he shuffled left and managed to hop his end of the filing cabinet forward a few inches.

Mitch heard a soft thump as something fell from behind the cabinet to the floor.

He dropped to the ground and peered beneath the filing case again. Unlike his last check, this time he found a pale-colored, hardbound book resting on the previously empty carpet.

"Violet?" he called, excitedly.

Mitch stretched out a hand and dragged the book toward himself. When he pulled it within range of the artificial overhead lighting, he saw the title on the front in all its red and black glory.

The Red Badge of Courage by Stephen Crane.

"Yes?" asked Violet, appearing in the aisle behind him.

Mitch held up the recovered item in triumph. "Got it. One ancient, haunted book as requested."

"Nicely done," she told him. "And we didn't have to turn the whole store upside down to find it. Did you see something that led you to the book?"

"No. Just got lucky doing a regular search."

"I guess it can be useful to have a police officer on the team. Thank you for your assistance, Detective Loman." Violet rewarded Mitch with a gentle golf clap.

Mitch stood and handed the book over to Violet, who accepted it and immediately began flipping through several of the interior pages. After a moment of casual perusing, she paused.

"Ah, here we are. Do you see it?"

She held the book where Mitch could observe it more easily. He peered closely at the lettering on the open page before realizing that the book itself was not what Violet wanted him to see.

A diffuse trickle of gray rose up from the novel, barely visible, like a wisp of steam escaping a cooling teapot. The trace of gray thinned the further it travelled from the book, becoming more difficult to follow, but never completely disappearing.

The trail rose upward a few feet before turning dramatically downward and vanishing into the floor.

"The poltergeist's tether," Mitch said.

Violet nodded. "Mm-hmm."

"Are we going to cut it?" He asked. "Like the echo in San Jose?"

Violet snapped the book closed and held it protectively against her chest.

"No," she said. "That would be a very bad idea in this situation."

"I don't understand. I thought that was what we were trying to do here."

Violet shook her head, then glanced toward the front of the store where the two owners waited. Both men stood behind the cashier counter, intently watching the interaction between the two ghost hunters in their store. Violet moved closer to him and lowered her voice to be sure their observers could not overhear.

"This thing is strong, Mitch. You haven't met anything like this before, but I have. We can't cut the tether and wait for it to go away. It could take months for a poltergeist this powerful to finally dissipate. In the meantime, if it isn't attached to the book, it could wander anywhere it wanted to go, and we would have no way to contain or control it. It also might decide to stay right here in the bookstore, which would probably not make the guys that hired me very happy.

"If we confront it face to face, there is a risk of one or both of us getting hurt. We found the book that it's attached to, though, so we don't have to fight it on its terms anymore. With the book in hand, we have two options."

"And those are…?" asked Mitch.

"Number one, we can get paid, take the book with us when we leave, and the poltergeist follows. We bury the book somewhere that hopefully no one ever finds it, and the poltergeist is free to exist among the surrounding trees and rocks and wilderness for as long as it likes, or at least until the book completely decomposes and the tether breaks naturally."

"That doesn't seem terrible."

"It's not," Violet agreed. "Unless someone digs it up. Then the whole haunting thing starts up again with a new victim. There is also the fact that this spirit has the ability to move the book by itself when it wants to. There's no guarantee it won't dig the book up from wherever we put it and relocate itself somewhere that it can do more damage."

Mitch did not like the sound of that at all. He wanted the poltergeist gone, not simply lurking somewhere, waiting for a new person to terrorize and harass.

"What's option number two?"

"It's a little more dangerous, but option two is we use the book to force the poltergeist back into the open, then sucker punch it while it's disoriented."

Neither option sounded ideal, but Mitch realized this wraith haunting the bookstore needed to be eliminated, not simply moved and hidden to become someone else's problem later.

"Sucker punch then," he told Violet. "How do you want to do this?"

"Have you seen those nature programs where a pack of hyenas harass a lion?"

Mitch nodded, confused. "Yeah. So?"

"The lion can only face one enemy at a time. Whichever hyena is at its back is the next to attack. When the lion turns, that animal retreats and another one jumps in to take a bite. That's what we need to do. But be careful. You only attack when you have its back. If it turns on you, retreat. Don't play hero. There won't be any room for mistakes."

"Got it," Mitch said. "No heroes here. Let's do this thing."

Violet placed a hand on Mitch's chest, indicating he should remain where he was, then she took five backward paces to create a space between them. She examined the book again, searching for the tether that bound the poltergeist to the tome. When she located it, she grasped the ethereal strand firmly while simultaneously being careful not to sever the bond by accident.

"Ready?" she asked, glancing at Mitch.

"Ready," he replied.

Violet pulled the tether. It stretched tight, resisting her efforts to draw it toward herself. Mitch watched her strain as she tugged the delicate filament, convinced it would break at any moment. It looked like a wisp of smoke, yet Violet struggled to move it so much as an inch.

A now familiar moan echoed through the interior of the store, and the poltergeist burst upwards through the floor, appearing suddenly between them. Though the man-shaped apparition had no face, it was clearly focusing its attention on Violet. She was the one who dared to touch the link tying it to the book, therefore she was the immediate threat.

The ghost's cry rose in intensity until it was almost a screech as it prepared to attack. Mitch did not waste any time. Before the poltergeist could rush toward Violet, he leapt forward. He extended his spirit into his right hand, letting his soul curl outward from his fingertips.

He slashed silvery claws into the apparition, swiping and cutting deep wounds into the creature's back. Mitch felt the specter's essence part reluctantly under his attack. The sensation was like dragging a dull knife through canvas cloth. The ghost felt much more solid than he had expected.

The poltergeist screamed in anger, or perhaps it had been hurt, though Mitch was unsure if the creature could actually feel pain. It whirled towards him. He barely had time to retract his soul before the ghost responded, flailing wildly in his direction. It swung one glimmering, translucent arm at him.

Mitch ducked, but he felt the limb brush through his hair and bounce painfully off the top of his head. Fortunately, the poltergeist only managed a glancing physical blow. Mitch's soul was once again shielded safely within his body.

Violet recognized her cue and jumped into action. Mitch saw a flash of silver as she slashed the poltergeist from shoulder to hip, forcing another wail of rage from the injured specter. It spun, refocusing on her. Mitch attacked its exposed back.

This time, he knew what resistance to expect, and he swung harder and cut deeper than he had during his first strike. He felt the poltergeist shred beneath his spiritual claws, pulling apart like thick tangles of cotton. Mitch wanted to go in for another handful, but Violet had warned him against taking unnecessary risks. He withdrew and waited for the ghost's counterattack.

The poltergeist turned to face Mitch but did not move closer. Instead, it rotated once again toward Violet as if anticipating her next flanking maneuver. The ghost was getting smarter, or perhaps it was simply panicking and unsure from which direction the next assault would come. The vaguely man-shaped cloud of fury lost cohesion, breaking apart and roiling uncontrolled for several seconds before drawing itself back together.

Mitch and Violet held their ground, neither attacking nor retreating as they waited for the poltergeist to decide its next move. The creature continued to circle, facing one opponent, then the other.

Mitch tried shuffling closer to the indecisive spirit, but when he did, the poltergeist bolted away from him, directly toward Violet. Surprised by the move, Violet dropped the book she had been holding and threw herself to the side to avoid the approaching ghost. The poltergeist changed directions at the last moment, but it was not following Violet's attempt to dodge. Instead, the ghost dove at the fallen book, disappearing as it passed through the pale, cardboard cover.

The book shuddered like a slumbering animal coming awake, then began to rise from the floor. Mitch bolted across the center aisle of the bookstore and slammed a foot down on the animated novel before it could levitate more than a few inches. It crashed back to ground, pinned to the carpet under his shoe.

Violet was also moving, crawling quickly to Mitch's side. She raised a hand, her palm bladed and fingers extended. Mitch saw a flash of silver as she extended her soul from the tip of her middle finger. He shifted his foot away, and she plunged the deadly point of her spirit blade through the center of the book. Violet raised her hand up, then stabbed down again, and again.

Four quick jabs and Violet rocked back, jumping to her feet. She placed a hand on Mitch's chest and forced him back two steps. Together, they stared at the book on the ground, waiting for the poltergeist to respond to her last brutal assault.

Ethereal gray smoke bled from the closed pages of the old novel. Mitch expected it to coalesce back into something human-shaped, but it merely drifted in the air over the book. The gray cloud shifted and eddied without direction for several long seconds, then faded from sight.

Mitch and Violet still did not move. They waited to be certain nothing new would come leaping toward them, either from the book or anywhere else in the store.

Tentatively, Violet stooped and retrieved the novel. She opened the front cover, then with her thumb and forefinger, she carefully flipped through each individual sheet of the two hundred or so pages.

"The tether is gone," she said.

"Does that mean the poltergeist is loose?"

She shook her head and smiled toward Mitch. "No. It means it's gone. We did enough damage to it that it fell apart. We got rid of it."

Mitch blew out a breath in satisfied relief.

"So, we're done here?"

Violet nodded her agreement. "We're done."

Hearing her pronouncement from their barricaded position at the front of the store, Aaron Pavali and Dayo Okoro left the protection of the cashier's counter and cautiously moved toward Mitch and Violet.

"The ghost is gone?" asked Aaron, making certain he had heard correctly.

"The poltergeist is gone," Violet confirmed.

"And it won't be coming back?"

"No," she assured him. "It will not be coming back."

Violet held up the hundred plus year-old copy of *The Red Badge of Courage*. "Would you like this back, or would you prefer I take it out of the store?"

Mitch watched Aaron with quiet amusement as greed and fear warred within the shop owner's mind. In the end, it appeared that greed won out.

"Why don't you set it down on one of those shelves there," Aaron finally said, pointing to a location close to Violet but at a safe distance from himself. "I'll deal with it later."

CHAPTER 3

After successfully removing the poltergeist from The Book Nook, Mitch and Violet treated themselves to an early lunch to celebrate. Carmel had several attractive dining locations in the area, and it only took them a few minutes of walking to find a place with a menu they both agreed upon.

The restaurant had four, two-person tables arranged outside, with a waist-high, wrought iron fence separating the patio dining area from the pedestrian walkway next to it. Each of the tables sported a wide cloth umbrella, mounted to shade customers from the overhead sun on warmer days. Violet requested one of the outdoor tables when they arrived, and Mitch nodded his agreement. The host indicated that they should help themselves to whichever seats they preferred as they were currently the only diners on the patio.

After placing their orders with a teenaged employee who looked like he should still be in school rather than hustling food on a Tuesday morning, they passed the time by people-watching and chatting about their recent adventure in the bookstore. Violet removed her black wig, freeing the shoulder-length blond hair underneath. There was little she could do about her makeup situation, at least until they went back to their hotel room where she could wash it off. Mitch didn't mind. He actually enjoyed her goth look, as well as the circumspect stares she frequently got from startled passersby.

"If you were by yourself, what would you have done with the poltergeist?" He asked.

Violet considered Mitch's question. She raked her fingers absently through her hair, removing a few tangles, before saying, "I would have taken the book out somewhere in the middle of nowhere, cut the poltergeist's tether, then run away as fast as possible. It probably would have rampaged a few weeks before it faded away, but in the desert, or deep in the woods, hopefully it wouldn't hurt anybody."

"You wouldn't have faced it head on, like we did together?"

"Absolutely not. It was too strong for one person to take on alone. With you there, we were able to keep it distracted and one of us always had an opening. If I had fought it by myself there was too much risk of it doing damage to me, physically and psychically."

Mitch smiled slyly at Violet. "So then, I was helpful today?"

Violet smirked back at the obvious play for approval.

"Yes, sweety. You were very helpful today," she said, using the same tone of voice she might use to praise an animal or a small child. Mitch almost expected her to reach across the table and ruffle his hair.

Unoffended, he accepted the praise. "You never thanked me, by the way," he said.

"For coming with me? That was the whole point of us being here."

"No, not for that. For saving your life."

"For…? Oh, right. Saving my life. That." Violet pasted a vacuous expression on her face and batted her eyelashes at Mitch. "Thank you for saving my life, my great big strong savior of a man."

Mitch's smile slipped away as the realization struck him. "You saw that bookend coming, didn't you? You didn't need me to stop it, you just *let* me stop it."

Violet sighed. "I knew you wouldn't let it hit me, but yeah, I saw it coming. I'm sorry if it bothers you that I trusted you so much I didn't deflect it myself."

The comment left Mitch feeling embarrassed at his assumption. He should have known that Violet would not be surprised by anything the poltergeist had attempted in the bookstore. At the same time, it made him feel somewhat better knowing she trusted him enough that she had not reacted to the heavy projectile aimed at her head.

"You don't stay in one piece doing this kind of work for as long as I have by being careless," Violet said, turning serious. "You are going to have some bruises from this morning that I hope taught you a few things for the next poltergeist you come across. Magic doesn't help much against ghosts. I think you figured that out when the poltergeist flew right through your shield. Magic can do a lot of great things, but you have to use and rely on your abilities as an exorcist when dealing with spirits at any level."

"I'm still learning about that kind of stuff," Mitch said, defensively. "I do have a great teacher, though."

Violet nodded, accepting the compliment.

"You've gotten pretty good at using shields. Our practice has paid off. You've gotten a lot faster at recognizing a threat and putting up your defenses. I'm happy about that. But…,"

"But…?" Mitch echoed.

"But I wonder if you are getting too reliant on shields. No matter how good you are with them, they won't work every time, and you need to be prepared to use other methods. I told you a long time ago you need to be ready to avoid an attack, deflect it, or disrupt it. You're not bad at avoiding, you've gotten really good at deflecting, but you haven't figured out how to reliably disrupt a magical assault."

"I don't really know how," Mitch admitted.

"I know. And that's my fault. I haven't pushed you to learn because I figured there were still too many other things we were working on. You have a lot of stuff to learn, that hasn't changed, but I think it's time we put a little effort into teaching you how to interrupt someone else's magic."

"Now?"

Violet shook her head. "Nope. Not now. We're on vacation, and I don't plan on ruining it by kicking your ass over and over. I want you to be in a good mood, not pouting because I spanked you like a toddler. There's plenty of time for that when we get back home. Besides, there isn't enough magic around here to…,"

Violet trailed off, staring at something over Mitch's right shoulder. Before he could turn to see what had caught her attention, a woman's voice rang out from somewhere behind him.

"Violet Rose? Is that you, baby girl? Please tell me it's really you."

"Be polite. Don't speak," Violet whispered quickly, then she stood up from the table, smiling as if she were greeting a long-lost family member.

Mitch turned his head to spy a stocky woman wearing jeans and a blue tank top walking purposefully towards them on the sidewalk. Mitch had never seen the woman before, but it was obvious to him that Violet knew her very well. It was also obvious from the tension in her bearing that Violet did not like the new arrival much.

Their visitor looked to be in her forties or fifties, with deeply tanned skin, wavy black hair and dark eyes. The woman grinned in surprised delight as she approached.

"Safia?" Violet said, her voice rising in apparent excitement. "Safia! What are you doing here?"

The two women embraced in a quick hug over the low metal fence, then separated. The dark-haired newcomer glanced toward Mitch where he remained seated at the table.

"You aren't in Sacramento anymore?" Safia asked, bringing her attention back to Violet. "Does that mean you finally left Alyssandra and formed your own coven?"

"No, I'm still with Alyssandra," Violet responded. "I came to Carmel to handle a haunting, but I'm headed back home tomorrow."

Safia gaze flickered again to Mitch. "And who is this lovely young man? I hope I'm not interrupting anything important."

"Sorry," said Violet, feigning forgetfulness. "Safia, this is Mitch Loman. He's actually a new member in our coven. Alyssandra asked me to take him with me on this job so he could see what I do." Violet waved a hand toward Mitch. "Mitch, this is Safia Bernal. Safia is part of the New York coven that Alyssandra and I belonged to before we moved to California."

Mitch nodded a greeting, mindful of the warning not to speak. Despite Violet's friendly demeanor with the New York witch, he could see a tightness around her eyes and wariness in her posture. This woman was not a friend, and Violet did not completely trust the circumstances that brought the older witch so far from the east coast.

The half-truth Violet told Safia about her relationship to him was further evidence to Mitch that silence was his best course of action. He did not want to accidentally let slip any information Violet herself was hesitant to reveal.

"How is Gail, by the way?" Violet asked. She looked over her shoulder at Mitch before adding, "Gail is the coven priestess back east."

"Not anymore," Safia said, her lips curving down into a frown that appeared to Mitch to be almost, but not quite, genuine. "Gail passed away very recently. Sad, but not terribly surprising since she was a little over a hundred and twenty years old. These things happen, you know."

"Who took over when she died?" Violet asked, surprised by the news of the old priestess's death."

Safia held out her hands in a modest "ta-daa" gesture. "Little old me," she responded. "Things are very different when you're the boss, but I'm sure you'll find that out for yourself eventually. Alyssandra won't be around forever. I'm actually surprised that you're still with her and haven't split off to form your own coven. You're strong enough to be in charge."

Violet waved away the compliment. "If you're the new priestess, why are you in California?"

"Why, for a much needed vacation, of course. I haven't had any time to myself in forever, and now with taking over the coven, I figured I deserved a few days of playtime in the sunshine. It's a shame you're headed back to Sacramento so soon. We could have spent some time together. You know, catch up on old times."

"Sorry about that. Bad timing. If I had known you were coming, I could have planned some extra time to show you around. As it is, Mitch and I have to head back home in the morning."

Safia tapped her chin as if considering something for the first time. “I don’t have to spend my entire vacation in Carmel. Maybe I’ll head to Sacramento tomorrow, too. I can pay my respects to Alyssandra, one priestess to another. Then, if she can spare you for a while, you can show me the sights and introduce me to the rest of your coven. I haven’t seen you in so long, I would hate to miss an opportunity to hang out.”

Violet smiled again, though the joyful appearance in her face never quite reached her eyes. Mitch was fairly certain he was the only one who noticed the forced expression, however.

“That sounds like a wonderful idea. I’ll talk to Alyssandra as soon as we get back and arrange a time to get together. Do you have a place to stay?”

“Not really,” admitted Safia. “My reservations for the foreseeable future were all here in Carmel.”

“Mitch? Any ideas?”

Mitch startled, then replied carefully, “Um, the Holiday Inn in Elk Grove is very nice, and they usually have rooms available for last minute arrivals.”

“There you go,” Violet enthused. “I’ll book you a room there. Of course, it will be our treat to host you while you’re with us. How long should I make the reservation for?”

“My original plans were for a week. Let’s start with that, then I can play it by ear. We might just have so much fun that I’ll never want to leave.”

Mitch almost laughed at the jousting match he was watching but managed to muffle it in a small cough. Violet had attempted to set a limit on how long Safia might be around, but the New York coven leader had neatly sidestepped the issue. He placed his chin on his fist and observed while Violet and her old coven mate exchanged phone numbers and promised to get in touch again tomorrow.

“Well, I should toddle along and let you two enjoy your lunch.” Safia leaned over the railing and gave Violet another brief embrace. “I can’t wait to see Alyssandra again. The two of us have a lot of old gossip to catch up on. I’ll see you in Sacramento.”

“Bye, Safia. It was really nice running into you.”

Violet sat back down at the table across from Mitch. They both watched the dark-haired witch walk away until she turned left and vanished down a cross street.

“We’re really heading back tomorrow?” asked Mitch when they could no longer see Safia in the distance.

“Yup,” Violet said. She continued staring at the corner where the woman had disappeared from sight.

“So much for our vacation.”

“Yup.”

“It must have been nice to see an old friend like that,” Mitch said. The corner of his lip quirked up mischievously.

Violet shifted her eyes to glare at him reproachfully.

“Could it be coincidence that she turned up today?” he asked.

“Maybe,” Violet demurred. “If I had to guess though, I’d say there’s something going on in New York, and for some reason Alyssandra and I are involved. Safia either needs to recruit us or eliminate us. I just have to figure out which one before it’s too late.”

“Do you really think it could be that bad?”

Violet laid her hands on the table in front of her and shifted uncomfortably in her seat.

“I always think it will be that bad. That’s how I stay alive.”

Chang'e knelt on the floor of her dilapidated studio apartment, finishing the details of the summoning circle she had drawn on the dirty laminate floor. The red stick of chalk in her hand left her fingers tinged with pink dust as she drew the final symbol at the southern point of the evocation sigil. There was almost no magic in this place from which to draw power, but she had conducted this particular summoning so many times over the past couple of years, she was confident in her results.

The fugitive witch missed her cozy California house, and the abundant magical energies that had flowed around it, but that evil cunt, Alyssandra, had deprived her of her home when she set it ablaze in the early hours of the morning only a few weeks ago. Chang'e had been hiding, terrified of being discovered and hunted down ever since.

Her flight from Alyssandra's attempts to kill her had landed her here, in this decaying cesspit someone had the nerve to call an apartment building. Maybe Chang'e would set fire to this place herself when she finally left. It would serve the owner right for the ridiculous rent he charged on six hundred square feet of mold-covered walls, rotting floorboards, and rust-colored water.

When the circle was complete, Chang'e set the chalk aside and dusted her hands on the folds of her skirt where they covered her thighs. Still on her knees, she placed the pad of her index finger between her teeth and bit down, drawing a small amount of blood. A bead of bright red welled up where she had broken the skin.

With external magic being so scarce, this summoning needed the amplification of a small blood sacrifice to activate the spell. Chang'e gazed at the oozing injury on her finger and internally cursed Alyssandra's name one more time.

Touching the drop of ichor to the last symbol she had drawn on the floor, Chang'e muttered a short incantation in her soft, child-like voice. Even to her own ears, she sounded like a six-year-old reciting nursery rhymes. She did not mind. She believed the affectation made her more mysterious and alluring to others.

Next, she called out to the demon advisor whose assistance she had sought so often in the past.

"Bala-Ahl, by our bond, I demand you appear."

There was a sudden pop of displaced air, and a tiny figure appeared at the center of the chalk circle. The creature was humanoid, in that it had two arms, stood on two legs, and had a round protrusion at the top that appeared to be some version of a head, but that was where the similarities ended. The demon's skin was red, with coarse brown hair covering most of the body. The head had no eyes or face to speak of, although it did have a mouth, if you could call it a mouth. Perhaps, more accurately, Chang'e would have described it as a tooth-filled, gaping crescent that parted the little monster's sorry excuse for a head almost in half.

"By our bond, I am here," the demon announced. Despite its size and appearance, the voice coming from the monstrosity was deep and melodious. "What would you ask of me this time?"

"I'm tired of hiding," Chang'e told the demon. "You promised this would only be for a short time."

"I did," the creature agreed.

"How much longer?"

The demon paused, considering the question. "Your enemies know you are still alive, so there is no need or purpose to pretending otherwise. The coven you so carefully gathered to you is beginning to fragment without your leadership. They will soon be seeking other locations, other covens."

"I'm aware of that. That's why I want to go back."

"Then go back," the demon suggested reasonably.

"Is it safe?" asked Chang'e.

The demon laughed; a loud basso rumbling that should not have been possible coming from such a tiny body. "It will never be safe for you again. There is only struggle ahead of you now."

Chang'e banged her fists on her legs in frustration. "That's not what I meant." She blew out a harsh breath. "What do you suggest then?"

"I suggest you go back. The time for running away is over. Confront your enemies. Make them see the truth."

"I didn't kill those witches," Chang'e insisted.

"I know that," the demon assured her.

"But they don't."

"No. They do not."

"How do I make them understand that I am also a victim in this?"

"You have me. I have been with you this entire time, and I know what you have done, as well as what you have not done. I can give support to your claim of innocence."

Chang'e paused, hope bubbling in her chest for the first time in weeks.

"Would anyone believe you? You're a demon. Demons are not considered terribly trustworthy."

"I suppose that there is only one way to find out."

"Go back home," Chang'e said.

"Go back home," Bala-Ahl agreed.

CHAPTER
4

As they had reluctantly decided, Violet and Mitch cut short their trip and returned to Sacramento the following day. Although it was normally a work night for Mitch, he was not on the briefing schedule for today due to the vacation he thought he was going to be enjoying with her on the beach. He had decided to remain at home for at least one more day rather than go in to work. Tomorrow, he would decide if he wanted to burn another day off or save the vacation hours for later by putting on his uniform one day earlier than originally planned.

That was his problem to figure out, however. Violet, on the other hand, did not have the luxury of simply hanging around the house and goofing off. She was on the clock the moment she arrived back in the city. Mitch dropped her off at home and, after she said goodbye and sent him on his way, she immediately picked up her phone to update Alyssandra on her chance encounter in Carmel. When that was done, she called to book a hotel room for Safia, then texted the confirmation information to the New York witch along with a time and location to meet for dinner later that evening.

Mitch was not on the guest list for this get-together. Despite his suggestions on the car ride home that he be there when Safia met with Alyssandra, Violet had insisted that this was coven business, and it was best that Mitch be nowhere around when the two coven leaders had their face to face. If Violet had her way, she would not be part of the meeting either, but unfortunately that option was not on the table. Both Alyssandra and Safia had been quite clear with their requests that she attend the evening gathering. With no recourse, Violet unpacked, showered and changed, then puttered around her house until it was time to head out for her unwanted dinner date.

At the appointed time, she drove into downtown Sacramento and found the restaurant she had selected as their meeting place. The diner was a chain restaurant with poor service and mediocre food, but the meal itself was not really the point of the location. It was neutral ground, in public, and they would be able to get a table at the last minute on a Wednesday evening without a reservation.

Violet pulled into a small parking lot behind the restaurant, exited her car and walked to the front entrance. Outside, on the sidewalk, she was exuberantly greeted by Safia, who had arrived several minutes earlier and posted herself at the front doors, scanning the surrounding area in anticipation of the arrival of her former coven mates. Alyssandra was still nowhere to be seen, and Violet suggested they go inside and grab a table while they waited.

As expected, there was no line inside, and a bored-looking server grabbed three laminated menus from a pile and escorted them immediately to a booth. The girl assisting them appeared far too young for the world-weary gaze in her eyes, and Violet watched her with curious compassion as she produced a cloth from her back pocket and did a perfunctory swipe over the surface of the table. The lacquered tabletop did not appear any cleaner from the attention, but the greasy smears illuminated by the far-too-bright overhead lighting were now travelling in a different direction than before. This appeared to satisfy the girl as she tucked the rag back into her pocket.

Violet thanked their server and slid into the booth. Safia followed suit on the opposite side.

"Do you want any drinks, or do you want to wait for the rest of your party to get here?" asked the girl, laying the stack of menus onto the table between Violet and Safia.

"I would love a glass of water," said Safia.

"Water is fine for me, too," Violet told her.

The girl wandered away without a word of acknowledgement to the request, leaving Violet wondering if she would be seeing her again any time soon.

"Alyssandra is coming tonight?" asked Safia, seemingly oblivious to the behavior of their zombie-like waitress.

"She said she was. I don't have any reason to believe she won't show up. I wouldn't be surprised if she shows up late, though. She doesn't like waiting for other people."

"She likes to make them wait for her," said Safia, finishing the unspoken part of Violet's thought.

Violet shrugged noncommittally.

"That's okay," Safia told her, pulling a menu in front of her and flipping it open. "She's always been like that, so I don't expect anything different just because I flew three thousand miles to see her."

"I thought you came to California for vacation," said Violet. "Wasn't running into you a coincidence?"

Safia flashed a small neutral smile. "Of course. I was only making a point. After flying for six hours, another four hours driving here, what's five more minutes? Let Alyssandra make her grand entrance."

"How is everyone in New York?" asked Violet, genuinely interested in hearing about her former covenmates.

"The coven is mostly the same old faces, with a few exceptions. Donna and Bernice quit a few years ago. They both got married, have kids, and decided to try to live like normies for a while. Alithia moved to Florida, and I already told you that Gail passed away. We picked up a new girl. Her name is Malta. She's extremely eager, though not very powerful. She's only been with us a few months, and we could use a few more people since we're currently down to ten."

"Not a very good number," Violet agreed.

"No, it isn't. It has been surprisingly difficult recruiting lately. Did you know that there are five covens operating in the city?"

"Five?" asked Violet, surprised. "There were only three when Alyssandra and I left. Why are there so many?"

"One of the old covens split during a war between the priestess and her number one, and a new coven moved in from outside. They came from Connecticut, or someplace like that. I'm not really sure. There is a lot of magic in New York, so it's incredibly attractive to all kinds of users."

"We have three here in Sacramento. One doesn't have any real power, but even so, there is always some friction between us. I can't imagine dealing with five."

"It's a big city," Safia said, dismissing the statement with a flap of her hand. "Yes, there is always conflict, but it really isn't any different than before."

The conversation paused as their waitress, against all odds, returned holding two glasses of water. She set the glasses down, noticed there was still one person missing from the gathering, and walked away without saying a word.

Safia rolled her eyes and chuckled. "Thank you for the water," she said to the empty air where the server had been.

Violet shook her head in mock disbelief, but she was also smiling. "That's why we come here," she explained. "The staff does their job, but pretty much leaves us alone otherwise. It lets us talk with some privacy without having to act all cloak and dagger out in public."

Violet caught a flash of movement out of the corner of her eye, and Safia's gaze travelled over her right shoulder. She turned in time to see Alyssandra appear beside their table.

Safia slid out of her bench and stood, spreading her arms in preparation for a hug. Alyssandra did not seem so inclined. Violet's coven leader stabbed a bony finger between Safia's breasts, giving the New York witch a push and forcing her to take a step back.

Violet caught a flash of anger in Safia's eyes, but to her credit, the east coast priestess reined in her emotions quickly and forced a smile back onto her face.

"You never were a hugger, Alyssandra," she said. "Still, I had hoped after all these years we might have a more sentimental greeting than a poke in the chest."

"How would you feel about my foot in your ass, Safia?" said Alyssandra, though her voice was low and calm.

Safia simply settled herself back into the booth. "It's nice to see that some things never change."

Alyssandra sat down next to Violet, across the table from Safia. She rested her hands in her lap and peered curiously at her old coven mate. "Why are you here?" she asked without preamble.

"As I told Violet, I was enjoying a visit to California, and I thought it might be nice to sit down with you two and reminisce about old times."

"You being here is purely coincidence?"

"Of course."

"And I suppose when maggots crawl out of a dead animal, that's coincidence as well? Cut the shit, Safia. What do you want?"

Violet sat quietly, not interrupting Alyssandra. She was not surprised by the coven leader's bluntness. Honestly, she had not expected anything different. Alyssandra always chose to attack directly, especially when her opponent appeared to be playing games. Violet watched and waited to see how Safia would respond.

The New York priestess laughed. It was an open and honest burst of amusement and joy, and it left Violet momentarily confused. Alyssandra must have felt the same, because her brows pulled tight together and her face twisted in displeasure.

"God, I forgot how much fun you are, Alyssandra," Safia said when the laughter subsided. "You are a bull in a china shop, my dear, and I do love to watch you crash through everyone else's attempts to be delicate. I thought I could spend a few days dancing around with you and working up to what I wanted, but I really should have known better. You were a blunt instrument when you left, and you have only gotten bigger and heavier since you moved to California."

Alyssandra seemed unmoved by the backhanded compliment. She growled, "Spit it out, or go back to New York."

Safia glanced toward Violet and winked. "You are right, of course. I didn't simply bump into you by accident. I came to California to find you two. My coven is dwindling. My best witches are gone, and I need to build us back up. I thought, what better way to recruit than bring back someone that was already with us. So, I came out here to convince the strongest witch I've ever known to come back and join me again."

Alyssandra scoffed. "I have no interest in returning to New York. I have my own coven, so why would I want to leave only to be subordinate to someone else?"

Safia burst out with another round of laughter. When she could control herself again, she said, "Oh, girl, the ego on you. Sorry, Alyssandra, but I wasn't talking about you. I was talking about Violet. I want her to leave Sacramento and come back to New York with me."

Alyssandra pressed her hands flat to the top of the table and leaned in toward Safia. Her eyes flashed and she bared her teeth. "Violet isn't going anywhere. And you are no longer welcome here, so I suggest you get on the next plane back to New York and be very grateful that I allowed you to leave in one piece."

"No, dear," said Safia, unimpressed with Alyssandra's display of menace. "Do you remember when Violet first came to us after that dreadful ordeal with her family?"

Violet froze. Her mind churned through deeply buried memories of sitting at the dining table, surrounded by blood and the writhing bodies of her family; of watching everyone that she loved die at the hands of three homicidal witches. Her breath caught in her throat, and for a moment she could not make herself draw air.

"I remember it clearly," Safia continued. "You brought this poor, traumatized little girl into our circle and asked us to take her in. She was hurt, broken, and oh so very angry. And who could blame her for that anger? Someone had murdered the only people that had ever cared about her."

"Safia." Alyssandra's voice was rough with suppressed rage. "Stop while you still can."

"I was thinking about this recently." Safia spoke as if discussing a picnic she had enjoyed years ago. "I was thinking about the witches that killed her family, and I was thinking about why they did that. Do you know? Why would they kill her parents, her brothers, and her lover, and then kidnap her? Did they think they could control her after doing something like that? Did they think she would simply join them and not try to retaliate at some point? Where was the logic in such an attack?"

"Safia," Alyssandra hissed.

"They didn't want me to join their coven," said Violet softly, the images of death and loss still flashing behind her eyes. "They wanted to bind me and use my power. They didn't care about me any more than they might care about a tool they stole out of someone's garage. A hammer doesn't have to like you, it only needs to strike where you aim it."

Safia nodded, acknowledging Violet's words while seeming to remain oblivious to the pain behind them. "That may be true, but it is an extremely shortsighted method. I don't think they would have been able to control you for very long. You would have turned on them eventually. If the witches that murdered your family were alive today, and you knew where they were, what would you do?"

"I would kill them," said Violet, her voice barely more than a whisper.

"Then it is a very good thing that Alyssandra already did that, so you no longer need to."

"Safia, you need to go," said Alyssandra.

"No, I don't think so. Just like the witches that killed Violet's parents, you cannot control her. Violet is free to come and go as she pleases. She's a grownup, and whether she stays here in Sacramento or comes with me to New York is completely up to her."

Violet stammered, “Safia, I-I don’t think…,”

Safia held up a hand, halting the statement. “Don’t answer now. I am going to be staying in Sacramento for a while. I plan to enjoy my free hotel room that has been graciously provided to me for the next week. We can meet and talk as many times as you would like during that time, and then, when I’m ready to return home, you can give me your answer.”

Their server chose this moment to reappear at the table. The girl, with the same bored expression she had displayed from the beginning, held a pad and pen in her hands, preparing to take their orders. Before Alyssandra or Violet could respond, Safia held up her menu to catch the waitress’ attention.

“I’m sorry, dear. I still don’t know what I want. I think we are going to need a few more minutes.”

CHAPTER 5

"Simon? Sorry to bother you."

Chief Jefferson glanced up from the supplies document on his computer screen to see his administrative assistant standing in the doorway of his office. Her feet were still outside the threshold, and she leaned forward until only her head and shoulders poked through into the room, almost as though she were afraid she might be trapped inside if she committed fully to entering.

"You're never a bother, Dot. You know that." Simon started to wave her into the office but paused when he saw the expression on her face. "What happened?"

"You have a phone call I think you should take," she told him.

"And...?"

"It's Chang'e. She says that it's urgent that she speaks with you."

Simon nodded his agreement to take the call, and Dot added, "Line two. Do you want me to listen in?"

Simon nodded again, and Dot retreated to her desk to monitor the call. When she had disappeared, Simon counted to five before picking up his desk line.

"This is Chief Jefferson. How may I help you."

"Chief Jefferson. Thank you for taking my call. Do you know who this is?"

Although he had been uncertain as to the legitimacy of this call before, as soon as he heard her speak he knew who he was talking with. The odd lilt to her statements, as though she was permanently distracted and could only devote half of her attention to any conversation, in addition to the high childlike pitch of her voice told him he was definitely on the phone with the demonic coven leader.

"Hello, Chang'e. Yes, I know who this is."

"Good, because I want you to hear this directly from me. I did not kill any of the witches that were assassinated last month. I certainly did not kill Zinea. That poor girl. She was one of my own, and I would never harm my own people."

"Of course not," agreed Simon. "You did not kill them directly. You used a spell or perhaps ordered someone else to carry it out."

"You aren't listening," she retorted angrily. "I understand that I can't convince you on the phone. I…, I need to speak to you in person."

Simon's eyebrows rose as he considered the request. "I suppose I could do that," he said after a moment. "Why don't you come down to the police department and turn yourself in. We can talk all you like, and I will carefully consider anything you have to tell me."

"No. No. If I come to you, you'll lock me up. You already think I'm guilty. I need to talk to you, and I need you to hear me when I do. I can prove I did not kill those witches."

"If you didn't do it, then who did?"

There was a long pause on the other side of the line. Simon could hear Chang'e's breathing. She was almost panting with frustration.

"I don't know," she finally admitted. "Maybe Alyssandra. She is certainly skilled enough to have done it."

"She is. But why would she? I don't think she had any motive to go after Mitch Loman, or either of the other two."

"Because she's always hated me, that's why. What better way to get rid of me than frame me for the murder of three people?"

"Nope. Sorry. That's banana oil and you know it, Chang'e. You and I both know Alyssandra is not that subtle. If she wanted to be rid of you, she would…, well, she would do exactly what she did. She would burn down your house with you in it."

Simon heard Chang'e moan softly into her phone. "I don't know who did it. I only know that I didn't. I must see you in person. I can show you proof."

"What proof?"

"I have … a, uh, witness of sorts. I'll explain everything when we meet. I'll come to the cemetery tomorrow morning. You can find me at the gates to the old North-West section at ten thirty. Chief Jefferson, please come alone. I will only talk to you. If you bring anyone else with you, I'll know, and I'll be gone before you find me."

"Chang'e, you can't believe for a second that I would show up alone…." Simon stopped talking. Chang'e had already hung up.

Simon placed the handset of his desk phone in its cradle. He leaned back in his chair and his office door immediately swung open. Dot let herself in and sat down in one of the padded leather visitors' chairs in front of his desk.

"You're not going, right?" she asked, knowing full well that he was.

"I know I shouldn't," he told her, avoiding the question.

"Darn it, Simon," Dot said, as close to swearing as she ever got.

He nodded. "Yeah. I know. Darn it, Simon."

Mitch went back to work Thursday night. There was too much happening with the coven for Violet to be free during the day, so he figured if he went to the cemetery, he would at least be able to see her that evening for training.

While in Carmel, she had insisted he needed to work on his techniques for dispelling magic. He had called her earlier in the day and reminded her of that conversation. After only a few minutes of pleading, he convinced her to meet him after shift briefing for some practice.

"Are you joining us for movies tonight?" asked Sergeant Smythe after beat assignments had been completed.

"Maybe the second one, Jorge. I'm meeting Violet as soon as I finish my first perimeter check."

"Then you're free to go," the sergeant told him. "Briefing is over. Everybody go to work and try not to get eaten."

"Why do you even bother to show up?" asked Tink, rising from the briefing table to begin his evening rounds. "Even when you're here, you aren't really here."

"Tink," barked Jorge. "Mitch is busting his ass, and you're pissed he's going to miss a movie? Your priorities are pretty messed up right now."

"No, he's right," said Mitch. "I've been chasing coven issues lately and haven't been a great shift partner. I'm sorry, Tink."

Tink sighed. "Nope. I'm sorry. That was a shitty thing to say, even if I did mean every word."

"Tink," the sergeant warned.

"I can't believe I'm saying this, but I think I'm a little jealous of all the stuff you're doing. You're out catching some really bad dudes, and I'm back here, walking the cemetery with only this stupid fucker to talk to." Tink jabbed a finger toward Brad Kodama. The other officer responded to the dig with a "who me?" gesture, and a comically hurt expression on his face.

"Things will calm down soon," Mitch said.

"Nope. I hope they don't," Tink told him. "It looks like you're having a lot of fun."

Tink clapped him on the shoulder hard enough that Mitch had to take a small step to keep from falling over. "Tell Violet I said, hello."

Brad and Tink exited the room, heading out to begin their patrols. Mitch started to follow, but Jorge called him back.

"Hey, Mitch," said the sergeant when the others were gone and safely out of earshot. "You might feel like you're letting the shift down by not being here, or by getting distracted by Violet and her coven, but I want you to know that you are doing exactly what you are supposed to be doing. You're training and getting stronger just like Simon asked you to do."

"I'm trying," he agreed.

"We all bring different things to the table," Jorge continued. "You, me, Tink, and Brad. That's what this job is really all about, helping people who can't help themselves by using the skills and resources that we have at our disposal. What you're training to do is something that none of us can help you with. So, instead of apologizing for what you aren't doing around here, I want you to become as good as you can possibly get at the things you *are* doing."

Jorge jerked a thumb toward the door the others had exited through. "Tink might be a little butthurt that his friend isn't around as much lately, but he'll get over it. Don't let that distract you from what Simon hired you for, and from what I expect out of you. You are exactly where you are supposed to be, and you're doing exactly what you're supposed to be doing."

"Thanks, Jorge," Mitch said.

"Go on. I have to go upstairs and set up the first movie. Tink and Brad have already started their rounds. Get yours done, then tell Violet I said hi, too."

Mitch left the police building and hurried through his early evening perimeter check. As on most nights, he found no signs of trespassers or issues with graffiti or vandalism along the outside fencing. Dasan's Terrace was not near town or any major residential neighborhoods, so there were very few people close enough to cause serious mischief on the cemetery grounds, even if they wanted to.

He completed his rounds in a couple of hours, then made his way toward the area of the cemetery known to the officers as Back Half. The sun had already set, but a bit of twilight glow still lingered on the horizon when he met up with Violet. He found her waiting for him near the eastern wall of Dasan's Terrace's older grounds.

Tonight, Violet had skipped the black wig and black dress she often wore during their training sessions. Mitch wondered if she had been too busy today to change, or if things with the coven had simply grown too tense for her to care about minor details like her usual love of witchy role-play. Regardless of her reasoning, he elected not to mention it.

Besides, he liked the way she looked in jeans and a tucked in t-shirt, so why would he ever want to complain?

"Hey," he said, giving her a quick hug and a peck on the lips.

"Hey, yourself," Violet responded. "You ready to work?"

"Sure. How did your meeting with Alyssandra and uh, what's-her-name go? Shasha?"

"We aren't talking about that right now," Violet told him flatly.

Mitch felt slightly taken aback by Violet's refusal to answer.

"That bad? Is there something…?"

Violet took one step back, giving herself some distance from Mitch. He saw a flash of yellow light appear suddenly in her hand and all hopes of further conversation fled his mind. She launched a spell toward him and Mitch was forced to dodge to his left to avoid being struck. The sphere of light impacted the ground several feet away and erupted with a muffled *whoomp*, launching dirt and debris into the air around a newly formed crater in the cemetery lawn. The attack had not been lethal, but from the displacement of earth behind him, he figured if it had landed, he would have been nursing several new bruises in the morning.

The time for talking was clearly over. Violet was in no mood to discuss coven business, and Mitch now had more important things on his mind. Things like keeping his head firmly attached to his body.

Mitch threw up a shield, using the magic barrier to deflect the next three attacks from Violet. When she was certain continued frontal attacks would be pointless, Violet changed her strategy. She tossed a bright green ball of magic into the air above both of them. The spell rose a dozen feet above the ground, then exploded like a firework during a Fourth of July celebration. The sparks that rained down from the detonation all unerringly cascaded directly toward Mitch.

He tried stepping back several paces, but the drifting motes followed, forcing him to create a new shield. The protective spell he shaped this time draped like the bell of an umbrella, protecting Mitch's head and torso down to his waist. When the first of the green sparks touched his shield, they flickered out, but not before eating a small hole in his defensive magic and leaving a gap in his protection. Mitch was forced to continually reinforce his barrier, suffusing it with additional magic as Violet's spell battered away at it.

While he focused on the attack from above, Violet sent a new spell at him, flinging it towards his exposed legs like a professional pitcher trying to kneecap a batter standing too close to home plate. Mitch skipped away, deftly avoiding the second attack while keeping energy flowing into the shield protecting his head from aerial bombardment.

An enemy was not limited to one attack at a time, and it was important not to get so fixated on one offensive strike that he did not see another one coming. Violet was an excellent teacher, and Mitch had already learned that lesson the hard way.

Violet smiled and rewarded Mitch with a quiet golf clap. "Very nice. Your situational awareness is definitely improving. Let's take this up another notch, shall we?"

She held her hands out to her sides, drawing magic to her and creating a red haze of power that swirled around both of her outstretched arms. Mitch groaned and braced himself.

For the next fifteen minutes, Mitch was pummeled, hammered, beaten, swatted, thumped, battered, and pounded by every manner of spell Violet could think of to throw at him. He avoided and deflected most of it.

Most of it.

After missing one of a series of ten attacks that seemed to come at him from all directions at once, Mitch pushed himself up from the ground, spitting dirt out of his mouth. He held both hands in front of himself forming a "T" shape, and announced, "Time out. I need a breather."

"In a real fight…," Violet began.

"Yeah, yeah. In a real fight, I couldn't call a time out. I know. But I'm also pretty sure that in a real fight with you, I would already be dead. I can tell you're still pulling your punches."

Violet relented. "You are getting much better. And while you're right that I'm not using my full strength, I don't think you are either. You know that I won't really try to hurt you, so your defenses are perfunctory, without any power behind them. I want you to start fighting me like your life depends on it. When I see that your shields are up to it, I will put more effort in as well."

"Okay. Five more minutes, then we go again?"

"No," said Violet. "We can work on shields another day. I think it's time we did a little training on what we talked about in Carmel."

"You mean disrupting magic?"

"Exactly. I think this is a skill you need. It could save your life when you don't have enough strength to hold a shield. I'm sorry I haven't already worked with you on this, but you have so much to learn, and it all takes time. I'm trying to show you everything I have practiced and trained with over the past ten years, and I can't cram all of that into a twenty-minute lecture."

"I know. I'm trying to pick this all up as fast as I can, but I know it's going to take years to get anywhere near as proficient as you are. If you promise to be patient with me, I'll try to be patient with myself, too."

The corner of Violet's mouth quirked up. "Promise," she said.

"Okay, so next lesson is how to disrupt a spell. How do I do that?"

Violet pulled magic from the surrounding energies in the cemetery and shaped it into a ball of white light. She held it out on her right palm as if offering it to Mitch.

"First point, if you're going to break up a spell, you have to do it before the spell is fully formed. Once it's been cast, all you can do is try to get out of the way."

"What am I supposed to do?" Mitch asked.

"Break it apart. Basically, knock it out of my hand so I can't use it against you."

Mitch mentally reached out toward the magic in Violet's hand, trying to pull it toward himself just as he did when he was gathering ambient power from the air around him. The ball twitched in her palm but quickly steadied itself again.

"No, don't pull on it. We aren't playing tug-of-war. Once the magic is in my hands, I have the advantage. The only way you can forcibly take it from me is if you are significantly stronger than me, and in this situation, that simply isn't the case."

"So, what am I supposed to do? How do I stop you from using the magic you already gathered?"

"By breaking it apart," Violet explained. "You have to guide a little bit of your own magic into the power I'm already holding, then use that to break up whatever spell I'm shaping."

Mitch tried again, this time directing a trickle of ambient magic into the ball Violet held in her hand. When the energy infused Violet's spell, he released it, allowing it to dissipate. As Mitch's gathered magic fell apart, Violet's remained completely intact.

"Closer," she told him, encouragingly. "But don't just release your magic. Once it touches mine, detonate it. Blow it apart. You have to completely disrupt my spell, otherwise I'll still be able to use it against you."

In demonstration, Violet tossed the sphere of magic directly at Mitch. He sidestepped the spell, and it flickered and fell apart as it flew past him. The magic had not been an actual threat. Violet was merely making her point.

"Gather up a small amount of magic," Violet said.

Mitch did as he was told and collected enough of the surrounding magic to fill the palm of his hand.

"Now, cast a spell. I don't care which spell. Anything you want."

While Mitch decided which spell he wanted to use, a flicker of new magic invaded the unformed power he held. A tiny burst of energy flared, and the magic broke apart, dissipating even as he struggled to hold it together.

"Did you see what I did that time?" Violet asked him.

Mitch thought about what he had witnessed and considered how he might be able to duplicate the effect. "I did. I'm not completely sure what I saw, but I did see … something."

"Good."

Violet pulled more power into her hands.

"Try again," she directed him. "Stop me from attacking you."

One of the first spells Mitch had ever learned was how to release magic in an explosive detonation. Brute force was the simplest way to manipulate magic, and therefore, was also the easiest trick to teach new witches. He had used the technique, albeit with questionable results, against an earth golem that had tried to kill him a few months ago.

Violet stood patiently, waiting for Mitch to decide how he was going to shape his next attempt at breaking apart her spell.

Mitch guided another trickle of magic into the sphere already collected in Violet's hand. When it entered, Mitch reached out with his senses through the trail of magic, trying to manipulate that invasive trickle into a percussive force that he could detonate at will. He felt the tracery of power he wielded spread through Violet's unformed spell. Suddenly, Mitch was not simply in control of his own magic, he could feel the power Violet had gathered responding to his will as well.

He commanded the magic to contract and condense.

"Bang," Mitch whispered, vocalizing his mental efforts.

The ball of white light in Violet's hand shrank, turning an angry dark-red color. Surprised by the unexpected change, Violet released her hold on the magic and dove to the ground, throwing up a blue blanket of protective power over herself. The ball she had released exploded in a shower of light and percussive force that could have blown her arm off had she not already gotten out of the way.

Mitch shouted out a whoop of excited delight.

"Like that?" he asked, pointing a finger at the afterglow of his explosion in unrestrained triumph.

Violet did not immediately respond. She lay on the ground with a stunned expression twisting her features, mouth open and eyes wide. Mitch's celebration gave way to concern, and he rushed over to Violet, kneeling beside her and laying a hand on her shoulder.

"Are you alright?" he asked, checking her for injuries. "I thought you were ready for that."

"I…. How…? What the hell did you do?" she asked. She stared at Mitch in puzzled wonder.

"I blew up your spell like you told me to," he said, uncertainty coloring his voice. "Did I do something wrong?"

"You blew up my spell," Violet told him. "You actually blew up my spell."

"You told me to," Mitch repeated. He was beginning to feel a bit defensive. "You told me to blow it apart."

"No, you don't understand. You didn't just break up the magic I was holding. You stole it from me, changed it, and blew the whole thing up."

"I wasn't supposed to?"

"Mitch. You shouldn't be able to do that. I don't know anyone who can do that. You shouldn't be able to change magic that I was already using. Breaking up spells is one thing. I have even known one really powerful witch that could pull magic out of my grasp to use it for herself, but even she couldn't change my spell while I was still holding onto it."

Mitch stayed quiet, unsure what to say or how to react to Violet's statement.

"What did you do?" Violet asked him.

"I thought I did exactly what you told me to. I put a little bit of my magic into yours, then detonated it."

"That should have only been enough to disperse my spell. You did more than that. How did you get control of it?"

"I…, I don't know," he said. Then he thought more carefully about what he had done, going over the sensations he had experienced in that moment. "I felt my magic filter through yours. After a moment, I felt my spell not just in the little bit of magic I had control of, but I felt it all through the magic you were holding as well. Is that normal?"

Violet shook her head. "It's incredible, but no, it sure as hell isn't normal." She smiled at him, a glow of pride shining in her eyes. "Every time you use your magic, you surprise me. You are really something special. I don't think we have even begun to understand what you are capable of."

Violet extended a hand, indicating that Mitch should help her to her feet. Upright once again, she brushed the dirt from her jeans and gave Mitch a gentle push to get some space between them. She created another ball of white light and held it up.

"Do you remember your ice spell?" she asked Mitch.

"Sure. I haven't used it much, but it's basically the same as a fire spell, and I'm pretty good with that one."

"Okay, let's try this again, but instead of blowing up my spell, I want you to try to use the magic in my hand to make ice. Do exactly what you did before, but with cold instead of kinetic force."

Mitch concentrated on the magic in Violet's hand. He tried mentally directing the power to dispel all ambient heat and freeze the moisture in the air. Nothing happened.

"It's not working," he said.

"I feel you fighting me for control of the spell," Violet told him. "You didn't do that before. Try to remember exactly what you did last time and do it again."

Mitch thought for a second, then realized his mistake. He was trying to use Violet's magic as if he already had control of it. That would not work. Instead, Mitch needed to infuse his own magic into hers before he could manipulate her spell.

As he had before, Mitch directed a tiny flow of power into Violet's own. He allowed the tendril to dissolve and suffuse throughout the white light until he could feel all of it in his mind. Through his extended senses, he could tell Violet was using the spell to create a small amount of extra heat, actively trying to combat what Mitch was attempting to do. It did not matter. As his awareness moved through the spell, he felt the magic begin to react to his presence. He repeated the cold spell he had previously attempted.

Ice crystals formed in Violet's hand. Shards of frozen water lanced outward from the spell she held, forcing her to drop the growing ice formation before it could pierce her skin or freeze her flesh.

"Well, fuck me bowlegged," Violet muttered, but there was a happy grin spreading across her face. "You really did it."

"Is that good?" Mitch asked with an excited smile of his own.

"This is amazing," Violet assured him. "And it's probably another thing we shouldn't be telling Alyssandra about. She would not like finding out you can do this kind of magic. She only trusts witches she is strong enough to control, and I don't know if you fall into that category anymore. I'm going to suggest we add this to the 'just between you and me' file."

Mitch nodded his agreement.

"I want to see how far this goes," Violet said. "Can you manipulate an already existing spell?"

"I have no idea. I didn't know I could do what I already did," Mitch replied.

"Let's find out then, shall we?"

Violet held out hand and pulled power toward herself. Instead of simply gathering unformed energy, this time she converted the magic into a small fireball hovering in the air a few inches above her palm.

"Can you take control of this?" she asked Mitch. "Try and convert my spell to ice like you did before."

Dutifully, Mitch guided a small thread of magic into the flame. He let the magic flow throughout the fire, trying to blend with it, but despite his best efforts, his own magic remained distinct from the already burning spell.

"It doesn't feel the same," he said.

"Try anyway," Violet directed.

Mitch mentally shaped the magic under his control, willing it to become ice. "Cold," he whispered, letting the word focus his thoughts on what he wanted the spell to do. Ice crystals formed within the flame, but rather than convert the fire, they battled with it. The combination of heat and cold hissed above Violet's hand, releasing small bursts of steam as the two elements struggled for dominance.

Neither ice nor fire could gain full control over the other, though they warred on until at last both spells guttered out and broke apart.

"I couldn't do it," Mitch said. "I couldn't get your spell to change."

"So, you do have limits," Violet said, though she did not seem at all disappointed. "You can't alter an already active spell. I didn't think you could, but then I didn't think you could convert magic I was holding either, so it was worth checking. It was still impressive, though."

"Was it?" asked Mitch.

Violet peered at him as if he might be joking. When she saw the sincerity in his expression, she said, "You might not have changed my magic, but you still managed to activate your own spell right in the middle of mine with enough strength to neutralize it. I don't know very many witches that have enough talent to even attempt that kind of trick."

"I did good, then." Mitch told her.

"You did very good," Violet agreed.

"Do I deserve some kind of reward?"

Violet slipped her arms over Mitch's shoulders and wrapped them around his neck, pulling him close. "I think a small reward has definitely been earned," she told him.

Violet went up on her tiptoes and Mitch bent forward to meet her. As their lips touched, a voice from the shadows startled them.

"I am so sorry to interrupt this special moment."

Mitch and Violet leapt apart, spinning toward the sound with hands raised and ready, magic swirling around them as they prepared to face any potential threat.

The New York coven leader appeared between two large trees; the pleased expression on her face visible as she stepped away from the shelter of the surrounding darkness and into the moonlight. Safia waved a hand at them as if beckoning them to continue.

"Go back to what you were doing. I can wait until you're done. Or should I leave you lovebirds alone and come back later?"

CHAPTER 6

"Safia," Violet blurted. "What are you doing here?"

"It's such a beautiful night, I thought I would get out and explore the area. The cemetery is quite old, isn't it? There is so much magic everywhere, I was simply drawn here. I understand why you and Alyssandra like this place so much."

"You went out to explore?" asked Violet with obvious skepticism.

"Mm-hmm," Safia agreed.

"We put you in a hotel in Elk Grove, and I'm supposed to believe you happened to stumble onto Dasan's Terrace twenty miles away? No way. Not possible. I think you're following me."

Safia gave a noncommittal little shrug. "I won't say I'm not happy to have found you here. I was hoping to talk to you again, preferably without Alyssandra around. Do you know, I don't think she likes me much. I'm not sure why, though."

"I doubt that's true, too," said Violet.

"That she doesn't like me?"

"No. That you don't know why she doesn't like you. You two have always been barely civil to each other, even when we were all in the same coven."

Safia waved her hand dismissively. "Nonsense. Sisters bicker, that's all. Nothing more than that. But what about, um... was it Mitch? Yes. What about Mitch?"

"What about him?" asked Violet, her shoulders stiffening with unconscious tension.

"When you introduced him to me the other day, you apparently left some things out. You told me he was a new member of your coven, but you didn't say he was a police officer, or that the two of you were ... friendly." Safia winked conspiratorially at Mitch.

"It was none of your business," Violet told her. "It still isn't."

Safia sighed as if her feelings had been hurt by the comment. "Such distrust. Look, I really don't mind if you two are a couple. In fact, I think it's wonderful. When you decide to come back to New York and join my coven, bring Mitch with you. I think he would make a wonderful addition. Warlocks are so rare and hard to find. We would be the envy of every coven in the area."

"I'm not going anywhere, and neither is Mitch," Violet said flatly.

I understand. You don't want to disappoint Alyssandra. She has been so good to you all these years."

"She has been," agreed Violet.

"I think you need to leave," Mitch interrupted. "The cemetery is private property, and you are currently trespassing."

"It was so good of her to take you in the way she did, after your parents were killed. She really has been like a replacement mother to you."

"You need to go," repeated Mitch, but Violet placed a hand on his shoulder, quieting him.

"Stop dancing around it, Safia. Say what you need to say."

"The witches that killed your family, they knew Alyssandra, right?"

"What do you mean?"

"I mean, they addressed her by name when she entered the house. I remember you told me that a long time ago. The witches called her by her first name."

"That doesn't mean anything," Violet told the coven priestess. "I know the names and faces of almost everyone in all three covens that operate in Sacramento. It's no surprise the New York coven members knew each other."

"No, I suppose it's not. Which means Alyssandra probably knew which coven they belonged to."

"She did," admitted Violet, finally seeing where this conversation was going.

"And did she ever tell you where the three women came from? Did she tell you which coven murdered your family?"

"She did not. When I asked her, she said she didn't want to risk me going after them before I was strong enough to protect myself. Alyssandra didn't want me to get killed trying to get revenge."

Safia nodded. "I suppose that makes sense. But what about now? You seem able to take care of yourself pretty well these days. Do you think Alyssandra would tell you which coven the witches belonged to?"

"I don't know," Violet said. "Maybe. I haven't asked about that in a long time."

"You should ask again. See what she says."

Violet hesitated, then said, "Do you know which coven they came from?"

"I do. But if Alyssandra still has reasons not to tell you, then I am going to respect her decision and let you two hash it out on your own."

"You and Alyssandra are in agreement." Violet barked a harsh laugh. "That's not something I heard very much back in New York."

Safia nodded agreeably at the jab. "No. It really doesn't happen often. Alyssandra and I don't see eye to eye on many things." Safia paused, looked thoughtful for a moment, then said, "I wonder why she didn't go in the house right away."

"What house?" asked Violet.

"Your parents' house. I wonder why she stayed outside after the other witches went inside. She knew they were after you, but she still waited before following them into the house."

"Stop it, Safia. I know what you're trying to do."

Safia blinked several times, appearing perplexed by Violet's accusation. "You do? What am I trying to do?"

"You're trying to put doubts in my mind about Alyssandra. You want me to move to New York, so you want to give me reasons not to trust her and to leave Sacramento."

Mitch stood to the side, quietly observing the back and forth between Safia and Violet. As he listened, a stray thought kept tickling at the back of his mind. Twice, Safia had stumbled across him and Violet, seemingly at random. Once in Carmel, and once here in the cemetery. Each location was improbable enough to make either meeting extremely unlikely.

But both? The odds were astronomical.

Violet had already realized Safia was following them. She was not stupid and had come to that conclusion long before Mitch had. There was more to it, though. Mitch was certain of that. Safia clearly wanted to talk to Violet, not him, so why didn't she simply follow and wait for a time that Violet was alone?

Answer: because Safia wasn't following Violet. She was waiting for Violet to turn up. Which meant…

"You aren't tracking Violet," Mitch said, interrupting the two women's heated conversation.

"What?" asked Violet, looking irritated at Mitch's intrusion into the argument.

"She isn't following you," Mitch repeated. He turned to face Safia. "You're following me, aren't you? Somehow, you are tracking my movements. You wanted to talk to Violet tonight, but you don't have any way of knowing where she is, so you came looking for me, hoping that she would show up."

"How could I possibly know that Violet would come to see you tonight? Or any night, for that matter?"

Mitch's eyes narrowed. Now that he had said it aloud, he knew he was right. Safia had been tracking him somehow. "You also knew that Violet and I have been dating. You weren't at all surprised to see us kissing. I don't know how or why, but you aren't in California because you suddenly decided you wanted Violet back. Someone sent you here."

There was a glint of anger in Safia's eyes. She covered it quickly, but not before both Mitch and Violet saw it.

"Why are you here Safia?" Violet asked.

Safia opened her mouth, but Violet quickly interrupted.

"Careful what you say. If you lie to me, I'm going to know it, and any hope you might have had of getting me to go to New York is gone. I will never follow you if I can't trust you."

Safia closed her mouth and flashed another glare at Mitch. Then she smiled. It was the grin of a grifter who had been caught cheating on a bet. She had tried to hide a critical card in her sleeve, but Mitch had seen it before she could completely tuck it away.

She held her hands up in surrender.

"Very well. No lies." Safia looked back at Violet. "I do want you to come back to New York, but…," she pointed a finger toward Mitch, "I want you to come as well."

"What do you know about Mitch?" Violet asked.

"A friend of yours, Violet, came to see me recently. She told me Alyssandra had attempted to kill her and had run her out of Sacramento. She wanted to go back home, but she could not do that unless she succeeded in weakening Alyssandra's coven enough to challenge her."

"Chang'e," Violet said. "Chang'e went to New York."

Safia nodded. "Yes, she did. She thought if I could convince you and Mitch to join me, it would leave Alyssandra vulnerable. Chang'e also told me that you and Mitch were in a relationship, and that if I found him, I would most likely also find you."

"How did you track me?" asked Mitch. He thought he might already know the answer to this question, but he waited for Safia's confirmation.

"Chang'e brought me a few stray hairs and some coins she said belonged to you. She took them from your car.

Mitch fumed internally. His car had been broken into several weeks ago, right before an unknown witch had attempted to kill him with a spelled knife. It appeared Chang'e had not only been responsible for the break in, but she had also helped herself to enough personal items to fuel several spells. Thank God Safia had only used her items to find him, rather than power any new assassination attempts.

"Is Chang'e still in New York?" asked Violet.

"She was still there when I left. I think she planned to stay until you left California. She never shared her plans with me, however, so I can't be certain."

"And that's everything? You aren't holding anything back?"

"Sweetheart, I never give anyone everything for free. But as far as why I'm here, I've told you the truth. Chang'e wanted me to break up you and Alyssandra, which I still think is a good idea if you would consider it."

"It's time for you to go," said Violet. "Go home, and don't come back."

"No," Safia demurred. "I think I'll stick around a little while longer and see what happens. You might change your mind yet."

"I can't force you to leave California," said Mitch, "but if you don't leave Dasan's Terrace right now, I'm going to arrest you for trespassing."

"Would you really do something like that? That seems awfully mean."

In response, Mitch unsnapped the case on his duty belt that held his handcuffs.

"Fine," said Safia in a huff. "I'm going. It isn't as if I can't tell when I'm not welcome."

The New York coven leader turned on her heel without another word and marched away, disappearing into the surrounding shadows of the cemetery. Mitch and Violet watched her go.

When they could no longer see her or hear the sounds of her footsteps through the grass, they turned to one another.

"Chang'e is coming for us," Violet said softly.

"Yeah. Shit."

"Shit, indeed," agreed Violet. "I need to talk to Alyssandra."

He nodded his understanding. "And I should go warn Jorge. Hey, Violet?"

"Yes?" she asked, one eyebrow rising in curiosity.

"We should have stayed in Carmel."

CHAPTER 7

Chang'e stood beside the wrought iron gates that separated the cemetery's publicly accessible areas from the federally protected, early tribal and pre-colonial burial grounds known to the denizens of Dead Town as North-West. Old growth oak and coniferous trees filled the North-West, along with scrub and weeds that blanketed the ancient gravesites and a few remaining, crumbling markers that had survived the centuries of erosion and neglect.

On Chang'e's side of the fence, there were also trees and many older gravestones that had seen their fair share of weathering and damage, but the grounds were better tended and most of the wild growth was kept under control. She had selected this as her meeting place with Chief Jefferson because this section of the cemetery did not have the tangling branches and treacherous footing of North-West but was still far enough from the main entrance that the likelihood of outside visitors wandering by and interrupting their private discussion was extremely low.

A summoning circle lay spread out before her, scratched into the earth at Chang'e's feet. Using a broken tree branch, she had carved deep into the dirt and patchy brown grass the symbols she used to bring Bala-Ahl into this world. The demon knew she had not been responsible for the death of two young witches and the unsuccessful attack on Mitchell Loman, and she hoped it might testify on her behalf to Dead Town's chief of police.

Demons were tricky, however, and had minds of their own, so this gambit had always been a risk. She simply had no idea how big a risk it would be.

Chang'e asked Chief Jefferson to meet her in this back corner of Dead Town at ten thirty in the morning. It was now twenty-nine minutes after ten o'clock. The chief had not actually agreed to meet with her, and it was certainly possible he would not show up today. It was also a possibility he would come with several of his police officers in a futile attempt to capture and arrest her. Many things might happen in the next few minutes, but she calmly waited to see how events might unfold.

Extending her awareness through the ambient magic of the cemetery, Chang'e searched for any activity that would indicate the arrival of other people, but the nascent powers around her remained undisturbed. Perhaps the police chief was not coming after all.

Then, something tickled her senses. Someone was close and approaching her location. At the same time that her magical awareness warned her of the new arrival, Chang'e saw a figure appear in the cemetery trudging in her direction. The distant shape grew larger, growing more distinct as it drew closer, and soon she recognized the stocky form of Chief Jefferson in his favorite tailored gray suit.

She thought it odd she had not sensed him sooner as she searched the magical eddies flowing through the cemetery. It was as if he had somehow disguised his approach until he was close enough to be seen. That seemed unlikely, however. The man was an extremely interesting character, but he was not a witch, and he had no magic of his own. Perhaps she had simply not been as diligent as she thought in her search.

To be certain there would be no more surprises, Chang'e focused and did another mental scan of the cemetery's magical landscape. She reached out further this time, pushing to the limits of her ability. Other than the approaching man she had already identified, she did not find any other people in the immediate vicinity.

As hoped, Chief Jefferson had come alone.

She watched him approach, noting the unhurried stride and his relaxed posture. In silence, she waited. Neither of the two figures acknowledged each other, although it was obvious the chief was aware of her. His eyes never left her face as he approached.

When he was less than a hundred paces away, he halted.

The chief stayed far enough away from her that he most likely felt safe from attack, but he was still close enough she could see the features of his face clearly. Despite the early hour, the July morning was already warm, and the exertion of walking almost two miles from the police department building to Chang'e's location had left a sheen of sweat on Chief Jefferson's brow.

"I'm here," he stated simply. "As you asked, I'm alone."

Chang'e nodded but said nothing.

Chief Jefferson waited a moment, but when it did not appear he was going to get any more of a response than the polite nod, he shifted impatiently. He swayed, moving his weight from one foot to the other, then back, as he mentally debated what to do next.

"You brought me out here," he said, finally. "You claim to have proof that you didn't kill those two girls or attack Officer Loman. I'm not in the mood for any games, so either show me your proof or I'm placing you under arrest and bringing you back to the police department with me."

Chang'e took one step forward, moving into the summoning circle in front of her. She placed her foot carefully onto the small rift she had created half an hour earlier, a slight tear that opened a pathway between this world and the world of the demonic. She felt the warmth of demon fire filling her body as it flowed from that other distant dimension.

Chief Jefferson desired proof? Well, here was all the proof he could ever want.

Chang'e extended one hand toward the chief. Fire erupted around him on all sides, insanely hot, glowing white as the magic of the demon realm fueled it to temperatures that earth magic could never match. The flame swirled, engulfing him in a vortex of manic destruction. Chief Jefferson was taken completely by surprise by the assault. He did not even have time to cry out before the fire fully consumed his flesh.

Chang'e felt the heat against her face. She blinked, and a single tear escaped her right eye and ran down her cheek.

The demonic fire dissipated as quickly as it had appeared, and in its wake there was only charred dirt, cracked stone, and a blackened skeleton curled up on itself on the scorched ground. Smoke rose from the burnt remains of Simon Jefferson, tainting the air with a sweet yet acidic odor that caused Chang'e's nose to wrinkle in disgust.

She stepped out of the circle, breaking her direct connection to the demon world. She no longer needed that link. The job was finished.

"I really thought he would put up more of a fight," she whispered regretfully.

Simon watched from behind a large oak tree. The pyrotechnics that consumed his body were indeed impressive, and his eyes widened in appreciation of the feat. He continued to mask his presence from Chang'e as she cast fire at his projected image. He observed the intense heat of those flames, and he was thankful he had taken precautions for his meeting with this crazy witch.

He had almost decided not to come today, but Sergeant Smythe called him late last night to update him on what Mitch had discovered about Chang'e and her meddling in a New York coven of witches. She was up to something, and whatever it was still involved Dasan's Terrace. He had decided the only way to find out what Chang'e truly wanted was to meet her as she had requested.

So, he had come, but he had not wandered into her grasp completely blind. As things turned out, that had been a wise decision.

The fire died away, and Simon altered the illusion of himself, replacing it with the image of a burned skeleton crumpled on the ground. He watched to see what Chang'e would do next. Would she laugh maniacally? Or would she go into evil villain mode and explain her ingenious plans to the smoldering corpse of her enemy?

To his disappointment, she did neither.

"I really thought he would put up more of a fight," he heard her say.

Okay. What did she mean by that?

Chang'e did not say anything further. Whatever else she was thinking she kept to herself. When it seemed she was about to leave, Simon decided it was his turn to act.

The smoking skull shifted on the ground, turning charred eye sockets to gaze at Chang'e. The surprised witch froze but did not flee as the crumbling, blackened mouth of the skeleton cracked open.

"Why?" asked the corpse. "Why kill me?"

Chang'e took a single step backward. She seemed uncertain how to react to this unexpected development.

"Why kill me?" the skeleton asked again.

"How are you doing this?" Chang'e said. "You should be dead."

In response to Chang'e's question, the immolated corpse climbed to its feet. Ash and chunks of burned flesh and clothing flaked away from the bones, fluttering lightly to the ground.

"Answer me first," said the skeleton. "Why do you want me dead?"

"You're in the way," said Chang'e. "You, and Alyssandra, and everyone here."

Despite her shock at Simon's miraculous resurrection, Chang'e's voice still had that distracted sing-song tone that unnerved Simon so much. The witch sounded like a child reciting nursery rhymes while playing in a sandbox. Was the affectation deliberate, he wondered, or was this woman truly mentally deranged?

"In the way of what?" Simon asked, forcing his attention back to what was important.

"Th-the magic," Chang'e sputtered.

Eyes appeared in the dead sockets of the skull, white orbs with smokey gray irises. The eyes rolled around without direction for a moment, then locked onto Chang'e.

“Magic? You mean Dasan’s Terrace?”

Chang’e’s face twisted with fear and revulsion at the appearance of the gray eyes in the skeleton’s head. “How can you…?”

The skeleton brushed at its body as though flicking lint from a shirt. Wherever it touched, ash flew away, revealing pink muscle and yellow blobs of fat underneath. Skin quickly followed, growing over the exposed flesh, dark and healthy as if it had never been damaged.

From his hidden location, the real Simon smiled devilishly at the scene he was creating. He should not be enjoying this as much as he was, he told himself, but the look on Chang’e’s face was too priceless not to relish.

The skeleton continued cleaning itself until a fully healed, but still quite naked, Chief Jefferson stood in the charred circle of ground.

“So, you are responsible for the murders?” asked Simon.

Chang’e waved her hand and a new rush of fire engulfed Simon’s image. It washed over the nude figure before guttering out. This time, he did not change his illusion after the flame extinguished itself. Chief Jefferson’s body remained unaffected by the demonic heat. The naked figure raised a hand and snapped his fingers. Once again, he was covered by a neatly tailored, unblemished gray suit.

“What do you plan to do with Dasan’s Terrace if you succeed in eliminating everyone else? Others will replace us. Other witches. Other police officers. It isn’t like brushing the pieces off a chessboard and keeping it all to yourself.”

Chang’e cast another spell, and this time the ground around Simon’s illusion erupted, spewing dirt and rock into the air. The phantom Simon ignored the disruption, moving to one side and back onto more stable earth. Chang'e growled with frustration.

Simon's apparition remained completely unharmed, but the cemetery grounds were taking a beating from Chang'e's attacks. Simon decided he needed to end this confrontation before she blew up something important or managed to set the entire cemetery on fire.

Keeping himself invisible to Chang'e's eyes and magical sight, Simon left the cover of the trees and moved toward her. He was carrying a gun, but he did not want to kill her. Chang'e clearly wished to kill him, but Simon had difficulty with the idea of shooting someone in the back, regardless of how dangerous they might be. It felt wrong to him. Besides, he had other options.

In his back pocket, he carried handcuffs that had been spelled by Alyssandra and Violet to repel ambient magic. Once the cuffs were secured to Chang'e's wrists, they would stop the witch from further manipulating any more power, preventing her from casting new spells.

Simon used his illusion to keep her occupied as he approached.

"Why don't you surrender and let me place you under arrest? You can't win here," the mirage continued.

Simon crept behind Chang'e while her attention remained on the projected image in front of her. If he could get close enough to grab her before she realized where the real threat was, he could pin her down and handcuff her. With her magic nullified, taking her back to the police department where she could be held and questioned properly would be a simple matter.

The plan worked better than he had hoped, and after a cautious, silent approach, he stood right beside the unaware woman. He grabbed her arms from behind and twisted to force her to the ground and onto her stomach. The woman was tall, about five feet seven inches, but she could not weigh more than a hundred and twenty pounds. She was rail thin, and it should have been a simple matter to wrestle her off her feet.

Instead of the easy tackle he had expected, Simon felt as if he had grabbed a fencepost, sunk into the earth and held fast with cement. Chang'e did not budge from where she stood.

Realizing she was facing an attack from an unknown source, Chang'e spun, lashing out with one arm to strike at her invisible opponent. The impact knocked the air from Simon's lungs and launched him through the air. He landed in a tumble of arms and legs, rolling like a rag doll for several feet after hitting the ground. Before he could stop his out-of-control tumble, pain flared through his head and he almost blacked out when his forehead, just above his left eye, made contact with a gravestone set flat in the grass.

The blow to his brow left Simon stunned. The illusion that kept him hidden, as well as the magic that animated his false image, fell apart when his mental control over them lapsed.

Simon saw stars. He felt dizzy and slightly nauseated, but he knew he did not have time to lie on the ground and shake the cobwebs from his brain. Chang'e could see him clearly now, and it would take only moments for her to figure out the truth of the situation.

"Ah, I see," she said, followed by laughter that suddenly sounded too deep and full to be coming from such a slender body. "Clever. It almost worked, too."

Another attack was coming. Simon could not actually survive anything like the spells she had thrown at his illusions. If her next assault landed, he would be a smoking, crisped corpse for real this time.

Simon pushed to his feet and bolted to the right, cloaking himself in a new illusion of invisibility. At the same time, he formed an image of himself darting away to his left. Chang'e hurled a ball of demon flame at the fleeing mirage, but an instant before it made contact, the false Simon dove downward, disappearing into the soil like an Olympic swimmer leaving the starting blocks at the sound of the starter's gun.

Chang'e hesitated, trying to decide if Simon had some bizarre ability to move through the earth or if this was another illusion similar to the smoking skeleton. Using her momentary distraction to his advantage, Simon picked up a fist-sized rock. Suddenly, there were six Simons standing around Chang'e in a circle, all holding rocks in their hands. They threw in unison.

Chang'e raised a shield of yellow light toward the figures in front of her. Simon's actual rock struck her in the lower back, undeflected by her attempt to protect herself. Chang'e should have been injured by the impact, but the witch hardly flinched. Simon had not held back when he hurled the heavy projectile, and the slender woman did not appear to be wearing any kind of body armor or other protection. Still, she barely reacted to the attack.

With no time to ponder Chang'e's odd display of unnatural durability, Simon was already moving before the witch could turn and orient on her real enemy.

She's insanely strong, Simon thought as he ran. He could not simply grab her and cuff her as he had originally hoped. He realized he might need to shoot her after all. Chang'e needed to be stopped, and he could imagine no other way to do it on his own and under these conditions. He really had not prepared properly for this confrontation.

Dot was going to be furious with him if he allowed himself to die after she had so adamantly insisted he not come here this morning.

Reluctantly, Simon drew his service pistol from the holster inside his coat. He sent three images of himself fleeing behind nearby trees. As Chang'e sent explosive spells after each one in turn, Simon positioned himself behind her, pointing the gun toward the exposed back of her head. He needed to end this in one shot. If he missed, or failed to drop her instantly, she would put up barriers that would prevent a second attempt. In that situation, a prolonged struggle between them would invariably result in Simon's demise.

Simon took a slow breath, steadying his hand as he took careful aim.

Before he could squeeze the trigger, Chang'e suddenly dropped to one knee. Simon relaxed his index finger barely in time to prevent firing a shot that would have gone harmlessly over her head.

Chang'e touched a hand to the ground and began twisting her fingers like she was attempting to claw a small hole in the patchy grass.

What is she doing, Simon wondered, but it did not really matter. He still needed to end this confrontation. He lowered the gun to point where she was kneeling and carefully aimed a second time.

Chang'e pulled her fingers from the ground and slashed her arm upward. A streak of light appeared where her right hand travelled, causing a ripple that warped the air around her. Something appeared. Something that did not belong in Dasan's Terrace. The image hovered in front of Chang'e as if a curtain had been pulled open and a hidden stage was suddenly revealed.

The gap widened and Simon realized he was looking at a portal to somewhere else. He stared into the opening, trying to guess where it led, and during his brief hesitation, Chang'e lurched forward into the breach, disappearing through it.

As soon as her body passed into the gap, it closed behind her, leaving Simon alone in the suddenly silent cemetery.

He holstered his pistol, grunting in frustration. He had missed his chance to stop this threat. Briefly, Simon wondered if Chang'e had sensed what he was about to do and fled, or if she had merely decided fighting illusions was a waste of her time. Either way, she was gone, and it did not seem likely she was coming back.

Simon knew this was only a temporary reprieve. He had been lucky enough to survive, but also unlucky enough to let Chang'e get away.

Eventually, she would return to the cemetery. Simon had no doubts about that. What happened when she did, however, was anybody's guess.

CHAPTER 8

Chang'e sat on the unmade bed in her seedy motel room, tears of frustration and confusion welling in her eyes as she tried to process what had happened in the past hour. The tan comforter loosely draped over the bed was tattered and stained from years of previous tenants and their questionable hygiene practices, but for the price, this squalid refuge was the best she could manage. Chang'e was afraid to use her credit cards or touch her bank accounts lest someone figure out how to find her, so for the moment, the limited cash she had in her possession was the extent of her financial means.

Besides, after her meeting with Chief Jefferson, the cleanliness of her room was the last thing on her mind.

Why did he attack me like that? she asked herself.

Chang'e had truly believed the police chief would give her the benefit of the doubt and allow her to at least tell her side of the events of the past few weeks. But he had not hesitated to attack the moment he saw her waiting for him in the cemetery. It wasn't fair. Was everyone here already against her? Should she have stayed in New York?

She picked up the cell phone resting on the bed beside her. She would try one more time to get someone to listen. If it did not work this time, she would….

She would what? Chang'e had no idea what she might do next.

Her home was nothing more than ashes on a concrete foundation. The members of her coven had fled the city or gone into hiding when Alyssandra attacked her. She had money, but she was afraid to leave any kind of paper trail that would lead her enemies to her.

What could she do?

She sighed, scrolled through her meager list of contacts, and selected the number labeled, "That Evil Bitch." She tapped the green call symbol and held the phone to her ear. Her call was answered after only two rings.

"You should be dead," growled the woman on the other side.

"It is very nice to hear your voice as well, Alyssandra. How have you been?"

"Why don't you come over and visit me? You can see for yourself how I am, and then I can finish what I started when I burned down your house."

"Why did you try to kill me?" Chang'e asked, trying not to rise to Alyssandra's baiting.

"This cannot possibly be why you're calling me," Alyssandra spat in reply. "I have wanted to kill you for a long time, but your attempt at assassinating one of my coven members was the final straw."

Calling Mitchell Loman a member of her coven was a stretch. The man had offered no loyalty to Alyssandra despite her willingness to teach him magic. Still, the warlock's coven status was not relevant to the conversation, and Chang'e elected to let the claim slide.

"I did not try to kill him," Chang'e said. "I didn't kill the other two witches, either. I'm being framed by someone. You must realize that, right? Look, I have proof this wasn't me. If we can meet somewhere, I can show you."

Laughter rang across the line, so loud and piercing that Chang'e had to hold the phone away from her ear for a moment. When the cackle finally died away, Alyssandra said, "You really expect me to believe that? I'm not as stupid as you seem to think I am."

"I tried to talk to Chief Jefferson, but he wouldn't listen. Please, just give me a chance to explain."

"Oh, yes. The police chief. I know all about your conversation with the Lost Child. He called me a few moments ago to warn me about you. He said you contacted him and wanted to talk. When he agreed to meet you, you attacked him and tried to kill him."

"I … what? He said that? He's the one who attacked me!" Chang'e shouted, at last losing her composure.

This was too much. After all she had gone through, now the chief of Dasan's Terrace was claiming she had tried to kill him. It had been completely the opposite. She had barely escaped from that madman with her life.

"Alyssandra. He's lying. I only wanted to talk to him, and he…,"

"The Lost Child is many things," Alyssandra interrupted. "One thing he is not, is a liar. When we meet again, Chang'e, it will not be to talk."

The line went dead as Alyssandra hung up.

"No. Wait," said Chang'e weakly, but it was already too late.

Chang'e dropped her cellphone on the stained comforter and let herself slip from the bed onto the floor. She knelt in front of a summoning circle she had shaped with sand on the balding gray carpet. In the center of the circle stood the hairy, red demon, Bala-Ahl. Though the small monstrosity had no eyes, it was clearly watching Chang'e closely.

"She would not talk with you?" the creature asked.

"No one believes me," Chang'e said, her voice sounding even more childlike than usual as she began to sob.

"No. It seems no one does. I suppose then that there is no longer any need for this ruse to continue."

Chang'e sniffled and wiped at her eyes. After a moment, the demon's words registered in her mind. "Ruse?" she asked. "What ruse?"

In answer, Bala-Ahl stepped outside of the summoning circle. Chang'e's eyes widened, and she flinched backward.

"You can't do that," she commanded. "I have not given you permission to leave the circle."

The demon chuckled, baring far too many sharp teeth in its wide mouth.

"You poor deluded witch," it said. "You have granted me access to yourself far too long and far too many times over the years. You surrendered any real control over me some time ago. Keeping you in the dark has been helpful so long as no one else was aware of what was happening. Now that your actions are obvious to everyone, I do not have to pretend anymore."

"Pretend? Pretend what?"

Bala-Ahl faded from sight, letting the small amount of corporeal flesh it possessed dissipate and leaving only its spiritual essence behind. The demon entered Chang'e's body. She felt its strength and power suffuse through her physical form like a powerful drug flowing in her bloodstream, before its consciousness settled into her head. She fought back, trying to mentally push it away, but the demon's will engulfed her own. It invaded her mind, taking control of her thoughts as easily as her limbs.

A block Chang'e had not known was there suddenly lifted, like a dusty shroud pulled aside to reveal the moldering corpse beneath. Suppressed memories came flooding back to her; memories of things she had done under the control of the demon's manipulations, memories that had later been hidden from her when Bala-Ahl was done using her.

In horror, she realized that she was guilty of everything the others had accused her of doing. She had raised ghouls in the cemetery. She had attacked Chief Jefferson unprovoked this morning. And the most unforgiveable sin of all, she had murdered people; two innocent girls in Sacramento, and one perhaps not so innocent woman in New York.

Chang'e screamed, but the release was solely an internal one. No noise escaped her mouth. Bala-Ahl had assumed full control of her body and mind, and Chang'e had become little more than a passive observer of her own actions. With the mental block removed, she remembered the many times that Bala-Ahl had manipulated her similarly in the past. They had all been terrifying experiences. She had been helpless to fight the demon's desires, left adrift in her own thoughts until the creature had surrendered her body back to her.

This time, however, it was much worse.

This time, Chang'e knew that Bala-Ahl had no intention of ever letting go of her again.

Mitch arrived at work a couple hours early. He wanted to catch Dot before she left to go home and ask her how the chief was doing. Violet had called Mitch to tell him that Chief Jefferson had been attacked by Chang'e that morning, but she did not have any additional information as to his wellbeing.

Mitch considered calling Jorge, but it was likely his sergeant was still sleeping and had heard nothing about the incident yet. With no other way to find out what had happened, Mitch decided to meet with Dot and get any relevant information about the fight directly from her. If anyone knew the details of that morning's confrontation, it would be Dot.

When he arrived at the police department, he found the chief's secretary at her desk. She sat back in her chair with a perplexed look on her face, scrolling through something on her cellphone. When she saw Mitch enter the administrative lobby, she set her phone down and greeted him with a friendly smile.

"Well, hello, Mitchell. I didn't expect to see you today. What can I do for you?"

"Is Chief Jefferson okay?" he asked without preamble.

Dot pursed her lips, caught a little off guard by the question. "He's fine," she said. "Why?"

Mitch exhaled a relieved breath. It seemed he had been worried about nothing.

"I heard Chang'e attacked him this morning and I wanted to be sure he wasn't badly hurt."

"Oh, yes. They did have quite the disagreement in the cemetery earlier. I'm surprised you heard about that already." Dot paused, then added, "I guess Violet called you after Simon called Alyssandra. That makes sense. The information grapevine moves quickly around here."

"Can you tell me what happened? Why was Chang'e in the cemetery?"

"I can try to answer any questions you have, Mitchell, but why don't you ask Simon? Get it straight from the old horse's mouth, so to speak. He's in his office."

Mitch startled and glanced toward the chief's closed office door.

"He's here?"

"Of course he's here. Where else should he be?"

"I just thought he might be home resting, or else getting treated at the…,"

"At the hospital?" Dot suggested when Mitch refused to finish the sentence.

"Yeah," he agreed.

"When he came back from meeting with Chang'e, he was pretty banged up, and I made him go straight to the hospital to get looked at. He went, but the moment the doctors said he was okay to leave, he came back here. You know Simon. He's stubborn. He's a lot like a certain detective we have working for us."

Mitch's mouth quirked, unable to completely suppress his amused reaction. "Can I talk to him, then? Is he busy?"

In response, Dot picked up the handset of her desk phone and pressed a series of numbers. After a moment of waiting, she said, "Hi, Simon. Mitchell Loman is here and would like to speak with you. Are you available?"

She paused another moment, and Mitch heard a few unintelligible words coming simultaneously from both the phone and the chief's office.

"'Kay," Dot said brightly, then hung up.

She smiled again at Mitch and told him, "Go on. He's waiting for you."

"Thanks, Dot."

Mitch shuffled around her desk and let himself through the door marked, "Chief of Police, Simon Jefferson."

Inside the office, the chief was waiting and waved Mitch toward one of the guest chairs. He closed the door behind himself and sat down.

"I'm glad you're okay," he said as he settled into his seat. "When Violet called and told me Chang'e had attacked you, I was worried it was going to be a lot worse."

"I'm fine," Chief Jefferson assured him. "I'm not as easy to take down as some people might think."

"Do you know why she went after you?" Mitch asked. "I knew she would be coming back to Sacramento eventually to deal with Alyssandra, but I didn't think she had any bad blood with you."

"I didn't think so, either," Simon agreed. "Chang'e is volatile and dangerous at the best of times, but I didn't expect she would come after me like that. That was poor judgement on my part."

"So, what happened?"

Simon rocked back in his chair, clasped his hands together and laid them across his stomach. "I don't exactly know. She wanted to meet with me in the cemetery, and I agreed to go. When I got there, she didn't say a word. She immediately started hurling fire at me."

Mitch's mouth dropped open. "She just attacked? Why?"

"I don't know. When I asked her about it, she was still pretty busy trying to kill me. She said something about me being in her way."

"In the way of what?"

Simon shrugged. "The magic," he told Mitch, using his fingers to make air quotes around the words.

"You're in the way of the magic," Mitch repeated. "What does that even mean?"

Simon shrugged again. This time, he gave a small wince along with the motion and touched his ribs gingerly.

Mitch saw the reaction and realized that the chief was not as unscathed as he appeared. He looked closer at Simon, examining his face and hands. They were completely unmarked. Dot had mentioned that the chief was hurt after the fight, and she had ordered him to get checked out at the hospital, yet here he was now, looking absolutely untouched except for some possible pain in his ribs.

Thinking about appearances, Mitch remembered something he had seen that he very much wanted to talk to the chief about. Assuming his boss was willing to discuss the matter with someone as far down on the food chain as a lowly part-time detective.

"Um, Chief. I have a question I've wanted to ask you for some time. It's kind of personal, and I'm hoping you won't fire me if I bring it up now."

Simon shifted forward in his chair and placed his hands on his desk. His eyes narrowed and his jaw flexed a few times.

"That is an interesting way to phrase a request. Do you really think I might fire you?"

Mitch glossed over the question. "I asked Violet once, but she got weirdly quiet and refused to answer. She said I needed to take this up directly with you."

"You have my attention, Mitch. I won't promise to answer this question of yours, but I'm willing to let you ask it without getting angry. Go ahead."

"When we met in the graveyard to hunt ghouls, I saw you talking to Violet and Alyssandra. I was too far away for you to notice me yet, but I was paying attention because I was watching Violet."

"I don't hear a question yet," Simon said, but his voice remained calm.

"I saw you change," Mitch said. "One minute, you looked like you normally do, standing there in the grass in your gray suit, then the next I thought I saw a kid talking to Alyssandra. By kid, I mean I saw a teenaged boy, thinner than you are but wearing the same gray suit. The suit didn't really seem to fit him very well either."

Mitch looked at Simon for an explanation, but the chief simply raised his eyebrows in anticipation.

"Right," Mitch breathed. "Question. Well, my question is, what was I seeing? Why did you change into a child right in front of my eyes."

The chief took a breath, organizing his thoughts before speaking. "Mitch, I'm one hundred percent, completely human, but I do have a few … um, abilities. One of these abilities is that I can create some small illusions around myself. These illusions are part of the reason I was able to escape from Chang'e this morning. At the time you saw me, I was practicing an illusion that made me look like a child. I was showing Alyssandra, and I did not realize you saw it as well."

"Stop," said Mitch, holding up a hand. "I understand if you don't want to tell me, but please don't lie to me."

"Lie?" asked Simon.

"When I saw you change, Dot, Alyssandra, and Violet were all looking at you, and none of them reacted to what I saw. They didn't see it. Also, that wasn't the first time I saw that boy. I saw him the first time when you came to visit me in the hospital." Mitch paused, building his courage, then rushed through what he had wanted to say from the beginning. "I think the boy is really you, and what I'm looking at now is the illusion."

Mitch hunched his shoulders forward, bracing for an explosion from the chief. Despite Simon's assurance, there was no way to know how he might react to the accusation. Mitch prepared himself for denial, recriminations, even an order to get the hell out of Simon's office. He did not expect what he actually got.

Laughter.

Simon laughed, slapped a hand on his desk, then pointed at Mitch as if acknowledging he had been the target of an exceptionally well laid out prank.

"You got me," said Simon. "No more lies. You're right."

The chief stood up, and suddenly Mitch was looking at a boy of about sixteen years of age. He still wore the gray suit, but it hung awkwardly on his slender frame. Above Simon's left eye, three butterfly bandages held closed a nasty cut he must have received while struggling with Chang'e. The boy's left cheek was also bruised and swollen.

One thing had not changed, Mitch noted. The boy stared back at him with the same pale gray eyes of Chief Jefferson.

Before Mitch could speak, the boy was gone and the chief was back, all two hundred pounds of the stocky adult he had come to recognize as Simon Jefferson. The chief sat back in his chair and held out his hands, palms up, as if to say, "Now what?"

"I'm not going crazy," Mitch said simply.

"You're not going crazy."

"Can you tell me how this happened?" Mitch asked.

Simon shook his head. "No. Some secrets are better left secrets."

Mitch sat quietly, debating if he should say what he wanted to say next. Then, realizing that he would regret not trying, he met Simon's gaze and spoke.

"When Lieutenant Delaney finally left Dasan's Terrace, he thanked me for finding the person responsible for killing him, and he told me that he owed me a debt."

Simon's eyebrows rose again. "And…?"

"And he told me that because he would not be around to repay that debt, that you would be the one to make good on it."

"And you are calling in that debt now," Simon suggested. "I owe you an explanation. Is that it?"

"No," Mitch said hurriedly. "Not at all. I'm saying that if you are willing to tell me who you are, how you got to be like this, then I would consider that information as full payment of the debt."

Simon did not speak for a long time. Mitch knew he had pushed as far as he possibly could and that to do any more would be to really risk making an enemy of the chief. So, he sat quietly and waited to hear what Simon might say.

"Okay, Mitch," Simon said at last. "I cannot settle the debt today. I will tell you a few things, however, on the condition that you never say a word to anyone else without my permission."

Mitch winced. "What about Violet?" he said. "I don't want to keep secrets from her."

"What I'm going to tell you, Violet already knows or suspects. Violet is fine."

"Then I promise. Not a word to anyone else."

"Good enough. The boy you saw is how I really look. Everything else that people see is a carefully shaped illusion. Although I look like a teenager, I am not a child. I have been around for a long time."

"How old are you?" Mitch risked asking.

Simon shook his head, but the gesture was not a refusal to answer the question. "I don't know. A hundred years? A thousand? I really don't know. What I will tell you, and then we are done with this conversation, is that I was born on December fourteenth, eighteen hundred and ninety-seven."

"Lost Child," Mitch whispered. Then louder, "Alyssandra knows, doesn't she? That's why she calls you 'Lost Child.'"

"That is part of it," Simon acknowledged. "But no more questions. I said we're done with this conversation, and I meant it."

"Thank you, Simon," said Mitch. "Seriously, thank you for trusting me with that."

"You had already seen through the illusion," the chief told him. "I couldn't very well have my best detective thinking he was losing his mind."

"I'm your only detective," Mitch said.

Simon only smiled and nodded.

"Now that we're done with that conversation, let's get back to the favor you owe me," said Mitch, clapping his hands and rubbing them together eagerly like a child preparing to tear open a carefully wrapped Christmas gift.

The smile faded from the chief's face, and he glowered at Mitch. "Where is this going?" he asked.

"How about authorizing some new patches for our uniforms?"

"I…? Patches?" asked Simon, completely floored by the change in direction the meeting had taken.

"Yes, patches. We have our own badges, but all of the officers here still wear Sacramento Sheriff's Office patches. I think Dead Town needs to have its own uniform patch. Is that something we can make happen?"

CHAPTER 9

Safia startled awake to the sound of a fist pounding on the door of her hotel room. She rolled onto her side in bed and touched the screen of her cellphone. The display immediately lit up to advise her that it was ten thirty in the morning. Not an outrageous hour normally, but much too early for someone who routinely went to sleep about the same time the sun came up each day.

"What the hell?" she groaned, groggily.

Instead of getting up, Safia buried her face back in her pillow and tried to ignore the interruption. A new spate of banging finally forced her out her comfy nest of sheets and blankets. She searched the floor until she found a pair of sweatpants, then pulled them on under the nightshirt she was already wearing.

"This had better be important," she growled.

Safia stormed to the door as a third round of knocking began. She snapped the locks off and jerked the door open.

"What?" she barked, then recognized the slender figure wearing all black standing in the hallway.

"Alyssandra," Safia drawled, eyes lidded and dangerous. "I'm sure whatever you want to talk to me about can wait."

She attempted to close the door, but Alyssandra slapped a palm against the painted wood and held it open.

"I'm here, so let's talk now," she said, pushing the door with a bony shoulder and forcing her way into the room.

The door bumped Safia backwards, and she grunted as she staggered into the wall behind her. Regaining her balance, she turned to glare at Alyssandra who now stood in the small hotel room kitchenette with her arms folded across her chest.

"Come on in," Safia grumbled. "Make yourself at home."

"You need to leave," said Alyssandra, ignoring further niceties. "Go back to New York. Go back today and never come here again."

"My reservation lasts a few more days, and I hate to give up a free room."

Alyssandra ground her teeth in frustration.

"What is it going to take to get you to see you aren't welcome here?"

Safia chuckled, although she was feeling anything but amused. She did not, however, want Alyssandra to see her ruffled. She needed to keep calm and control this conversation.

"I am very aware that I am not welcome here, but unfortunately for you, here is where I am going to remain. For a few more days, at least. I have business to attend to, and I am not free to leave until it has been fulfilled."

"I know what your business is. You want to drive a wedge between Violet and me. You want to take her back to New York with you."

Safia tilted her head and widened her eyes in mock surprise. She did not attempt to deny the accusation. What would be the point? Alyssandra was absolutely correct. She was here to take Violet back to New York, and she had been directed to accomplish that goal by any means necessary.

"The only way that Violet would ever turn on me is...," Alyssandra paused.

"If she found out what you did," Safia finished the sentence.

Alyssandra cleared her throat. "Yes. But you can't do that."

"Can't I?" asked Safia.

"No. You swore an oath to me and to Gail that you would never say a word to Violet."

"Gail is dead," said Safia sharply. "I run the coven now, and I do as I please."

Alyssandra took a menacing step towards her. Safia wanted to move away, but she knew she could not show any fear now or Alyssandra would gain the advantage. She stubbornly held her ground, not allowing her rebellious feet to shuffle backwards.

"I am still very much alive," Alyssandra said, her voice growing deeper with emotion. "Break your oath to me and I will make sure that every witch in your coven knows you cannot be trusted to keep your word."

Witches lied and broke their promises every day, Safia knew, but not to their own coven mates. When she had sworn her silence to Alyssandra they had both been sisters under Gail's leadership. Breaking a vow to one of your own was not something that was tolerated in the magical community, and if word spread that Safia had broken an oath to one of her coven members, she could lose her standing as coven priestess, maybe even be cast out of the coven altogether.

"I haven't told her anything," Safia said. "I haven't broken my oath. However, it is not my problem if Violet comes to a few conclusions on her own."

Alyssandra's shoulders drooped. Some of the anger leaked out of her, and the look of fury on her face mellowed to one of puzzlement.

"Why, Safia? Why come after Violet now, after all this time? I know Chang'e put you up to this. Violet told me what you said to her. But you don't know Chang'e, and you certainly don't owe her any favors."

Safia opened her mouth to answer, but paused before she could say anything rash. Should she tell Alyssandra what she had been about to admit? Speaking now, there would be no going back. If she showed Alyssandra any sign of weakness, would the woman be sympathetic, or would she go on the attack?

Safia was in a fight she had no desire to be in, but she also knew she had already come too far. There was no easy retreat. She could only push forward.

But, perhaps, she did not have to continue forward alone.

"Chang'e killed Gail," Safia told Alyssandra.

Alyssandra's face screwed up in confusion. The confession surprised her.

"I thought you said she died of old age?"

"No," Safia clarified. "I said she died, and I said she was old. Both are true. I can't be responsible for the assumptions you make based on what I say."

Alyssandra began to look angry again, and Safia hastened to mellow her tone. "Chang'e killed Gail, and when I became the new priestess, she told me she wanted me to come to California and turn you and Violet against one another."

"And you agreed to do it because you felt you owed her for making you the new coven leader?" asked Alyssandra.

Safia shook her head slowly, her eyes lowering to the floor. "I agreed to do it because she told me if I didn't she would simply ask the next coven leader after me to do it."

"Ahh," said Alyssandra, finally seeing the full picture. "You're afraid of her."

"The bitch is crazy, and she clearly isn't bothered by murder. I agreed to do it because I thought it was safer than telling her no."

"One more question," said Alyssandra. "How did Chang'e know about … about what happened?"

"She doesn't. Not exactly what happened anyway. But she suspected there was a reason you took Violet and left New York, and she thought I could use that to drive some sort of a wedge between the two of you."

"She doesn't know?" Alyssandra repeated.

"No."

"Then there's no reason we need to discuss this any further. With Chang'e here in Sacramento, you can go home and…,"

"No," Safia interrupted. "I am still going to try to do what I told her I would do."

Alyssandra sputtered, struggling to find words to respond to the unexpected declaration.

"But you…? Why did you tell me all of this if you're still going through with it?"

"Because Chang'e is still a threat to me. I don't want to make an enemy out of her. However, now you understand my full motivation, and if you choose to do something about it, then perhaps my reason for being here might disappear."

Alyssandra turned and paced away from Safia, sliding a finger along the plastic surfacing of the kitchenette counter. "Are you asking me to go after Chang'e for you?"

"I am not asking anything from you, Alyssandra. I am simply explaining to you that if something were to happen to

Chang'e, something permanent mind you, then I would have nothing preventing me from packing my bags and going home."

Alyssandra stood stiffly straight, using her height advantage to gaze down her nose at Safia. "I think we have an understanding," she told her.

"Do we?" asked Safia. "That would be wonderful, particularly if it meant that you would leave my room and allow me to get some sleep."

Mitch arrived at work at his usual time Saturday night. It was his long work week, which meant he was here at the police department while everyone else in the county was enjoying their Fourth of July evening festivities; barbequing with neighbors and setting off fireworks after dark, or going to a park to watch a professional pyrotechnics display put on by one of the many companies that were happy to take their admission fees and charge exorbitant prices for slightly warm beer.

This particular holiday didn't mean much to Mitch, particularly since he had no family nearby to share it with, and his closest friends these days were the other police officers who also had to work today. At least this Fourth of July would be an easy night's work. No one wanted to spend their holiday in a cemetery to celebrate. A few people might visit during the day to pay their respects to loved ones who had passed on, but these were not people likely to cause trouble. They would enter, spend a few minutes at one of the gravesites, then leave to attend whatever plans they had made for the evening.

Tonight would not be like when he had worked a patrol job for Sacramento County. Fourth of July nights for beat cops were pure misery. It was nonstop call after call of kids setting off illegal fireworks, accidental fires, and drunken brawls among individuals that suddenly decided their next-door neighbors, or their brothers-in-law needed a solid punch in the nose.

No, not tonight. Mitch was fully prepared for twelve hours of boredom and wandering the cemetery grounds looking for nonexistent trespassers.

Lunch this evening was also something he looked forward to. The police department owned an old Weber grill that they kept in the employee parking lot. All the shifts had equal access to the charcoal barbeque anytime they felt the need to fire it up for a little team-building meal, and Jorge had volunteered to bring in some hamburgers to grill for Code-7 that evening. Of course, Tink had immediately nixed the hamburger idea and said he was bringing in a couple tri-tip roasts for the team.

A quiet night and a tri-tip meal? Yes, please. This was looking like a pretty good Saturday despite having to work on a holiday.

Briefing was short. Chief Jefferson's confrontation with Chang'e had been discussed in detail the night before, and with no additional activity in the cemetery, paranormal or otherwise, there was little to talk about. The three officers left to handle their foot patrol duties after Sergeant Smythe's nightly admonition not to get eaten, then reconvened a couple of hours later in the parking lot.

"That tri-tip smells amazing," said Mitch, watching the thick slabs of red meat sizzle over the glowing coals in the grill. "Thanks for bringing it in."

"No problem," Tink told him. "Your share is twenty bucks."

"Um, what?" asked Mitch, surprised. No one had discussed paying for the meal previously.

Tink was already laughing, unable to keep a straight face for more than a few seconds. "Um, what?" he mimicked Mitch's startled response. "Kidding, man. The meat is totally on me."

"How much longer, Tink?" asked Jorge. "I have a green salad and macaroni salad upstairs in the fridge. Let me know when I should go get it."

"We've got a little while, Sarge. No rush."

The portable scanner Jorge carried on his equipment belt crackled to life with yet another noise disturbance call for the Rancho Cordova officers. They all listened as the unlucky patrolman acknowledged the request, then shook their heads in sympathy.

"Poor bastards are getting run ragged tonight," said Brad. "Makes me glad to work for Dead Town."

"Me, too," agreed Mitch. "It's too bad…,"

Mitch's cellphone vibrated in his pocket, interrupting his thought. He pulled out the phone and saw Violet's name on the screen.

"Hey. I guess Violet's having a slow night, too," he said, showing the screen name to the other officers. He slid the green icon to answer, then held the phone to his ear. "Hey, Violet. Were you missing me?"

Violet's voice spoke in his ear, sharp and clipped. She sounded out of breath.

"Mitch, someone is in the cemetery. I think it's Chang'e."

"What? Wait, how do you know someone's in the cemetery?"

"After Simon was attacked, Alyssandra and I placed a net over the entire grounds. We set it to send us an alarm if anyone uses a large amount of power. A few seconds ago, someone started manipulating a huge amount of magic. Most of it is earth magic, but some of it is demonic."

"Demonic? That's why you think it's Chang'e."

"Who else would it be? She's in Back Half, somewhere near the west wall. I can't really give you more specifics than that. Watch the flow of magic on the ground when you get close, and the movement should lead you right to her."

"Where are you?" Mitch asked. He could hear a hum and vibrations that sounded like she was calling from her car.

"Alyssandra and I are both headed to Dead Town. I'll probably beat her there, but I'm still at least twenty minutes away. Be careful."

"I will. See you soon."

Mitch hung up and met the confused stares of the rest of his teammates.

"We have to go. Chang'e is in Dead Town and she's up to something. We have to find her."

"Find her where?" asked Jorge.

"Back Half. Somewhere on the west side."

Meal plans temporarily put on hold, the night shift officers and their sergeant headed toward Back Half at a fast walk. Mitch felt the urge to hurry, to run, but he knew as well as the others that none of them would be of any use in a fight if they all arrived at the location exhausted and panting for breath. The price of a few lost seconds was worth showing up physically ready to deal with whatever they found when they located Chang'e.

Mitch filled the other officers in on Violet's portion of the phone call as they walked, sharing her suspicion that Chang'e was working on something that required a lot of power.

Entering Back Half, Mitch scanned the grounds, examining the ambient magic. He noticed an abnormal flow toward the north. Ordinarily, the earth magic that filled Dead

Town hovered or drifted like low fog on a windless day. Now, it was definitely moving to a specific destination.

"What do you see?" Tink asked.

"This way," Mitch responded, pointing and urging them all forward.

Because Mitch was focusing his attention on the surrounding magic, Jorge was the first to spot Chang'e in the distance. With only a crescent moon in the sky, there was little natural light to see by, but Chang'e was kneeling in an area with almost no surrounding foliage or tall gravestones, and the beam of the sergeant's flashlight found her easily.

Chang'e was on her knees, leaning forward and holding her palms flat against the ground. Despite the flashlights now trained on her and the sounds of the approaching officers, she gave no indication that she was aware of their approach.

As the only member of the team that could manipulate magic, Mitch tried to move in front of the others and take the lead position. Jorge stopped him with a hand on his shoulder.

"I'm going first," the sergeant told him.

"You can't see magic," Mitch warned.

"No, but I am your boss, so get behind me."

Mitch reluctantly backed down.

When only a dozen or so yards separated them from the kneeling witch, Jorge raised his voice and announced their presence.

"Chang'e. Stop whatever you're doing and lie down on your stomach. Put your hands out to your sides."

The woman remained motionless, her attention still fixed on the dirt and grass beneath her.

Jorge took another step closer. "Chang'e. I know you can hear me. Stop doing whatever it is your doing right now."

There was still no reaction from Chang'e. She seemed fully engrossed in something on, or perhaps beneath, the earth.

Jorge gestured for the others to spread out in a half circle and stay close behind him. When they were in position, he rushed forward to make first contact. He placed a hand on Chang'e's shoulder and tried to push her chest to the ground. The witch did not collapse under his weight as he had hoped. Instead, she merely turned her head and glared at him.

"Get off me," she snarled.

A burst of green and red light that only Mitch could see radiated from her, shoving Jorge away. The sergeant shouted as he tumbled to the ground, and he began slapping at his chest as if something were burrowing through his clothing and trying to bite him.

Mitch leapt forward and dropped down beside Jorge, searching for the problem and ready to throw up a shield to protect his supervisor if Chang'e attempted another attack. He saw something glowing in the center of Jorge's chest. A clear stone amulet hanging from a gold chain around the sergeant's neck flared with a bright red light. The stone had been under Jorge's shirt a moment ago, but it burned outward through the man's clothing and was still smoldering where it sat in a melted pocket of Kevlar from his ballistic vest. If not for the soft armor between the amulet and his bare skin, Jorge might have been badly burned by the activated stone.

Mitch tried to remove the amulet, but Jorge stopped him.

"It's okay. It's cooled down already. Simon gave me this talisman to ward off magic attacks. It shouldn't have gotten so hot, but she's not just using earth magic."

"Demon magic," Mitch said, then said it again loud enough for the others to hear.

Jorge ordered the team, "Look for a demon, or some kind of portal she's drawing magic from. Be careful, she's going to be a lot stronger than she normally should be."

Mitch scanned the area, first with his flashlight, then again by feeling the magic where it drifted around him. "I don't see a demon, or a portal," he said.

Jorge climbed to his feet.

"Chang'e," he said to the witch.

She had gone back to studying the ground beneath her and ignored him.

Jorge searched the area near his feet and found a small rock. He picked it up and threw it at Chang'e. It was not the most chivalrous thing to do, but Jorge clearly did not want to get within touching distance of her again.

The rock did not hit Chang'e. It skipped along the ground between her hands and knees. She noticed the stone go past and turned her head to glare at the sergeant.

"What are you doing here?" Jorge asked her when he seemed to once again have her attention.

"You ruin everything," she whined at them. "You kill my ghouls. You frighten my witches and send them fleeing and into hiding. I need an army, but you continue to get in the way."

"Army?" asked Jorge.

Mitch heard the sound of steel sliding along hard leather. Brad had drawn his katana.

"She's making new ghouls," said Brad. "We have to stop her."

"Mitch," said Jorge. "Look again. Do you see any demons or glowing rips in the air? Or maybe on the ground?"

Mitch did another scan of the area but again came up empty. He said so to Jorge.

Jorge addressed the witch again. "Where is Chang'e?" he asked.

Mitch was confused by the question, but apparently Chang'e was not.

"Gone," she said. "She served her purpose, but that is over."

"Shit," whispered Jorge, barely loud enough for Mitch to hear. Then, louder, "The demon is inside her. She's been possessed."

"What the hell do you mean possessed?" asked both Tink and Mitch at the same time.

"Simon warned me that something seemed really off about Chang'e when she attacked him. That's because it wasn't Chang'e. She's been taken over by whatever demon she thought she was using."

"If you want to survive the next few minutes," said the thing inside Chang'e, "you will leave me in peace immediately. If not, your deaths will be your own doing."

Brad moved closer, leveling his katana into a fighting position. Chang'e's eyes flicked toward him, and Mitch saw her hands tense, ready to lash out.

"Brad, don't," warned Mitch. "She isn't going to let you get close enough for that."

Mitch decided it was time to get involved. Instead of focusing on Chang'e, he concentrated on the magic she was wielding. She was pulling an extraordinary amount of power from the surrounding area and pushing it down into the earth. Tracing the flow with his mind, he realized she was sending the magic into a gravesite, attempting to revive the mass of bones and tissue in the coffin below. In addition to the outside magic taken from the cemetery, Chang'e was releasing a small flow of internal power as well.

The internal stream of energy pulsed a sickly red and yellow color in Mitch's vision. This was the magic the demon exuded, the magic that had the ability to animate the dead.

Mitch pulled magic around himself, holding it ready but not yet shaping it. He extruded a small tendril of power toward Chang'e. She saw the spell as it approached, but when it touched her own and there was no immediate reaction, she ignored it. Mitch sighed in relief, then pushed a bit more effort into his weavings.

He felt his magic meld with Chang'e's, suffusing through it. Part of his spell was burned away by the demon's power, but he added more ambient magic to account for what was lost. The magic Chang'e sent into the ground was not fully shaped. Her spellworking was all happening six feet beneath them and was mostly unformed, otherwise what Mitch was attempting probably would not work.

When he could fully sense Chang'e's magic as well as his own, he remembered what he had done when training with Violet. He tried to feel what he had felt back then.

"Bang," he breathed, and sent a mental image of the reaction he wanted.

Everyone heard the *whoomp!* of a muffled explosion beneath their feet. The ground shuddered, and Mitch had to take a step backward to keep on his feet. That reaction had been much bigger than he had expected. The other officers looked toward each other in confusion as they tried to figure out what had happened. They probably thought it was Chang'e's spell that had caused some sort of detonation.

Chang'e, however, knew instantly what Mitch had done. She felt the sudden loss of control. Her head snapped to the side and her eyes blazed in fury and frustration.

"Always in the way," she screamed. "Always!"

Mitch was not finished. Even as Chang'e screamed out her rage, he guided the percussive force of his spell up through the ground, tracing the magic trail Chang'e had laid. Fire and raw disruptive energy blew up and into the witch's face.

Chang'e screamed again, this time in pain and surprise. She threw herself backwards away from the explosion, sensing the danger in time to evade the brunt of the initial impact, but too late to avoid it completely.

Mitch cursed silently. He had hoped for a knockout punch but had only landed a grazing blow.

Chang'e scrambled to her feet and pointed a slender, accusing finger at Mitch. He braced himself and prepared to throw up a shield, but the witch's gesture was merely dramatic, not magical.

"You should have died. How did you avoid my knife? Who are you, and why are you here?"

Mitch did not like that at all. The demon inside Chang'e knew who he was; knew he was the one who had escaped its assassination attempt. It also seemed to think there was a lot more to his survival than simple luck. That was bad for several reasons. One, it was probably going to try to kill him again. And two, it would take a lot more care in any future efforts to eliminate him.

Mitch had to end this here and now. Chang'e needed to be in custody, safely behind enchanted bars where she could not make another attempt on his life.

Mitch collected more ambient magic and cast out several lines of power that snaked out in a growing cobweb of light. It was an entangling spell. He did not have much experience using it, so it moved slower than he would have liked, giving Chang'e plenty of time to employ her own defensive maneuvers. She waved one hand, glowing with yellow magic, back and forth in front of her, and where it touched Mitch's spell, it burned away the strands like fire touching spider's silk.

With the immediate threat gone, Chang'e launched her own offensive. It was a broad cone of flame meant to engulf all four members of Mitch's team at once. Fortunately, because it was not directed at any one of them in particular, Mitch was able to cover them all with a protective shield. The widespread screen of blue magic was not as strong as his smaller, more condensed workings, but it did not have to be against Chang'e's wide ranging attack.

As the flames died away, Brad leaped forward, raising his katana for a strike against Chang'e. She did not let him get closer than ten feet before aiming another spell directly at him. Mitch cried out, trying to erect a new shield to protect him, but Brad was too fast and had already moved too far away for Mitch to help him.

Mitch prepared a counterattack when he realized that he could not save Brad. At least, while Chang'e was distracted, he could take her down and protect the rest of his team.

The new spell was never launched. It fell apart in his hands, his concentration broken as he watched Brad Kodama drive his sword forward, piercing the oncoming bolt of magical energy.

What Chang'e's spell was supposed to be, Mitch could not have guessed. The magic broke apart and flared outward in multiple directions, like a bursting rocket at one of the local fireworks shows.

Brad continued rushing forward, ready to drive his blade through Chang'e's ribcage. The witch, startled by the failure of her attack, only had time to dodge and retreat from the reckless charge. The possessed woman twisted and flailed as she threw herself aside, contorting in a manner that no human body should have been able to accomplish. Watching the bizarre manner in which she writhed away from Brad's sword was deeply unsettling to Mitch.

If he still had any lingering doubts regarding demonic possession, they disappeared as he watched Chang'e crab-crawl and scuttle to safety.

Chang'e was on the defensive, but the witch was not ready to concede defeat. She assessed her enemies one at a time, scrabbling a safe distance away and peering back at the group that had come to challenge her. Mitch watched her eyes slide from Brad and his katana to Jorge and the glowing talisman on his chest. She glared at Mitch next, and he shuddered at the pure malevolence in her gaze.

He readied another shield spell, but Chang'e did not attack. Instead, she fixed her attention on Tink, the only member of the group opposing her who had not yet demonstrated an ability to counter her magic. The weak link.

"Tink! Watch out," Mitch shouted, anticipating Chang'e's next move.

He ran toward his partner, trying to put himself between Chang'e and the defenseless man, but the witch was already weaving her next spell. Tink could not see magic, so had no idea of the danger he was in.

Mitch raised a shield wide enough for both himself and the oblivious officer, but he was still too far away. The area he needed to cover to include Tink inside his defenses at this distance would spread the magic too thin, and he did not know if it would withstand a focused attack from Chang'e. The broad range spell she had cast at the entire team had been one thing, but with all her efforts centered on Tink, her energies would be gathered to a single point.

Mitch pushed as much power into his shield as he could manage. The spell around him and Tink brightened as Chang'e cast a single bolt of condensed magic. The attack appeared as white light tainted throughout with deep veins of dark red. Her spell moved slower than he expected, but it struck Mitch's shield like a charging bull, blowing his defenses completely apart.

Chang'e's magic was blunted by the shield, but not stopped, and the remaining energies engulfed Tink, swallowing him in a net of red and white power.

Tink screamed and dropped to his knees.

Mitch and Brad charged Chang'e, Brad leveling his katana and Mitch shaping magic in preparation for another percussive spell. Mitch did not know how to help Tink, but he understood if there was any hope for the downed officer's survival, they needed to stop Chang'e from launching a second attack at him.

Chang'e expanded a bubble of force around herself that battered against Mitch, knocking him from his feet and onto his back. Brad was also pushed away for a moment, but he waved his sword through the spell and the bubble popped like a fragile film of soap blown by a child on a windy day. With the barrier temporarily removed, Mitch rolled onto his side and released the magic he held, willing it to burn fast and hot.

"Fire," he whispered, shaping the spell.

Chang'e raised a new barrier in time to protect herself from the worst of the heat, but she was forced to take several steps in retreat. Brad continued stalking forward, ready to cut through her second shield as he had the first, and then hopefully to take a pound of flesh in retaliation for her attack on Tink. Chang'e dropped to the ground and scampered away from the threat on all fours, moving impossibly fast.

Mitch positioning himself between Tink and the demonically controlled witch, preparing for her next attack. His partner was no longer in apparent pain, but he had not yet risen from the ground either.

Chang'e did not cast another spell. She paused and cocked her head as though listening to something she could barely hear, something calling out to her from a great distance away. She turned her back on the group of officers, her attention fully absorbed by whatever had distracted her.

"Always in the way. Witches and humans." Chang'e turned suddenly toward Mitch and snapped, "Always in the way."

Power flowed from her hand, drawn from deep inside Chang'e rather than pulled from the ambient earth energies around her. The witch held her arm out in front of her and swept her palm downward, leaving a smear of magic in the air, almost as if she were fingerpainting on a blank page of paper. The smear ripped and widened until it revealed a new landscape behind it.

Mitch saw houses, an asphalt street, and trees. It was a residential neighborhood, but he did not recognize the specific location.

With one last hateful glance at the ones responsible for thwarting her yet again, Chang'e stepped into the rift, disappearing as it closed behind her.

Mitch did not waste time staring at the empty spot where Chang'e had been. He hurried to check on Tink. Jorge was already beside the fallen officer, pulling at the buttons on his shirt.

When Mitch reached them, the sergeant was examining a crystal pendant around Tink's neck. The amulet was identical to the one Jorge wore, but Tink's stone was blackened and cracked. The crystal fragmented and fell to pieces in Jorge's hand as he examined it.

"He's okay," Jorge said as Tink groaned and tried to get up.

Mitch helped him into a sitting position.

"Fortunately, whatever Chang'e had done was enough to break through the amulet's protection, but not enough to do much damage to Tink after the crystal had failed."

Mitch thought about the shield he had erected and how much Chang'e's attack had been weakened before it hit Tink. He might have saved the man's life. Mitch did not say anything about it though to either Jorge or Tink. He was simply happy everyone was still alive.

"What are these amulets?" Mitch asked. "Why do you both have them?"

"We all have them," said Brad, pulling a gold chain from under his shirt. At the end of the chain hung a clear crystal. "The chief issued them to everyone on the department right after Chang'e's house burned down and she disappeared."

"I never got one," said Mitch.

"You were gone the night I handed them out to the team," Jorge said, although the sergeant looked a bit embarrassed as he said it. "They're only good for one or maybe two hits before they break, and I figured you didn't need one since you're better at protecting yourself from magic than anyone else on the department."

"So, the chief didn't give me one?"

"No, he handed out enough for everyone on the department, including Dot," said Brad, always happy to deliver the hard truth with a smile and an evil wink. "Jorge made the decision not to give you one."

"I thought we could hold onto it as a spare," Jorge quickly explained. "Do you want yours?"

Mitch thought about it, then sighed. "No. You were right. Give it to Tink to replace the one that broke. If it's only good for a couple uses, you should probably get a new one, too."

Jorge nodded. "Probably."

Mitch's confusion about the amulets had been cleared up to his satisfaction, but there was still one mystery in the cemetery he desperately wanted an explanation for.

Hey, Brad," he asked, "how did you block the demon's magic? I didn't think you could even see it, much less break through it like that."

"That wasn't me," Brad answered lightly. He drew his katana from its scabbard. "That was all Tenshi."

"Tenshi?"

"Brad, are you sure?" asked Jorge cryptically.

Brad cocked his head casually, as if to say, "why not?"

"Mitch has been with us what, six months now? He's trusted us with a lot, so I think it's safe for us to trust him with Tenshi."

"What is Tenshi?" Mitch asked a second time.

"This is Tenshi," said Brad, holding the bare blade up where Mitch could see it more easily. "Tenshi is the angel that inhabits this sword."

"Um…, angel? Angels are real?!"

"Yup." Brad cut the air a few times with the blade, then noticed Mitch's expression of disbelief. "What? Demons you believe in, but angels are a problem?"

"Uh, I…. Good point," Mitch was forced to concede. "So, there's an angel in your sword?"

"Well, not quite. The story I was told was that about eight hundred years ago, a demon was rampaging through Japan. No one was able to stop it. Finally, a samurai summoned and made a pact with an angel to get help facing the demon. The angel agreed to bind with the warrior's blade. The samurai, with the aid of the angel in his sword banished the demon."

"That's the same blade?" asked Mitch, incredulous at the thought of how old the sword in Brad's hands must be. "And there's an angel in it?"

"Well, like I said, not quite. The angel isn't actually still here. It returned to its own realm after the battle, but it did leave a fragment of its spirit in the sword. That fragment still connects the katana to the angel and the powers of the angelic realm. The blade will never break, never get dull, and it will disperse any demonic energies it comes into contact with. In addition to that, I look like a total badass carrying it."

"The angel's name was what? Tenshi? And it beat another demon. Is there a way to get Tenshi to come back and help us against Chang'e?" Mitch was suddenly hopeful that there might be an easier way to stop the threat to Dead Town than fighting the possessed witch to a draw every time she came into the cemetery. This angel could give them the advantage they needed.

"No," said Brad, throwing cold water on Mitch's excitement. "I have no idea how to bring the angel back, or ask it for help, or even talk to it. I don't even know the angel's real name, for that matter. Tenshi is the name the Samurai gave the sword after the angel departed. Tenshi is the Japanese word for angel. The sword's full name is 'Tenshi No Migite.' It means, The Angel's Right Hand."

"I see. So, no actual angel." He sighed, accepting the bad news. Then, with a little more enthusiasm, he asked, "But the sword still works against demons, right?"

"It does," agreed Jorge. "And we will use the sword again if we have to. But Mitch, the chief and this team are the only people who know the truth about Tenshi, and it needs to stay that way. Understand? If word gets out about its capabilities, we will have to lock it up in the property room so it doesn't end up in the wrong hands. As long as people think it's just a regular sword, we can keep using it."

"Wrong hands? If it fights demons, whose hands would be the wrong hands?"

"Angelic magic is just as dangerous as demonic magic in its own way. If it's misused, it can do a lot of damage in our realm. So again, Mitch, please, not a word."

"Mitch!"

The shout came from somewhere behind him. It was Violet's voice, and Mitch searched the gloom of the surrounding grounds looking for her. She appeared from the south, her figure silhouetted by the electric lights illuminating Front Lawn in the distance.

Mitch quickly nodded at Jorge. "Okay. I won't say anything." Then he turned and called out to Violet, "Here. We're all right. Chang'e left in a hurry. Thanks for getting here so fast, because honestly, I think she only bolted when she felt you coming."

When she reached the group of officers, Violet hugged Mitch, then gave him a quick head-to-toe check to be sure he was not trying to hide any injuries from her.

"What was she doing here?" Violet asked. "She was pulling a lot of power for some reason."

"She wanted to make more ghouls," Brad said. He still held his katana in his hand, but as Mitch and Violet watched, he casually resheathed it and slung it into its customary position across his back.

"What does Chang'e want with ghouls?" Violet asked.

"It isn't Chang'e anymore," said Mitch. "Something has taken over her body, and whatever it is, it wants to take Dead Town. Apparently, it thinks it needs an army to do it."

"Something has…? What?" asked Violet.

Jorge gave Tink a reassuring pat on the shoulder, then approached Violet.

"Chang'e uses demonic magic, right? She summons demons to power her coven. That's why Simon has never given her access to Dasan's Terrace."

"Right. She's been doing it for years," agreed Violet.

"Well, she pushed her luck too far," Jorge said. "One of the demons has broken loose from her control and taken over her body. She's been possessed."

Violet's face fell. "How did it happen?"

Jorge shrugged. "How does it ever happen? She starts trusting that she has the demon completely under control, then she gets sloppy. What matters now is, how do we stop her?"

Violet shook her head. "I don't know. Alyssandra specifically forbids any of her coven from summoning demons because of this possibility. It keeps us safe, but at the same time it means that I don't know the first thing about dealing with creatures from the demonic realm."

"I might have an idea," said Mitch.

When everyone turned to face him, he corrected himself. "I mean, I might know someone who might have an idea. I helped him out a while ago when some of his property was stolen. You remember the golem?"

Jorge and Brad nodded.

"This is the guy that originally owned the creation stones. He teaches ancient mythology. Maybe he knows something about demons."

"I suppose it's worth talking to him," said Jorge. "When can you do it?"

"I'm off tomorrow, so I'll pay him a visit. Hopefully, he can tell us what we need to do next."

CHAPTER 10

Mitch sat in the kitchen at a small, oval breakfast table across from Professor Solomon Schick. He had called the man early Sunday morning, and despite the holiday weekend and extremely short notice, Solomon had immediately asked Mitch to come visit him at his home. Violet requested to come along as well, both for the information they were seeking, and because she feared leaving Mitch alone and unprotected while Chang'e was still at large. The professor had happily extended his invitation to her as well.

Solomon was a pleasant older man in his late sixties. His appearance was the epitome of the college professor that he was, with a shiny brown head, bald but for a thin fringe of white hair around the temples, and heavy smile lines around his eyes and mouth. A pair of John Lennon inspired, round spectacles perched low on the bridge of his nose to complete the look. Mitch had spoken with the professor a few times in the past, most notably after the man had lost a particularly powerful set of stones capable of raising earth golems. He had found him pleasant and easy to talk to, if perhaps a bit overly garrulous at times.

A hot cup of tea, that he had not wanted but had been too polite to refuse, was cradled between Mitch's hands. He enjoyed the warmth it provided, if not necessarily the taste. Coffee would have been more to Mitch's liking, but it had not been offered, and Mitch did not wish to seem ungrateful.

The professor sipped absently from his own cup while he carefully considered the question Mitch had posed a moment earlier.

"What do I know about demons?" he mused. "Quite a bit, and yet not a great deal. I suppose it depends on specifically what you are trying to find out. In my personal studies, I have devoted a great deal of time to religious mythologies, and specifically the stories involving the demonic and angelic realms."

The professor slipped the tiny, round, rimless spectacles from his face and held them toward the overhead lighting. He wiped the lenses with the tail of his blue button-up shirt, then replaced them on his nose. "You obviously realize that demons are real, or you would not be here today asking these questions. The thing to remember, Officer Loman…,"

"Mitch, please," Mitch corrected for the third time that morning.

"Ahem, well, Mitch. The thing to remember is that human religions, particularly the Judeo-Christian religions, did not invent the idea of demons and angels. Stories of their presence on our plane go as far back as the earliest discovered writings of mankind. These creatures exist in their own realms, but occasionally cross over into ours. When these events occurred, ancient religious scholars confronted by supernatural beings attempted to define what these creatures were to the best of their abilities, using the admittedly limited framework of their own understanding of the world."

"So, according to you, and what you know today, what are they?" asked Mitch.

"They are creatures of immense magical ability that come from another dimension. Occasionally they stumble into our world, or else are forcibly drawn here by human beings with enough knowledge and power to open portals between our realities."

Violet blew across her teacup and took a small sip.

"This is very good, Solomon. Mitch, you should try yours."

"Thank you," said the professor, beaming. "It's one of my favorites. I discovered it years ago in Syria, but I was fortunate to find an online boutique in Canada that sells it. I try to always have some on hand."

Mitch reluctantly sipped his tea. It tasted like every hot tea he had ever tried. The brew was bitter and tasted like someone had floated grass clippings in water. He checked the table for sugar or milk, but neither was available. He set the cup down and folded his hands around it again.

"If demons leave their realm and come here to ours, how do we get them to go back?" he asked, bringing the conversation back to its original topic.

"That's the easy part," Solomon said. "Think of a demon, or angel for that matter, as a person who has jumped into deep water. Maybe to be more accurate, they have been pulled into the water against their will. They cannot breathe while they are submerged, so they must return to the surface after a short time or risk perishing."

"So, the demon will go back on its own. All we have to do is wait."

"Yes and no," Solomon said. "When the demon is drawn to our world, a portal is opened to bring them through. As long as this portal is open, the demon can draw strength and remain in our dimension. If you close the rift, severing the connection, the demon is simultaneously pulled back to where it belongs. Unless, of course, something traps it here first, in which case it will eventually die."

"Okay, so there is a portal keeping the demon here. We need to find it and close it. How do we do that?"

"No," interrupted Violet. "We're straying from the current problem. This demon is not dependent on a portal any longer. It has possessed a human body."

"Ah, I see," said Solomon, taking a moment to sip again from his teacup. "That is a whole new set of parameters to the issue."

Mitch looked back and forth between the professor and Violet. "I don't know anything about this stuff, so what am I missing? What are you two talking about?"

"Remember the water analogy?" Solomon asked. "Let's expand on that. When a demon possesses a human host, it is like … ah, it's like…,"

"It put on a SCUBA suit," finished Violet.

"Yes. Perfect description. The demon is protected by its human host. Instead of minutes, the demon can survive days without an open portal to its own realm. In addition, when it begins to weaken, all it needs to do is reopen that portal for a short time to reinvigorate itself for the next few days. It can repeat this cycle indefinitely, staying in our world until the death of the host."

"Damn it. That's a problem. But ultimately that doesn't change my question. Is there a way to make it go back home?"

"It depends on the demon in question. Do you know how powerful this one is?"

Mitch looked to Violet. "Any idea?"

"Alyssandra told me that Chang'e and her coven have three different demons that they used in the past to draw power from. I don't know which one this is, but none of them are major demons. All of the demons Chang'e uses are lower-level creatures, otherwise she would never have had the strength to pull them into our world."

"That's good," said Solomon. "That is to our advantage. Sending a lesser demon back is comparatively easy to do."

"Great," said Mitch, seeing a small hint of light at the end of the tunnel for the first time in this conversation. "What do we need to do?"

"You need to conduct an exorcism," Solomon said.

Mitch looked toward Violet questioningly.

She shook her head at him. "He doesn't mean that. What we do is also called exorcism, but it's completely different. The professor is talking about the old-school, crosses and holy water kind of exorcism."

Solomon nodded, paused, then shook his head. "Not quite, but yes. First, to understand what you must do, you need to understand exactly what an exorcism consists of."

"Do we need a priest? And if we do, do you know anyone that has done something like this before?" asked Mitch.

"You don't need a priest," Solomon chided. "Religious organizations have practiced exorcisms for a very long time, and throughout history they frequently added a great deal of ceremony and mostly unnecessary symbolic items into the process. Catholics use holy water and prayer. Hindus chant mantras and attempt to trap the invading entity in vessels made of precious metals. Muslims believe that an exorcism can only be carried out by one who prays daily and is morally pure."

"And those don't work," said Violet.

"They do work," insisted Solomon. "They are merely unnecessary."

Mitch ran a hand through his hair, then scratched his head in growing exasperation. "You are starting to get a little confusing, Professor," he said. "They work, but they're not necessary? I don't understand what you're trying to tell us."

Violet nodded her head in agreement, equally puzzled by the seeming contradiction.

"What I mean to say is that each of these religious groups have methods that successfully exorcise an afflicted person, but their specific tactics aren't why the demonic entity leaves. For example, let's talk about Catholic exorcism. You mentioned a priest, Mitch, so let's stick to that illustration. The priest finds a person who has been possessed by a demon, so what does he do?"

Solomon paused like the teacher he was, gazing back and forth between Mitch and Violet and waiting to see if either would volunteer an answer.

When Mitch realized what the professor wanted, he cleared his throat and said, "I have only seen stuff like this in movies, so I have no idea what actually happens."

Solomon accepted the non-answer and continued. "The movies are a bit dramatic, but they have the general idea correct. The priest secures the afflicted person so they cannot escape or cause harm to themselves or others. Next, he sprinkles holy water on the victim and reads prayers from the bible, all the while commanding the demon to depart. Usually, he orders the demon away using the name of Christ or God, or sometimes even a specific saint known for assisting with exorcisms. The entire process takes a great deal of time, but usually after one to three days of constant prayer and attendance, the demon at last relents and withdraws."

Solomon paused again, waiting for the point of his explanation to sink in. Mitch thought about it carefully, but still did not fully understand if a priest was necessary or not.

"So, yes or no on the priest?" Mitch finally asked, defeated by his inability to figure out what the hell Solomon was telling him.

Solomon, for his part, seemed to be enjoying his role as the cryptic advisor. He wanted his students to come to their own conclusions.

"Remember what we talked about first?" he asked his captive audience. "Demons don't belong in our world. They cannot exist here on their own. By possessing a human host, they are only delaying the inevitable, and they will eventually have to return to their own realm. You wanted to know how to force a demon to leave. I'm sorry, but the short answer to that question is that you can't."

"Damn it, Professor," Mitch blurted, reaching the limit of his patience. "If there's no way to get the demon to leave, why have you been wasting our time? You could have said that as soon as we got here."

"Mitch," said Violet, placing a hand on his arm. "I think I know what Solomon is saying. We can't make the demon leave using any kind of force, but then again, we don't have to."

Solomon tapped the side of his nose with an index finger, indicating Violet was headed in the right direction.

"We can't leave the demon in Chang'e," Mitch argued.

"No, we can't," Violet agreed. "We have to catch Chang'e and keep her immobilized for a few days."

"Precisely," said Solomon brightly, clapping his hands together. "Keep her under control so she can't harm herself or anyone else."

"Keep her from accessing a new portal, so the demon can't recharge itself," Violet continued.

The light bulb finally went on in Mitch's head. "And after one to three days, the demon won't have the strength to stick around. It will have to either take off and go home, or else stay and die."

"Exactly," Solomon concluded. "The bible, the priest, holy water, and prayer, they're all simply ceremony to cover the true exorcism. Keep the demon from rejuvenating itself and it will have no choice but to flee."

"Capturing Chang'e is not going to be easy. She's strong and will be difficult to control," Violet said. "And that is assuming that we can even find her if she doesn't want to be found."

"She will come back to the cemetery eventually. She made it pretty clear she wants it for herself. In the meantime, we could set up some kind of trap."

"The last one didn't work as well as we'd hoped," Violet reminded him.

"Well, that wasn't so much a trap as an alarm. We weren't ready to deal with her yet, especially not with that demon already inside of her. We need to set a real trap. Maybe even close Dead Town to the public until this is over." Mitch glanced at Solomon. "Speaking of Dead Town, Professor, why is this demon so fixated on taking over the cemetery? Why does it even want to stay here instead of going home?"

"Most demons do prefer to go home," Solomon stated. "They often possess a host for the sole purpose of punishing the person that dragged them away from their realm in the first place. They do as much damage as possible for a short while, then leave."

Violet stared at the table, searching for answers that weren't there. "This demon is different, though," she said thoughtfully. "It wants to stay. Why?"

"You said that it is drawn to the cemetery. I know the golem stones were used in Dasan's Terrace, so there are magical energies there. Is the magic very strong in the cemetery? More so than anywhere else in Sacramento?"

Violet and Mitch glanced at each other. Dead Town's magical resources were not advertised, but then again, they weren't exactly a secret, either.

"It is," Mitch admitted. "It's the strongest source of natural magic on the west coast, maybe even the whole country."

"Mm-hmm. That makes sense, then," said Solomon. "Demons in their own realm are chaotic and anarchistic by nature. There are no leaders per se. No presidents, no kings, no rulers. There are only the strong and the weak. This particular demon is most likely part of that latter group. It is accustomed to being subjected to the whims of its more powerful brethren. Now, however, it has accidentally stumbled upon a pool of great power, a source of immeasurable strength, and it sees an opportunity to grab that power for itself. This demon wants an opportunity to be a leader for a change, rather than a follower."

"And it will do anything it has to do in order to claim Dead Town and keep control of it," said Violet.

"Like raise an army."

"What?" asked Violet.

"The demon told us last night it needed to raise an army."

"We need to stop it fast, before it can figure out how to get that army," she said. "How about it, Professor? Do you have any handy tips for how to trap an absolutely crazy, homicidal, demon-possessed witch?"

"Have you tried summoning the demon and trapping it in a circle?"

"Isn't it a little late to do a summoning?" asked Mitch. "I mean, the demon is already in our world, so what would it accomplish?"

Solomon chuckled. "That will not be a problem. Summoning a demon is not predicated on that demon being in its own realm. A demon can be summoned at anytime from anywhere by a person with sufficient magic and ability. All you need is the creature's name. I imagine it might even be possible to summon a demon that is trapped in someone else's summoning circle, if the summoner is stronger than the one currently holding the demon. Although, in all honesty, I have never heard of such a thing happening. It would be an interesting experiment to try. We would, of course, need to practice with an extremely low-level demon since there is always the possibility of it escaping. We could set up a circle…,"

"Professor, I'm sorry," interrupted Violet. "Maybe we could discuss hypothetical experiments another time. We still need to figure out how to capture this particular demon, and unfortunately summoning isn't going to work. We, um, don't actually know the demon's name. Chang'e is the one who summoned it originally, and she has not shared the thing's name with anyone outside of her own coven as far as we know."

"That shouldn't be too much of a problem," Solomon assured them.

"No?" asked Mitch. "How is that not a problem?

"You said the demon has taken possession of this coven leader, correct?"

"Yes."

"Well then, as long as the demon wishes to maintain control of her, its essence is going to remain inextricably linked to the witch's soul. Instead of summoning the demon, you summon the witch, and the demon will be towed along with her. Wherever your host goes, the demon goes as well."

Mitch and Violet were stunned into silence for several seconds. When he found his voice again, Mitch asked, "You can summon people?"

"Absolutely," insisted the professor. "Any being from any realm can be summoned if sufficient magic is used."

"I've never heard of a person being summoned," said Violet.

"No. It is extremely rare. Not necessarily because it doesn't work, but rather because there is little reason to expend the necessary effort to summon a human being. Witches summon demons and angels because they can gain power from doing so. Creatures of other realms are not going to waste their time and effort to pull a human out of this realm. There is no reward commensurate with the energy expenditure. Human beings can't grant wishes, or provide magical strength, or any of the things that would make summoning worthwhile. In addition to that, they are extremely fragile. We would tend to die quickly, and rather nastily, in most other realms."

"What would we need to summon Chang'e?" asked Mitch. He was beginning to grow hopeful again. Perhaps this visit would be the turning point in their battle with the demon.

"The same things you need to summon a demon. You need a name, a circle to hold them when they arrive, and sufficient magic to power the capture and containment spells."

Mitch looked to Violet. "Do we have Chang'e's full name?"

Violet's shoulders slumped slightly. She shook her head. "Chang'e isn't even her real first name. It's the name of a Chinese moon goddess, and Chang'e has been using it for as long as I've known her."

"Is that enough, Professor?" asked Mitch, turning to Solomon. "Can we summon her using that name?"

Solomon frowned regretfully. "No. That will not be enough. You need her real name, the name she was given at birth, not simply a pseudonym she uses."

"What about angels?" Mitch asked, remembering Brad's sword. "Do you need their names, too? Or can you summon them with an item that they're connected to?"

"How do you mean connected?" Professor Schick asked, shifting forward in his chair with genuine curiosity.

"Um, like, if it once inhabited an object, then left a fragment of its magic behind when it left."

Violet leaned close to Mitch and whispered in his ear. "What are you talking about? Do you know something?"

"I'm sorry," Mitch responded quietly. "I promised not to say,"

Violet, accustomed to secrets, and having enough faith in Mitch to be willing to accept the cryptic statement, at least for the moment, let it pass without further questions. Mitch was grateful for her discretion, though he knew she would expect at least a little more explanation the next time the two of them were alone.

"Fascinating," muttered Solomon. "And you know of such an object?"

"I can't give any specifics. Just assume something like that existed," said Mitch, giving the professor basically the same answer he had given Violet.

"Well, I imagine the item would be quite powerful, as well as potentially very dangerous. But as a focus for a summoning, I do not think it would be of much use. You would still need to know the name of the angel you were attempting to call. Would you, er, hypothetically, have that angel's name?"

"No," Mitch admitted, then cursed under his breath. "I thought we might have something with this summoning trick. Damn. That can't be it, though. Right? There has to be another way to locate and force a demon to come to you, even if we don't have its name. Can you think of anything else that might help us catch her? Maybe something non-supernatural that we haven't considered yet?"

Solomon raised his teacup. "I'm sorry, but I am no help to you with that problem. Capturing rogue witches is not my area of expertise. Of course, if you can't apprehend her, there is another method of exorcism that generally works. It is a bit extreme, however."

Mitch tapped the handle of his own cup with a fingertip. "And this extreme method is…?" he prompted.

"I am not sure whether or not this is the proper way to address your current problem. I don't know this, um, Chung person myself. I don't know how important she is to you two. You see, the second method of exorcism is to kill the demon's host, ejecting the entity out of its protective shell and forcing it to return to its home dimension."

Mitch thought about it for a moment. He did not like Chang'e, but he also did not necessarily want to kill her. "I would like to avoid that outcome if we can," he admitted.

"I don't know. It's certainly worth considering," said Violet. She shrugged lightly, then took another sip of her tea.

Mitch paused, waiting to see if she was joking. Violet continued to sit quietly, contemplating the flavor of the tea and the idea of having to kill Chang'e as though neither thought was more pressing than the other.

"Professor, can you…?"

The sound of Violet's phone ringing interrupted Mitch.

Violet slipped her phone out of her pocket and glanced at the screen.

"Alyssandra," she said to Mitch, then she turned to Professor Schick. "Sorry, Solomon, but I need to take this."

She stood and wandered into the next room, answering the phone as she left.

Mitch cleared his throat when she disappeared, then started again. "Professor, can you tell me, if we do end up having to kill Chang'e, how do we do it? Is there some special ceremony, or something we have to do drive the demon away?"

"No," Solomon said. He shook his head slowly as he answered. "When a person is possessed by a demon, they are stronger, faster, and most definitely more dangerous, but they are ultimately still human. Any method you can think of that would kill a human being will also work on a demonic host."

"Mitch, we need to go," said Violet, striding back into the kitchen. Chief Jefferson is calling an emergency meeting for both the police department and the coven. Since you happen to be part of both, you've been ordered to be there."

"What's the meeting about?" he asked.

Violet gave him an irritated look.

"Right. Chang'e. Of course," he said after a moment's thought.

Mitch stood, and Professor Schick rose to his feet with him. Clearly sorry to see his guests leaving so soon, Solomon reluctantly shook hands and said goodbye to both Violet and Mitch.

"Thank you for talking with us on such short notice, Professor," Mitch said. "I'm sorry, but it looks like we have something important we need to get to."

"Of course. Of course. I hope I was at least somewhat helpful."

"You were very helpful, Solomon," said Violet. "Thank you for your time."

"And if we have any more questions…?" began Mitch.

"I am at your disposal," the professor assured them. "You have my phone number, and you know where to find me if you need anything. Even if you simply want to come by and enjoy another cup of tea."

CHAPTER 11

Mitch and Violet found Chief Jefferson in the largest conference room on the second floor of the police department building. The chief wanted plenty of room to accommodate the people he had invited, and his office, or any of the smaller meeting rooms, would have been a tight fit for the gathered group.

In addition to the chief, Mitch, and Violet, Dot was also in the meeting, as was Alyssandra, and Willa, one of the strongest witches in the coven after Alyssandra and Violet. Willa was a short stocky woman with what seemed to be a permanent frown affixed on her face. Her hair was braided in close cornrows pulled tight along her scalp that did nothing to lessen the severity of her expression. She seemed to glower at Mitch as he entered the room.

From the police department staff, Simon had reached out to each of the four shift sergeants. Mitch recognized Sergeant Alonzo Ricci from the B-Days shift and Sergeant Teresa Bulgado from A-Days, but he had never met the young, blond woman sitting next to Jorge. He assumed she must be Elizabeth Donair, the team leader on A-Nights.

Since Mitch and Violet were the last to arrive, the meeting began as soon as they claimed seats next to Alyssandra and Willa at the far end of the table.

"Thank you everyone for making time to be here," began Simon. "I don't normally ask for meetings like this, but I'm afraid this is a rather unique situation we have on our hands. Chang'e, a very powerful witch in our area...,"

Alyssandra snorted derisively at the description, but when Simon paused to see if she had a comment, she waved him on.

"As I was saying, Chang'e has announced her intentions to take over Dasan's Terrace and to eliminate anyone she considers to be in the way of that goal. That includes all employees of the police department as well as every member of Miss Alyssandra Freid's coven. It isn't often that both of our priorities align so closely that I would propose a joint operation between our two organizations, but this is definitely one of those times. The last time we coordinated at this level was during our recent hunt to eradicate the ghouls in the cemetery. As it turned out, that event was only a prelude to what is still coming."

"I'm sorry, Chief, but I don't think I understand," said the young nightshift sergeant. "I thought Chang'e was run out of town last month. Even if she came back, how is she any more of a threat to the department than any of the other magic users in the area? Can't the witches take care of their own problems?"

The woman threw a dark glance toward the end of the table where Alyssandra and her people were seated. Mitch noted uncomfortably that the sergeant's glare seemed to also include him.

"That is what this meeting is to address, Liz," said Simon. "Now, if you'll show a little patience, I think all of your questions will be answered. To get everyone up to speed on where we are today, I think Jorge should brief us on what occurred last night. Jorge?"

Sergeant Smythe remained seated, but he leaned forward far enough that he could see, and be seen by, everyone at the table.

"Last night, my team received a phone call from a member of Miss Freid's coven. The call was to let us know that someone had entered the cemetery and was manipulating a large amount of magic. The person in question, and their purpose for being in Dead…." Jorge hesitated and flicked a quick glance toward Chief Jefferson before correcting himself. "I mean Dasan's Terrace, were as yet unknown."

"Why are the witches monitoring the cemetery?" asked Sergeant Donair. "Since when did they become our early detection alarm system?"

"Liz. Thank you, but I am going to ask you to hold your questions until Jorge is finished. If you keep interrupting, we are going to completely lose the thread of why we are here in the first place."

The chief's voice was as soft and calm as always, but everyone in the room felt the rebuke in his tone. Sergeant Donair sunk into her chair and folded her hands in her lap, embarrassed at the sudden amount of attention on her.

"Since we first discovered that Chang'e was coming back to Sacramento, Miss Freid's coven took it upon themselves to watch and notify us of any unusual activity within the boundaries of Dasan's Terrace," Jorge clarified, addressing the night shift sergeant's question even though she no longer seemed interested in the answer. "Last night, when we were notified that someone had entered the cemetery, my shift responded out to the area identified. We found Chang'e at a gravesite casting a spell that required a massive amount of magic.

"Mitch Loman," and Jorge gestured toward Mitch at the end of the table, "was able to disrupt Chang'e and stop her from completing the spell. When I tried to ask her what she was doing, she admitted that she had been the one responsible for creating the ghouls that infested the cemetery last month. She was trying to make new ones when we stopped her."

Jorge paused to be sure that everyone in the meeting was paying attention. When he saw that all eyes were on him, he continued. "Chang'e said that she needed to raise an army. She isn't going to quit until she has taken control of Dasan's Terrace and eliminated everyone that might get in her way."

An outbreak of private discussions erupted around the table, leading to a general din in the room. Simon allowed it to continue for a moment, then brought everyone back to order with a rap of his knuckles on the conference table. The knocking cut through the growing noise.

"Yes, that's bad," he agreed as the conversations died. "But it is exactly what we already knew, or at least suspected. Jorge discovered something else last night. Something worse and infinitely more dangerous." The chief gestured toward Jorge, who waited patiently in his seat. "Please continue."

"We attempted to take Chang'e into custody, but she fought back. It was during this fight that I realized that we were no longer simply dealing with an ambitious witch. We have known for a while that Chang'e uses demons to amplify her power. It is one of the primary reasons she is banned from Dasan's Terrace. What I discovered last night, however, is that one of those demons has broken free of her control and taken over. Chang'e has been demonically possessed."

Another surge of questions and statements came from the attendees around the table. Simon quickly waved the noise down.

"Chang'e has always been a problem," the chief said, reclaiming the floor, "but until today, we have been able to deal with her. Now, there is no way to know how dangerous she has become. We do not have any idea of the capabilities of this demon that has taken possession of her. What we do know is that the demon has already created ghouls in our cemetery and that it has been responsible for at least three deaths."

"Four," clarified Alyssandra. "Chang'e murdered another witch while she was in New York."

"Four," Simon echoed. "At least four deaths."

Jorge removed an object from his shirt pocket. He laid it on the table in front of him and slid it out to where the others could see. It was a gold chain and three pieces of blackened crystal.

"I have some good news, and some bad news," Sergeant Smythe said, poking at the burned shards. "The good news is that the amulets Chief Jefferson issued to all of us work. This one here saved the life of one of my officers. The bad news is that because we are facing demonic forces, the crystals will not help for long if we get drawn into a prolonged fight."

He poked at the gem pieces again. "This is what's left of an amulet after it took one hit."

"What happened to Chang'e?" asked Sergeant Bulgado. "How did she get away?"

Jorge laughed, but there was not much humor in his voice. "Get away? We're lucky she didn't stick around and kill us all. We fought her to a standstill for a couple minutes, but we were taking multiple hits while she was mostly untouched. Violet showed up and somehow Chang'e sensed her coming, so she took off before she got too badly outnumbered."

"Violet?" asked Bulgado. "Who is Violet?"

Jorge pointed toward the end of the table, and Violet held up one hand in quiet acknowledgement.

"Another witch?" snorted Sergeant Donair. "Are we just handing the cemetery over to them?"

"Mind your tone, Sergeant," warned Simon. "That witch has done more for Dasan's Terrace than you, or me, or anyone else at this table." He glanced at his administrative assistant. "With the possible exception of Dot," he amended.

Dot lowered her head, hiding a sudden blush.

"Now that everyone here is aware of how bad our situation is, we need to start talking about what we can do to fix this problem."

Several people began to talk at once, but none of them could be understood as they each attempted to raise their voices over the others. Teresa Bulgado remained silent but raised her hand to catch Chief Jefferson's attention.

"Quiet," called Simon, banging his knuckles on the table again.

When the room came back under control, he pointed toward Bulgado. "Teresa, what do you want to say?"

"If the demon possessing Chang'e is the problem, then we need to get rid of the demon. I think that means our first priority is figuring out what is necessary to kill it. Has anyone at this table ever faced something like this? Or ever heard of someone else who has?"

The room went still. No one had an answer to the sergeant's question.

"If we can't kill it," Bulgado continued, "then is there any point to this meeting?"

Simon opened his mouth to speak, but paused, unsure what to say.

"We don't have to kill the demon," Mitch interjected into the pause.

All heads turned toward him.

"Another witch?" asked Sergeant Donair, derision clear in her voice.

"Detective Mitch Loman, Dasan's Terrace Police Department," said Mitch, his tone sharper than he had intended. The night shift sergeant was really getting under his skin. "If you don't know the people that work for you, maybe you shouldn't be a sergeant."

"Mitchell," said Dot disapprovingly.

Mitch was immediately ashamed of himself for rising to Donair's bait. More so than if the chief had been the one to call him out on his behavior. He mouthed a quick, "sorry," to Dot, then turned back to Sergeant Donair.

"We don't need to kill the demon," Mitch repeated. "Before we came here, Violet and I were meeting with Professor Solomon Schick, an expert on religious mythology and demonology."

Simon and the other people at the table perked up at his pronouncement. "What did he tell you about the demon?" the chief asked.

"Demons can't survive in our realm," he told the gathered members of the group, then he went on to repeat what he had learned from the professor about demons that had been pulled out of their own world and brought into this one.

When he finished, he summed up his understanding by saying, "The key isn't the demon itself, it's Chang'e. We need to force it to leave its host and return to its own home. Therefore, we need a way to capture Chang'e."

"Or kill her," Violet added.

Mitch sighed unhappily but agreed. "Yes. Or kill her."

"So, how do we do that?" asked Sergeant Ricci. "Aren't we still dealing with the same question: how to kill a demon?"

"No," Mitch told him. "The demon may be too strong for us, but Chang'e herself, her physical body, is still human. She can be captured or killed like anyone else. Once it is forced out of her body, the demon will have to leave our realm and return to its own."

Simon spoke next. "Which means our job, all of us in this room, is to come up with a plan to locate and capture Chang'e. That is ultimately the purpose of this meeting. I am open to hearing anyone with ideas."

"Chang'e summoned the demon in the first place," said Jorge. "Can we do the same thing? Bring it to us?"

"In order to summon a demon, you must first know its true name," Alyssandra responded. "We do not know the demon inhabiting Chang'e's body."

"Professor Schick said something about using magic to summon people," said Mitch, "but that would also require us to know the person's full name. Unfortunately, Chang'e is just a title she uses, so it doesn't help us. If we can figure out what her real name is though, maybe we could use it to bring her to us. That would give us the demon as well. Where the host goes, the demon has to follow."

Mitch saw Alyssandra purse her lips and nod her head in contemplation. She did not say anything, however."

"Okay. If we can't bring her to us, how do we get to her?" asked Simon.

Sergeant Donair said, "When I was a detective and we needed to find a missing person, we started with phone and financial records. These might help us figure out where she's been and where she might be staying. I assume she has a phone, and everyone needs money to eat. I can contact a judge on Monday and get warrants for those records."

"Thank you," said Simon. "Do that. With any luck, we might be able to figure out where she is and go get her before she does any more damage. In the meantime, does anyone have an idea for finding her a little faster? The longer Chang'e is roaming around loose, the more time she has to plan her next attack and build up that army she wants."

"Call her," said Alyssandra. "Call the bitch directly and challenge her to come to us."

Simon peered at Alyssandra, unsure if the old witch was joking or not.

"Do you honestly think that will work?" he asked.

"I have no idea. I know she has a phone. She called you and she called me in the last couple of days. Call the number she contacted you from and demand she come speak with you. Or challenge her to a fight. Or maybe, call her a coward for running away last night. Who knows how this demon will respond? It might agree, it might not."

"What if you just piss it off?" asked Donair. "You could make this whole thing worse."

Alyssandra shrugged. "Worse how? Is the demon more dangerous if it is angry at us, or if it is calm and rational and has the advantage of knowing where we are? It will attack us either way."

Sergeant Donair did not have a response to Alyssandra's logic.

"Perhaps," mused Simon. "If I call, we might get lucky, and this demon will tell us what it has planned. It may want to boast about what it will do next. The worst-case scenario is Chang'e tells us nothing, and we are right back to where we are now. I hate to say it, but I think Alyssandra is right."

Simon removed his phone from his pocket, then scanned through his recent calls list. He found Chang'e's number.

“Okay, then. By a show of hands, who here thinks this is a bad idea?”

CHAPTER 12

The question had been mostly rhetorical, although a couple people in the room seemed uncertain if Simon should make the phone call and voiced their concerns. Simon acknowledged the objections, but with nothing much to lose, he still agreed with Alyssandra. They might learn something by talking to Chang'e, and if not, the worst that would probably happen is that they would be in the exact same position they were already in.

Simon turned on the conference call speakers mounted in the center of the meeting room table. He wanted everyone present today to hear this conversation. Maybe if they heard the witch for themselves, they would understand a little better what they were facing. When the speakers were ready, he allowed them to synchronize with his personal cell phone.

"I'm going to call Chang'e now," Simon announced. "I will do the talking. If anyone here has something relevant to contribute, I ask that you raise your hand before speaking so we don't end up with everyone talking at once. Is that understood?"

Simon gazed around the room. No one appeared to object to the directive, so he took that as agreement.

"Good."

He tapped the number in his call history from when Chang'e had reached out to request a meeting with him in the cemetery. The phone immediately began ringing, the sound of the outgoing call audible to everyone through the conference speakers. The phone rang three times with no response. On the fourth ring, Simon began to wonder if Chang'e had discarded the phone since their last contact. It was also possible the demon recognized the number he was calling from, and it simply did not want to speak with him.

Halfway through the fifth ring, someone answered.

"Yes? Who is this?"

"Chang'e?" asked Simon. "This is Chief Simon Jefferson of the Dasan's Terrace Police Department. Do you remember me?"

"Oh, I remember you, Simon. I remember you very well."

The voice was Chang'e's, and yet it wasn't. Simon recognized the sound of her speech, but Chang'e's normally childlike, nasal tone, and her distracted way of conversing were now gone. The person on the other end of the line spoke low and direct, with obvious malice dripping from every word.

"Have you called to tell me you surrender? You are leaving the cemetery to me?"

"No, sorry," Simon responded, trying to sound confident and in control of the conversation. "I was actually reaching out to see if you were ready to turn yourself in."

The laughter that echoed through the room grated in his ears. He felt a cold chill run up his spine, and he struggled not to let it show to the others at the table.

"Thank you, Simon," Chang'e said when the laughter died away. "I haven't enjoyed anything that amusing in a very long time. Surrender?"

The laughter started again but did not last as long as the second time.

"You can't have Dasan's Terrace," Simon told her. "We are not going to walk away, and you aren't strong enough to take it away from us."

"Of course I am, Simon," Chang'e argued. "It's you that isn't strong enough to stand against me. When I am ready, I will destroy you all and take the cemetery and its magic for myself."

"Now you're the one telling amusing stories," he said, trying to irritate the demon. "You couldn't get away fast enough last night when my officers caught you in the cemetery. And I seem to recall running you out of here all by myself not that long ago."

"I was not prepared for a drawn-out battle last night," the demon growled. All hints of amusement in its voice were gone. "And you and I recall our confrontation very differently. I don't remember being chased. I do remember you running and hiding from me until I got so bored I decided to leave."

"You ambushed me. You made the first attack and were unable to so much as put a scratch on me. Remember it however you like, it doesn't change the fact that you lost."

"I have lost nothing." The demon was angry now.

Simon wanted the creature unsettled. Maybe it would accidentally slip up and reveal something that they could use against it. He had to be careful, however, not to upset it to the point it simply hung up on him.

"Maybe not," Simon agreed. "But I would argue you haven't gained anything yet, either."

"What is your name, demon?" Alyssandra interrupted.

Simon pursed his lips in agitation. No one was supposed to speak without letting him know their intentions first. But of course, Alyssandra would consider herself to be above any such restrictions imposed on the others here in the room. He wanted to say something, to put Alyssandra in her place, but he could not risk letting Chang'e hear any dissent in their ranks. He sat quietly, and let the question go.

"My name?" It responded. "Why would I be so careless as to give you my name?"

"I grow tired of pretending I am still talking with Chang'e. That careless witch is gone. Who are we speaking with? I demand your name."

"Alyssandra Mondari Freid," the demon drawled, demonstrating its advantage over the coven priestess. "I do not care what you demand. My name is none of your concern, as you are well aware. I must admit, however, I did not expect you and Simon to be working together on this. You two so rarely agree on anything. Although, perhaps I should reconsider my surprise at this outcome. You both are very protective of that land and its magic, so, I suppose it only makes sense. Enemy of my enemy, and all that."

Alyssandra looked briefly shaken by the demon's use of her full name. This conversation was veering too far away from the original idea and Simon needed to get it back on track. He jumped in, cutting off whatever reply Alyssandra intended.

"You need to remove both of us if you plan on taking over Dasan's Terrace," he said. "There is nothing surprising about the two of us coming to that same conclusion and choosing to combine resources. The fact that we have is only further proof that you don't have any chance of winning."

"Is that it?" asked Chang'e. "Did you call merely to gloat and preen? You're wasting your time, but I am happy that you think you have the slightest chance of coming out on top. It simply means I will enjoy your defeat so much more when I bring you down."

“Actually, the reason I called was to invite you to meet with us. We can talk about what you want, and what we are willing to give up in order to end this conflict between us.”

“You propose a parlay?” asked the demon, its voice rising in surprise.

“Yes,” agreed Simon. “We meet in a neutral location and try to find a way to end this stalemate.”

“There is no stalemate from my perspective,” said Chang’e. “It is simply a matter of time before I have what I want. Besides, why should I trust you to keep your word? I would be walking into some sort of trap, and we all know it.”

“I trusted you when you wanted to talk.”

“And it was a trap,” laughed Chang’e. “The only difference between you and me is that I know what I would be getting into if I agreed to show up.”

“Forget the parlay, then,” snapped Alyssandra. “You think you hold all the cards, then agree to face us in one last battle. No ambushes. No surprises. You face the Lost Child and his people, as well as me and my coven. You can bring whatever ghouls or creatures you have at your bidding, and we will see, once and for all, who owns this land.”

A low chuckle issued from the conference speakers. Simon felt the hair on top of his head prickle uncomfortably.

“At least your proposal is more honest than Simon’s friendly get together. Thank you for your directness, Alyssandra.”

“Then you accept?”

“No. I don’t,” said Chang’e. “Why would I let you dictate terms to me when I hold all the advantages? That would be foolish.”

“You’re afraid,” insisted Alyssandra. “I knew it. You want to lurk in the shadows, reaching out from the rock you’re hiding under in the hopes of catching one of us unawares. You should tuck your tail between your legs and run for home. It would save you the embarrassment you will face later."

"Careful of your tone, witch priestess. I will tear your heart out and eat it in front of you before you die."

The demon sounded angry, Simon thought. Alyssandra must have really struck a nerve with her last comment.

"Then prove you aren't afraid of us," Alyssandra said, ignoring the threat. "If you do not want us to set the terms, then you do it. You tell us when you wish to face us. You choose where. Or is that still not enough for you? Should I tie my hands behind my back? Wear a blindfold? You don't have to tell me your name, demon. I have already figured it out on my own. Your name is *coward!*"

Chang'e did not respond. The call went quiet except for the sound of her labored breathing over the line. She was furious. Alyssandra's accusation had sounded a painful cord within the demon, and there was no telling how the creature would respond. Simon waited, saying nothing and wondering if the next sound he heard would be the call disconnecting.

Chang'e calmed herself on the other end.

"Well done, Alyssandra," Chang'e said, the angry edge to her voice gone. "You did a wonderful job of getting under my skin, and I applaud you for it. Very well. We can meet, and I will set the terms for that meeting. But first, tell me where you are right now."

"You want to do this here? Right now?" asked Simon.

The possessed witch laughed, sounding as relaxed as when she had first picked up the phone. "No, not at all. It is only idle curiosity. Where are you calling me from?"

"I do not think I will tell you," said Alyssandra.

"Who is the coward now?"

"We are at Dasan's Terrace. In the police department's main conference room," Simon announced.

"Thank you, Simon. You see, Alyssandra? That was not so difficult, was it?"

"What do you want the information for?" asked Alyssandra, still suspicious of the question.

"Nothing really. As I said, it was idle curiosity. But enough foreplay. You wanted me to set terms? Here they are. I will meet both of you, Simon and Alyssandra, and anyone else you wish to bring with you. I will be in Dasan's Terrace on … oh, let's say Wednesday. Is that the eighth? I think it is. I will be there on Wednesday the eighth, at nine o'clock at night. That will be a little after sunset. Do you agree so far?"

Alyssandra nodded tightly, and Simon said, "We agree. Location?"

"I choose the old cemetery. The ancient area you call North-West. I will meet you inside the gates by the northern wall."

"We accept," Simon announced. "Is there anything else?"

"Yes, there is, actually," Chang'e said. "I will meet you there if, and only if, both Alyssandra and Violet Rose are present when I arrive."

Simon paused, unsure how to respond to the stipulation. It seemed obvious to him that both Alyssandra and Violet would be there. Why wouldn't they be? But the way Chang'e had made the request caused him to hesitate.

"We agree," said Alyssandra, "but I do not want to waste my time. Swear that you will also be there, demon, and that before then, you will not take any action against us. Swear it by your name."

"What is your fascination with my name, witch? You do not know it, so what would be the point of making such an assurance?"

"The point is that I do not believe you will show up. I think you are playing a game with us. If you are serious about your promise to meet us, you should have no problem swearing by your name. Otherwise, Chang'e, you can save us all the trouble of this charade and admit to being the coward I know you are."

A soft growl floated out of the speakers. "Damn you, witch. I will kill you last for your insolence."

"Not if you never show up."

"Very well. As you wish. Given that you meet my conditions, I will arrive in Dasan's Terrace on Wednesday this coming week, at nine o'clock that night, again so long as both of you, Alyssandra and Violet Rose, are there to meet me. I swear it on my name."

"And…?" prompted Alyssandra.

"And I will take no direct action against you or your coven, or anyone with the police department until that time. Satisfied?"

"Then we are done. Until Wednesday." Alyssandra pointed at Simon, indicating he should break the connection with Chang'e.

Simon hated letting Alyssandra take control of the situation away from him, but he tapped the red button on his phone as directed and ended the call. It appeared that Alyssandra had achieved exactly what they had hoped when he made the call in the first place, and remaining on the line could only jeopardize that accomplishment.

As soon as the call disconnected, the assembled sergeants all began firing questions at him.

"Are we ready to face her?"

"How are you going to stop her?"

"Is three days enough time?"

"How do we fight a demon?"

The words all blended together, and Simon could not focus on any of them. Instead, he banged his hand on the table to subdue the anarchy.

"We have a date and a time. I suggest we start talking about our game plan next. We need to be prepared to capture or kill Chang'e as soon as she is in the cemetery. We cannot afford a long-term, protracted battle with a demon. We can't win that kind of a fight."

"Don't be stupid."

Simon turned his gaze on Alyssandra. He had endured just about enough of her disrespect.

"Stupid?" he asked. "And what, may I ask, is so stupid about preparing for Chang'e's arrival?"

"Because she isn't coming," Alyssandra said. "She has absolutely no intention of showing up. There is no compelling reason to keep her word."

"She swore on her name," argued Sergeant Donair. "You were the one that went out of the way to make her do that."

"The oath means absolutely nothing if we don't know the demon's name. We need to find that out before we can force the creature to uphold its promise."

"And how do we do that?" asked Sergeant Ricci.

Alyssandra pointed directly at Elizabeth Donair. "You were so good at finding people when you were a detective. Go find the members of Chang'e's coven. At least a few of them will know the name of the demon we are dealing with. I imagine they were present on numerous occasions when it was summoned."

"You don't have the authority to tell me what to do," Sergeant Donair shot back. "Don't treat me like one of your witch underlings. I could have you arrested."

"You could try," Alyssandra responded.

"Stop it. All of you," Simon ordered, bringing silence once more into the room.

He glared at Elizabeth. If she was going to be a burr under his saddle every time a major event occurred, he might have to reconsider his decision to put her in charge of a team. Despite her rank, her inability to control herself and see the bigger picture was clearly a problem.

"Alyssandra is correct. If we can't compel Chang'e to keep her word, everything else we do is pointless. It's time to start planning and dividing up tasks. Mitch is our detective, so I think we should start with him trying to track down the missing coven members."

Bala-Ahl glared at the cellphone in its hand. The human that called itself Alyssandra Freid had hung up without warning. Bala-Ahl was unsure why it was so angry at the dismissal, but it felt the trapped soul of Chang'e seething in outrage at the disrespect, and so, it too was upset. Still, there were matters to attend to, and they must be done quickly. Repayment for the insult would come, but it would have to wait for now.

Dialing a new number, Bala-Ahl raised the phone to its ear and waited for a response.

"Chang'e? What do you want?" answered a female voice on the other end of the call.

"Safia," grunted Bala-Ahl, not bothering to disguise the harsh demonic voice. The witch already knew what she was a part of, and there was no longer any need to hide its control over Chang'e's body. "Violet Rose has not left Alyssandra Freid's side.

This was the sole purpose of sending you here, and you continue to disappoint me."

"I-I'm sorry, Chang'e. I've been trying, but I'm bound by my oath. I can't tell Violet directly what I want her to know."

"Not my problem," Bala-Ahl sneered. "You have one last chance to make this right, or your time as coven leader will end as fast as it began."

Safia swallowed. The sound of her distress was clear to Bala-Ahl even over the phone line.

"What can I do? Tell me."

"Alyssandra and Violet are both at the Dasan's Terrace Police Department at this very moment. Go there immediately. Finish the task I gave you and finish it today."

"Yes. Of c-course. I'll...,"

Bala-Ahl disconnected the call before Safia could finish her sentence. The action made the demon feel a tiny bit better about Alyssandra doing the same thing to it. The creature smiled, stretching the lips on Chang'e's face as far as they could physically go and reveling in the slight pain it caused.

Bala-Ahl searched the phone directory a second time, locating a new number. It tapped the call icon and again waited for a response.

"Yes?" said a woman, speaking softly, almost hesitantly as she answered.

"Hello, Delilah," said Bala-Ahl. This time it spoke using the high, lilting voice of the body it controlled. "I'm so glad you're still okay."

Delilah Dearlove was the oldest member of Chang'e's coven and had been her second in command for most of the past twenty years. She had ordered the other members of the coven to scatter and hide themselves after Chang'e was burned out of her house.

"It's good to hear from you," Delilah responded. "Is everything okay now? Is it safe to go back home?"

"No, dear. Not just yet. You and the others need to stay hidden a little longer, but there is something I need to discuss with you immediately."

"Of course, Chang'e. What do you need?"

"No," said Bala-Ahl. "Not over the phone. We need to speak in person. I don't want to be overheard."

"Should I come to you?" asked Delilah.

"That isn't necessary," Bala-Ahl told her. "Stay where you are, dear. I'll come to you."

The meeting continued for an additional half an hour following the end of Simon's phone call with Chang'e. It was decided that additional officers would not be assigned to the cemetery on Wednesday night. None of the men and women working for Dasan's Terrace had any particular affinity for magic, other than Mitch of course, and the chief decided that they were more likely to end up hurt or killed rather than provide any significant aid in stopping Chang'e.

The sergeants were all dismissed to brief their teams on the outcome of the meeting, and to take any steps they felt necessary to protect their people in case the demon sent any nasty surprises their way. Alyssandra advised that she felt confident the creature would adhere to its promise of not acting directly against the cemetery until Wednesday, but she also thought it was possible it might cause trouble in some indirect manner, and the officers working the next few days should be on their guard.

Jorge elected to stay behind with the chief, Dot, Mitch, Alyssandra, Violet, and Willa. It was his shift that would be affected by the demon's next appearance, and he announced to the assembled group that he would be damned if he wasn't going to be there with his team to fight back. Chief Jefferson had applauded his enthusiasm, if not his common sense, and allowed him to remain.

The discussion that followed was direct and to the point. The primary goal was to determine the demon's name and hold it to the promise it had made to Alyssandra. Simon gave Mitch the task of hunting for the members of Chang'e's coven. If anyone knew the name of the demon, it would be one of her own people. The witches had all gone into hiding after Alyssandra had attempted to kill Chang'e, and since her return, they had not yet made a reappearance. Simon was confident Mitch could locate at least one or two of the missing women in the time frame given.

Next, Jorge was tasked with searching through the property room for any magical items that might be of use to them when facing the demon. Upon hearing this, Mitch immediately raised his hand and asked if he could assist the sergeant.

"No," Simon told him. "Officers are not allowed into the property room, and you know it. Besides, I already gave you an assignment. Stick to that."

Reluctantly, Mitch agreed.

The last assignment was for Alyssandra and her coven. They would be responsible for setting traps in North-West prior to Chang'e's arrival, as well as countering the demon's magic on the night of the confrontation. Simon gave Alyssandra and her people special dispensation to enter the cemetery over the next few days to facilitate their goal.

There was nothing more any of them could do. Everything now hinged on locating the demon's name and forcing it to abide by its oath to show up on Wednesday. Without it, any other preparation was wasted effort. Chief Jefferson concluded the meeting, and the remaining attendees filed out of the conference room and made their way out of the building.

As the group exited the main doors of the police department and stepped out into the front parking lot, Mitch and Violet walked together, heads bowed in discussion as they tried to figure out the best way to hunt down the scattered members of Chang'e's coven.

"I can look for bank activity," Mitch said. "Withdrawals, or credit cards being used might give me a general location of where to look, but that's only if I can get cooperation from the banks without getting a subpoena first. Cell phone records are the same problem. If I have to go through a judge to get them, it might take too long."

"If you know where they lived before they went into hiding, we can search their homes," Violet suggested. "If I can find something personal that belongs to them, I can do a tracing spell to find them, assuming of course they haven't warded against being tracked. Unfortunately, if they really are afraid that Alyssandra was coming after them, they might have done exactly that."

"That would be a good start. I can find the most recent residence for each of them if I have a name and an age to do an internet search. Um…," Mitch hesitated.

"Yes?"

"I don't actually know any of their names," he admitted. "Do you know the members of her coven?"

Violet smiled and gave Mitch a gentle pat on the cheek. "I do," she said. "I know most of their names because Alyssandra feels it's important to know the competition. I'm not as certain of their ages, but I'm sure we can figure it out. Besides, Alyssandra probably knows.... Oh, now what the hell is she doing here?"

Mitch paused at Violet's question and looked up to see what had caught her attention. He spotted the problem immediately.

Standing in the parking lot, leaning against the side of the beat-up green sedan that she had rented upon her arrival in California, was Safia. The woman was wearing sweatpants and a white t-shirt that looked wrinkled and unwashed. Her hair looked similarly unkempt, as if she had hurried out of her hotel room without time to check her appearance first, but the witch waved toward Voilet with a pleasant smile on her face as though she were merely out for a pleasant stroll and had stumbled upon a dear old friend.

"What the hell is she doing here?" Mitch echoed Violet.

"Chang'e," said Violet. "Of course."

"What?"

"Chang'e asked Alyssandra where she was while they were on the phone. Now we know why." Violet pointed at Safia. "She sent her to meet us."

"Why would she do that?"

"I'm not exactly sure, but I have a feeling when I find out, I'm not going to like it much."

Violet took a step toward Safia, but Alyssandra had also spied the New York witch and positioned herself between the two of them.

"What do you want, Safia?" Alyssandra asked. Her voice was low and rough, menace echoing in every word. "I thought we had an understanding."

"We do," the New York coven leader said airily. "When Chang'e is no longer a threat, I can go home. Is Chang'e gone, then?"

Alyssandra glared but said nothing.

Safia nodded, taking confirmation from Alyssandra's wordless response.

"Then you know what I'm doing here," she said. "I'm trying to keep my head firmly attached to my neck."

Safia moved around Alyssandra and approached Mitch and Violet.

"Violet, dear, so good to see you again. Hello, Mitch."

"I'm not in the mood for pleasantries right now, Safai," Violet warned. "You have been running around, chasing after me ever since you got here. When I ask you what you want, you say I should go back to New York with you, then you make vague, shadowy suggestions about Alyssandra and why I should leave her. I wish you would get to the point, or else go home. So, what's it going to be?"

"I can't really do either," Safia admitted. "I'm in a bit of a bind."

"Damn it, Safia! If you have something to say to me, why don't you say it?"

For the first time that Mitch could remember, Safia's composure broke. Her eyes narrowed and she bared her teeth in anger.

"I have been trying very hard not to say it," she blurted. "Don't you get it? I'm not allowed. You have to see it for yourself, but you're being so goddamned stubborn that I can't tell if your stupidity is intentional or not."

"Safia," Alyssandra shouted, trying to get the witch's attention away from Violet.

"If you won't listen, then I have to try something else," Safia said.

The New York witch raised one hand in a fist. "Cut," she said aloud, and released four simultaneous bolts of magic. The spells fled from her hand in four different streaks of red, flying toward Alyssandra, Willa, Violet and Mitch. The other three witches immediately cast defensive conjurations; only Mitch was too slow to recognize the threat in time to defend himself.

The spells Safia launched toward Alyssandra and Willa died out as the two women easily deflected them away. Fortunately for Mitch, Violet erected a field of protective force large enough to cover both of them. He watched Safia's magic blink out of existence as it struck the erected shield. Although he had been too slow to protect himself, Mitch belatedly realized he was under attack and needed to retaliate immediately. He pulled at the surrounding magic and prepared to launch an assault of his own.

"Wait," Violet said, resting a hand on his arm.

"Wait? Why? She just tried to kill us."

"No," Violet told him, staring curiously at Safia. "She didn't. There was no power in that spell. Even if it hit us, it wouldn't have done anything."

Mitch considered this for a moment. He realized Violet was right. The attack launched toward him had been pale and fragile, barely a spell at all. He had enough experience sparring with Violet to know what a feint looked like, and Safia's attack had been little more than a light show compared to a real magical onslaught.

He released the power he had gathered, letting it drift away unused.

"That is all I will tolerate from you," raged Alyssandra. "Leave now, or I promise you, the spell *I* cast will not be simply a warning."

Safia ignored her, keeping her attention instead on Violet.

"Do you understand?" she asked, almost pleading.

"Understand what?" asked Violet, exasperated with the puzzles and riddles and half-statements. "What is there to understand?"

"How did you stop my attack?" Safia begged. "Why did you have time to defend yourself?"

"Because I don't trust you," Violet told her. "And because I'm always on my guard around you."

"Yes!" Safia crowed, excited. "Alyssandra and Willa stopped it, too. How?"

"Because they know better than to let their guard down around you, too."

Safia pointed at Violet in agreement. "Yes, they do. Any witch with any common sense," and Safia took a moment to glance sideways at Mitch, the only one of the four who had not been able to protect himself, "is always ready to defend against hostile magic."

Violet grunted in acknowledgement but still seemed confused. "What is your point, Safia?"

Safia sighed, then took a step toward Violet. Her eyes were cold and direct as she stared at the younger witch.

"The three women that killed your family, they knew who Alyssandra was. You said they spoke her name."

"Yes. So what? Witches know each other. That's nothing remarkable."

"Safia," Alyssandra hissed, the fury clear in the sound of her voice. "Stop this now."

Safia ignored her.

"Alyssandra killed all three of them with one spell. Is that right?"

"Yes. What the fuck do you want Safia? Spit it out."

"Were those three witches stupid, incompetent, or…?"

Violet froze. Mitch wanted to ask her what was wrong, but he understood there were times to butt in, and there were times to stay silent and mind your own business. This was one of those moments he needed to stay quiet.

"Or did they trust her?" Violet whispered. "They didn't try to defend themselves because they didn't expect an attack."

"Violet," Alyssandra said, speaking quickly. "Don't listen to her. She's trying to confuse you and drive us apart."

"Did you?" Violet asked.

"Did I…?" said Alyssandra.

"Did you kill my family?"

"No! Absolutely not. You know I didn't. You were there."

Violet nodded, then rephrased her question. "No, you didn't kill them. I saw who killed them. I'm asking you, Alyssandra, when you saw the three witches come into my house, did you know that they were going to murder my family? Did you know they would kill everybody in the house, and did you wait outside until they were done slaughtering everyone I cared about?"

Alyssandra stared at Violet, visibly urging the girl to trust her. Her face was calm and stoic. "Violet," she said softly. "I had no way of knowing they would hurt your family. If I knew they planned to kill your parents, I would have stopped it."

Violet turned her head so she could be heard by the people behind her.

"Dot?"

It was Alyssandra's turn to freeze. She knew what was about to happen. Mitch did, too, and turned to look toward Dot and the chief.

"Yes, Violet?" asked Dot. There was no curiosity in her question, only resolution.

"Is Alyssandra telling me the truth?"

The chief's assistant was an empath, an aura reader, and no lie could ever slip past her undetected. Mitch had seen her abilities displayed in the past, and he had never known her to be wrong.

Dot gave one small shake of her head. "No. She's not."

A white brilliance blossomed around Violet, clearly visible to Mitch even in the bright light of midday. Swirls of magic coalesced around the woman that he loved, quickly taking shape into something fearsome and terrible. Mitch knew that what came next would not be a mere warning, easily blocked or parried.

What came next was that someone was about to die.

CHAPTER 13

Magic flared bright around Violet, reflecting the rage emanating from her broken heart. Alyssandra, the person who had been resolutely in her corner since the death of Violet's family, the person who had been by her side, supporting and protecting her for the past twelve years, was also the reason her parents, her boyfriend, and her brothers had died.

Mitch saw the power explode from her, and he took an involuntary step backward. Everyone else in the parking lot did as well, except for Jorge and Dot, the only people present unable to see the hostile magics emanating from Violet. The two non-magic users glanced around at the others' reactions and tensed, understanding that something important was happening, even if they could not see it.

Red and blue waves of power flashed from Violet hands toward Alyssandra. Mitch could feel the heat of the spell even from his position standing behind Violet. With the amount of magic pouring from her, he fully expected Alyssandra to be immolated in the blast, but he greatly underestimated the power of the old witch. Alyssandra stood her ground, seemingly unphased. A glittering dome of air closed around her, taking the brunt of the magically fueled flame and leaving her untouched.

"Violet," said Alyssandra, trying to keep her voice calm.

Violet did not listen, instead she released another bolt of intense power, followed in quick succession by two more.

Out of the corner of his eye, Mitch saw Safia dart behind her car and duck down behind the passenger side fender. From her position of relative safety, her head appeared over the top of the hood as she peered at the pyrotechnics her words had initiated. Apparently, her work was done, and now she only needed to sit back and observe the outcome of the battle. Anger boiled inside Mitch, and he wanted to run over to Safia and beat her senseless with his bare hands. She had caused this confrontation intentionally. This had been her plan all along.

He resisted the urge.

At least she was staying out of the fight. Keeping her a passive observer for the moment was probably for the best.

Someone else, however, chose that moment to join the mele. A burst of orange magic erupted around Violet. What the spell was meant to do, Mitch had no idea as Violet was able to easily diffuse it while continuing to launch her own assault against Alyssandra.

Mitch searched the parking lot for the source of the new magic and saw Willa drawing power around her in preparation for a second strike on Violet. Mitch did not wait for her to finish. He reached out with a trickle of his own magic, touching the growing spell in Willa's hands.

Repeating the technique he had so recently used against Chang'e, Mitch detonated Willa's spell before she could finish forming it. It was easy, almost too easy. When he had practiced the trick against Violet, he had struggled to pull her magic apart. He had experienced the same difficulty when battling Chang'e in the cemetery. Willa's magic, however, detonated as easily as touching a match to gunpowder.

As her spell exploded in her face, Willa reeled backward, falling to the ground. Watching her spill onto the parking lot pavement, Mitch realized something for the first time. He could feel Willa's strength when he touched her magic. The moment his own spell came in contact with hers, he understood instinctually that she was not as strong as he was. In fact, Mitch was more powerful than Willa by several magnitudes.

Violet had told him that many times, but he had never believed her. Every time they mock battled, she beat him almost without trying. The depressingly regular defeats had left him feeling amateurish and weak, but as he discovered how easy it was to disrupt Willa's magic, he at last understood the hierarchy of witches, and even a little bit about where in that hierarchy he stood.

For months Mitch had been training with Violet, one of the most powerful witches on the west coast, perhaps in all of the country. Of course he had seemed weak in comparison to her. Facing a lower-level witch in Alyssandra's coven made Mitch see exactly how fast he had progressed. He still needed time and practice to build his skill levels before he could ever hope to match Violet, but in a simple confrontation of pure strength, he did not need much skill to deal with Willa.

The shorter witch was trying to climb back to her feet, her dark eyes narrowed as she gazed in shock in Mitch's direction. She had not expected him to interfere, or at least, not quite so effectively.

Mitch wasted no time and sent an impact spell in her direction. He hoped to knock her out of this fight quickly so he could focus on helping Violet. Willa was dazed but still managed to put up a shield fast enough to deflect Mitch's initial attack.

Mitch responded by sending a second, similar spell, this time taking an extra second or two to increase the strength of the assault.

The resulting explosion obliterated Willa's shield and sent her rolling along the asphalt like a limp rag carried helplessly in a hard wind. Mitch grimaced, hoping he had not injured her too badly, but he did not have time to go check on her.

He turned his attention back to Violet and Alyssandra. Alyssandra had given up on trying to reason with her protégé and was hurling magical attacks in response to each of Violet's spells. Neither woman seemed able to pierce the protections of the other, and the deadly bolts of magic continued to flare, gutter, and die out as they met the opposing shields.

Mitch considered trying to speak to Violet but gave up before opening his mouth. There was no hope of discussion or resolution in this battle. The lines of warfare had been clearly drawn, and this confrontation would not end until one opponent lay broken and defeated at the feet of the other. There was no changing Violet's mind. All he could do now was support her.

Pulling as much power from the surrounding magic as he could hold, he shaped it into an explosive force and launched it at Alyssandra. The spell he directed at the coven leader was twice as powerful as the one that had leveled Willa, and it struck Alyssandra in the chest with perfect precision.

Instead of a blinding explosion and an end to the fight, Mitch's spell was snuffed out before it could detonate. Alyssandra continued trading blows with Violet, completely ignoring Mitch's attempt to get involved. It was as if he was not even there. He was so insignificant that he had not gotten so much as a glance of acknowledgement from Alyssandra.

In an instant, Mitch went from feeling strong and powerful right back to fully understanding how weak he truly was in this melee. As far above Willa as he might be in magical status, he was probably equally that much below these two battling titans.

Still, he did not give up. It was not in his nature to stand by and wait for an outcome to occur. He needed to be involved. He needed to help Violet.

He needed to *protect* Violet.

Mitch ducked and ran through the parking lot, approaching Alyssandra from the side. He sent multiple impact and fire spells at her, but they did no damage to her or her protective barriers, and she continued to ignore his existence.

Magic attacks and defensive spells flared and died, flared and died. The two combatants were so preoccupied with each other it was as if the outside world had simply disappeared. As he moved closer to Alyssandra, Mitch did a quick check of his own surroundings. Willa remained down for the count, and Safia crouched behind her car, content to continue observing rather than get involved. Simon, Jorge, and Dot had moved to a, hopefully, safe distance away to wait for this clash of magical giants to conclude.

Mitch reached Alyssandra, close enough now to feel the peripheral heat and percussive force of Violet's spells as they connected with her coven leader's defenses. He could not afford to waste magic or time erecting shields to protect himself from the unintended backlash of the spells' detonations. Violet and Alyssandra had the experience and ability to launch powerful aggressive attacks while simultaneously maintaining defensive shielding, but Mitch did not. He only knew how to cast one spell at a time. Mitch envied their skill, and he figured these were abilities that he should attempt to learn at some point in the future.

That was assuming he survived the next sixty seconds.

Alyssandra's shield was too strong to break by normal magical means. Mitch knew that. He had thrown everything he had at it, and Alyssandra had not so much as noticed he was there. Violet's defenses were at least as strong, perhaps stronger than Alyssandra's, and that's what gave Mitch hope.

He remembered, many weeks ago in the cemetery, when Violet had broken down and closed herself off from the world, figuratively and literally. Her magical defenses had seemed impenetrable at the time, but through sheer desperation and will he had managed to push through the seemingly impassible barrier. At the time, he did not know how he had done it, he simply had. Necessity dictated that he must get through to her, and he had done exactly that. Failure simply had not been an option.

He knew he had to do the same thing again today.

Drawing power to himself, Mitch gathered and shaped the spell around his right hand. He condensed it, forming a small ball of force that hovered over his knuckles. He focused on making the bead of magic as dense as possible, then he drew in more magic to add to it. Several times he added to the collected power, then compressed it back to a sphere no larger than a marble.

Mitch was sweating, and some of the hair on the left side of his head had been singed by stray fire, but he did not move away. He also did not hesitate when his spell was ready. As the tiny bead of magic glowed above his fist, he stepped to within four feet of Alyssandra. This time, appearing so close to her, she could not help but take notice of him. Her eyes shifted in Mitch's direction, glanced at the magic he wielded, then turned back to face Violet. The dismissive sneer on Alyssandra's face told Mitch what she thought of his interference.

"Pierce," Mitch muttered, shaping the spell one last time in his mind.

He slammed his fist into Alyssandra's defensive shielding, striking the wall of magic in front of him like he was slugging a boxer's heavy punching bag.

The pellet of force broke through her magical barrier. The impact did not dismantle her defensive spell, but the penetration by Mitch's magic created the slightest disruption to her shield which he immediately capitalized on.

"Expand!"

The tiny ball of magic widened, not a lot, and not quickly, but it did grow, increasing the area of failing magic until it was barely large enough to let Mitch's hand through. He thrust his arm into the hole all the way to his shoulder and felt his fingers brush the flowing material of Alyssandra's dress.

Mitch grabbed the witch's clothing and jerked her towards himself, at the same time putting more effort into holding open the hole he had created.

"What…?" Alyssandra cried out, pulled off balance.

"Break!" shouted Mitch, attempting to smash the shield completely.

Alyssandra's defenses held against his onslaught, but he had at least succeeded in gaining her full attention this time. Mitch felt her magic coalescing as she prepared to blow him into tiny pieces. He did not have time to protect himself. First, he would need to release the energy he was already manipulating to hold Alyssandra's shield open, and if he did that, he would most likely lose his arm.

Mitch released Alyssandra's dress and jerked his arm back through the opening he had created. Alyssandra raised her hand, her newest spell glowing in her palm, ready to release. There was no time to put up a shield. There was no time to dodge.

There was no time.

Alyssandra screamed. The magical energies in her hand and all around her erupted, scattering in the wind like tiny shards from a shattered mirror. The force of the explosion lifted the coven leader off her feet, tossing her mercilessly onto the hard asphalt of the parking lot.

Violet had attacked while Alyssandra was distracted by Mitch. The woman's inattention, along with the damage Mitch had done to her magical defenses had left her vulnerable to Violet's attempts to overwhelm her.

Although Alyssandra's defenses had protected her from the worst of the magical attack, the priestess was still an old woman, and her frail body was not capable of absorbing a great deal of direct physical punishment. The initial impact and shock of striking the hard asphalt had hurt her.

Alyssandra groaned where she lay on the ground and raised one hand toward Violet. She was either trying to put up a new shield, or cast an attack, but neither actually happened. Mitch realized she was too injured to focus her magic effectively.

Violet did not waste time trying to assess Alyssandra's condition. She threw another bolt of fire, intending to destroy the old woman once and for all. Without stopping to think or consider the consequences of his actions, Mitch stepped in front of Alyssandra and raised his own shields. Violet's spell struck his barrier, burning hot and bright, and for a moment he thought it might break through. Mitch pushed more magic into his defenses and managed, at last, to defuse the attack.

Violet was not playing games. That spell had been meant to kill Alyssandra, and Mitch had barely been able to stop it. He knew the next one she sent would be stronger than anything he could defend against.

Fortunately, Violet did not attack again. Although the look she gave him almost made Mitch wish she had simply killed him and Alyssandra both.

It was not anger Mitch saw on Violet's face. She was shocked and in pain, and her cheeks were wet with tears. She had been crying during the battle, mourning her family and feeling her heart break into pieces even as she tried to kill the woman she had thought of as a surrogate mother for the past twelve years. But now, instead of directing that pain at Alyssandra, all of the hurt, bitterness, and betrayal was redirected toward Mitch.

"Mitch? Why…?" she asked. Her voice cracked, and she had to swallow heavily before speaking again. "Why are you protecting her?"

"I'm not protecting her," he said, pleading for her to understand. "I'm trying to protect *you.*"

"She killed my family," Violet told him, as if he didn't realize what Alyssandra had done.

"I know," Mitch said. "And she is going to pay for that. I promise."

"She…," Violet's voice broke again. "She has to die. I … I need her to die."

"You can't kill her," Mitch begged. "Please. If you kill her, you will never forgive yourself. It will break you. I know it will, and I can't let that happen."

Violet hesitated. Mitch knew what she was thinking. He had seen into her soul, and he knew without question what she would say next.

Violet sniffed, wiped at the tears on her face with her fingers, and straightened her shoulders.

"She killed my family. She destroyed everything and everyone I loved. She has to pay for that."

Alyssandra tried to say something, but Mitch quickly stepped behind her, placed a foot on her back and pushed her flat to the ground. She cried out in pain as he shifted his weight onto her, crushing her chest against the pavement.

"Quiet," he ordered. "We're all done listening to you."

Mitch reached to the back of his waistband and lifted the tail of his shirt. He removed his off-duty weapon from the leather holster secured in the small of his back and aimed the 40-caliber pistol at the back of Alyssandra's head.

"Okay," he said to Violet. "If you want her dead, say the word. I'll kill her."

"Mitch." This time the voice belonged to Simon. He had almost forgotten anyone else was in the parking lot with them. Mitch glanced up from Alyssandra and saw his chief take a step toward him. "What are you doing?"

"Stay there, Simon," Mitch told him. "When this is over, you can arrest me. I won't fight you. But right now, don't get in the way."

Mitch saw Dot lean toward Simon and whisper something. The chief nodded, frustration painting his face. "I know. I know," he barked, but he did not attempt to speak with Mitch again.

Mitch turned his attention back to Violet. "Should I end this?" he asked softly.

"What are you doing?" Violet asked, echoing Simon's question.

"I'm trying to give you what you need," he explained. "If you kill her, even though she deserves it, you will never forgive yourself for murdering the woman who took care of you all these years."

"She lied to me," Violet cried, her hands balled into fists. "For twelve years she looked me in the eyes every day and lied to me."

"I know. But she was also there for you. Whatever reasons you have for wanting her dead, you will still hate yourself if you're the one that does it."

"So, I should let her live? Forgive her, just like that?" asked Violet. Her voice had gone flat and cold.

"No. That's not what I'm saying. I'm saying if you want her dead, I will do it for you. That way, you can hate me, but you'll be able to live with yourself. I am willing to carry this for you so you never have to."

"Mitch...," Violet started speaking, but stopped, uncertain how to continue.

Mitch pulled the hammer back on the pistol.

"This isn't an ultimatum," Mitch told her. "I'm not trying to trick you. I will give you whatever you want. Say the word and I will put a bullet in her head. Or, if you think you can find a way to move on, I will let Simon arrest her and put her in prison for the rest of her life. She isn't getting away with anything. I promise. Tell me what you want me to do."

Violet stood silent for several long moments, considering what she wanted. At last, she dropped to her knees and began to cry. She covered her face with her hands and moaned.

"Mitch," she whimpered. "I can't kill her. I can't let her go. I don't know what to do."

Mitch waited, his gun still pointed at Alyssandra's head. His aim never wavered.

"I can't lose you, too," Violet sobbed.

"You will never lose me," he said.

"Promise me."

Mitch slipped the gun back into the holster at his waist. He rushed to kneel beside Violet and wrapped his arms around her.

"I promise. I will always be on your side. You can count on that."

As Violet cried into his shoulder, Mitch took a moment to point at Jorge and then gesture toward Alyssandra. Simon and

Jorge understood his meaning and hurried to take Alyssandra into custody. Simon removed from his pocket the handcuffs he had tried to use on Chang'e and secured the stunned witch's hands behind her back.

To his relief, Mitch noticed that Willa was once again on her feet and did not appear to be too badly injured from her run in with him.

He squeezed Violet tighter.

"I know you feel lost right now. But I might have to go away for a while."

Violet clutched at his shirt desperately. "Why? Where are you going?" she asked. Mitch could see panic in her eyes.

"I, um, threatened my chief, and told him I was going to kill someone. I think I might be in a little bit of trouble for that."

"He can't touch you," Violet hissed, anger and fear giving her new strength. She straightened and peered around the parking lot for any new threats. "I won't let him."

"Nobody is touching anyone," said a soft voice nearby. Mitch glanced up to find Dot standing over him. "The way I see it, you did something that no one else here could have done. You protected Violet and arrested someone for a crime that New York PD left unsolved for the last twelve years. And nobody got hurt. Heck, I think Simon should give you a medal."

"You sure?" Mitch asked.

Dot nodded. "Mm-hmm. Don't you think so, Simon?"

"Sure," the chief agreed. "I mean the protecting Violet and making the arrest part," he amended. "You aren't getting a medal."

Jorge and Simon took Alyssandra into custody and transported her to a holding facility in Rancho Cordova. The facility had been designed and modified years ago to hold supernatural entities, so Alyssandra would be detained safely and securely within those walls until arrangements could be made to transfer her back to New York.

Mitch and Violet did not remain at the cemetery. Before Alyssandra was even out of the Dasan's Terrace parking lot, Mitch had Violet in his car and was leaving the scene of the confrontation.

Safia made one last attempt to speak with Violet, but a look from Mitch sent her scurrying in the opposite direction, suddenly recalling somewhere else that she urgently needed to be. He was in no mood to let her come within ten feet of Violet, and Safia was not stupid enough to miss the murderous glower on his face when she tried to get too close.

Mitch drove Violet to her home. He sat her on the couch in her living room and wrapped a blanket around her, then, when she was settled and comfortable, he searched through the cupboards in the kitchen until he found teabags and a mug. The tea kettle was already full, and he clicked the stove burner underneath it to the on position. A few minutes later, he joined Violet on the couch, and the two sat peacefully while she sipped absently at the hot beverage in her cup.

They did not speak for a long time. There was little that needed saying. Mitch understood the emotional pain that Violet was suffering, and he knew asking questions would not make her feel any better. When she was ready to talk, she would. It was as simple as that. For now, he sat beside his exhausted girlfriend, letting her know that he was with her, both physically and emotionally.

"Thank you," Violet said after almost half an hour had gone by.

"Of course. I thought you would like the tea."

"Not the tea," she said, a tiny smile flickering on her face at his deliberate misunderstanding. "For … everything."

"Of course," he said again. He laid a hand over one of hers. "Anything you need, all you have to do is ask."

"What will you do now?"

Mitch paused, unsure what Violet meant by the question.

"Nothing. I'm staying with you tonight. I'll sleep on the couch if that's what you want, but I'm not going anywhere."

Violet shook her head. Her blond hair hung over her eyes, hiding the upper half of her face.

"No. Not tonight. What will you do about Chang'e?"

"Chang'e?" asked Mitch. He had not given Chang'e a second thought since Violet's attack on Alyssandra in the cemetery parking lot. Other matters had become more pressing than the possessed witch and her attempts to take over Dasan's Terrace.

"I'm not doing anything about Chang'e right now. When the time comes, I'll face her, but my focus today is you. You are more important to me than some demon that may or may not show up again."

"It will show up," Violet said. "And it will attack the cemetery, and the officers there. Your friends."

"Like I said. I'll deal with that when I have to."

"What if you didn't have to deal with it" Violet asked him. "Could you walk away? Leave everyone else to fight Chang'e alone?"

"What are you asking me, Violet?"

"I can't stay here," she said, setting her tea mug on the low table in front of the couch. She pulled the blankets tighter around herself despite the fact that the room was not even remotely chilly. “I’m leaving Sacramento as soon as I can sell the house and arrange the financials to move.”

“Are … are you moving back to New York?”

Violet shook her head, vehemently. “No. I don’t know if Safia was in on the plan to kill my family, but she knew about it and kept it from me. I don’t want anything to do with her or Alyssandra ever again. I need to find someplace that isn’t California and isn’t New York. I don’t know where yet, but I need to get out of here.”

Violet glanced toward Mitch, peering at him from behind the curtain of hair in her face.

“Will you come with me?”

“I will,” said Mitch without hesitation. He spoke the words like he was agreeing to make more tea; without emphasis and without any doubt that he would do whatever she asked.

Violet curled up against him, pressing her head to his chest. She let out a small breath, releasing the internal tension she had bottled up before she knew what his answer might be.

“Thank you,” she whispered.

He wrapped an arm around her shoulders and held her close.

“Tomorrow, we’ll go to Chief Jefferson and let him know that I’m resigning,” Mitch told her. “Tonight, though, the only thing I care about is being right here with you.”

CHAPTER 14

Mitch and Violet strode into the administrative reception area the next morning a few minutes after eight o'clock. Mitch knew that Simon was usually at his desk at this time, but even if he wasn't, Dot would certainly be there. The diminutive assistant arrived at work each morning by seven-thirty without fail.

As expected, Dot was at her desk, opening emails on her computer and prioritizing tasks for her workday. She glanced up as Mitch and Violet entered and greeted them happily.

"Hi, guys," she beamed. Her expression became more somber as she asked, "Violet, how are you feeling?"

Dot was the smallest and youngest person in the room, and yet she always managed to take on the concerned parent role whenever anyone needed it. Perhaps as an empath, she was simply a natural nurturer. Regardless of how she did it, Mitch found her presence comforting. So apparently did Violet.

Violet walked around the desk, and Dot rose to meet her. She threw her arms around the younger woman, and the two held the embrace for several long seconds.

When Violet at last pulled away, Dot commented, "That felt like a goodbye. I hope I'm wrong about that." The welcoming smile was completely gone from her face, replaced with a look of concern.

Violet's lips curled up in sad acknowledgement.

"You're not wrong, Dot, and you know it. You're never wrong."

"I don't know what to say, Violet. I understand yesterday was simply awful, but it doesn't mean you don't still belong here. Me and Simon aren't upset at you, and Mitch still works here, so you can come see him anytime you like."

"No, Dot. You don't understand. I'm not just leaving Dasan's Terrace. I'm leaving California. And as for Mitch, he's agreed to come with me."

Dot's eyes grew wide, and Mitch could have sworn he saw a hint of sheer panic in her expression. She blinked several times, attempting to pull her emotions under control, then she snatched at the phone on her desk, fumbling the handset briefly. Mitch had never seen her this unsettled, and it worried him. After pressing a button, she spoke.

"Simon? Can you please step out here? We have a problem and you really need to be here."

"Dot? Are you okay?" Mitch asked.

"Are you really leaving with Violet?" Dot asked him. "Is that why you came here today? To quit?"

"I…. Well, yes. I came here with Violet to let you and the chief know that we're leaving. I'm not sure exactly when, but…,"

"What's the problem, Dot? Oh, hello, Mitch. Violet." Simon exited his office, joining Dot where she stood beside her desk. "Is everything all right?"

"Everything is fine, Chief," Mitch said. "Violet and I only came in this morning to let you know that I'm resigning from

Dasan's Terrace. She wants to leave the state, and I promised to go with her."

Simon's face turned serious. "I'm very sorry to hear that. I would really hate to lose you, Mitch. Either of you, actually," he amended, looking toward Violet. "Are your minds made up?"

"They are," Mitch said.

"Then, I wish you the best. Wherever you end up…,"

"Simon," Dot interrupted. She placed a hand on his arm and pulled at his coat sleeve. "They can't go. Mitchell and Violet, they're the ravens. They're the two ravens. They have to stay."

"Ravens?" Simon asked, momentarily confused. Then his eyes widened, exactly as Dot's had done moments before. "Ravens! Are you certain? There's no mistake?"

Dot grasped the chief's sleeve tighter. "No. No mistake. I'm sure of it."

"Ravens?" asked Violet, sounding as lost as Mitch felt. "What ravens are you two talking about?"

Dot glanced toward Simon and the chief nodded at her, indicating she should speak freely.

"Mitchell, you know that I see auras and can read people's emotions."

"I do," he said.

"What you may not know, though, is that I also have dreams, or maybe visions would be more accurate."

"You see the future," said Violet matter-of-factly. She clearly knew more about Dot than Mitch did. Just as she knew more about Simon, and probably more about everything to do with Dasan's Terrace than he did.

"Yes, but it's never that simple. The visions aren't direct images of the future. They are more like suggestive representations of people and events. I don't always understand what they mean until after something has happened, so they aren't always exactly helpful."

"You've recently had one of these dreams?" asked Violet.

"I have," Dot agreed.

"And it has something to do with me and Mitch." This time, Violet was not asking a question.

Dot spoke quickly, trying to get the explanation out of her head as fast as she could put the words together.

"I've had the same dream every night for a week. I'm positive it means something. There are three ravens. One, a red-eyed raven, has to be Chang'e. I've been certain of that since yesterday. The other two must be you and Mitch. Yesterday, I thought they might be you and Alyssandra for a while, especially after the phone call when Chang'e said she wanted you together in the cemetery on Wednesday. But when the ravens left, they flew off in the same direction rather than separating, so that had to mean they were leaving together. That means that it's you two, not Alyssandra."

"Hold on, Dot. Wait a minute," Mitch interrupted. "You completely lost me. Ravens leaving? What are you talking about?"

Dot took a few breaths and tried again to organize her thoughts. "Sorry. Simon and I have been working on this for a week, but it's the first time you guys have heard this. Let me start from the beginning. Last week, I had a dream…,"

Dot explained her premonition to Violet and Mitch as she had to Simon so many days ago. She did not leave anything out or try to abbreviate any of the elements. She needed them to understand how important they were to the future of Dasan's Terrace. When she finished with her vision, she explained what she believed each element meant as best she understood them. Mitch and Violet listened quietly until she was finished.

"So, the red-eyed raven is Chang'e," Mitch repeated.

"Yes. The red eyes indicate something inside the raven is different from the others. When we found out that Chang'e was possessed by a demon she had summoned, I realized the connection."

"The other two ravens are me and Violet? How do you know it isn't Violet and Alyssandra, like you thought before?"

"I originally thought it was Violet and Alyssandra because they are the strongest witches in the cemetery, but when Violet and Alyssandra ... um, had their disagreement, I remembered that when the ravens left, they both flew off in the same direction. That would not have been true if one had been Alyssandra. They should have gone in separate directions."

"But because they went in the same direction, you realized this morning that the second raven was me."

Dot nodded. "I believe so. Nothing is one hundred percent certain in my visions, but I am almost positive that if you and Violet leave Dasan's Terrace, something terrible is going to happen to the cemetery and all the people connected to it."

"I don't owe anything to Dead Town," said Violet.

"No, you don't," agreed Simon.

"It's unfair of you to ask me to stay."

The chief said nothing, but his silence was admission enough. It was unfair of them to make the request, but still they were asking her to help.

Violet remained quiet for a long moment, thinking. Finally, she turned to Mitch.

"And what about you? What do you want to do?"

Mitch knew this question was much more important than it seemed. She had asked it simply, almost casually, but his answer would be critical in determining how Violet responded next. The query was a land mine hidden beneath flowers. Violet was not asking for his opinion but rather gauging his allegiance. Was his dedication to Dead Town greater than his commitment to her? Could she rely on him to always support her when she needed it?

He weighed his words carefully before speaking. Violet was one of the strongest people he had ever met. In magical prowess, yes, but also emotionally. She had survived personal adversity that would leave most others broken and defeated, and she had come back from it with more heart and courage than most people ever started with. Despite that immense strength, Violet was also fragile. She was a diamond, capable of withstanding immense pressure, yet one well-placed strike could shatter her into a thousand pieces, leaving her forever unable to reassemble her remaining humanity.

Mitch did not want to be that final strike. He loved Violet, and he desperately wanted to support her in all things. He also knew he needed to be completely honest with her, or his support would ultimately mean nothing.

"I want to stay and fight for Dasan's Terrace," he said. "I care about the people here, and I don't know if I could ever forgive myself if my leaving is the reason they get hurt or killed. I also know that my feelings aren't what's important right now. Yours are. I won't force you to stay, and I will never let you leave on your own."

Mitch took one of Violet's hands in both of his own. "Say the word, and we'll both leave right now and never look back."

"What about Dead Town?" asked Violet.

"If it's the only way I can be with you, let it burn."

Violet nodded, then, as if laying her last card on the table in the highest stakes poker game of her life, she whispered, "And Denny?"

Mitch's throat grew tight, and his heart suddenly felt as if it were being crushed in his chest. The lost spirit of his son was trapped here in Dead Town. He had not forgotten about Denny, even now, but hearing his son's name touched a wound so deep inside of him, so much a part of him, that he feared it might never heal. Mitch had promised Denny he would find a way to free his soul from its imprisonment here, and Violet knew how important that promise was to him.

"I will save my son," he told her. "I will figure out how to free him from whatever is keeping him trapped here, but I don't have to work for Dasan's Terrace to do that. I can be there for you and keep my promise to Denny at the same time."

Mitch looked into Violet's clear blue eyes, holding her gaze. He needed her to understand how serious he was, that he was ready to do anything to stay in her life. He raised his voice loud enough to be heard clearly by everyone in the room and said, "Dot? Tell me, am I lying?"

Mitch did not look away from Violet's face, so he saw the tear that rolled down her cheek when Dot said, "No, Mitchell. You aren't lying."

Violet quickly wiped away the unwanted tear, composing herself despite the emotional turmoil Mitch knew was churning inside of her. He waited for her to speak, to announce the path they would take from this day forward. Simon and Dot similarly remained silent as they waited for Violet to pronounce the fate of Dasan's Terrace.

"As long as I have you, I think I can withstand anything," Violet told Mitch. "You are the only reason I am still standing today. You stepped in to protect me from Alyssandra, and you took care of me afterward when my entire world collapsed around me. How could I abandon the people who brought you to me?"

Violet paused long enough to sniff and wipe away another errant tear. When she was ready, she turned to face Simon. "We will stay until Chang'e is dealt with. After that, I can't promise anything. We'll have to see what things look like."

Mitch put his arms around Violet, and she hugged him back. Over her shoulder, Mitch saw Dot furtively wiping at her face. Apparently, Violet was not the only one that did not want to be seen crying.

When they released their embrace, Dot hurried over and hugged Violet as well.

"I didn't like the goodbye hug," she announced, "so, I need another one. Thank you for staying," she whispered in Violet's ear.

"Now that we still have a chance," said Simon to Mitch while the two women were occupied, "you need to find us a name for that demon."

"I know," said Mitch soberly. "We've already lost a day we couldn't afford to lose. I only have a couple days left, but I think I know someone that can help me with the search for Chang'e's old coven members."

"Whatever you need to do, I suggest you do it soon. If we don't force Chang'e to show up on Wednesday, we've lost our only chance at preventing a future ambush attack."

"Hey there, Sergeant Minhas. I'm surprised you still have time to answer the calls of a lowly detective like myself."

"Careful, Mitch. You're going to jinx this promotion. I haven't even taken the written test yet."

"I have faith. Besides, how can the department not promote the guy that solved a thirty-year-old homicide against one of their own lieutenants?"

Detective Ali Minhas worked for the Sacramento Sheriff's Office in their homicide bureau, and he had helped Mitch with a few big investigations since Mitch had moved to Dasan's Terrace. In repayment for those favors, as well as for a few more personal reasons, Mitch had handed off an arrest recently that was beginning to draw all kinds of positive attention to Ali from the men and women higher up on the food chain.

Mitch was perfectly content where he was and did not resent Ali's sudden push into the spotlight. In fact, Mitch was happy he had been able to do something to relieve a little of the guilt he felt for not being able to share all the details with Ali of the kinds of cases he worked for Dead Town.

"Solved?" asked Ali. "I seem to recall somebody else solved it and dropped the suspect in my lap at the last second."

"Doesn't matter how it happened," Mitch said. "What matters is the right guy got the arrest."

"Okay, so are you done lubing me up? Is it time to push it in now?"

Mitch laughed. "Why, Ali, I have no idea what you're talking about."

"If you were going to ask me out for a beer, you would have done it already. This is starting to sound like one of those 'Ali, I need something,' phone calls," Ali said, though Mitch could hear the amusement in his voice.

"Yeah, you got me. I do need a favor."

"I don't have a lot of free time right now," Ali responded. "Is this something easy, or am I going to have to push a couple other cases to the back burner? I know I owe you one, but I really am slammed right now."

"I'm hoping it isn't going to take too much of your time. In fact, I only have two and a half days before everything I'm doing becomes moot. So, for good or bad, by Wednesday it'll all be over. Besides, you don't owe me anything. Delaney's homicide investigation barely makes us even in my book, so now I'll owe you one again."

"Well, I do like the way you pay back your debts. What do you need?"

Mitch hesitated. What he needed was simple, but explaining why he needed to find eight witches was a little more complicated, especially since Ali would either think he was getting punked, or that Mitch had completely lost his mind. Mitch did not want to lie to Ali, but it was necessary to keep some details to himself.

The best lies, however, are the ones that include as much of the truth as possible, so Mitch did his best to be as honest with his friend as he could.

"I'm looking for eight women who have gone into hiding. I don't have time to wait for warrants to come through on phone and banking records, so I'm brute forcing this thing. I'm looking at any registered addresses, phone numbers, and family members I can find online or in our records."

"Playing gumshoe, huh?" asked Ali.

"Pretty much."

"Why are they in hiding, what do you need them for, and why the time limit?"

Mitch smiled to himself. Ali did not pull any punches. He got right to the heart of the matter, as any good detective should.

"I'm trying to find a witch priestess," Mitch said, then waited for Ali to digest the statement.

"Um, do you want to say that again?" Ali responded after a long, uncomfortable silence.

"I am trying to find a woman who has committed at least two murders that I am aware of. She claims to be the leader of a coven of witches, and she says that she can command demons."

"So, this lady is a complete bag of cats," said Ali.

"Yeah. I guess that says it pretty clearly," Mitch agreed. Chang'e was angry, unpredictable, and dangerous, just like ... well, just like a bag of cats. "Her name is Chang'e, although that isn't her real name. It's just what she calls herself. I have reason to believe that she is going to attack police officers at Dasan's Terrace on Wednesday. That's why we have a time limit."

"Why Wednesday?"

"That's what she told us, and I have no reason to believe she won't do what she claims. If I can't find out some information on her before then, I think she's going to be responsible for a lot more deaths."

"Okay. So, how do the other women fit in?"

"The other women are witches in Chang'e's coven. They follow her and do her bidding. I believe they have information that will help me find Chang'e and stop her before she can hurt anyone else."

"Sounds like a sort of cult thing," mused Ali. "And you need them to tell you where Chang'e is? Are you sure they would help you even if you found them? And why are they all hiding, anyway?"

Mitch sighed. He was wading into muddy water, and he had no idea how Ali was going to respond to much more of the truth. As long as the detective thought Chang'e was crazy and simply believed that she was a witch, maybe he could risk sharing a bit more.

"I told you that Chang'e has killed some people already, and I also told you that she claims to summon demons."

"Yeah," agreed Ali.

"Here's where shit gets really weird, and this is why I need your help. Chang'e got possessed by one of the demons she summoned. It's why she committed the murders."

"The devil told her to do it." Ali laughed out loud. "I've heard of people saying that before, but I never worked a case where my suspect believed it."

So far, so good, thought Mitch. *We're most of the way there.*

"When she started killing people, another witch priestess tried to kill her to make her stop. That attempt on her life is why all of her followers went into hiding. They thought they might be next, so they scattered all over the map."

"Hold on, hold on," interrupted Ali. "*Another* witch priestess? How many fucking witches are you chasing? What the hell are they putting in the water over there at your cemetery?"

"I know, right?" said Mitch, trying to joke the question away. "But don't worry. We already caught the second priestess. She's in jail and totally out of the picture at this point."

That was not completely true, but it wasn't exactly a lie, either. Alyssandra was currently in custody and no longer involved in trying to kill Chang'e.

"The coven members are still hiding, though, and I need to find them as soon as I can."

"So they can tell you where this Chang'e person is?"

"Yes. That, and…," Mitch trailed off.

"And what?" asked Ali. "What crazy shit haven't you told me yet?"

This was it. The last piece of information that would either have Ali shaking his head but ready to help, or else it would be the point that he realized Mitch was pulling his leg and he hung up the phone.

"I need them to tell me the name of the demon that possessed Chang'e."

The words came out in a rush. Mitch could not think of a better way to phrase it, so he blurted the sentence, then waited to see what kind of response he would get from Ali.

"Mitch, I don't know what you've been smoking, but the next time we get together, you have to share it with me."

The answer was not exactly helpful, but at least Ali was still talking to him. He was still on the phone.

"I'm serious, Ali. I need that name."

"Why? What does this demon's name have to do with anything? I'm not saying that I won't help you, but I would love to understand what it is that we would be doing here. It might be easier for me if I knew exactly what we were trying to accomplish."

"Chang'e believes she is possessed by this demon," Mitch explained. "She doesn't respond to the name Chang'e anymore. In her head, she is playing a completely different game than the rest of us, so I think if I have any chance of catching her, I have to play by her fucked up rules. One of those rules is that I have to find out the demon's name so I can gain some control over her. I might even be able to get her to surrender with the right … um, use … of the demon's name. I think the members of her coven are the best chance I have of finding that name."

There was silence on the line as Ali considered his explanation. Mitch could hear the other detective's soft, steady breathing as he mulled over the request.

"Weird shit is right," Ali finally said. "I don't totally get it, but then I've never been totally fluent in crazy. If you need a demon name, I guess I can try to get you a demon name. What information do you have on the witches?"

Mitch breathed a quiet sigh of relief. The hard part was done.

"Not much," he admitted. "I have first and last names that may or not be one hundred percent correct, and I have approximate ages, but no birthdates."

Ali whistled. "Yeah. That's not a lot to go on. You probably couldn't get a warrant with that information even if you had the time."

Mitch nodded his agreement, then remembered that Ali couldn't see the gesture over the phone. "I know," he said.

"You said you had eight witches." Ali paused to chuckle at the word. He still thought this was a bunch of mentally disturbed cult members play acting, and that was fine with Mitch. "You want to give me four of them? Or were you planning to dump the whole pile on me?"

"No. I was hoping you would take half. Thanks, Ali. I appreciate this."

Mitch glanced at a slip of paper on the desk in front of him. Violet had written a list of the names and ages of the members of Chang'e's coven for him. Her information had been mostly third hand, since she had only met a few of the women in person. She could not guarantee the accuracy of her recall, or even the spelling of a few of the names she did remember. Still, it was all they had to work with.

He gave Ali the first four names on the list, along with a warning that any, or all, of the information might be bad.

"Got it," said Ali. Mitch could hear a pen scribbling on a notepad. "Possible misspelled names and wrong ages. Why should helping you ever be easy? I'll get started as soon as I hang up. Is there anything else?"

"Anything else?" laughed Mitch. "That wasn't enough?"

Ali chuckled back. "I gotta admit, Mitch. You do have a way of making my life more interesting. I'll get back to you as soon as I can."

"Thanks again. If you ever need anything, let me know."

"Oh, I can guarantee I will."

Mitch hung up the phone and looked back at the list of names in front of him. He tapped the spacebar of the keyboard on his desk and his computer monitor came to life.

"Okay, Jessica Lassiter," he said to himself out loud. "About thirty-five years old. Let's see if any search engines have ever heard of you."

CHAPTER 15

Mitch worked through Monday and most of Tuesday morning, pausing only to eat and get a few hours of sleep. Violet had come home with him after their meeting with Simon and Dot because she had not wanted to be alone. After everything she had gone through in the past two days, Mitch did not blame her. In fact, he was happy for the company.

While Mitch researched the members of Chang'e's coven, Violet sat quietly on the couch, reading a book or simply watching him work, content to be close enough to see him, but never bothering him while he searched for the missing women. Occasionally, she would offer suggestions or add additional physical description to a name if she knew it, but mostly she stayed out of his way.

Mitch checked every version he could think of for each of the names on his list, trying different spellings as well as possible nicknames. He checked them through the Sacramento County databases, federal databases, and he ran them through a dozen different online name search programs. During the past day and a half, he had located dozens of potential addresses and phone numbers, as well as generating a hundred new names of possible relatives that he then put through the same search parameters.

He had made countless phone calls. Most had gotten him only confused responses and claims that they had never heard of the person he was looking for. A few calls earned him cold acknowledgements of familial connection, followed by variations of the statement, "I haven't spoken to her since she started claiming to be a witch, and I have no idea where she is now."

The remainder had been disconnected numbers or answering services. Mitch had dutifully left messages on every machine, but no one had yet bothered to call back with any helpful information.

On five occasions, Mitch found addresses in the Sacramento region, and he had dutifully driven out to each of them to meet the current residents. Violet had joined him on those trips, not wishing to remain at home alone. Other than the chance to get out of the house and spend a few peaceful hours chatting and pretending they were a normal couple out for a casual drive, those expeditions had unanimously been a waste of his time.

Mitch was growing discouraged. He did not want to let Chief Jefferson down, but it was looking less and less like he would be able to produce any of the missing women in the timeframe allotted. Maybe if he had a week to get access to credit card activity and identify cell phone services for his targets things might be different. Unfortunately, he did not have the luxury of that kind of time.

If they missed their window to force Chang'e to appear at the cemetery on Wednesday, Mitch would, of course, follow up on those types of leads. He simply doubted the demon would grant them much of a reprieve to hunt for its name before staging another assault on the cemetery.

With little hope of a better result than he had been getting for the last twenty-four hours, Mitch dialed yet another phone number he had located online.

"Yes?" came the response after only one ring.

"Hello. I was hoping to speak with Jova Medina. Is she available?"

"This is Jova," the woman replied. "Who is this?"

"Hi, Miss Medina. My name is Detective Mitch Loman. I work for the Dasan's Terrace Police Department."

"Did you find something? Do you know who did it?" the woman asked. Her voice was high, excited. She sounded almost frantic after Mitch identified himself.

"I'm sorry. Who did it? I don't...,"

"Who killed my niece? That is why you're calling, isn't it?"

Mitch needed a moment to get his brain moving. He had been getting all kinds of responses to his calls, confused, irritated, bored, even amused, but this one was a first. There was obviously something happening in this woman's family that involved the police, and she thought he was part of whatever that situation was. He needed to clarify his position quickly.

"Ma'am, I apologize for the confusion, but I think there's some mistake. I'm not investigating a death. I'm simply trying to find someone that you might know. Are you related to, or do you know anyone by the name of Marley Serrano?"

"Yes," Jova said, enunciating the word clearly and distinctly. "My niece. Marley. She was murdered on Sunday."

"I-I didn't know that. I'm so sorry. May I ask where it happened?"

"What the hell is wrong with you?" the woman shrieked into the phone. "Don't you people ever talk to each other? You should be calling to tell *me* what happened, not asking me to do your job for you."

Before Mitch could say another word, the line disconnected. Jova Medina had hung up.

Mitch set his cellphone on his desk, stunned by what he had just learned. He had finally succeeded in finding someone who knew one of the people he was searching for. He supposed that should be considered a small victory. Unfortunately, that victory was tainted by the fact the subject of his search was dead.

Could that be coincidence, he wondered. Although if it was, it was a pretty disturbing coincidence.

Maybe, instead of searching for relatives and old phone numbers, he should be checking crime blotters and obituaries. That was a gruesome thought, but it wouldn't be completely surprising, would it? He knew the demon was dangerous. It had killed before.

As Mitch considered his next move, his phone vibrated on the desk, announcing someone was trying to reach him. He picked it up and glanced at the caller I.D. screen before answering.

"Hey, Ali. Please tell me you have good news for me. I really need it right about now."

"Hey, Mitch. I guess it depends on what you consider good news."

Mitch sighed. "Did you find any of the women on your list?" he asked, without much actual hope.

"I did, actually," Ali told him. Mitch could hear a note in the detective's voice announcing that there was another shoe about to drop. "I found two of them."

"But they're dead," Mitch stated. "Am I right?"

"Yeah, man. They are. How did you know? Wait, let me guess. You found a couple of yours, too?"

"I found one. She was murdered on Sunday. I can only guess that the ones we haven't found yet are going to turn up dead, too."

"Holy hell. My two were killed on Sunday, too. This is not random."

"No, it's not," Mitch agreed. "Chang'e anticipated what I was going to try to do, and she decided to get there first."

"Wow, Mitch. You really have a knack for sucking me into shit, don't you?" Ali did not seem upset. If anything, the detective sounded excited.

"Yeah. I'm sorry about this."

"What do you mean you're sorry? This is fucking amazing!"

"Wha-?" Mitch had no idea what was so amazing about all of his potential witnesses being murdered on the same day.

"One of the women killed on Sunday had her head torn clean off in Carmichael. That makes it a County investigation. I went to my lieutenant when I found out and told him about what you were looking into, and he immediately gave me the case to investigate. You know what that means, don't you?"

"He dumped a mess on your desk," Mitch said.

"No, he didn't. With the two murders you told me about, plus potentially eight more if this woman got to everyone in her coven, that means he put me in charge of investigating a serial killer. A serial killer! And a female serial killer, too. Do you know how rare those are? Not just in Sacramento, but anywhere in the world?"

"You're … happy about this?" Mitch asked.

"You're not?" replied Ali. "Buddy, if arresting Delaney's killer doesn't get me stripes, this sure as shit is going to do it. Hell, they might make me a captain."

"That's great, Ali," although Mitch was struggling to find any real enthusiasm. He did not see the positive aspects of this case the way Ali did. He simply knew too much the other detective did not. "Take a beat, though. We still need to catch her."

"I know," Ali said. "But we already know who she is. It's just a matter of time before we get her."

Ali was still operating under the assumption that Chang'e was a crazy woman who had gone on a demented killing spree. Mitch knew the truth, and the danger, about the reality of demonic possession and how difficult it might be to stop Chang'e before she could do a lot more damage.

While Mitch considered his options, Ali continued talking. "Send me the rest of that list of names. I'll figure out if any of the eight women are still alive. If not, I'll get reports on all the homicides and start building a joint file with the other agencies. Unless of course…," He trailed off.

"Unless?"

"Am I overstepping? Do you want to take lead on this?"

"No. In fact, I would appreciate it if you take this case. None of the deaths occurred in Dasan's Terrace, so I don't have any jurisdiction to run the investigation. Besides, my priority is catching Chang'e before she kills anyone else."

"Perfect. You flush her out, and I'll take point on the investigation for the County. Oh, by the way, I'll need the names of the first two victims you mentioned."

"I'll email you everything I have. Can you give me copies of any reports you manage to dig up? I don't know if they'll help me, but I still need to find this demon's name. Without it, I'm playing blind out here."

Demon. Right, I forgot about that. Man, that is truly some weird shit," said Ali.

"Yeah. Weird shit," Mitch repeated. "Look, Ali. I need to go. I have to call my chief and let him know this whole thing just went egg-shaped. I'll send you those names right after I call him."

"Do that. I need to give a call to Roseville and let them know they have a piece of our case. The second woman I found was killed in their jurisdiction."

"Good luck."

"You too. Talk to you later."

Mitch disconnected the call and set his phone back on his desk. He rested his face in his hands and breathed slowly in and out. He stayed that way until he was confident he wasn't going to scream.

Violet noticed his distress and left her seat on the couch to stand behind him. Concerned, she laid a hand on his shoulder.

"Mitch? Are you okay?"

He wanted to reassure her, to tell her everything was going to be fine. Instead, all he could say was, "Fuck."

Simon walked into the Rancho Cordova branch office of the Sacramento County Jail. The East Office, as it was referred to by the few who knew of its existence, was not officially recognized as part of Sacramento County's detention facilities, primarily because the people typically held there were also not officially recognized. The security was as tight as any maximum-security prison, plus a few added non-standard safeguards.

Simon showed his identification to three different officers before he got further than the front lobby. He was also subjected to a pat-down search when he set off one of the magical wards in front of the elevator doors. The security guards found his magic nullifying handcuffs, but no other suspicious items in his possession, and they seemed confused as to why the wards continued to insist Simon was trying to bring magical objects into the facility.

He could have told them the ward was responding not to anything he was carrying, but rather to his own magical aura. He remained quiet, however. That was not a secret he cared to share. In the end, it required a phone call to the facility commander who personally vouched for Simon before he was allowed onto the third floor and to the detention cells where Alyssandra was being held.

Simon was visiting the East Office because Alyssandra had asked to see him. More than asked, actually. She had insisted. He did not like feeling like he was being summoned into her presence, particularly not when she was a prisoner here and he felt she should be treating her situation with a little more humility. Still, even with his reservations, he had agreed to come.

Dasan's Terrace needed Alyssandra, and he had to play nice. For a little while longer at least. If they ever managed to determine the demon's name, they needed both Violet and Alyssandra at the cemetery to force the creature to abide by its promise. That would be hard enough already with Violet as upset as she was. He did not want to also antagonize Alyssandra any more than he absolutely had to.

He needed her help, that was true, but he had not forgotten that Alyssandra was also a murderer, so Simon was in no mood to coddle the witch, either. Especially after his phone conversation with Mitch. With Chang'e's coven members all murdered or missing, it did not look like they would be able to find the demon's name by Wednesday as he had hoped. While Dasan's Terrace had been chasing its own tail, Chang'e had been busy cleaning up loose ends, and it appeared she had been rather thorough.

A smooth-faced young deputy that did not look old enough to have graduated high school escorted Simon along the third-floor corridor to Alyssandra's cell. The chief of Dasan's Terrace had to remind himself not to make any biased judgements about a person's capabilities based on their age. Given his own situation, he was the last person who should be evaluating others based solely on their appearance.

A single chair had been placed on either side of the reinforced metal bars and plexiglass divider that marked the boundaries of Alyssandra's new living quarters. The guard escorting Simon gave a quick admonition not to touch the barrier and not to give or accept any items from the prisoner. When Simon nodded his understanding, the deputy gestured toward the chair outside the cell, indicating he should sit down.

"I'll give you some privacy, but I'll still be close enough that you can yell if you need anything and I'll hear you."

"Thank you," said Simon. He sat down, dismissing the deputy.

Alyssandra already sat in her chair on the other side of the barrier. She wore a gray flannel t-shirt under a baggy orange shirt, and matching orange pants with overly long legs that had been rolled up at the ankles to prevent their wearer from tripping on them. Seeing Alyssandra in inmate orange made Simon much happier than was probably seemly, but he had never really liked the old witch much, and he had always believed she would end up here eventually.

"Alyssandra," Simon said in greeting. "I'm here. What did you need to tell me?"

The woman glowered at him. "You have made your point, Lost Child. It is time to end this game and let me out of here."

Simon's eyebrows furrowed in puzzled surprise. "Game? This is not a game. You killed Violet's family. You are going to pay for that. I'm amazed you think you can talk to me like you still have any leverage here."

"I did not kill her family, and that is the truth. Whatever I may or may not have known before it happened is irrelevant, and you have no proof of anything. I cannot be convicted of anything, and you are wasting both of our time by keeping me here instead of allowing me and my coven to deal with this demon that is coming after all of us."

Simon remained calm in spite of Alyssandra's tirade. He had the upper hand, and he was not about to allow his own emotions to change that. Getting angry would only give her the satisfaction of seeing him lose control.

"As far as being convicted of anything, you are counting on two things that, unfortunately for you, neither of which is true. First, you're assuming I would charge you through normal channels, in which case you are probably right, a good lawyer would likely prevent you from being convicted. Instead, I could simply hand you over to Federal authorities as a supernatural threat to human safety. There is certainly enough evidence to support that accusation."

"You wouldn't dare," Alyssandra raged, though she did not sound completely certain of her assertion. "There wouldn't even be a trial. They would execute me out of hand. You couldn't live with yourself if you did that."

Simon relented. "I know. And you're right. I probably won't do that. But I don't need to, either. This brings us to your second incorrect assumption. I can still turn you over to the State of New York for prosecution. Let's not forget that although you did not kill Violet's parents, you did in fact kill three witches in that house. Witches that were at the time working for you. Those murders have never been officially solved, and should a witness come forward, a witness that was in the house with you that day, I don't think they would have any difficulty putting you in prison for a long, long time."

Alyssandra quieted, staring petulantly at the floor as she tried to think of a way out of her situation.

"What do you want from me?" she finally asked.

"I don't want anything from you, Alyssandra," Simon told her honestly. "It's Violet that wants something. She wants you to pay for what you did to her family."

"You still need me to get Chang'e into the cemetery on Wednesday. I can't do that if I'm locked up here."

Simon shook his head, sadly. "That demon hunted down and murdered every member of Chang'e's coven to protect its name. We can't force it to show up whether you're there or not. Unless, by some miracle, we find someone who knows its name, your last bargaining chip has been played."

Simon was about to stand up and tell Alyssandra goodbye, but the witch stopped him with her next words.

"I can still get it to show up on Wednesday night."

He paused, settling back into his chair.

"How?" he asked.

"The demon is inside of Chang'e. Its essence, its soul if you will, is intertwined with hers. When I demanded the demon swear by its name, I addressed it as Chang'e. It accepted the name I called it, meaning that when it swore its oath, it bound Chang'e to that oath as firmly as it bound itself."

"That helps us how?" Simon thought he knew where Alyssandra was going with her argument, but he wanted to hear her say it.

"The two souls are linked, so we can force the demon to appear on Wednesday by its own name, or by Chang'e's. Either one should be sufficient."

Simon considered the information carefully. This was good news, but it was not everything they needed.

"That helps," he admitted to Alyssandra. "The problem remains that we don't know Chang'e's real name, either. We still have no way to enforce the oath."

"I know Chang'e's name," Alyssandra said. She looked into Simon's eyes, holding his gaze with her own as she said, "I have known it for many years."

"How? How did you learn her name?"

"Know thine enemy, Lost Child."

"Sun Tzu," said Simon. "The Art of War."

"Exactly. Years ago, when I first decided that Chang'e was going to be a problem for me, I hired a detective to dig into her past. There wasn't much to find, but he did manage to locate her parents. They were immigrants from China, and they settled in Florida where Chang'e was born two years later."

"Were?" asked Simon.

Alyssandra shrugged. "They are both dead now."

"Did Chang'e…?"

Alyssandra shrugged again. "She may have. I don't know for certain. What I do know is that the investigator found Chang'e's birth certificate, and he gave me her real name. I can hold her to the oath the demon made."

"What is her name?" asked Simon.

"Oh, no," said Alyssandra, shaking her head and baring a sly, canary-killing grin. "I give you nothing for free. I can bring the demon to Dasan's Terrace on Wednesday, but in return I want all charges against me dropped, never to be brought up again. Not here, not in New York, and especially never with the federal authorities."

"I can't do that," said Simon.

"You can't? Or you won't?"

"I won't do that to Violet," Simon amended. "This has to be her decision. If she agrees, then I'll make it happen. If, however, she tells me she wants you to rot in prison, I will do everything in my power to lock you away forever."

"You would choose her over me?" asked Alyssandra.

"Every time," said Simon without hesitation.

"You would choose her over Dead Town? Over all of the people there that look to you for protection?"

Simon smiled and slowly shook his head. "Violet and you both must be in the cemetery to make this work. If I free you over Violet's objections, she will leave Dasan's Terrace. I will be in exactly the same situation I am now. The only difference will be that you will be out of prison. I don't like that trade."

Alyssandra stood up from her chair and moved further back into her cell. There was not much room, and she could only take a few steps before she reached the far wall, but the action was a symbolic gesture.

"I suppose we are done, then. No agreement, and no name. I suggest you take my offer to Violet. She can accept it or not, but the outcome will be on your heads, not mine."

CHAPTER 16

Mitch hung up his phone, staring at the display screen as if the answers to his new problem might magically appear if he only watched it long enough.

"Damn it, Simon. Right now? You're really doing this to me right now?"

Chief Jefferson had spoken with Alyssandra, and the wily witch had dropped a bomb on him. She knew Chang'e's real name, and she believed she could force the demon to keep its promise to show up at the cemetery tomorrow, but she would only agree to help if….

"Damn it," he said again.

He shoved his phone into his back pocket. Why was this his problem? Just because the chief didn't have the guts to ask Violet directly, why was it Mitch's job to tell her what Alyssandra wanted?

He sighed. He understood why the chief had done it this way. If he were Chief Jefferson, he would have done the exact same thing. Violet would tell Simon no before the question was halfway out of his mouth, but if Mitch was the one who approached her, she would at least listen to the full story before making a decision.

Mitch felt like a sacrificial goat, tied to a stake and waiting to be devoured by an approaching predator.

"Who was on the phone?" asked Violet. She wandered down the stairs into the living room, toweling her hair dry with one of Mitch's guest towels. She wore a fluffy yellow bathrobe she kept at his house, but she had not bothered to tie the front closed. The robe hung loose on her, leaving a six-inch gap of visible flesh from her neck to her knees.

Mitch stared for a moment at the exposed skin. It was still slightly pink and damp from the shower. Violet noticed the direction of his gaze, but she made no effort to cover herself.

Damn it, Simon, Mitch thought again, but he did not say it aloud this time. *You're about to ruin what might have been a really nice evening.*

"That was Chief Jefferson," he told her.

"What did Simon want?"

"He wanted to ask you something, but I told him you were busy."

Violet stopped drying her hair, holding the damp towel in her hands and leveling a quizzical look at Mitch.

"Should I get dressed and go see him? Or call him back?"

"No. That isn't necessary. He told me what he wanted."

"And…?"

"Sit down," Mitch said, gesturing at the couch.

"Mitch?" Violet asked, a note of concern in her voice.

"Please. Simon went to see Alyssandra today."

Violet draped the towel over her neck, and Mitch watched crestfallen as she pulled her robe closed and secured it with a cloth belt attached at the waist. Violet settled onto the couch, pulling her knees up and tucking her feet beneath her.

"I'm sitting," she said. The ice in her tone chilled the room around Mitch.

Mitch sat down beside her, leaving enough room between them that they did not touch, but where he could easily reach her if he needed to.

"The good news is that Alyssandra believes the demon will respond to its oath even if we use Chang'e's real name instead of its own. The better news is that Alyssandra already knows Chang'e's name. We don't have to keep searching."

"The bad news is that now Alyssandra has to be in the cemetery with us tomorrow night," Violet added.

Mitch almost rested a hand on Violet's knee, but he hesitated. He did not think the gesture would be wanted or appreciated, so he stayed where he was.

"The bad news, actually, is that Alyssandra has refused to tell us her name and will not go to the cemetery tomorrow unless Simon drops all charges against her and lets her go free."

Violet was on her feet in an instant. Her normally calm blue eyes flashed bright and hot.

"He can't do that!" she shouted. "Mitch, you call him back right now and tell him he can't do this. Alyssandra has to pay for what she did."

Mitch raised his hands in surrender, trying to calm Violet's anger. He remained on the couch and continued to speak softly.

"He's not. I promise you, he isn't doing anything. Alyssandra is still in custody, and she's going to stay there as long as you want her to."

Violet had begun to pace through the room, but she stopped when Mitch told her Alyssandra was not going free. She peered at him, suspiciously. She knew there was more to this story, and she was not sure she wanted to hear it.

"So then, why did he call? Just to tell me everything is fine, and Alyssandra is still behind bars?"

Mitch glanced down, finding it difficult to meet Violet's gaze. He felt as if he were betraying her by having this conversation, but he had promised the chief he would at least ask Violet if she would consider Alyssandra's deal.

"Chief Jefferson asked if, based on the information and help that Alyssandra is offering, would you be willing to let her go."

Mitch stood and spoke quickly, wanting to make sure she understood what Simon was asking. "The chief won't do anything if you say no. He said it is absolutely your decision, and if you want her to stay locked up, then she will. He would completely understand."

"I don't think he understands anything," Violet said. She glared at Mitch, and his heart broke a little at the thought that he was causing her more pain than she had already suffered. "If he understood what that woman did to me, then he would *understand* that she has to pay for her crimes. She needs to suffer for her actions. If Simon understood, he should have known what my answer was going to be, regardless of the fact that he didn't have the balls to come to me directly and had to send his errand boy to do his dirty work."

"You're absolutely right," Mitch said.

"About what part?" snarled Violet. Her eyes shone wet with anger and pain. She wiped at her face with the towel before any tears could escape.

"About all of it. Alyssandra hurt you, and she has to pay for that. And Simon is a coward for going through me instead of talking to you directly."

"He's like everyone else I've ever known," Violet said. The anger ebbed, and with it, the strength seemed to drain from her body. Violet dropped back onto the couch, shrinking into the corner as far from Mitch as she could get. "He says he cares, but the second he wants something, he throws anyone else under the bus. Their feelings don't matter."

"That isn't fair," said Mitch softly. "You know Simon better than that. Everything he does, he does for the people he cares about. He tried to take on Chang'e by himself because he thought he could protect the rest of us from her. In fact, do you know what he told me before he hung up?"

"What?"

Violet's question was so quiet, and she looked so defeated. Mitch felt a burning lump forming high in his chest. He tried to breathe it away, but the pain only grew more persistent, pressing around his heart and beginning to squeeze. Despite his own misery, he forced what he hoped was a reassuring smile onto his face.

"He said that Dot told him Dasan's Terrace could only be protected if you and I stayed. Her prediction doesn't include Alyssandra at all. She does not matter. Simon said if you want Alyssandra buried in a deep hole for the rest of eternity, he would be happy to drop the first shovelful of dirt on her head."

Mitch leaned closer, and this time he did reach out to Violet. She allowed him to take her hand in his own.

"Simon thought Alyssandra might help us take out Chang'e, that is the only reason he called to tell us what she said. But he also made it very clear that you are the only one who can make this decision. You are the only one he cares about, and if you say no, then the answer is no. No further questions asked."

Violet looked so tiny and helpless that Mitch wanted to gather her up in his arms and never let go. He was so accustomed to the beautiful and powerful witch that had so often been his protector, that it was painful to see her this fragile. Still, he loved her for her vulnerabilities as much as for her strengths, and this moment only made him realize more than ever that the two of them needed each other.

"You were right, you know," Violet told him. "When you stopped me from killing Alyssandra. As much as I despise her, and can never forgive her for what she did, I also know that she has been the closest thing to family that I have had in over a decade. If I had killed her, I would hate myself forever. You are the only reason that didn't happen. So, thank you Mitch, for that, and for being on my side."

"I'm always on your side. You know that."

"I do."

Violet gave him a sad smile that made him want to build a mile-high wall around the house and never let the world get close to her. He would do anything to erase the pain from her face, to protect her from ever being hurt again.

"I love you for that," she continued. "But as much as I appreciate that Alyssandra is alive, I also need her to be punished. Maybe you think that's evil, but I can't stomach the thought that she can steal from me everyone I loved and then walk away without paying a price. I can't just let her go. No matter what she could do to help us. I can't."

"I won't ask you to. You're not evil. You're human. I want her to pay for what she did to you, too."

Mitch had a sudden thought. Maybe there was a way to get Alyssandra's assistance, and see that Violet got the justice she so deserved. It would require a bit of work, and he would need Simon's cooperation to make it all happen, but he did not think the chief was in any position to negotiate with him at the moment. If anything, he should jump at the chance to save Dasan's Terrace and stick it to Alyssandra at the same time.

Mitch squeezed Violet's hand with new hope blooming in his heart.

"What if we could have it both ways?" he asked.

Violet looked at him as if he might be losing his mind.

"No, really. What if we can get Alyssandra to help us take down Chang'e, and you can still see her punished. Not a slap on the wrist kind of punishment either. I mean you can hurt her the same way that she hurt you."

"I don't even know if she has any family," Violet said. "And if she does, I don't think I can…,"

"I'm not talking about that," Mitch said, hurriedly. "No one gets hurt. Well, no one except Alyssandra."

"What are you talking about?"

Mitch shifted closer to Violet on the couch.

"Alyssandra took something precious away from you," he said.

He felt her hand shaking in his and it made him angry, but it also firmed his resolve. Violet should have the opportunity to take some action on her own behalf, not remain a passive observer of whatever discipline others decided was sufficient for Alyssandra.

"She deserves having the same thing done to her," he continued. "So, would you consider it enough of a punishment if you could take from her everything that she cares about in this world?"

CHAPTER 17

Standing in the shadows of the old growth trees that filled North-West, Mitch and Violet watched the members of the coven prepare for the coming confrontation. The group of witches sat on the ground in two rows of five. The front row consisted of the strongest remaining magic users of the group, with Willa leading the team. Behind them were the women who could not directly manipulate magic but had been trained by Alyssandra and Violet to support the true magic users, lending strength and control to the coven's spellcasting.

Jorge and the B-Nights team were also on the grounds. Tink was kneeling in front of a large mound of dirt, reading from a tiny, black notebook, while Jorge and Brad stood nervously scanning the surrounding area. Brad had his katana drawn and ready, while Jorge held a two-foot-tall crucifix in his hands. The cross, similar to Brad's sword, had been blessed by an angel to help ward demons away. The blessing was weaker than the fragment of trapped spirit from an actual angel, but the metal cross could still be quite effective at dispelling demonic magic. It was one of the carefully selected, powerful relics the chief had approved to be removed from the department's property room.

Simon stood beside Alyssandra, the two adversaries speaking in hushed tones while trading dagger-sharp glares at one another. Dot was not present. Her talents, though remarkable, did not lend themselves to battle, and so Simon had forbidden her to be on cemetery grounds tonight.

Though the sun had set almost half an hour earlier, there was still light on the horizon, and no one had yet needed to resort to flashlights or other artificial lighting sources with which to see. An almost full moon was already above the trees to the east, giving its own faint glow to assist the assembled men and women of Dasan's Terrace.

Mitch took Violet's hand. She was adorned in her long black dress, goth makeup and black wig, ready for a night of witchy mayhem. Mitch had opted for his short-sleeved officer's uniform, complete with ballistic vest and equipment belt. Although he knew this battle would be more magical than mundane, he still felt more prepared to fight in his police gear than if he had worn his street clothes. Besides, he was also technically at work tonight. He was expected to be in uniform.

He glanced at his watch. "Two minutes left. If she keeps her promise she should be here any second."

Violet nodded, scanning the grounds nearby for any signs of threat.

"I don't think she's coming."

"She promised," Mitch reminded her.

"Her word is worthless. The demon only agreed because it was certain Alyssandra and I would not both be here. It was almost right about that."

"But you are both here. It has to come."

Violet squeezed his hand, then released it. "I think it will only come when Alyssandra compels it. Either way, though, we need to win tonight. I don't think we'll get another chance like this."

"I'm concealing us," announced Simon. "Don't panic when you can't see the others. Be ready and stay alert."

Violet dimmed beside him, and Mitch realized that Simon was using his magic to hide them all behind a shadow illusion. The others in the cemetery also faded from his view. The chief wanted Chang'e to see nothing when she arrived, hopefully giving them the advantage of surprise when they launched their ambush.

Despite not being able to see everyone else, Mitch could observe himself perfectly clearly. It made him wonder if the illusion spell had not worked on him. No one else said anything about him still being visible, however, so he assumed everything was going according to their plan. He looked again at his watch, following the second hand as it swept past the twelve.

One more minute.

Mitch felt his stomach tighten with the tension of waiting. Thirty seconds left. Then ten.

Then it was nine o'clock and…

Nothing moved or appeared out of place. Mitch also heard nothing other than a slight wind rustling the needles of the trees overhead. The second hand continued its next sweep around the dial of his watch.

A minute passed. Then another.

At five minutes past nine o'clock, Simon dropped the illusion and announced, "She isn't coming. Alyssandra, you're up."

"This may not work," Alyssandra said, "but I will do what I can."

"You'll make it work, or the deal is off," Simon said coldly.

"I'm here, as I promised. That was the deal."

"No," Simon corrected her. "The deal was you knew Chang'e's name, and you could summon her if she failed to show up on her own. I'm not going to stand here and watch you pretend to try and be satisfied with that. Now, summon her, or I'll stick you back in your tiny little cell."

"You go too far, Lost Child," Alyssandra warned.

"Alyssandra," Violet said softly, though loud enough that her voice carried clear and true to the witch priestess. "Do not make me break you again in front of the entire coven. It would be unseemly."

Alyssandra opened her mouth as if to retort but thought better of it. Instead, she dropped to one knee and began drawing in the dirt with an index finger. The figure she drew was a simple, growing spiral, starting from a central point and winding in ever growing circles along the ground. When she finished the spiral, she placed both hands palm down in the soil to either side of the crude drawing.

Mitch saw the surrounding energies Alyssandra drew toward her, filling the spiral image with pale white light.

"Chang'e, you are bound by your oath," Alyssandra intoned. "I hold you to your promise by your given name, Eng Wingshan. By your name, show me where you are. I demand you reveal yourself."

The light swirling in the spiral lashed outward in every direction. It looked like a fan of glowing strings unfurling in a perfect bloom around Alyssandra.

"Chang'e, you are bound by your oath, and by your name, Eng Wingshan. Show yourself to me."

Several of the white lines began to flicker and die out. Gaps appeared in the glowing fan. Mitch though the binding might be failing as more and more of the strands disappeared, but he soon understood exactly what was happening. As some lines faded away, others began to glow brighter. In fact, one strand in particular was thickening as well as increasing in brilliance.

Alyssandra repeated her command a third time, and now there was only one thread remaining. She sat up, raising her hands from the ground and grasping the final glowing filament.

"I see you, oath breaker," Alyssandra said.

She began wrapping loops of the shining thread around one hand.

"Chang'e, by your oath and by your name, Eng Wingshan, I command you to fulfill your promise. By your oath and by your name, Eng Wingshan, I command you to fulfill your promise. By your oath and by your name, Eng Wingshan, I command you…,"

Alyssandra suddenly pulled at the strand in her hand. The white light responded in her grasp, writhing like a living creature and deepening to a sickening, bruise-like, purple color.

"…fulfill your promise!"

An opening appeared in the air, a jagged tear in the fabric of the cemetery's reality. Mitch could see a room on the other side of that rip, an oddly normal looking space inside someone's home. He saw a couch, a coffee table, and a stretch of gray carpet. He also saw … her.

"Simon," Mitch warned. "She's coming. Cover us up."

The invisibility illusion settled back onto the assembled team in the cemetery. Violet, Simon, and all the rest of the people around him faded from Mitch's view as the portal Alyssandra had created continued to widen.

Chang'e appeared in the opening as she was forcibly pulled from wherever she had been comfortably hiding moments ago. She screamed, her face contorting as she was dragged from her previous location into the waiting cemetery. The were no words in her verbal defiance, the sounds more closely resembling the bestial denials of a trapped animal rather than anything remotely human.

Chang'e emerged fully into Dasan's Terrace, standing in the ankle high weeds of North-West, her angry figure backlit by the low hanging moon. The gap through which she had been snatched from her lair closed behind her.

"Nooo!" Chang'e shouted when she realized where she was. "How could you? No one else knows."

"Willa," Violet shouted. "Now."

Yellow and green streams of magic launched from seemingly nowhere to drape over Chang'e like a colorful net. Chang'e formed a barrier around herself, but the web was created to contain her, not injure her. The shield did nothing more than add an extra layer of magic between her and escape.

"Tighten the lines," Violet called.

The magical net shrank, squeezing against Chang'e and her defenses, pushing her to the ground and holding her in place. As the interlacing lines of magic touched the witch's shield, they began to flare red and burn away. The demonic magic emanating from Chang'e was already countering their attack.

"More power," Violet directed the witches. "Secure that web."

New lines launched, adding to the already existing net and bolstering the containment spell.

"Tink, you're up." It was Mitch's turn to direct his portion of this fight.

He could not see Tink under the chief's illusion, but the mound of earth the officer had earlier been kneeling beside bucked and jerked. The soil pulled together around an invisible central force, compacting into a roughly humanoid form. It clambered up onto two stumpy legs. The creature was an earth golem, and Tink had used a set of spelled gemstones to raise it from the cemetery soil. The stones were items Mitch himself had collected recently, and they too had been liberated from the mysterious selection of items in the police department's storage room.

"Hold her down, and don't let her go."

Mitch heard Tink giving the golem directions. The massive, animated collection of dirt and sod turned toward Chang'e and lumbered in her direction. The possessed witch saw the golem approach. Recognizing the creature as a real threat, Chang'e tried pushing to her feet, but the constantly reinforced magical net kept her pinned flat on her stomach.

Chang'e's hands glowed with an internal light as she began shaping a new spell.

"Jorge! We need you. Get in there," Mitch called. "She's trying to cast something."

Jorge rushed forward wielding the heavy angelic crucifix in his hands. He laid the cross over Chang'e's back. Although Mitch could not see his sergeant, he could see the results of the man's actions. Mitch watched the spell in the demon's hands burst like an overheated lightbulb, fragmenting into harmless splinters.

"That did it. Good job, Sarge. Stay on her," Mitch encouraged.

The golem reached the struggling demon and slammed both hands down on top of it, crushing the already pinned creature more securely to the ground. Mitch winced. Chang'e was a small, willowy woman, fragile looking and waiflike. The golem looked like it was capable of snuffing the life out of her simply by poking her with one massive finger, and here it was leaning its entire weight on top of her. Still, Chang'e struggled. The demon possessing her body gave her incredible strength and superhuman durability.

"Simon. Handcuffs," directed Mitch when everyone else had completed their tasks and they had Chang'e trapped and helpless.

The chief removed the handcuffs from his pocket and approached Chang'e, trying to find a good angle that would allow him to grab her hands and secure them behind her back. Mitch realized he could see Simon now. He could see everyone in fact, the witches, the other officers. The chief must have felt confident enough in their tactical situation that he had let the illusion spell lapse.

The plan was working beautifully, exactly as they had hoped when Violet and Simon had initially come up with it. Once the handcuffs were on, there was little the demon could do. Although the creature was strong, the golem would easily be able to control it while the demon was denied any access to magic.

Not only had they captured Chang'e, but they had managed the feat with no casualties to anyone on their team.

"Hurry," warned Jorge, disrupting Mitch's sense of impending victory.

Something was wrong. As Simon tried to grab one of Chang'e's hands, the crucifix Jorge held began to smoke, then glow red. Mitch could see pain on Jorge's face as he tried to hold the cross in place despite the unexpected heat burning his hands.

A deep red aura pulsed around Chang'e and Mitch realized the demon was once again connected to a source of power. The blessing bestowed on the crucifix had reached its limit and finally failed. The cross was now nothing more than a useless, smoldering chunk of metal in Jorge's grasp.

"Jorge, drop it," Mitch shouted at the sergeant. "The blessing failed. It's not working anymore."

Jorge cried out in relief as he released the blistering hot object. He stepped away from the demon, and Brad moved smoothly around him, preparing to use his katana to bring Chang'e back under control.

The web holding Chang'e down sparked in several places with dancing red motes, burning away as it touched the demonic aura growing stronger beneath it.

"Reinforce the net," called Violet, and the witches hastened to add more power to the remaining trap, as well as casting more lines of force to hold the struggling demon in place.

"Don't let her get up," shouted Tink at the golem.

The creature was already exerting tremendous pressure on the slender frame of Chang'e, but remarkably the possessed witch continued to thrash and twist underneath its massive hands. The golem leaned forward, trying to crush the squirming thing in its grasp.

Chang'e lashed out with one hand, pointing a finger toward Brad who had raised his katana over his head. He angled the point of the blade downward, preparing to pierce through the demonic energy growing around her. Though Brad could not see the magic, he had watched Jorge toss aside the crucifix, and he knew he needed to intervene before Chang'e could mount a counterattack.

The demon must have recognized the new complication that the sword represented because all Chang'e focus turned now on the approaching katana and its wielder.

"Burn," cried Chang'e, her voice rough and deep under the strain of fighting the forces arrayed against her.

Fire lanced from her hand, striking Brad in the chest and shoving him backward. The officer shouted in surprise as his uniform smoked and burned. The angel-imbued katana intervened, protecting Brad from the worst of the demon's scorching magic, but even the residual heat was enough to cause the officer pain.

Brad dropped to the ground, slapping at the smoldering patches of his shirt, trying to put out the flames before they could burn through to his skin underneath.

With the katana-carrying officer momentarily distracted, the demon turned its attention to the next greatest threat, namely Simon and the handcuffs he was attempting to place on its wrists. The demon pointed at the chief, but after witnessing the attack on Brad, Simon wisely stepped backward and enveloped himself in a spell of invisibility.

The demon shrieked, angry at losing sight of its second target. Still, there were plenty more annoyances at which to direct its wrath.

Three balls of blood-red light appeared, circling the pinned demon's head. They spun in their tiny orbit like planets around a raging sun before launching toward the dirt golem. Two of the spheres struck the golem at each of its wrists, breaking the arms and causing the massive hands to collapse back into the harmless piles of soil from which they had been formed.

The third ball of light, the largest of the three, struck the earth giant in the chest, punching into the magic-hardened torso before erupting. The blast punched a hole the size of a bowling ball entirely through the golem's body. The creature opened its mouth, roaring silently as it tried to understand what was happening to it.

Finally unimpeded, Chang'e made her move. As soon as the golem's hands were off of her, she pushed up from the ground. The coven's net continued to hold her in place, but it could not prevent her from gaining her feet. What had only moments ago seemed the perfect plan to capture a rogue demon was now completely falling apart before Mitch's eyes. Catch and detain, their primary goal at the beginning of this fiasco, was suddenly no longer a valid option.

If Mitch, the police officers, and the witches all wanted to survive to see the sun rise in the morning, they had to stop this demon, permanently, and they had to do it before the creature broke completely free of its restraints and turned the full force of its powers against them.

Mitch collected magic as fast as he could draw it to himself, then launched a flame attack against the possessed body of Chang'e. Violet must have reached the same conclusion as he had, because she began hurling percussive spells at the creature at the same time. Their dual attacks flashed and detonated with impressive pyrotechnic force, but they failed to penetrate Chang'e's protective shelter.

When the fireworks began, Tink shouted to the golem to renew its efforts to stop Chang'e. He, too, realized this mission of detention had suddenly become one of seek and destroy.

"Stop her. Smash her," Tink told it.

The golem, damaged but a long way from defeated, began to rain down blows on Chang'e's head with its truncated arms. The strikes landed with deafening impact, but they did not quite reach the demon's host. Chang'e had full control of her magic, and her defensive spells were locked in place. Although they were taking a beating from the combined attacks of Mitch, Violet, and the rampaging golem, the glowing shields held.

The demon was strong. Dasan's Terrace had thrown everything they had at this monster, and it was not enough. Chang'e grinned in fierce triumph from behind her magical defenses. The twist of her lips and her bared teeth no longer looked human. The essence of the demon inside the woman's body was becoming more and more apparent in its outside appearance.

"Alyssandra, we need your help," said Simon to the coven priestess.

Alyssandra had not yet joined the attack. She stood to one side, silently observing the desperate attempts to subdue the demon, as well as the creature's systematic destruction of each of those attempts. At Simon's urging, Alyssandra only took a few steps further from the fray.

"Damn it, witch. Help us," the chief demanded.

"Help yourself, Lost Child. I've done everything I promised I would. The rest is not my problem."

Mitch continued to throw every bit of power he could control against the demon's defenses. His fire and impact spells had no effect. The demon ignored him the same way Alyssandra had ignored him during her battle with Violet. When this comparison occurred to Mitch, it gave him an idea.

"Violet, cover me," he said. "I can't hold a shield and fight, too, but I need to get close to Chang'e."

Violet simply nodded, never taking her attention away from Chang'e. She expanded the protection spell she had already erected around herself to include Mitch.

Chang'e stood in the middle of the mele observing the activity around her. As the tide of battle turned, she seemed almost amused at the pitiful attempts to subdue her. She glanced toward the golem as it continued to hammer its broken arms against her defenses. The earth giant did not fatigue, and as long as it was able, it would continue trying to smash her as it had been commanded.

"Disrupt," Chang'e said, waving a hand dismissively at the golem.

The creature froze in mid-swing, one of its huge broken stumps raised over its head. As Mitch watched in horror, the giant collapsed backward, crumbling to useless soil, rock, and grass as it fell. The magic animating the golem from within deactivated, returning the creature to its basic elements.

Next, the demon began firing bolts of flame toward the gathered witches. The five women in the front line threw up defensive barriers and were able to protect themselves and their sisters from the assault. However, as the witches were now forced on the defensive, they were momentarily unable to continue reinforcing the net that held Chang'e.

The demonically possessed witch saw her opportunity and extended glowing wands of power, one from each of her hands. Chang'e swept the fiery rods through the air like she was wielding dual swords, slashing the bindings still clinging to her with arcs of bright light. The strands of magic previously ensnaring her parted easily wherever the light touched. A few deft strokes, and she was free of all restraints.

Simon dropped to the ground and dug his fingers deep into the soil. Mitch could not see precisely what the chief was doing as he was still focused on trying to get closer to Chang'e, but as Simon gripped the dirt in front of him, tree roots and thick tendrils of manzanita burst from the ground. The wooden appendages coiled and lashed about until they found purchase around the possessed witch's legs.

Violet and Mitch redoubled their efforts to get closer as Simon's new gambit distracted the possessed woman.

Mitch focused power at the end of his fist. As he had done while fighting against Alyssandra, he balanced as much magic as he could hold, then compressed it into a ball small enough to easily sit atop his fingertip. When he had the spell stabilized, he added more power to it, compressed it again, repeating the process as he rushed toward Chang'e.

The demon did not react to Mitch and Violet's presence. It was too busy grasping handfuls of the writhing tree roots and tearing them out of the ground. The other witches in the coven began lobbing fire and impact spells, as well as a few lethal looking ice shards. Mitch could see the ice attacks coming from a witch named Rachelle, who specialized in water-based spells.

Unfortunately, every spell broke harmlessly against Chang'e's shield. Mitch hoped the witches would not give up. Even though the steady barrage did no damage, it did keep the demon from turning its attention towards him and Violet.

When he was close enough, and he believed he had sealed enough power in his spell, Mitch punched his fist into the defensive barrier surrounding Chang'e.

"Pierce," he growled, releasing the magic in one glorious burst of energy.

The reaction to his punch was instant and dramatic. He had expected the shield to break and create a hole that he could reach through. What he had not expected, however, was a complete detonation of all the magic surrounding Chang'e. The resulting explosion knocked Mitch, Violet, and Chang'e in three different directions.

Mitch rolled on the ground, grunting uncomfortably as a sharp lance of pain stabbed through his chest. His ribs, broken only a few months ago, were reminding him that they were not completely healed. Silently thanking God that he had put on his protective vest that evening, Mitch took several shallow breaths, assessing how much damage he had taken. It did not feel like he had rebroken anything.

But damn, it really did hurt.

He wrapped his arms around himself, trying to protect his torso from further damage as he forced himself to draw and release air. His attempt to bring down the demon's magical barrier had been successful, but Mitch had also effectively taken himself out of the fight, at least temporarily.

The coven witches renewed their attacks at the momentarily defenseless demon, and Brad rushed forward with his sword raised, ready to deliver a final blow to end this battle.

Although its magical shield was gone, the demon was still agile and fast. It leapt side to side, dodging each successive magical attack, while simultaneously keeping its distance from Brad and his slashing sword. The demon lashed out, sending a series of its own combat spells back toward the assembled witches and forcing them to change once again to defensive tactics.

Violet regained her feet before Mitch. She released a shower of green stars at the leaping demon. Even at close range, she was too late to take Chang'e down. The demon had a new shield in place by the time the flashing stars found it. As each green mote reached the nimble monster, they winked out against its newly erected defenses. Mitch watched in dismay as the creature began to laugh.

Brad made another attempt to stab the demon through its black heart, but a swipe of the creature's hand threw the officer aside like a toy victimized by a child's tantrum. When he landed, Brad did not move. His body lay still in the weeds and grass of the cemetery, unconscious. Or worse.

Mitch did not have time to check on the fallen officer. Nor was he sure he could move right now even if he did have time. The fight was still on, but the good guys were starting to fall, one by one.

Chang'e dragged a finger through the air, and a pale line of fire emerged, ripping a hole in the air that hovered three feet from the ground.

"Watch out," Mitch called, wincing at a new jolt of pain in his chest. "It's a portal. Stop her. She's trying to get away."

Chang'e laughed again. "So foolish. Why would I want to leave? I'm winning," the witch cackled.

Mitch realized the demon was telling the truth. It made no effort to move through the opening it had created. The demon had created the portal for a completely different reason.

From his position on the ground, Mitch could see through the hole in the air, but beyond the tear he saw only a sickly yellow-green light. Then, something red and oddly shaped emerged, crawling slowly into Mitch's line of sight. The amorphous thing paused for a moment, seeming to sniff at the unfamiliar air on the other side of the rift before dragging its lumpy form through the gap.

The malformed creature flopped to the ground, wet and slimy, like a newborn animal thrust from its mother's womb into the light of day. But this thing was like no animal that had ever existed in this world.

"Another demon," Simon shouted.

The newly summoned demon looked like a bulging lump of cancerous flesh, with no visible arms or legs, and no head that Mitch could identify. Despite its lack of appendages, it bolted forward, propelling itself along the ground with a combination of slithering and rolling movements. The thing moved so much faster than it should have been able to given its physical morphology, and it apparently had set its sights on Jorge.

The sergeant saw the danger coming toward him. He drew his service pistol and began firing, the gun discharging rounds in a rapid fire staccato. Most of his shots went wide, but a few slugs struck the attacking demon. The impacts did not slow the thing's approach. A few feet from Jorge, the shapeless demon leapt into the air, striking the sergeant in the chest and knocking him off of his feet.

Violet continued trading spells with Chang'e, too distracted to notice the sergeant's plight, and the coven witches were too far away to attack the new demon without risking injury to Jorge. Simon was the only person close enough to help. He ran past Brad, who remained unmoving in the sparse grass of North-West, snatched up the fallen katana, and sprinted toward Jorge.

The tiny demon pinned Jorge to the ground, flattening across his chest in a boneless, gelatinous pool before suddenly slithering down his left arm. The red blob wrapped a portion of its anatomy around his wrist, then tried to flee, bounding along the ground and pulling Jorge behind it in a series of violent jerks. Sergeant Smythe could not get his feet under himself, and his free hand was unable to find purchase on anything that would halt their progress.

The monster headed toward the portal. It was trying to drag Jorge into the demons' home dimension. If it succeeded, there would be no chance of bringing him back in time to prevent him from dying there. Professor Schick had been quite insistent that the demon realm was completely inhospitable to human life.

Jorge's blindly clutching hand at last snagged the corner of a grave marker. As the sergeant clung to the stone with all his strength, the demon dragging him found itself wrenched to a sudden stop. The thing emitted an irritated squeak, then pulled at Jorge's arm again, this time twisting on the ground as it tried to move him.

Jorge cried out in pain, but he kept his hold on the gravestone.

Simon arrived a moment later, stabbing the point of Brad's katana downward through the top of the struggling demon. The blade cut through the monstrous blob, and the tip of the sword stuck in the ground beneath it.

The demon squeaked again as the sword pierced completely through. The malformed creature burst into a cloud of pink mist before disappearing altogether. The rift in the air beside Chang'e closed at the same time the demon came apart.

Demons were difficult to kill on Earth, but they could be physically damaged to the point that they would be forced to return to their own dimension. This little creature had been a very minor demon, and the single blow from Brad's angelic sword had been enough to banish it.

Chang'e noticed the loss of her summoned helper and immediately ripped open another portal. This time two new demons scrambled through into the cemetery. These creatures were not bulbous, unformed things like the first, but appeared humanoid in shape. They stood on two legs, although instead of arms, a cluster of appendages like tentacles extended from multiple points along their torsos.

"Simon," called Mitch, as he at last gained his feet. His chest still hurt if he breathed too deeply, but he finally felt capable of getting back into the fight. "There are two more. Can you handle them?"

"I can try," said Chief Jefferson, raising Brad's katana to face the smaller demons.

As its two minions faced off with the police chief, the demon possessing Chang'e turned toward the rows of witches who had again begun firing spells in its direction. Instead of attacking directly, however, this time the demon began disrupting the ground around its opponents. Explosions at the women's feet launched huge chunks of earth upward. The coven witches were tossed into the air along with the eruptions of soil and rock, disrupting their concentration and effectively stopping their coordinated efforts to battle the demon.

"Run!" shouted Violet when she saw her coven mates tossed into the air like so much debris. "Get somewhere safe."

Violet sent a vortex of yellow light at Chang'e. The magic flickered and died harmlessly on the demon's protective barrier, but the attack at least drew the possessed witch's attention away from the now defenseless women running for their lives. Chang'e sent streams of magic toward Violet, the lines of power glowing red as they wrapped themselves around her as snugly as the skintight black dress she wore.

Violet brushed a hand across her stomach as though removing an unsightly smudge of dirt, and Chang'e's attack snapped like so much red thread.

Violet waded closer to the demon, her hands glowing bright white as she came within arm's length of her opponent. Violet punched the witch's shield, using both her strength and her magic to try to bludgeon the protective barrier down.

Mitch watched the carnage around him. The scenery was grim as he assessed their chances of defeating the demon now that their initial plan had fallen apart. Jorge and Brad were down and unable to rejoin the fight. Violet's coven had fled, and Alyssandra was nowhere to be found, having apparently left the battlefield after refusing to help.

Simon continued battling the two lesser demons, but the nasty little creatures were darting left and right, avoiding the swinging sword as they relentlessly drove the chief backward. Violet was the only one other than Tink still standing and uninjured, and Tink was useless in a magical battle.

Mitch did not know what else to do, so he did the only thing he could think of. He drew his duty pistol and began shooting.

When Tink saw Mitch firing at Chang'e, he drew his own weapon and followed suit. He knew he could not fight the demon hand to hand, but this much he could still do. The rounds sparked as they struck the demon's shield, but they did not penetrate, and they did not slow the creature down.

"Mitch," Violet panted as she continued to punch at the demon's defenses. "How did you break its magic before?"

"Focus your magic into the smallest point you can. Don't try to break the shield, you're only trying to poke a hole into it."

Violet paused, shrinking the glow around her hands into pinpoints of light. She was forced to release some of the magic to deflect another attack from Chang'e, but she managed to hold the spell she had cast on her right hand without losing too much power.

Mitch fired the last bullet in his magazine. Without a new round to chamber, the slide of his pistol locked backward. He stopped to eject the emptied magazine and pull a fresh one from his belt. While he slammed the new ammo clip into his pistol and released the slide, Violet threw one more punch.

The magic she wielded did not have the same results as Mitch's shield breaker spell, but it had enough force in it to cause a ripple through Chang'e's defenses. The demon's magical barrier flickered, though only for a second.

Three gunshots rang out as Mitch raised his weapon to begin firing again. Tink emptied the last of his own rounds at the exact moment that Violet attacked the demon's defensive wall. Two bullets sparked on Chang'e's compromised shield, deflecting harmlessly away. The third round found the tiniest gap in her magical armor and sailed through without hinderance.

Chang'e's head rocked back on her neck, causing her to take one staggering step backward. Her heel caught against something, tripping her, and she toppled to the ground like a felled tree, making no effort to arrest her fall. The magic around her flickered again, then blinked out of existence. The rift she had made into the demon realm closed as suddenly as her shields failed, leaving only calm, unblemished sky behind. The demons harassing Simon also disappeared when the portal vanished. Relieved, the chief rested his hands on his knees, lowered his head and panted in exhaustion from the prolonged melee.

Chang'e remained motionless on the ground where she had fallen, her eyes open but unseeing, her arms thrown wide at her sides. A hole in her forehead leaked a trickle of blood that trailed into her left eye before pooling on her cheek.

"Is she…?" asked Mitch, letting the question trail off. He still had his pistol in his hand, ready to shoot if necessary. He did not dare holster it yet.

Violet knelt beside the still body and touched two fingers to the side of Chang'e's throat. Next she laid one hand flat on the witch's chest and the other on the top of her head.

"She's dead," Violet said. "No pulse, no heartbeat, and her brain is … shredded. It's over."

Mitch was too tired to celebrate the unexpected victory. Besides, it did not feel like much of a win. They had been unable to capture Chang'e as they had hoped, and eventually had been compelled to kill the witch to stop the demon inside her. Even that outcome had only been a fluke of timing and good fortune. Prior to one lucky bullet, the entire team of witches and officers fighting the demon had been getting their asses handed to them.

In the quiet that followed, the coven witches that had run for cover under the demon's assault returned to the battlefield. Most of the women had sustained minor injuries and bruising from their participation in the fight. Three of them had cuts that were serious enough they would require stitches, but overall, the coven was in remarkably good shape.

Brad at last sat up, and Simon returned his sword to the dazed officer. Brad would definitely need a trip to the hospital to get checked for a concussion, Mitch decided. He had taken quite a blow to the head to have been unconscious for so long.

Jorge was also sitting upright, but his left arm hung uselessly at his side. The sergeant grimaced as he clutched the injured appendage and hugged it to his chest.

"Let me see that," said one of the coven witches to Jorge. She was an older woman, though perhaps not quite as old as Alyssandra. Mitch remembered Violet had introduced her to him some time ago as Audie.

"I'll be okay," protested Jorge.

Audie tsked and knelt beside him. She grasped the injured arm, and Mitch saw a blue aura surround her.

"It's dislocated," she told the sergeant. "This might hurt a bit."

"What…? Aah!" Jorge shouted as the aura brightened around Audie, though he sounded more shocked than actually hurt. Suddenly, he relaxed and began to move the arm tentatively. "That … that feels a lot better. Thank you."

Audie beamed, pleased at the results. Without another word, she rose and returned to her sisters.

"I thought magic couldn't heal people," said Mitch to Violet. She had left the corpse of Chang'e and was now checking Mitch for injuries, poking experimentally at his chest.

"It can't," she replied. "But magic can put things back where they belong. Audie put his shoulder back in its socket, but Jorge will still need to heal on his own."

"So you can't do anything about my ribs?" he asked, teasingly.

"You're fine," Violet reassured him. "They aren't broken this time. Just bruised a bit. Don't be such a baby."

Mitch laughed, then stopped when the pain in his sides returned.

"No," said a shocked voice nearby.

Mitch searched for the source of the comment, glancing left and right. He spotted Simon, still standing with Brad, but suddenly looking pale and frightened. The chief's eyes were wide, and he was staring at something behind Mitch.

"Oh, no," breathed Mitch when he too spied the problem.

Chang'e was sitting upright.

Clearly she was not as dead as Violet had believed. The witch turned her head slowly, taking in the people around her. A garish red streak of blood ran from the open hole in her forehead, trailing over her left eye and down to her jawline. The trickle of scarlet looked like warpaint, applied carelessly and in a great hurry. She blinked, and her left eye stuck closed in the sticky gore covering her face.

The resurrected witch raised a shaking hand and clawed at the air as if trying to grasp something no one else could see. Her fingers twisted until they appeared to entangle themselves with the empty space around them, shredding open a new portal beside her. She said nothing but sneered briefly at the men and women who had laid her low. Fortunately for all of the injured combatants in the cemetery, Chang'e did not seem inclined to continue fighting.

Unsteady, but determined to push her damaged body into action, she crawled through the hole she had created.

The portal sealed shut behind her as she made her escape.

CHAPTER 18

"I thought you said she was dead," Mitch muttered.

"I did," said Violet, equally stunned by the escape of what she thought had been a corpse. "She was. I mean, she is. There was no pulse and no heartbeat. Chang'e's body was dead."

Simon approached Violet and Mitch. He pointed at the empty space where there should by all rights have been a dead witch.

"How did this happen? Where did she go?"

"I don't know," said Violet, answering both questions. "We were told that when the host dies, the demon is forced to return to its own realm. Chang'e is dead. I know she is. Her brain was scrambled by that bullet. There's no way she should have gotten up."

"I handed her to you on a silver platter, but you still managed to screw everything up."

Alyssandra emerged from behind the trees she had been using as cover during the battle. The priestess had contributed nothing in the fight, but she acted entitled to criticize those that had risked their lives to confront the demon.

"Nonetheless, the final outcome doesn't matter," she continued. "I brought her here, like I promised. Everything can go back to normal now."

"Nothing is normal until this demon is dealt with," said Simon. "Are you going to help us?"

Alyssandra waved a dismissive hand. "As I said, the final outcome doesn't matter. You will deal with the demon as you see fit, but me and my coven will no longer be assisting in any way. This is a problem for Dasan's Terrace to handle on its own."

Simon stared at Alyssandra, shocked at her declaration. Then, as if realizing that he should have expected no different, his face went calm, and he quietly cleared his throat.

"Maybe that's true," he said, "but as Chief of Police of Dasan's Terrace, I have decided to ban you from the cemetery. You are no longer welcome here, Alyssandra. Any attempts to enter the grounds will be considered trespassing and you will be arrested on the spot."

Alyssandra's eyes narrowed. She glared at the chief. "You know you cannot do that, Lost Child. You have made agreements and promises that you are not at liberty to break."

"I made agreements, that's true," agreed Simon. "However, I made those agreements with the coven. They, as a group, are still welcome per the contracts we established. It is only you that is never permitted to enter the cemetery."

"This is ridiculous. You cannot allow a coven access and deny the priestess."

"Again, you're correct. I can't," Simon told her. He gave her an enormous grin. He was obviously enjoying this moment. "Violet is, of course, allowed to enter with her coven as she sees fit."

"Violet?" snapped Alyssandra, confused. "What does she…?"

"I have officially recognized Violet as the coven priestess. As far as Dasan's Terrace is concerned, you no longer have any such standing."

"You do not have the authority to remove me. Only the coven can remove a priestess."

"And they have," said Violet, gazing at Alyssandra coldly. "All ten members have accepted me as their new leader. You no longer have their trust or their loyalty. In fact, you have no position within this coven at all as of this moment."

"You are not allowed to do that without a proper challenge," Alyssandra argued.

"That challenge already happened," Violet retorted. "And I beat your ass into the ground. Willa was witness, to both your confession that you murdered my family and your defeat at my hands. There's nothing left for you here, Alyssandra. In fact, Simon, were you able to take care of that matter for me?"

"I was," said the chief.

He removed a slip of paper from his coat pocket and handed it to Violet. Violet did not unfold it but handed it directly to Alyssandra.

"This is an eviction notice. You have thirty days to vacate the house you're staying in and find new lodging. Preferably someplace far, far away from here, because I've decided to stay, and if I ever run into you again it will not end well for you."

"You can't take my house," insisted Alyssandra, but her tone of righteous anger had degraded to little more than confused pleading.

"It's not your house," Violet said. "It is an asset belonging to the Thirteenth Circle. You signed the house over to the company when we took over paying your mortgage years ago, if you'll remember. As you are no longer a member of this coven, you are also no longer an employee of Thirteenth Circle. The house is for employees only, and therefore it is not available to you."

"You can't do this. I don't accept it. You have no rights to do this to me, and I won't simply walk away."

"Yes, you will," Simon warned her. "You will walk away, or I'll throw you back in prison."

"We had a deal," Alyssandra jabbed a bony finger in the chief's direction. "You will honor it."

"I'm not talking about that," Simon replied mildly. "I'm talking about the attempted murder of Chang'e when you burned her house to the ground."

Simon removed a second slip of paper from his coat.

"This is an agreement with the District Attorney's office to grant full immunity from prosecution to two as yet unnamed eyewitnesses for their testimony that you orchestrated the entire attack on Chang'e in her home. If you choose to stick around, I will move forward with this."

Alyssandra turned toward the assembled coven members. Her gaze found Willa and Audie in the group.

"They wouldn't dare," Alyssandra said in utter disbelief.

Willa stared at the ground, not wanting to meet her former coven leader's eyes. Audie however, glared right back at Alyssandra.

"You're goddamned wrong about that," the woman told Alyssandra. "After what you did to Violet's family, I'll tell the cops everything they want to know. I'll even make up some shit if that's what it takes."

Violet smiled quietly at Audie's remarks, turning her head to one side so no one would see. Mitch, however, caught the expression. He was smiling, too.

"What will it be?" asked Simon. "Disappear with your tail between your legs, or prison?"

Alyssandra peered at the people surrounding her, pausing a long moment to stare at each face.

"I'll leave. I give you fair warning, though, this isn't over."

The small smile on Violet's face vanished. Her expression turned deadly serious.

"It had better be over," she said, moving to within two feet of Alyssandra. She leaned in until their noses almost touched. "If you try to harm me or anyone I care about.... No, that's not good enough. If I so much as see you or hear your name ever again, I will hunt you down, and I swear to God, this time not even Mitch will be able to stop me from finishing what I started."

Alyssandra stood mute for several seconds. When she started to open her mouth, Violet interrupted.

"Whatever you're thinking, don't you dare say it. It will only piss me off, and you don't want that. Forget thirty days. You need to disappear tonight. Get the fuck out of my life, Alyssandra."

Mitch stood behind Violet, backing up her threat. To his surprise, Simon stepped behind them both, indicating his agreement with Violet's ultimatum.

Alyssandra wisely stayed quiet. Without another word, she turned and stalked away. They all watched as her slender silhouette disappeared into the darkness of the surrounding cemetery. When she was gone, Violet's shoulders slumped as if the energy had completely drained from her body. She turned and leaned into Mitch, who caught her and held her tightly against himself despite a twinge of complaint from his injured ribs.

"It's okay," he told her. "I've got you."

"I know," she whispered. "Thank you."

Mitch felt her shudder against him. Adrenaline letdown and fatigue combined to leave her absolutely exhausted.

"That didn't feel as good as I thought it would," Violet whispered.

"If it had, you wouldn't be the person that I know you are," Mitch reassured her. "Besides this wasn't about feeling good. We did this so you could find some measure of closure."

"Closure?" she said, then laughed with absolutely no amusement in her voice. "What closure?"

"Can you live with this?" Mitch asked simply. "Can you accept, knowing everything you now know, that this is the only punishment Alyssandra will receive? And can you move on without the burden of wishing you had done more?"

Violet did not speak for a time. Her steady breathing did not change as she leaned against his chest. If she had not still been on her feet, Mitch might have thought she had fallen asleep.

"I think so," she said, at last. "At least, I can if I know you're with me."

He squeezed her again. "Of course I am. Always.

Mitch felt a hand settle on his shoulder. He turned his head to see Simon watching him gravely.

"Do either of you have any thoughts about Chang'e?" Simon asked. "We dealt with one problem tonight, but that demon is still out there."

Mitch sighed. All he wanted to do right now was take Violet home, curl up in bed with her and sleep for the next week. But they did not have a week. Mitch had no idea how long it would be before the demon made another attempt to take Dasan's Terrace. All he knew for certain was that they would not have any control over when the next confrontation occurred. The demon had complete autonomy over its next move.

"We have people here that are hurt," Mitch said. "First, let's get them taken care of."

Simon nodded. "Agreed. Then I need to start making calls to the sergeants. I'm doubling up patrols in the cemetery. Two teams on at all times, twelve-hour shifts without days off until this demon is dealt with. Violet, can your coven help?"

Violet nodded against Mitch's chest. "Yes. I can keep two witches in the cemetery as long as you need them. I'll have them relieve each other every eight hours so no one gets too tired."

"Thank you," Simon told her.

"I need to get Violet home," Mitch said to his chief. "As soon as I drop her off, I'll come back. With Jorge and Brad hurt, it will only be Tink and me until you can get the other night shift team to come in."

"No," Violet argued, looking up at him. "If you're staying, I'm staying."

"Okay, but I'm putting you in the break room and you need to try and get some sleep. First thing tomorrow, we need to go talk to Professor Schick again. Maybe he can tell us what the hell just happened, and hopefully, he'll have some ideas about how to fix it."

CHAPTER

19

Early the next morning, Mitch called Solomon Schick and asked for another meeting. The professor was enjoying his summer break and had no current classes to teach, so he promptly agreed to see Mitch and Violet as soon as they were available to visit.

After a short drive, Mitch found himself once again in the professor's immaculate kitchen, sitting at the same small breakfast table where they had gathered only a few days ago. Solomon and Violet both held hot cups of tea, but Mitch had declined the offer this time and instead had a glass of water on the table in front of him.

"And you are quite sure she was dead," Solomon asked after taking a thoughtful sip from his cup.

"She was dead," Violet repeated. "I checked and there was no heartbeat. I couldn't find any activity in the brain either."

"This is very bad," said Solomon. "It means you were wrong before."

"Wrong about what?" asked Violet.

"Wrong about the demon. You told me that this, uh…,"

"Chang'e," Mitch supplied.

"Yes, this Chang'e person, you said she only summoned minor demons. Reanimating a body is not something within the abilities of a minor demon. Whatever she summoned was extremely powerful. In fact, in order to claim a host after the soul has fled would require a creature of quite high rank. Your friend got herself involved with something she had no hope of controlling."

"She wasn't a friend," Mitch clarified. "Regardless, we have no idea what to expect next, and we were hoping you could help us."

Solomon nodded absently, gazing around the kitchen as he pondered the request.

"I can tell you that there is both good news and bad news. Although, it is mostly bad news I'm afraid."

"Mm-hmm," said Mitch, emotionally and physically drained from the past few days. "Go on."

"I suppose I should start by explaining what the demon is doing."

The professor paused again, and Mitch waved a hand, indicating Solomon should continue.

"Demons are spiritual creatures, first of all. They can only stay in our world as long as they have a link to their own realm. After the gate through which they have entered is closed, they are in most situations compelled to return. When a demon takes over a host body, they intertwine themselves with the soul of their host. This gives them the ability to remain here even after their gate has closed. They still require contact with their own realm periodically to um, recharge, I guess you could say, but as long as they have a host, they are difficult to remove."

“We know that much,” said Violet. “You told us the same thing last time we talked. You also told us that if we killed the host, the demon would be forced out of the body and it would have to return to its own realm.”

“Yes, I did. What I did not tell you, because I had no idea we were dealing with such a powerful creature, is that a few demons have the ability to stay in their host even after the soul of that body has fled. In order to do this, they have to, in essence, evolve into the new spirit animating the physical body. They must become that body’s missing soul.”

“Are you saying that the demon isn’t just occupying Chang’e anymore, but it has actually become her?”

“No, no, no,” said Solomon. “You misunderstand completely. The demon is not becoming Chang’e. Chang’e’s body is becoming the physical manifestation of the demon in our world.”

“What does that mean?” asked Mitch. “In practical terms. In plain English.”

“Chang’e is gone,” said Solomon. “The demon exists physically in this realm now. We can’t force it to leave. It will only return to its own dimension when it chooses to.”

“That’s bad,” said Mitch.

“Yes,” agreed Solomon. “That’s bad.”

“So, that’s the bad news,” said Violet.

“Oh, no. That is only some of the bad news. There is much more.”

Mitch took a long drink from his water glass. He was not particularly thirsty, but his mind was telling him to drink from the glass or throw it across the room, and under the circumstances he felt the first option would be more polite.

When he put the glass back on the table, he said, “Professor, please tell us the rest. What are we facing?”

Solomon raised his own cup, glanced at it, and realized it was almost empty. Rising from the table he collected the teapot from his stovetop and poured himself more tea. He held the pot out toward Violet, and she accepted a refill as well.

"I suppose the best way to explain it is this," Solomon said, replacing the pot on the stove then returning to his chair. "As long as the demon inhabits a physical body, the body cannot be killed. The demon has the power to repair almost any damage short of complete dismemberment or immolation. In addition, as long as there is a physical body to inhabit, there is no way to force the demon to return to its own realm."

"We can't kill it, and we can't make it go home," Violet summarized. "So, we've already lost? Should we give up and hand over Dasan's Terrace?"

"That would be one solution," Solomon agreed, blowing on his tea to cool it.

"Wait a minute," said Mitch, rubbing the bridge of his nose with his thumb and forefinger. He could feel a headache coming on, and this conversation was only making his situation worse. "You said there was good news. What is it?"

"I said there was mostly bad news, but yes, there is some good news."

"And…?" Mitch was getting tired of having to pull information out of Solomon. He wished the old man would cut out all the professorial oration and simply get to the point.

"It will take the demon a few days to gain full control of its new body. After the original soul leaves, the demon must take control by brute force. It will be a while before it has fully integrated with its stolen physical form."

"If we find it before it's fully in control, we can stop it somehow?" Mitch asked.

"No."

"But maybe we can still force it to leave?"

"No."

"Then how the hell is this good news?" Mitch slapped his hand on the table in frustration.

"Mitch. Calm down," said Violet, laying a hand on his arm.

"The demon will be distracted, getting accustomed to its new body. It most likely will not come back to the cemetery until it is confident in its control. That gives you a few days to rest and plan."

"That's it? A few days to rest?" Mitch took a deep breath, then released it slowly, trying to bring his blood pressure back down. "So, we get a few days before this demon comes back and takes over the cemetery. That's pretty lousy good news."

"No, Mitch. It actually is good news. The demon needs some time. In fact, I'm willing to bet it will be more than a few days before it comes for us again."

"How do you figure?"

"We have managed to chase it off two…, no, three times in the past week. It knows we aren't going to let it have the cemetery without a fight, and that we are currently ready to face it if it comes back. If I were that demon, I wouldn't be in such a hurry to try again."

"You would wait for us to get tired. Maybe let our guard down a little," suggested Mitch.

"Right. Since the demon can stay in this realm as long as it likes, what's the hurry? It can sit tight and watch until we get sloppy and give it an opening. If it's patient enough, it might wait weeks, or months."

"Years," said Mitch.

"I wouldn't count on that, but yes. The point is, we have a little time, and maybe we can take advantage of that window."

Violet turned to the professor and gave him her most admiring smile. She batted her eyelashes, the perfect damsel in distress. Mitch knew the look. She usually turned it on him when she was trying to get him to do something he did not want to do.

"Solomon," said Violet. "You know a lot about this sort of stuff, don't you? Demons, angels, and other realms?"

"More than most, yes," the professor agreed. "I don't know everything there is to know, but I have devoted a significant amount of my life to studying the origins of the mythological and religious beliefs of our world."

"Then you must have heard of something, of some way we can still fight this demon. We can't kill it, and we can't force it to go home, but isn't there any way of protecting Dasan's Terrace? Can we … I don't know, bargain with it, or convince it to leave?"

"Hmm. Probably not," said Solomon, tapping a finger to his chin. "It seems to be quite keen on taking over the cemetery. If you haven't convinced it to leave you alone already, I don't see any way to change its mind now."

"Solomon," Violet said, leaning forward and lowering her voice to a confidential level, as if she were attempting to share a secret with the professor. "Help us. Is there anything you haven't told us? Is there something out there, even if it's a long shot, or seems foolish to try?"

"There may be one thing," Solomon admitted. "I don't know if it will work. I have never tried it myself, or even seen it attempted. It certainly isn't anything that I would recommend except under the most dire of circumstances. Which, I suppose considering our position, these might be."

"I think we have reached that point," said Violet. "What are you referring to? Is it something that might help us stop a demon?" she asked in the same conspiratorial tone.

"The demon can't be killed or forced home, but I do know of a … particular sort of box, or um, artifact, that is capable of imprisoning a demonic spirit. I don't know much about it personally, but I have been told it is quite effective if operated properly. The source of that information is, however, as you might say, um, dodgy."

"Dodgy?" Violet asked. "How do you mean?"

"I mean, the owner of this item is a, ahem, collector of antiquities who uses some questionable means to obtain his pieces. He also is not a believer in the arcane, and simply gathers his prizes because of their monetary worth, rather than their magical value."

"Have you seen it? asked Violet. "The box? Do you think it's real?"

"Why didn't you tell us about this box last time we were here," Mitch growled. Violet glared at him. "What? I just want to know why we couldn't use it the last time we ran into this demon. Maybe we would already be done with this whole mess."

"I did not think to tell you about it then," began Solomon, "because, as I said, I cannot speak to the artifact's efficacy. The owner of this box is not an expert on the demonic, and I have only been able to examine the trap superficially. Also, when you came to me last time, I seem to remember that you were still trying to save the woman the demon was using as its host. Imprisoning a demon in this device while it inhabits a living human being would have dragged the human soul into the trap along with it. I didn't think that was what you wanted to accomplish. Third, and most importantly…,"

"You didn't think of it then," Violet said, finishing the professor's sentence.

"Um, well, yes. I only just now remembered it," Solomon said, embarrassed by the confession.

"That's okay. We know about it now," Violet told him. "And since Chang'e's soul is already gone, do you believe we can use this box safely?"

"I don't see why not," Solomon mused. "And by that I mean, you can use the box. I would not say it is safe. Nothing dealing with demons is safe."

"On that, I think all three of us agree," said Violet.

Mitch nodded.

"Do you think you can convince your friend to give us the box?" he asked.

"This man is not my friend. I would barely call him an acquaintance. But yes, I do believe he would sell it to us. As I said, he is more impressed with the money these items can bring than he is with the ethereal or historical value. When he showed me the demon trap, he offered it to me for five thousand dollars. I believe the offer would stand. Providing, of course, he has not already sold it elsewhere."

Mitch blew out a surprised breath. "Five thousand. Chief Jefferson is not going to like taking a hit like that to his annual budget."

"Dasan's Terrace has funding for exactly this sort of thing," Violet assured him. "Besides, if Simon doesn't want to cover it, Thirteenth Circle will. Solomon, please arrange to purchase the demon trap as soon as possible. This afternoon, if possible. I would like to have it in my hands with enough time to figure out how to use it."

"If it works," Mitch said, gloomily.

"Yes," Violet acknowledged. "If it works. And if it doesn't, I want to have enough time to go find this collector friend of yours and beat him unconscious with his own fake trap."

"I will reach out to him immediately," Solomon promised. "Is that everything, then?"

"No, not quite," Violet told him. "We still have the same problem we have had from the beginning. We don't know how to summon the demon. Do you know anyone that has done a summoning, or at least knows the basics on how to do it?"

"I do, actually. I myself am familiar with the technique. I own a journal written in the fourteenth century that outlines the process in quite a bit of detail."

Mitch almost erupted at the table but caught himself at the last moment. He breathed through his frustration until he could speak with some civility, then asked, "Again, Solomon, why are we only hearing about this now? Why didn't you tell us you knew how to perform a summons last time?"

"Because you told me you did not have the demon's name," Solomon said blandly. "Without the name, you cannot summon a demon at all. Why would you need a summoning ritual? Also, you did not ask last time. I will not be held responsible for not providing information you did not ask for."

"Solomon," Violet said quickly, "Mitch is sorry. He's under a lot of pressure to protect the people he cares about. He's on edge. We all are, actually. Mitch?"

"Yeah. Sorry about that. You have been a big help to us, and just because I'm feeling helpless, doesn't mean I should take it out on you."

"I am sorry, too," said the professor. "Perhaps I have been viewing this entire situation through too much of an academic lens. I haven't been fully understanding of what is truly happening to all of you. I will endeavor to do better. In fact, let me offer you this as an olive branch."

Solomon stood up and left the kitchen. He wandered upstairs and out of sight for several minutes. Mitch and Violet remained at the table and waited impatiently for the professor to return. Before long, Mitch began to grow restless, and he was about to go looking for Solomon when the older man returned holding a small black notebook.

"This," said Solomon, holding up the book, "is a detailed accounting of how to conduct a summoning."

"It doesn't look seven hundred years old," Mitch commented, gesturing toward the notebook.

"This?" laughed Solomon. "Oh, no. The original book is far too fragile to be handled without great care. Besides, it was written in the Francien dialect, a medieval form of French. You most likely would not be able to read it. No, this book is my own translation of the original journal, complete with illustrations and personal notes. It should give you everything you need to conduct a summons. Before you leave, I will walk you through each step until I am confident you understand it as well as I do."

"Thank you," Violet told him. "That will be very helpful."

"When we are finished, you may take the book with you, if you like. I wouldn't recommend attempting the summoning from memory. Especially with a demon as powerful as … what was its name, by the way?"

"We don't actually know its name, yet," admitted Violet. "We're still trying to figure that out."

"I don't understand. I thought you said you were able to force it to comply with its oath. I assumed that meant you had its name."

"No. We managed to learn Chang'e's real name, and Alyssandra was able to compel the demon using that."

"But we still can, right?" asked Mitch. "I mean, the demon is Chang'e now, so her name should still work."

Solomon shook his head and opened his mouth, but Violet spoke first.

"Weren't you listening? Chang'e, the real Chang'e, is gone. Even though it is still using her body, the demon is not bound to her anymore, and attempting to summon it using her name won't work. We need the demon's true name this time."

Solomon sat down and placed the notebook on the table. He slid it gently toward Violet.

"Please, take my notes. We can review them until you're comfortable that you understand the process."

Violet accepted the book. "Thank you. We should go ahead with our plan as best we can while we search for the demon's name. All we can do is hope the pieces come together in time. Otherwise, we…,"

Violet did not finish the thought. Instead, she opened the notebook and glanced at the first few pages.

"Okay," she said. "Let's start with this diagram. What do we need for our summoning circle?"

CHAPTER 20

Mitch and Violet sat in Chief Jefferson's office. It was late in the evening, long after the chief had normally gone home for the day, but under the circumstances, Mitch had not been surprised to find him still at work. Dot was also at her desk, seeming to have no plans to leave before her boss. When Mitch and Violet arrived in the upstairs lobby asking to speak with Simon, she followed them into the office and claimed the third empty chair in the room for herself.

A few minutes later, the detective, the witch, and the office administrator sat in a row, watching intently as Simon turned a block of wood over and over in his hands. The block appeared to be constructed from a single piece of dark wood, with no hinges, cracks or visible seams. The six outside faces were meticulously inlayed with silver, gold, and bronze filagree, twisted and shaped into various images and symbols.

"Seven thousand dollars for this?" grunted Simon, placing the item carefully onto his desk.

Solomon had been successful in obtaining the demon trap from his "dodgy" companion that same afternoon. Upon the professor's inquiry, the collector advised he still had the box and was happy to arrange a meeting later in the week. Solomon had urged that they meet as soon as possible, advising that time was a bit of a factor for this purchase. Unfortunately for the professor, Mitch, and Violet, as soon as the dealer saw how eager they were to obtain the trap, the price went from five thousand dollars to seven.

"We can share the cost with you, Simon, if that's a problem." advised Violet.

"Of course not," the chief replied. "This is to protect Dasan's Terrace. The Sheriff isn't going to give me any grief over a lousy seven thousand."

"I'll make sure your professor friend gets reimbursed tomorrow," Dot told Mitch. Simon grunted agreement.

"Do we know this will work?" asked the chief.

"It sort of has to," answered Mitch. "It's all we have left. Unless anyone can think of a better option?"

The room settled into a gloomy silence.

"Professor Schick vouched for it," said Violet finally. "He examined it closely after we bought it, and he advised that from the markings he is familiar with and able to translate, the trap seems legitimate. He sounded like he knows what he's doing, so I am willing to put my faith in him."

"Because we have nothing else?" asked Simon darkly.

Violet pressed her lips together grimly. "Because we have nothing else," she agreed.

"Assuming the trap works," said Dot, "do you think it has ever been used before?"

"I would think so," said Mitch. His eyes narrowed as he considered the question. "Why would anyone go to the trouble of making the thing if they didn't have an immediate need for it? I'm guessing whoever created the trap had a demon problem, or at least knew someone who did."

"So, there is probably at least one demon already inside it?" continued Simon's diminutive assistant. "Or more."

"Dot?" asked Violet, knowing the woman was not simply talking for the sake of talking. Dot was friendly and chatty in normal situations, but she would never speak without specific purpose in a meeting like this one. "Where are you going with this?"

"I was wondering if there is a limit to what this trap can hold. Has it already reached that limit, and how would we know? Most importantly, what will happen if it is used after it's already full?"

All four sets of eyes settled on the box sitting on the chief's desk. The last question had not needed to be asked, as they were all thinking the same thing, but Dot was not one to leave something so important unspoken.

Simon settled back into his seat, collapsing into the cushions and looking utterly exhausted.

"I think we come back to our initial assessment," he said. "We have nothing else. Mitch, where are we on finding this demon's name? Have you got any leads?"

"No, Chief. Sorry. I've been working with Professor Schick on learning how to do a summons, and then we were waiting all day for him to get us the demon trap. I haven't been looking for the thing's name. In all honesty, Simon, I'm not even sure where to look anymore. My best leads have all dried up. The demon got to the coven witches before we did."

"It got all of them?" asked Simon.

"I think so," Mitch replied.

Dot turned to him with an inquisitive look on her face. “Mitchell,” she said. “Do you think so, or do you know so?”

“I … I think so,” he told her. “I handed off the search to a detective friend of mine that works in Homicide. Ali Minhas. I’m sure he would have called me if he found anything. He knows how important this is.”

“Does he know specifically what we need from him?” asked Dot, not relenting in her cross examination.

“He does. I mean, I didn’t explain everything to him, he doesn’t believe in any of this stuff, but I gave him enough that he would reach out to me if he found any of the coven members alive.”

“Okay. If you’re certain it’s a dead end, we all trust you.”

Mitch heard an edge to Dot’s voice. It wasn’t harsh, or disapproving, but it reminded him of the times his mother would ask him to clean his room. She would come in an hour or so later to check on him, look around at the mess he hadn’t touched and say to him, “If you think this is clean, I guess it’s clean.” Then she would walk out without another word.

Mitch would then clean his room for the rest of the day until it was absolutely spotless.

That same vague feeling that he had disappointed his mother was how he felt now. Dot’s pronouncement left him wondering if he had been a bit lax, and because of it, maybe he had missed something.

He pulled out his cellphone.

“If nobody minds, I think I’ll call Ali and check in.”

Dot’s expression did not change. She was far too smart for that. Mitch did notice, however, a small smirk on Violet’s face.

Ali answered his call on the first ring.

“Hey, man, how’s it going on your end?”

"Not great, Ali. We actually got our hands on Chang'e last night, but she slipped away."

"Damn. That sucks. Do you think she took off, or is she still going to be a problem for you?"

"She's definitely going to be a problem. After last night, she went back into hiding, but she won't stay underground for long. Which is why I'm calling. I was wondering if you found any of the women on that list. Alive, I mean. I was hoping that Chang'e missed at least one of them."

"No, man. I'm sorry, but I haven't found any of them alive."

Mitch looked at the others in the room and shook his head. He could feel the hope evaporating throughout the office.

"She got all of them, then?"

"Out of the eight names, I've already found six bodies," Ali said. "The other two, I can't find any trace. I'm thinking if they managed to get away from your crazy demon witch, they're probably so well hidden we won't find them anytime soon. Between you and me, though, I'm guessing their bodies are going to turn up in the next couple days. Your girl was pretty thorough."

"That's what I was afraid of," Mitch responded. "I really needed that demon's name, but I guess it isn't going to happen now."

"You're still looking for that name?" asked Ali, his surprise clear even over the phone.

"Yeah. It's what we've been looking for the whole time."

"I know you were looking for it when we talked Monday, but I thought you told me you needed it by yesterday or it wouldn't matter."

"Well, yeah, we did need it yesterday," Mitch explained. "Chang'e got away from us, though, so we still need it."

"Shit. I didn't realize that. Sorry, man. I thought it didn't matter anymore. I should have called you this morning."

"Why?" Mitch asked. "What happened this morning?"

"I've been searching our victims' homes, trying to find anything to tie them to your … what did you call her? Witch priestess?"

"Yeah. Coven Priestess."

"Anyway, I found a bunch of stuff that shows these women were into some creepy shit. Not just witchcraft and demon worship, but some other fucked up underground dealings. This morning, I found a journal at one of the houses written by one of these weirdos. She wrote about everything they were doing with our killer."

"Have you read through the journal?" asked Mitch.

He felt his heart beating faster. This could be the lead they needed. He tried not to let his excitement show, however, either to Ali or to the others in the room. He did not want to get anyone's hopes up until they had a solid lead, especially not his own.

Ali laughed. "Yeah, I've been flipping through it. It lays out how all nine of them were working together. It even mentions the girl that got killed a few weeks back. Zinea. The one you told me about. This book is going to make our case for us."

Ali laughed again, then Mitch could hear him over the phone rustling around as if searching for something.

"Anyway, you gotta read this thing. It's got dates, locations, it even lists a few things they did that we didn't know about. We can add them to the charges on Chang'e when we catch her. Best part though, Mitch, is this book is full of names."

"Demon names?" he asked, his excitement winning out over his pragmatism this time.

Violet's eyes widened, and Dot and Simon both leaned forward in their seats.

"These ladies were grade-A wackos," Ali said, "but this girl, Jessica Lassiter, sure knew how to keep records. Hang on."

Mitch heard the phone click as it was set down on something hard, then the shushed sound of pages turning. He waited, keeping quiet only with difficulty. He wanted to shout at Ali to hurry, but he knew that would not help matters. He chewed on his lip with impatience and kept his mouth shut.

"Here it is. Jessica wrote that this coven of hers regularly summoned demons. They would use the demon's magic to fuel spells because they did not have ready access to other sources of power. She said you guys have lots of magic at the cemetery, but you won't let them in to use it. Hey, is that why this Chang'e nutjob is so mad at you all?"

"That's part of it," admitted Mitch. "The demons, Ali? Did Jessica write down their names?"

"She wrote that Chang'e had somehow figured out the names of three demons. They managed to summon all three, but two of them were pretty weak, so whenever they needed something big, they would use the third one. The names were…,"

"Wait a sec," said Mitch. He looked at Simon and made a scribbling motion in the air. The chief handed him a notepad and pen. "Sorry. Go ahead. I'm ready."

"The names were Mortic, Persuphil, and Bala-Ahl." Ali spelled the names out for Mitch as he said them.

"Just the three? There weren't any others?"

"Not according to the journal. These three were the only ones Jessica knew about, and from all the detail in this journal, I'm guessing there wasn't a whole lot going on in this group that Jessica wasn't aware of."

"And how sure are you on the names? The pronunciation, I mean."

"Pretty sure," Ali assured him. "This crazy lady wrote the names with phonetic explanations on the pronunciation. I guess she thought knowing the right way to say them was important. I suppose if you're calling a demon, you don't want to get its name wrong, huh? Anyway, she wrote Mortic like it was 'more-tick.' Then Per-sue-fill. And Bah-lah-Ah-hull."

Mitch wrote the names down, including Ali's phonetic pronunciation. The homicide detective did not understand, but getting the demons' names exactly right was indeed critical.

"Did Jessica mention which one was the strongest demon? Or say which was Chang'e's favorite?"

"The strongest one was Bala-Ahl. Jessica wrote that none of the coven members were allowed to even try to summon that one without Chang'e around to oversee it."

"Thanks, Ali."

"Does any of this help you?" Ali asked.

"More than you will ever know," Mitch assured him. "When we catch Chang'e, yours will be the first number I call. You're looking at another big notch in your gun."

Mitch could almost hear the homicide detective's grin over the phone.

"When this is over," Ali said, "I'm buying the first round of beers."

"When this is over, yes you are."

Mitch hung up, then tapped the notepad eagerly.

"We got it," he announced. "We have everything we need to finish this."

Simon clapped his hands and began rubbing them together in anticipation. "Then we need to get planning. We can't let what happened last night happen again. I think it's time to reach out to a few friends for some outside help. Dot, can you call the department sergeants and have them here for another meeting tomorrow morning? Let's say ten o'clock. I have a few calls of my own to…,"

"Simon, wait."

Violet's voice was soft but firm as she interrupted. She glanced toward Mitch, who nodded his agreement.

"Mitch and I have discussed this at some length before we came here. We didn't have the demon's name, so I wasn't going to bring it up as it seemed a bit premature. Now that we are moving forward, I think it is important that Mitch and I face the demon alone this time."

"What?" asked Simon, astounded at the request. "No. Absolutely not. Last night was a disaster, and we had sixteen people out there. I can't let the two of you go alone. It would be suicide."

"Chief, please," said Mitch. "Like Violet said, the two of us talked about this a lot before coming here. There are two major things you should know before you tell us no."

Simon crossed his arms across his chest. "I'm listening," he said, although his posture suggested otherwise.

"First, that box is not just the best chance we have. I think it's the only chance. Solomon…, Professor Schick, made it very clear that this demon is too strong to defeat in a direct confrontation. The problem with the demon trap is that it isn't simply a one-way device. When we activate it and attempt to pull the demon into that box, it will open in two directions. It will become a battle to drag the demon into the trap, and if we fail, we don't get to try again. We will be the ones sealed inside forever."

"We don't know if only the ones using the box are at risk," added Violet. "If we have several people in the cemetery when we open it, I am afraid all of us might be caught in the snare. Neither Mitch nor I want to risk anyone else when we attempt this."

Simon paused, but he still did not seem completely convinced. "And the second thing?" he asked.

Mitch turned to Dot. "Your premonition," he said. "I think there is more to what you saw than what you told us. You said that if Violet and I leave Dasan's Terrace, then the demon will win. Right?"

Dot nodded uncertainly. "I think so. That explanation makes the most sense to me. You don't agree?"

"No, I agree," Mitch hastened to say. "But I wanted to ask you, was there anyone else there besides the demon, me and Violet?"

Dot considered for a moment, then said, "No. There were three ravens. I didn't see anyone, or anything, else."

"Is it possible that what you saw was a fight between only the three of us? Could your vision mean that Violet and I have to face the demon by ourselves? We tried combatting it as a group, but we failed. Maybe the only way to defeat this demon is if Violet and I fight it alone. What do you think?"

"I...,"

Dot hesitated, then turned toward Simon. The chief watched her closely, visibly wanting her to say no. Every line in his body screamed at Dot to tell Violet and Mitch that they were wrong, and they should accept all the help Dasan's Terrace had to offer them. Dot mouthed a small apology to him, then dropped her eyes to her lap.

"It is possible," she finally admitted. "I want to say it isn't, but I still struggle sometimes to interpret the things I see. You're right though, Mitchell. There were only you and Violet in Dasan's Terrace facing the demon. That doesn't mean there can't be more people involved, but ... I ... I don't think there are. The more I think about my dream, the more I think this confrontation is about the three of you specifically."

"This is a mistake," insisted Simon.

"Maybe," Mitch agreed. "But then again, maybe the mistake is not trusting Dot's vision enough to try. If Violet and I never face the demon alone, we may already have lost."

Simon closed his eyes, defeated but still reluctant to send two people on a mission that could leave them dead, or worse.

"When would you do this?" he asked.

"We have everything we need," Mitch told him. "We have the trap, the demon's name, and Solomon's notes on conducting a summoning."

"Professor Schick mentioned that summonings are at their most effective on a full moon," said Violet. "The next full moon is on Monday, four days from now. I'm reluctant to wait that long, since every day we hesitate, the demon is going to grow more secure in Chang'e's old body. I believe we should move while the demon is still adapting to Chang'e's death."

"We will try to bring the demon to us tomorrow morning," Mitch told the chief. "Not early. A little bit before noon. We'll do this in North-West again. Chief, please make sure the day shift team is aware and stays as far away as they can."

"I'll do that."

"And one more thing. Do you mind if I take the night off? Violet and I…. Well, this might be our last…."

"Of course. No need to say anything else. Go home. Spend tonight together."

"Thanks."

"Thank you, Simon," said Violet.

Simon inhaled and released a shaky breath. His eyes were wet, as though he had just done something he knew he was destined to regret. He looked at Violet, then at Mitch, and forced a more relaxed look onto his face.

"Good luck," he told them.

CHAPTER
21

Friday morning was hot, even for a typical July day. As he wiped at sweat beading on his forehead, Mitch briefly regretted not waiting for nighttime when the temperature would be more reasonable.

No, he chided himself. The night might be cooler, but he did not want to face this demon again in the dark. Wednesday night had gone poorly. Maybe he would do better when it was easier for him to see what was happening.

In deference to this heat, both Violet and Mitch had forgone their usual outfits; Violet's black dress, and Mitch's police uniform. Today, they wore loose T-shirts and shorts. They might lose a few points for stylishness, but if this was going to be their last day on Earth, they could at least be somewhat comfortable.

Mitch watched patiently as Violet knelt on a mostly bald patch of ground. She had brushed away most of the surface litter and debris to create a flat, useable space in which to work.

"How does that look?" she asked, leaning backward and sitting on her heels to allow Mitch a clearer view of her efforts.

She had finished drawing the primary summoning circle using salt to create an outline. Violet had opted for this ingredient since, as she told Mitch, it was easy to manipulate, cheap to get in large quantities, and the compound element already had some minor affinity to magic.

"Okay," said Mitch, tracing a finger along a line of text in the notebook. "Solomon's notes say to attach four smaller circles to the main ring at the north, south, east, and west edges. The circles must touch but not overlap at all."

Violet followed Mitch's directions, pouring neat, steady lines using the small metal spout on top of the salt carton. When she finished to her satisfaction, she paused, waiting for further instructions. Reading the written explanation in front of him, he told her to fill the secondary circles with different symbols, each meant to convey a specific action during the summoning. He showed Violet the page in question, and she dutifully copied the images Solomon had drawn. When that was finished, they stood at opposite ends of the configuration and admired their handiwork. Mitch glanced at a diagram in the notebook, then at the ground. What he saw seemed to match, and he gave a nod of approval.

"I think that's it," he said. "Is the trap ready?"

"Violet pointed to the filigreed box that currently sat in the dirt on the south end of the summoning circle.

"I'll activate it when the demon is in the central ring. As soon as I give you the word, drop the barrier and help me power the trap. From what Solomon told us, it's probably going to take everything both of us have to get the creature inside."

"Probably," Mitch agreed. "Okay. Let's do this thing. Which demon should we call first?"

"I am almost positive that Bala-Ahl is going to be the demon we want, but maybe we should start with one of the others. A kind of test run, if you will."

"That's not a bad idea. We don't know for certain what's going to happen. Starting with one of the weaker demons seems a smart way to go."

Violet gestured toward the symbol drawn in the northern quadrant of the diagram. The image consisted of a spiraling line that began in the middle of the attached smaller circle and ended when it contacted the edge. The spiral mirrored the image Alyssandra had used when she had brought Chang'e to the cemetery. Professor Schick had explained that this symbol was a guide to help the summoner locate the demon he or she wished to call.

"Go ahead. Power it up."

While explaining the directions in his notebook, Solomon had lectured them about how little natural magic was necessary to power a summoning gate. It was one of the reasons that weaker magic users sought out demons. It took minimal exertion to call them, and in return, the summoner could gain a great deal of power from the imprisoned spirit. Bringing this particular demon to the cemetery, now that it held a physical body, was going to be a different matter. Pulling it from wherever it currently hid and into Dasan's Terrace would take a significant effort for Mitch and Violet to achieve.

To begin, Mitch allowed a small trickle of magic to flow into the spiral image. In his mind, he scanned outward, searching for signs of any demonic presence.

"By your name, I seek you, Mortic. You cannot hide from me. I know you, and by your name, I seek you."

The fan of magic Mitch had seen encircle Alyssandra on Wednesday night, now surrounded him. He could feel tiny vibrations along each thread as the summoning cast outward in search of the named demon. The odd sensation left Mitch feeling like a spider, sitting at the center of its web and waiting for a trapped insect to signal its location.

"By your name, I seek you, Mortic," he repeated. The sensations around him became brighter, more insistent. Several threads of magic flickered and died as they failed to find any purchase in their search, leaving others still questing. "By your name, I seek you, Mortic."

Seconds ticked past, and now only five lines remained bright and active as all the others dimmed and winked out. He felt tugs in each direction, but they were faint, like the touch of a curious fish on a dangling hook. Another thread blinked out of existence, leaving four. Then three.

Finally, one strand of magic remained, and Mitch could feel a definite pull in that direction. He was connected to … something.

"I have it," said Mitch. "I think I do, anyway. I'm not sure what this is supposed to feel like."

"Bind it," Violet said.

Mitch released the first pattern, and the glowing spiral went dark. He began feeding magic into the second symbol, located in the east circle.

"I bind you by your name, Mortic."

The light touch he felt at the end of the remaining thread now became a desperate thrashing. Whatever sat at the end of that filament was ensnared by the magic Mitch continued to pour into the binding symbol. Because he had no idea how much power he needed for the binding to take effect, he kept sending magic into the symbol until he felt his target go quiescent.

When all active resistance ceased, he glanced toward Violet.

“As near as I can tell, this thing is caught. Unless I’m missing something, I’m going to start reeling it in.”

“Do it,” she told him. I’m ready to help if you need it.”

This time Mitch did not stop feeding power into the second symbol before activating the third. Solomon’s notes indicated that failing to keep both circles active might allow the ensnared demon to escape. He kept the binding fueled while simultaneously sending energy into the southern circle.

The thread attaching Mitch to the bound creature on the other end tightened suddenly. He felt it stretch thin and threaten to break, but by incrementally increasing the amount of magic he sent into the third symbol, he was able to strengthen the tie and keep the connection intact. Mentally, he reeled in the cord, drawing whatever he had captured toward him.

As the line shortened, the amount of magic necessary to maintain it lessened. Collecting his prize became faster and easier with each pull.

“I think it’s close,” he warned Violet.

“Tell me when, and I’ll activate the final symbol.”

“I’m not really sure…,”

There was a soft sucking noise, like air being drawn into a vacuum. At the same time, a yellow light appeared in the center of the summoning circle. The glow expanded until it formed a jagged rip in the air within the main circle.

“Uh, now, I guess,” Mitch finished lamely, as a tiny, green, multi-legged creature appeared in the gap. The miniscule demon squeezed through the hole and plopped to the ground with an audible groan.

Violet activated the final symbol as Mitch released his own magical hold on the second and third summoning elements. The central circle of the diagram flared silver and white for a moment before going quiet once again.

"Did it work?" asked Mitch.

"It looks like it," Violet answered, her voice rising and making the statement sound more like a question.

The demon righted itself awkwardly, struggling to drag its many legs underneath itself and stand up. The thing in the circle reminded Mitch of an octopus stranded on land, assuming of course that an octopus was green, possessed a dozen or more legs, and had a tiny face that looked like an angry baby.

The creature peered at Mitch, then at Violet, trying to gauge the amount of trouble it might be in. It lifted one slender leg and poked it forward experimentally. The tip of its limb touched the limits of the conjuring circle and came to an abrupt stop.

"Fuck," the demon muttered as it gave the barrier a few more experimental taps. It glared at Mitch. "Fucking amateurs. How the hell did you get my name?"

"Is that any way to speak to the person that controls your freedom?" Mitch responded disapprovingly.

"You don't control shit," the demon spat. "You gotta let me out eventually. In the meantime, you can go fuck yourselves."

"How about we snap that portal shut behind you and see if we can hang on to you for a while," Violet suggested. She spoke cooly, without any hint of concern. "See how much you enjoy being stranded here. I know it won't kill you, but it might be fun watching you suffer for a while before you get pulled back into your own realm."

The demon's wrinkled little face smiled at her. "Easy there, sweety. No need to do anything mean. I was only kidding."

"Why did Chang'e summon you?" Violet asked the demon. "What did she ask you to do?"

"Chang'e, huh? She gave you my name? I thought she could keep a secret better than that. I might have to have a little chat with her the next time she rings me up."

"Chang'e is dead," Violet told it. "What did you do for her the last time she summoned you?"

"Sorry. That's privileged information. I'm not some genie that has to grant you wishes just because you asked. Although, if you want to do a little rubbing on my lamp, I wouldn't be completely opposed to that."

Violet scoffed and looked at Mitch. "Why would anyone choose to deal with demons?" she asked him. "They're nothing but trouble, if you ask me."

"I agree. What do you suggest? Send him back and move on to the next one?"

Violet shook her head and pointed toward the demon trap.

"Maybe we should practice using this thing on it. At least it will tell us whether or not the trap works."

"Good idea," Mitch agreed.

"What trap?" asked the demon, sounding more nervous now than curious. "Seriously, what are you guys talking about?"

"You open it, and I'll drop the barrier. It shouldn't be too hard to stuff this thing in there, and it will be a good trial run for the main show."

"Hey, now!" shouted the green creature, waving multiple legs to get Violet and Mitch's attention. "You don't need to open any traps. You were asking about Chang'e? I can tell you anything you want to know."

"I don't care about Chang'e anymore," Violet told it. "The trap sounds like more fun."

"I'm sorry if I said anything that upset you," it continued, talking fast. "You need something, I can get it for you. We can make a deal. You called me here so we could make some kind of deal, right? Why don't we do that right now?"

"Ready?" Violet asked Mitch.

"Hold on a minute," he suggested. "Maybe there is something old Mortic here can do for us."

"I can," the demon insisted. "I can do anything you want. Name it."

"Do you know Persuphil or Bala-Ahl?" he asked.

The demon hesitated for only an instant before responding, but Mitch noticed the pause.

"Persuphil? Bala-Ahl? Sure, I know them. I can find them for you. I can do anything you want me to do to them. Just say the word, and I'm your guy."

Mitch sighed theatrically. "You have no idea who they are. Oh well. Too bad."

"Wait, wait. You gotta give me another chance," the demon pleaded. "I don't know them, but I can find them. I can find out anything you want to know."

"Let's do this," Mitch said to Violet.

He stepped around Violet to pick up the demon trap, then searched the sides of the box until he found the specific image Solomon had pointed out to him. This was the activator that opened the trap. Mitch placed the block back onto the ground with the trigger facing up and announced he was ready.

"Now," he told her.

Mitch drew magic from his surroundings and directed it into the gold wiring on the top face of the trap. The wire absorbed the power and began to glow. The box did not open so much as it transformed. The wooden sides elongated until it formed a rectangular tube, and the two end pieces that previously held it closed faded away as if they had never existed. Gray tendrils, roiling like smoke or low-hanging fog, drifted from both openings.

The fog from one end of the box split into two, one end trailing toward Mitch and the second toward Violet. The opposite end sent one questing extension directly toward Mortic.

"Drop the barrier," Mitch said, and Violet dragged the toe of one foot through the salt, breaking the largest circle.

The instant the circle opened, Mortic darted for the open rift beside it. The demon did not get far. The snaking trail of mist from the trap caught hold of it and began dragging the struggling form back toward the box. At the same time, Mitch felt himself pulled toward his own end of the trap.

His first reaction was to pull back against the force dragging him forward. He braced his feet, digging his heels into the ground. When that did not work, he tried using magic to erect a shield between himself and the trap. His shield shattered the moment it touched the adorned wood that formed the box. Mitch slid forward several more inches toward the opening.

Pulling away was not going to work. Mitch could not fight against the trap directly. So, how did this work? How was he supposed to make sure the demon was trapped, but he and Violet were not caged inside as well? Was it a timing thing? Did they simply have to stay outside the trap longer than Mortic?

No, that did not seem right. Solomon's explanation had not made it sound like a race. The professor had said it would be a challenge, and they would need to fight the demon, but he had not been able to explain what that actual challenge would be. Now that Mitch was experiencing the weapon firsthand, he still had no real idea of what he was supposed to do.

Others had used this trap. The person that created the box had probably not intended the item to be inescapable for everyone that activated it, so there must be a way to save himself and Violet from being dragged inside.

Mitch glanced toward Mortic and was relieved to see the demon was not faring much better. The creature was scrabbling in the dirt frantically with all of its many legs, trying to run away from the gray mist that dragged it inexorably closer to its end of the trap. As he watched, the demon slipped, tumbling onto its back and skidding several inches toward the opened snare. At the same time, Mitch felt the hold the fog had on him loosen. It was only a slight cessation of force, but it had definitely happened, and the timing of it was no accident.

In order to stay out of the trap, Mitch and Violet simply needed to be sure the demon went in. At the same time, they couldn't rely on the demon to go willingly. They were going to need to help this process along. Put a thumb on the scales, so to speak.

"Violet, come here. Hurry."

She moved to stand beside Mitch without hesitation. Mitch was closer to the trap entrance than she was, but she trusted him enough to join him in spite of the incessant pull of the box.

"We have to force the demon into its side of the trap," he explained. "We need to grab it and drag it towards us, but I think we have to go through the box to do it."

To demonstrate, Mitch sent a stream of magic into the trap, letting it flow into the opening on his side and out through the far gap. Unlike his shield spell, which he had attempted to use directly against the box itself, the passive magic he sent through now was not broken apart. It drifted through the length of the open trap undisturbed. As it exited the far side, he grabbed the struggling demon with his spell and drew it back toward himself.

The demon squealed in distress as it felt itself dragged more forcefully toward its demise.

"No, no, no, no, no," it chittered angrily.

Violet followed Mitch's lead and cast her own entanglement spell. With both of them compelling the hapless demon toward the trap, the forces pulling against them eased, giving them the freedom to take a few precious steps backward, away from the sucking abyss.

The demon at last realized what was happening to it, and why. In retaliation, it reached toward Mitch with its own magic, trying to snatch him up and pull him into his own side of the gilded box.

Violet cut the demon's spell before it could take hold, and Mitch took the opportunity to pull harder on his own tether.

The demon screeched, then went silent as it popped through the open end of the demon trap. Suddenly, the pressure on Mitch and Violet halted. Without warning, the wooden block snapped back into shape, once again as solid and unblemished as when they had received it from Solomon.

Mitch stood with his feet braced, leaning away from the trap when it closed. The unexpected release caused him to stagger backward several feet before falling onto his butt. Violet stumbled as well but managed to catch her balance before she fell.

Cautiously, Mitch climbed to his feet, tensing in case the box should make one more desperate attempt to snatch him up. Everything remained quiet. It appeared the ordeal was over.

"That was certainly interesting," Violet commented.

"Mm-hmm," Mitch agreed, swiping at the dirt on the seat of his shorts. "Interesting is one word for it."

"I'm glad we decided to experiment before going toe to toe with a stronger demon."

"We know what to do now, at least," said Mitch. "The demon that took Chang'e isn't going to go so easily, though. We're going to have to be ready for a hell of a fight."

Violet put a hand on Mitch's shoulder and went up on her tiptoes to kiss him on the cheek.

"We're ready. Should we try to summon Persuphil next?" she asked.

Mitch shook his head. "I don't think so. We're both sure the demon we want is going to be Bala-Ahl. I think we're ready to take it on. As ready as we can be, anyway. And if I'm wrong, and the demon we want is Persuphil, we can go after that one next."

Violet considered a moment, then said, "Agreed. Bala-Ahl it is. Should we investigate the summoning circle and make any repairs? I'm betting Mortic probably messed it up pretty badly."

Mitch grinned at the memory of the little multi-legged thing scrambling around on the ground, trying to escape as they pulled it into the trap.

"Probably," he agreed.

Ever the gentleman, Mitch gestured toward the summoning circle. "After you."

CHAPTER
22

Violet cleaned the summoning circle, repairing scuffed symbols and closing lines that had been brushed away during their struggle with the first demon. She placed a fresh layer of salt on the main circle to be certain it was intact across the entire circumference. It would not do to have any gaps that would allow Bala-Ahl to escape their control.

Mitch was feeling much more confident about their chances against a more powerful opponent. The encounter with Mortic had proved that the demon trap was legitimate, and that they were capable of using it. It had been more of an ordeal than Mitch had expected to ensnare the tiny demon, but at first they had not fully understood how to use the magical box.

Now that they did, he believed they held the advantage in the coming confrontation.

Bala-Ahl would not go down as easily as Mortic, but Mitch was certain that between Violet and himself, they could defeat the stronger demon as well. Of course, it would not do to become careless. This would still be a fight to the bitter end, and losing would mean….

Well, it was not worth considering what losing would mean.

"Everything looks like it's back in order," Violet announced, standing and brushing dirt and salt from her hands.

She wiped sweat from her forehead with the back of her wrist and left a smudge over her right eye. Mitch used a thumb to brush at the smear but only managed to spread it around.

"Did you get it?" Violet asked.

"Sort of," he said, with a shrug. "What's a little dirt, anyway?"

Mitch opened the notebook to the summoning diagram and did a quick comparison between the drawing on the page and Violet's designs. Everything seemed ready. She had reconstructed the symbols without needing to reference the book, and her memory had been picture perfect.

"I know Bala-Ahl might not be the demon we're looking for," Mitch said, "but you and I are both pretty certain that it is. The next few minutes will probably determine the fate of Dasan's Terrace."

"Ours, too," Violet said, speaking aloud what Mitch was thinking.

"Yeah. Ours, too."

"The circle is ready. The trap is ready. How about you?"

Mitch hesitated for about three heartbeats before nodding. "I'm ready. Same routine, okay? I'll bring it here and you put up the barrier. When I say go, I'll activate the trap and you drop the circle."

Violet gave Mitch a thumbs up and positioned herself at the west end of the summoning circle.

She nodded when she was ready, and Mitch began pouring magic into the seeking symbol, casting his awareness out in all directions in search of their target.

"By your name, I seek you, Bala-Ahl. You cannot hide from me. I know you, and by your name, I seek you."

He repeated the mantra he had used to find and then to bind Mortic. He felt the magic take hold, locating the greater demon and securing it at the far end of his questing tether. Mitch could tell immediately that the target he had captured was much stronger than the demon he had snared on his first attempt. This creature pulled harder and struggled much more fiercely, compelling Mitch to funnel considerably more power into his binding spell than he had used previously.

Several times, the connection between Mitch and his quarry stretched thin and almost broke as he pulled the reluctant demon toward him. Each time it did, Mitch added more magic into the tether to keep it intact.

"It's close," Mitch warned Violet.

The amount of effort to drag the demon lessened the closer it came to him, and Mitch could feel that it was almost on top of them. Like before, a rift appeared in the air over the summoning circle; a vertical yellow line that elongated then stretched outward.

"As soon as you see it, power up the barrier," Mitch announced, though he realized as he said it that the comment was unnecessary. Violet knew what to do.

Something moved within the gap, and Mitch shifted to one side to see what he had caught. A hand appeared, thin and fragile looking, followed by a slender arm. Behind the arm, Mitch saw the face of Chang'e glaring out at him from the hovering opening. The demon appeared truly outraged to be forcibly dragged into Dasan's Terrace for the second time in three days.

Rather than fall through the hole as Mortic had done, Bala-Ahl stepped gracefully through the tear in space, alighting in the center of the summoning ring as though its arrival had been by choice rather than compelled by Mitch's force of will.

Violet erected the barrier and Mitch released his hold on the tether, watching it blink out of existence.

The demon that looked like Chang'e stood calmly in the circle, hands clasped behind its back. It attempted to appear unfazed by its sudden imprisonment, but Mitch recalled the anger he had seen in its eyes only seconds before. Bala-Ahl was furious but did not want its captors to know the extent of its agitation.

"Are you in such a hurry to die?" Bala-Ahl asked, peering first at Mitch, then at Violet. "After our last encounter, I was feeling content to leave you be for a time. I think you should have accepted my beneficence and enjoyed your small, peaceful respite."

"Until we grew too complacent, and you attacked again?" asked Mitch.

Bala-Ahl shrugged, unconcerned. "There is that, of course. I would not stay away forever. Still, if you drop this silly attempt to … ah, do whatever it is you think you are doing, I would be willing to leave and grant you the few days grace I had already planned to allow."

"While that is a very gracious offer, I think we'll pass," Mitch told the demon. "I'm happy to settle this problem between us right here and now."

"Problem?" asked the demon. "There is no problem. I will take possession of this place and all the magic that it holds, and I will kill everyone in my way when I do it."

Mitch sighed. This discussion was staying pretty predictable.

"Look, I'll make you a deal," he said. "You leave the body you stole, return to your own realm, and promise to never to come here again, and we'll drop this whole thing. Violet will let you out of the circle and you'll be free to go."

Bala-Ahl glanced toward Violet, then back at Mitch.

"Okay," it said.

Mitch blinked. This response was not at all what he had expected. He figured the demon would continue directing threats at him and calling him names, not give up so easily.

"Okay?" Mitch asked, still a little off balance. "You agree to that?"

"Yes," Bala-Ahl said. "I agree. Let me out of the circle and I will abandon this body and all my plans to take Dasan's Terrace."

Uncertain how to respond, Mitch remained silent. Violet, however, was not so surprised by the demon's words.

"You will, of course, swear to this on your name," she said. "Won't you, Bala-Ahl?"

The demon smiled, then began to laugh. As it did, the creature waved a single finger at Violet like a parent correcting a wayward child.

"Oh, you clever witch," it said when the laughter had died down to a chuckle. "You caught me. I was lying. I still intend to kill all of you."

Mitch suddenly felt stupid. Of course the creature was lying. Why had he thought for even a moment it would consider backing off? To hide his embarrassment, Mitch cleared his throat and stood straighter.

"Get ready. I'm going to open the trap," he announced, trying to regain control of the situation.

"Trap? Did you weak little things build some sort of trap for me? This should be interesting."

The demon glanced around the immediate area, searching for the promised snare. Its eyes soon locked onto the gilded box resting on the ground.

"Is that a demon trap?" Bala-Ahl asked, concern suddenly audible in its voice. "Where did you get that?"

"Doesn't matter where we got it. What matters is that we have it," Mitch said. "And we are about to stick you inside of it."

Bala-Ahl held up its hands, palms out. "Wait. Wait. Let's not get crazy," it said. "We can find some room to negotiate. Is it too late to make a deal?"

Mitch paused again. "Deal?" he asked. "The only deal I'll consider is you swear to us on your name that you'll abandon Chang'e's body and go back to your own realm."

Bala-Ahl smiled again. "No, not that deal. I mean, the deal where you let me out of here right now and I'll kill you quickly rather than torture you until you beg me to die."

Mitch cursed. That was twice he had allowed the demon to distract him, making him think there was a chance of negotiating a way out this confrontation. This was going to come down to a fight, and he knew it. He needed to stop letting his hopes for a peaceful disposition get in the way.

"Demon trap it is," he said, moving toward the box.

"Do you know what the fun thing about summoning circles is?" the demon asked.

"I know what the fun thing about sticking you in a box will be," Mitch retorted.

Bala-Ahl continued as if Mitch had not spoken. "It's the fact that they were created to trap beings of magic and spirit. They are very good at doing what they were designed to do. However, whenever you ask them to do a job they weren't intended for, things can go wrong."

"The time for talking is done," Mitch said, wishing the demon would shut up. "And for that matter, so are you."

"For example, when you ask a spirit barrier to contain a physical body, you must use additional spells to reinforce it. If you forget this principle, any creature with physical extremities, borrowed, stolen, or otherwise, can interfere with the spell."

Mitch was trying to ignore the demon's words, but something the creature said caught his attention. Something about physical bodies interfering with spirit barriers. He turned toward Bala-Ahl.

"Violet. What is it saying?"

"I'm saying, witch, that you made a mistake."

Bala-ahl pushed one black-slippered foot to the edge of the containment circle. Instead of finding a solid barrier, the creature's toes passed through the magic animating the summoning circle and slid through the line outside drawn in salt. The moment the salt border was disturbed, the containment shield held by Violet dropped, disappearing and leaving Bala-ahl completely unrestrained.

"Violet," Mitch shouted. "Open the trap."

Although springing the demon trap had been Mitch's job, Violet was closer to the box, and there was now no time to lose. If Bala-Ahl attacked before they could trigger the enchantment, they might not get another chance to activate it.

They might not get another chance to do anything.

Violet raised her hand to start the spell, but Bala-Ahl moved faster. The demon cast a stream of demonic magic too fast for either of them to stop it. To Mitch's relief, the flow of power from the demon was aimed at the box, not at Violet.

That was fine, he thought. It did not matter who opened the spirit catcher, it would become a two-way funnel that latched onto everyone in its vicinity regardless of who activated it. All

Mitch and Violet needed to do in that case was exactly what they had done before: drag the demon through its side of the trap before they were pulled into theirs.

The demon's spell struck the box. The silver, gold, and bronze images on the side began to glow, and Mitch waited for the box to elongate and spring open. To his horror, the box did not react as it had the last time. It began to smolder and blacken. The spell Bala-Ahl cast was not meant to activate the trap, but rather to destroy it.

Helpless, Mitch and Violet could only watch as their last hope of banishing Bala-Ahl from Dasan's Terrace caught fire and burned. Mitch caught glimpses of something bright and fast ejected from the box as flames engulfed it. It took him a moment to realize he was seeing ghosts fleeing from the damaged trap. He saw demons leap free and immediately disappear, pulled back into their own dimension the moment they were released. He also observed more than a few human spirits emerge from the confines of the box; poor souls that had been unable to capture the demons they had attempted to ensnare. Unfortunate magic users who had themselves been drawn inside.

One brilliant flash of white light burst up from the burning box, flying into the sky at incredible speed before blinking out of existence. Was that a…? No, Mitch thought. It couldn't be.

Who would want to trap an angel?

A few final spirits drifted out of the trap and fled before what was left of the wooden block crumbled to ash. The metal filigree that had once been so beautiful and ornate, now bubbled and puddled into slag in the dirt.

Mitch moaned in disbelief at the destruction of the trap. Violet, however, did not waste time worrying about things that were already gone. She launched a volley of offensive spells at the demon.

Her attacks came too late. Bala-Ahl had already encased itself in a shell of defensive magic.

Mitch experienced flashbacks of their battle two nights earlier. They had already played this scenario out to its conclusion, and Dasan's Terrace had lost. What was the point of going through it all again?

"Mitch, help me," Violet shouted, casting spell after spell at the protected demon.

Her voice snapped Mitch out of his stupor. This was no time for pity and self-doubt. He pulled magic around himself and began throwing percussive and fire spells as fast as he could form them. Bala-Ahl did not counterattack. It merely stood in its protective bubble and watched the humans waste their strength and magic. It was clear that it felt no threat from the witches, and that it was enjoying the futility of their efforts. The only real threat, the box, had already been eliminated, and there was nothing left in this pathetic display of defiance that could harm it.

"Violet, cover me. I have to get close."

Mitch had an idea. He did not know if it would work, or how effective it would be, but it was the only plan he had left. During their previous contest, he had managed to blast the demon's shield with a piercing spell. For a moment, the creature had been unprotected. If he could do that again, and Violet could launch her most devastating strike at the same time, they might manage to … to do what?

Win? That seemed unlikely.

Could they even hurt it? Mitch didn't know. But it was all they had remaining to try.

Mitch gathered as much magic as he could hold, then condensed it to a single point as he had done before. He did not have the experience to build one spell while holding another, so he was relying on Violet to keep him shielded from the demon's attacks as he drew closer.

Violet continued her own assault on Bala-Ahl while she covered Mitch's approach. Mitch continued to grow and condense the magic balanced at the end of his fist until the last possible moment. Curiously, Bala-Ahl watched Mitch move closer, though it took no action to stop him. It made Mitch nervous that the demon seemed more inquisitive about his actions than actually concerned, but it was too late to back out now.

"Get ready," he told Violet. "We have to time this right."

Mitch yelled, a wordless howl of fear and desperation as he leapt forward. He raised his fist and slammed his hardest punch into the demon's shield. "Pierce," he cried, willing the magic to disable Bala-Ahl's barricade.

When the breaking spell hit Bala-Ahl's defenses, the magic erupted. Mitch felt heat and pressure exploding all around him, pushing him backward. But all of that released magic came from his own spell, thrown back at him by its encounter with the immovable object that was Bala-Ahl. The demon's shield did not so much as flicker. It remained intact, and Bala-Ahl continued to watch Mitch impassively from behind its fortifications.

"Is that all you have?" the demon asked.

Bala-Ahl had seen Mitch's breaking spell before, and the demon had taken steps to counter it this time. Or perhaps, the demon was simply stronger after taking full control of Chang'e's body. Regardless of the reason, the result was the same. There was nothing Mitch could do so long as Bala-Ahl could protect itself so completely. They had gambled on the demon trap, and they had lost.

They had lost everything.

Mitch backed away, defeated and unsure what to do next. Bala-Ahl continued to watch him, ignoring Violet's continuous barrage of spells. The demon smiled, revealing rows of sharp teeth that were eerily out of place in Chang'e's mouth..

"Yes, that does seem to be all. That means it is my turn. Is that not correct?"

Mitch tensed. He raised a shield of his own in preparation for what the demon might throw at him.

Bala-Ahl did not cast any magic at Mitch or at Violet. Instead, it reached out a hand and began tearing holes in the reality around itself. The demon paced slowly forward, and as it walked, it continued ripping openings into its own realm. As each new rift occurred, demons began to pour into Mitch's world. Red, green, and yellow bodies flopped to the ground and immediately began to scurry toward the only two humans in their vicinity. The new creatures were smaller and weaker than Bala-Ahl, but there were so many of them Mitch could not even keep count.

They continued to crawl and squeeze through the openings as he watched, monsters of all shapes and forms, running, loping, or writhing through the dirt to swarm toward him and Violet.

Violet redirected her attacks to the new threat. Several of the smaller demons were broken apart by her spells and vanished, their essences sucked back into their own realm, but more continued to come. For every one she destroyed, three more emerged into the cemetery.

Violet next turned her attention to the rifts hanging in the air all around Bala-Ahl. She managed to close a few of the portals, but Bala-Ahl simply tore open new ones to replace those that had been sealed.

Mitch had no idea how portals worked, and even less understanding of how to close one. He was useless to Violet in this respect. But he could still help her fight. He dropped his shield and began casting fire at the creatures surrounding him. The attacking demons shrieked and wailed as he burned them, but there were always more in the ranks behind to replace their stricken companions. He was barely slowing their advance.

Violet cried out, and Mitch turned to see her fall, pressed to the ground under a mass of malformed multi-colored bodies. He saw her shield burning with bright red embers as the magic fueling the demons' bodies ate away at it. Violet desperately tried to reinforce the slim barrier, adding new layers to the damaged ones, but the weight of the demons on top of her made it difficult to shape her spells. The creatures continued to pile onto her, pressing closer.

"Violet!"

Mitch tried to run toward her, but he was tripped up by more of the creatures surging around him. He felt teeth and claws tearing through his clothing and puncturing his skin. All of Mitch's magic had been focused on offence. He did not even have a shield to protect himself from the tiny, vicious creatures.

Violet screamed again, this time a cry of pain.

"Violet," Mitch called out to her a second time.

Mitch had been so certain they could win this battle today. Dot's dream had given him hope that he and Violet were meant to be victorious. All they had needed to do was face Bala-Ahl together and they would walk away triumphant. Instead, his stupid bravado had led him and Violet into a death sentence.

They were going to die. And worse, he would not be with Violet when that happened. He could not get to her. She was buried under writhing creatures trying to rip her apart, and he was pinned to the ground by more of the tiny monsters, unable to help. Mitch had promised Violet he would be there for her. He told her he would protect her and support her, but most importantly, he would always be at her side.

Now, she was alone, afraid, and helpless, and he could not reach her. In the last moments, he could not even get close enough to hold her hand as she died. In all ways possible, he had utterly failed her.

Mitch's vision narrowed as a directionless fury rose in his chest. He could not die like this. He was not afraid of death, but he was afraid to let the woman he loved think he had broken his promise to her. He decided he would be at her side at the end no matter what it took to get there.

Mitch reached deep inside himself, feeling for the core of his being. When all of his focus settled upon his truest self, tendrils of his soul extended, reaching out from the center of his body and trailing out along his arms. His essence filled his hands until they glowed, spirit energy escaping and curling from his fingertips like ethereal claws.

Demons were not ghosts, but they were not born of this physical world either. Violet had never mentioned using their gifts against creatures from another realm. The fact she had not used her own unique powers in this battle suggested she did not believe it would make any difference. Mitch had no idea if this desperate act had any hope of working, but it was all he had left. He was an exorcist, and this is what an exorcist did.

Demons were creatures of spirit, he told himself. He had shredded spirits before, and he could do it again.

Mitch lashed out, screaming his final defiance against the multitudes piling onto his trapped body and burying him. Grabbing the first demon he could catch, he wrapped his fingers around what might have been a neck. He buried his claws into the monster and squeezed.

The demon burst in his hands.

The creature did not vaporize like the demon Simon had pierced with an angelic sword. No, this little monster burst like a balloon, releasing black ichor that splashed all over Mitch and the other demons surrounding him.

Mitch realized instinctively that he had not banished the demon back to its own realm. He had killed it.

He had exorcized it.

Shrieking with a glee that bordered on insanity, he snatched up another demon, shredding it with his claws and showering more of that thick dark blood on the ground. When the third demon died in his hands, its companions began to notice that something was not right with this situation. They were watching some of their own be destroyed. Demons were only supposed to be banished, they must be thinking as Mitch slashed his ethereal talons through their ranks. They weren't supposed to actually die.

This realization changed the tide of battle rapidly. Demons were by nature cowards, and when faced with their own mortality, the multitude of colorful marauders suddenly decided they wanted nothing to do with Mitch or his wild rampage. The creatures swarming him bounded away, seeking the portals they had come through in an attempt to get back home while still in one piece.

At last, able to scramble back onto his feet, Mitch ran to Violet's side. The demons pinning her to the ground were unaware of the change in the battle rules and of the mass exodus of their fleeing comrades. They had not seen their fellow warriors exploding under Mitch's claws, so they were unprepared when he began pulling them away from Violet and physically tearing them apart.

Mitch grabbed and squeezed, grabbed and squeezed, killing demons in both hands as he attempted to free Violet from the mountain of squirming bodies. He was careful not to let his claws get too close to her. They could do the same damage to

Violet's soul as they were currently inflicting on the demon infestation.

Once again, as the creatures realized what was happening, they decided fleeing was a smarter option than continuing to fight the madman that was murdering their kind one by one.

When the last demon had died or fled, Mitch examined Violet closely, checking her for injuries. Blood soaked her shirt and covered her right arm. The calf of her right leg was also badly cut in several places.

"Are you okay?" he asked, stupidly. He could clearly see she was hurt.

Violet nodded, her eyes wide as she stared up at Mitch.

He did not wait for any further response. There was still an immediate threat he needed to deal with. Violet could not be safe until Bala-Ahl was destroyed and out of their lives forever.

Mitch turned to face the greater demon. It was still opening portals, trying to coax demons through to help it, but the flow of fleeing demons heading back to their own realm impeded the entrance of new combatants.

Mitch held up his hands in front of him, feeling the sensation of his spirit claws stretching from his fingertips, eager to tear into more demon flesh. He wanted to rush forward and leap onto Bala-Ahl, rend him to pieces, but he paused.

Bala-Ahl's shield was still up. Mitch knew he could not push through it. The barrier was too strong. His previous attempt to break it had been less than futile.

A thought came to him, or rather a memory returned. He recalled his scuffle with a feisty poltergeist in Carmel. In that bookstore, he had thrown up a shield trying to protect himself from the ghost, but the nasty little spirit had flown right through his defenses, striking him in the chest. Violet had later explained that earth magic had little effect on ghosts or spirits.

And what about demon magic, he wondered.

Could Mitch extend his soul through the magical protections Bala-Ahl had erected around himself?

Even if Mitch's claws could penetrate the demon's magic, there was still another problem to overcome. The extended tips of his soul only extended a few inches from his fingers. They were too short to reach Bala-Ahl. His hands would stop the moment they hit the barrier. If he had any hope of success, he needed to extend his spirit far enough to reach the demonic presence hiding behind both the spell barrier and the physical shell of Chang'e.

He thought of Brad's katana, and he wished he had possessed the foresight to bring it with him. A pointless wish, however. He did not have the sword, and he had no way of retrieving it now.

But … did he have something else? Another sword of sorts?

He had never done it before. He had never tried to extend his soul outside of his body more than he was doing right now.

Mitch was angry, and perhaps still not thinking straight. Violet had always told him it was dangerous to let his soul extend too far beyond the protection of his human flesh. He was vulnerable when exposed. He should never overextend himself that way. She had not, however, said he *could* not do it.

Mitch allowed his claws to melt away. He directed more of his soul into his right hand, letting as much of his essence leave the shelter of his body as he could. His soul drifted from his palm, and as he felt it exit his flesh, he shaped it. No mere claws would do this time. He needed something much longer, and much more deadly.

Standing in the dirt and grass of Dasan's Terrace, surrounded by the gore of dead demons, Mitch felt the full extent of his abilities for the very first time. He raised his right hand and closed his fist around a silvery handle of pure soul. Rising from that handle shone a blazing sword of spirit fire.

He did not simply see the soul blade he had created; he could touch it and feel it. It was a physical manifestation in his hand, and with it, he would cut this demon into pieces and rid the world of Bala-Ahl forever.

Mitch ran toward Bala-Ahl. With a start, the demon took a step backward, uncertain what had changed. There was genuine concern in the demon's expression for the first time since it had been summoned into the cemetery. In a flurry, it began casting spells in Mitch's direction. It finally saw the lowly human as a real threat.

Although Mitch had never learned the trick of holding a shield while casting offensive spells at the same time, the soul blade did not require any magic to wield. It was part of him. So, it was an easy matter to cast a shield spell as he ran, deflecting every attack that came his way.

Bala-Ahl decided now might be a good time to run away, but Mitch was already on top of the demon. The creature turned its back to flee as Mitch swung the glowing sword. The blade of pure soul passed through the creature's magic without slowing. At the first touch of Mitch's weapon, the spell protecting Bala-Ahl tore, then burned away, leaving the demon completely defenseless.

Completing his cut, Mitch's spirit weapon slashed through the corpse of Chang'e, leaving no marks on the dead flesh. The demon within, however, was not so fortunate. Bala-Ahl screamed in pain as it felt the blade slice through it, trying to extinguish its very existence.

Mitch swung again, then a third time. Each cut tore a new piece out of the demon, leaving it weakened and dying.

Chang'e's body collapsed to the ground, and Mitch saw the demon Bala-Ahl's true form emerge from the human husk. The creature had a head, but no eyes or nose. Only a gaping mouth full of daggerlike teeth adorned what should have been a face. The body was damaged, and leaking the same black blood that had poured from its smaller brethren.

Bala-Ahl fled. It did not pause to hurl threats or cry out in defiance. It was dying and needed to evade this unstoppable foe immediately or be vanquished for good. Mitch pursued, trying to deliver one last finishing cut, but the demon leapt through one of the rifts it had created, making its escape with mere inches to spare.

As soon as Bala-Ahl disappeared through the portal, all of the openings it had created closed, vanishing one after the other until not a single rift remained. When the last of the holes to the demon realm was gone, Mitch at last allowed himself to relax. The glowing sword in his hand faded as his soul settled back into the safety of his body.

He suddenly felt tired, exhausted actually, but he could not rest yet.

Mitch hurried to Violet's side and checked on her again. The cut on her upper arm seemed the most serious. The laceration ran from her shoulder and down almost all the way to her elbow. He needed to stop the bleeding, and the injury would require stitches to permanently close it, but although it looked ugly, Violet did not seem to be in immediate danger.

With the fighting over, Mitch began to feel the pain of his own wounds as well. He had dozens of punctures and cuts all over his torso, arms, and legs from multiple teeth and claws, and there was one large laceration in his back where something had stabbed him a few inches above his right kidney.

He was going to need some medical attention himself, he realized.

"I'll get us some help," he said to Violet, smiling to reassure her that everything was going to be okay.

He paused when he saw the look on her face. Violet appeared … afraid.

Afraid of me? he wondered. No, that was impossible. She would never have a reason to fear him. Mitch was about to tell her that, but Violet spoke first.

"Chang'e's body," she said, pointing toward the lifeless corpse lying among the weeds and cemetery stones. "If Bala-Ahl manages to return, it can reclaim her. You need to burn her. Destroy the body completely. Make sure the demon can never come back."

Mitch understood her concerns immediately. Professor Schick had warned them that in order to stop a demon holding a human body, the remains would need to be completely dismantled or burned. Only after the physical tether was permanently destroyed would the demon be safely trapped in its own realm. If the host remained intact, there was always the risk that it might be used as a portal through which the demon could return.

Mitch cast a fire spell over Chang'e's corpse, raising the heat of the magical flames until even her bones had been reduced to ash.

"Done," he told Violet, kneeling once again beside her. "Can I get you some help now?"

"No. Wait," she said. "Mitch, we have to talk before anyone else gets here."

"Talk? About what?"

The only thing Mitch could think of was that Violet wanted to break up with him. What else could be so important that she wanted to talk about it now? He looked into her eyes and found that same fear he had seen a moment ago.

"Violet. A-are you afraid of me?" he asked, not really wanting to know the answer but unable not to ask the question.

Violet shook her head and placed a comforting hand on his cheek. "No, Mitch. I'm not afraid of you. I'm afraid *for* you. What you did to Bala-Ahl and those other demons, you shouldn't have been able to do."

"Maybe no one has done it before, but that might be because no one else has tried."

"No, Mitch. Listen to me, please. I was wrong. You're not an exorcist like I thought. Exorcists can't kill demons. I can't kill spirit creatures."

"But I am," he insisted, confused by her explanation. What was Violet trying to tell him? "I've exorcised echoes and poltergeists with you. You've seen me do it."

Violet sniffed. Her eyes grew shiny with unshed tears. "I know you have," she said. "You can do everything an exorcist can do, but you are obviously so much more than that. This explains so much. How you can see the essence of your own soul when other exorcists can't. The way you can break through the protective shields of magic users who should be much stronger than you. You can steal magic right out of another witch's hands. But, most of all, I saw how you wielded your soul against Bala-Ahl just now, letting it flow from your body so completely. No one else can do that."

Violet gave him a sad, very tired smile. "Mitch, you are something unique; something the world hasn't seen in a very long time. You are a spirit hunter."

"A…? What are you talking about?"

"Exorcists can deal with human souls. That is a really rare ability. When we met, I saw some of that strength in you and I assumed you were an exorcist, like me. You're not. Spirit hunters aren't limited to human ghosts, or even human magic. They are the ultimate killers. They can manipulate or destroy anything that exists in the spirit realm. Demons. Angels. Anything."

Mitch thought about what Violet was saying.

"That's good, though. Right? I stopped a demon today."

"It's not good. And you can never tell anybody else what you can do."

"Violet…,"

"You don't understand," she interrupted fiercely. "I have never met a spirit hunter before. I have only heard of them. They don't come along very often, and when they do, they don't tend to live long. Demons and angels don't like having to be afraid of something, and they often decide to kill whatever it is that they are afraid of."

Tears were falling as Violet spoke, leaving wet tracks on her cheeks.

"Bala-Ahl escaped. It may not know what you are yet, but if it ever figures it out, it will tell others. Most creatures will be too afraid to confront you directly if they find out, but that doesn't mean they won't try to kill you in other ways."

"That's why nobody can know."

"Right," Violet agreed. "That's why nobody can know. Dangerous people attract dangerous people."

Violet wrapped her good arm around Mitch's neck and held him close. Blood from her injured bicep soaked into his shirt, wet and warm, as she hugged him. The sensation was oddly comforting. It reassured him she was alive.

Violet raised her lips to his ear and whispered.

"And Mitch, you might be the most dangerous person on the planet."

CHAPTER

23

"I'm glad to hear that Violet will be okay."

Mitch sat in one of the guest chairs in Chief Jefferson's office. He had wanted to speak with the chief immediately after the battle with Bala-Ahl, but Simon, with Dot's staunch support, had insisted he and Violet get to the hospital to be treated, and then take the weekend to rest. Mitch had chaffed at having to wait, but after Simon had heard that Bala-Ahl was gone and would not return, there did not seem to be much urgency other than Mitch's own sense of impatience.

He had reluctantly complied with the orders, but first thing Monday morning, Mitch showed up at Dasan's Terrace bright and early for debriefing.

"Twenty-two stitches to close the cut," Mitch told Simon. "The doctor doesn't think there will be much of a scar. Personally, I think a scar would make her look as badass on the outside as I know she is on the inside."

"She should wear that scar with pride after what she managed to accomplish," Simon commented."

Mitch nodded but said nothing. He and Violet had agreed that they would tell anyone who asked that Violet had been the one to banish the demon. It was not an ego thing for her. The real issue was that if anyone learned it had been Mitch that defeated Bala-Ahl, it would lead to too many questions that he was not prepared to answer.

Besides, being known for taking down a major league demon like Bala-Ahl certainly did not hurt her standing as the new priestess within her coven. It cemented her position with any of the witches who might still have doubts about supporting her over Alyssandra.

"I finished my report and submitted it to Jorge," Mitch said. "Bala-Ahl is gone for good. We burned Chang'e, his last physical tether to the cemetery, and unless there is someone out there that knows his name and is stupid enough to summon him back, he is stuck permanently in his own realm.

"Good to know, but I thought I told you to relax this weekend. Jorge shouldn't be working, either. The doctor wanted him to take two weeks to let his shoulder heal."

"You know I can't relax until after the paper is finished," Mitch retorted, laughing ruefully. "And, honestly, I don't think the sergeant has even looked at it. I sent it to his e-mail and haven't heard anything back. I do have a question about what we give to the homicide detectives, though."

"Go ahead."

"Ali Minhas has been working Chang'e's case ever since he found out about the coven murders. I already told him that she was killed trying to get away from us, but he asked me for a copy of the coroner's report when it's finished. What am I supposed to tell him?"

"That won't be a problem," Simon assured Mitch. "There's a medical examiner employed by the County that I've worked with before. I'll give him a call. Cause of death will be gunshot wound to the head from Adam's gun, fired in self-defense."

"Adam? Oh, right. Tink. You know, sometimes I forget that his parents gave him a real name when he was born. Nobody calls him Adam."

"Is that right?" asked Simon. "Should I be calling him Tink?"

Mitch waved a hand in the air negligently. "You can call him whatever you like. You run the place."

Mitch paused for a moment, remembering something.

"Speaking of running the place," he said. "I think I owe you an apology, Chief."

"You do?" asked Simon, looking puzzled. "For what?"

"A while ago, I asked you about your secret, thinking that I was somehow entitled to know because of some stupid debt. That was arrogant, and I'm sorry. I'm still willing to listen if you ever want to share it with me, but I also know now that it isn't my place to ask, or to expect anything. We all have things we keep to ourselves for our own reasons, and the only person who has the right to decide when we share those things is the person holding that secret. I hope you can forgive me for overstepping."

Simon pulled open the top drawer of his desk and reached inside.

"There's nothing to forgive," the chief told him. "Forget it ever happened. Now, speaking of paying off debts, I have a few duties as Chief of Police I need to take care of right now."

Simon removed a silver badge from the drawer, set it on his desk and slid it toward Mitch. The seven-pointed star looked identical to the one Mitch had pinned on his uniform shirt downstairs in his locker. It was a Dasan's Terrace police badge, and it even had Mitch's officer number, 23, in the middle. The only difference was this star had a silver banner affixed at the top with the word "detective" etched into the metal.

"I'm sorry it took so long to get this to you, but as of now you are officially the first detective working for the Dasan's Terrace Police Department. Congratulations, Mitch."

Mitch picked up the badge, angling it so the overhead lights made it flash as he ran a finger over the detective banner admiringly. "Thank you, sir."

"Don't thank me yet," the chief told him. "I have one more gift for you. I hope you like this one as well."

Simon reached back into the drawer, and this time he brought out a piece of cloth. He held it toward Mitch, who accepted it, not quite sure what he was being handed. He flipped the cloth over to look at the front, then realized what he was holding.

"A shoulder patch?" he asked.

"Our shoulder patch," Simon corrected him. "You asked, and I went out and made it happen. You said we should have something distinctive for Dasan's Terrace, and I agreed. By next month, this patch will be on the sleeves of every uniform in the department."

The patch was rectangular, taller than it was wide, and the top corners were rounded giving the cloth a distinctive shape.

"Tombstone," Mitch said with a chuckle. "That's a nice touch."

Simon gave a small nod of his head. "I thought so."

The image on the front of the patch was a willow tree, reminding Mitch of the tree in Dot's vision. It seemed an apt representation for the department, and Dot would be happy when she saw it, assuming she had not already gotten a sneak peek. Above the tree, the words, "Dasan's Terrace" were stitched in yellow thread, while the word "Police" was stitched below. At the base of the willow tree, leaning against the trunk was....

A tightness formed in the back of Mitch's throat. He tried several times to swallow it, but it refused to go away.

"That looks.... It looks like a teddy bear," Mitch said, touching the tiny image. "It looks like Denny's teddy bear."

Simon watched Mitch. His eyes were hard and serious. "The patches were your idea, Mitch. I thought it was fitting that there be something on them that was of personal importance to you. I hope you're okay with what I chose."

Mitch shook his head, for a moment unable to speak. "I'm more than okay with it. I.... Thank you, Simon."

The chief relaxed into his chair and smiled. "Good," he said loudly, breaking the somber mood in the office. "Because I already ordered two hundred of those damn things, and it's too late to return them."

Mitch laughed and tried to surreptitiously wipe at the moisture in his eyes. He was pretty sure the chief saw the gesture, but his boss was kind enough not to comment.

Mitch held up the patch. "Debt paid," he announced. "This officially makes us square."

Simon chuckled. "Oh, I'm not so sure about that. After what you and Violet did for us last week, I'd say I still owe you at least one."

"I was only doing what you pay me to do, right? It's part of the job. But if you're serious about wanting to repay me, there is one thing I'd like to ask."

"Name it, and if I can reasonably make it happen, I will."

"Do you think I could get a few days off? Violet and I never got to finish our vacation in Carmel. Plus, her birthday was last week." Mitch's shoulders hunched, and he appeared sheepish as he admitted the oversight. "With everything going on, I sort of forgot, and I'd really like to spend some time with her."

"Done," Simon announced. "You have the next two weeks off. Grab Violet and take her somewhere where there are no murdering witches, demons, or book-eating poltergeists. Go have fun."

"No, I don't need two weeks," Mitch protested. "I was thinking…,"

"Two weeks!" Simon repeated. "That's an order. If I see your face at the police department before then, you're fired."

Mitch jumped to his feet, clutching his new badge and shoulder patch. He hurried to the office door and pulled it open. Before stepping out, he paused long enough to look back at Simon.

"Thanks, Chief," he said again. "I guess I'll see you in two weeks."

About the Author

G. Allen Wilbanks, an internationally best-selling author, was born and raised in northern California. For twenty-five years he worked in law enforcement to pay the bills while writing horror and fantasy fiction during his free time to keep himself sane. In 2016 he decided to retire from real life and live in a fantasy world of his own making full time. For additional information about G. Allen, including where you can find more of his writing, please visit his website at www.gallenwilbanks.com.

Made in the USA
Las Vegas, NV
13 August 2025

26280420R00204